E. E. 'Doc' Smith

Second Stage Lensmen

The fifth novel in the Lensman series

Panther

Granada Publishing Limited
Published in 1973 by Panther Books Ltd.
3 Upper James Street, London W1R 4BP

First published in Great Britain by
W. H. Allen & Co. Ltd. 1972

Made and printed in Great Britain by
Richard Clay (The Chaucer Press), Ltd
Bungay, Suffolk
Set in Linotype Plantin 9/10

To F. Edwin Counts

Contents

Second Stage Lensmen

Foreword

A couple of billion years ago, when the First and Second Galaxies were passing through each other and when myriads of planets were coming into being where only a handful had existed before, two races of beings were already ancient. Each had become independent of the chance formation of planets upon which to live. Each had won a large measure of power over its environment; the Arisians by force of mind alone, the Eddorians by employing both mind and mechanism.

The Arisians were native to this, our normal space-time continuum. They had lived in it since the unthinkably remote time of their origin. The original Arisia was very much like Earth. Thus all our normal space was permeated by Arisian life-spores, and thus upon all Earth-like planets there came into being races more or less like what the Arisians had been in the days of their racial youth.

The Eddorians, on the other hand, were interlopers. They came to our space-time continuum from some horribly different plenum. For eons they had been exploring the Macrocosmic All; moving their planets from plenum to plenum; seeking that which at last they found—one in which there were enough planets, soon to be inhabited by intelligent life, to sate even the Eddorian lust for dominance. Here, in our own universe, they would stay; and here supreme they would rule.

The Elders of Arisia, however, the ablest thinkers of the race, had known of and had studied the Eddorians for many cycles of time. Their integrated Visualization of the Cosmic All showed what was to happen. No more than the Arisians themselves could the Eddorians be slain by any physical means; nor could the Arisians, unaided, kill all the invaders by mental force. Eddore's All-Highest and his Innermost Circle, in their ultra-shielded citadel, could be destroyed only by a mental bolt of such nature and magnitude that its generator, which was to become known as the Galactic Patrol, would require several long Arisian lifetimes for its building.

Nor would that building be easy. The Eddorians must be kept in ignorance, both of Arisia and of the proposed generator, until too late to take effective counter-measures. Also, no entity below the third level of intelligence could ever be allowed to learn the truth, for that knowledge would set up an inferiority complex that would rob the generator of its ability to do the work.

On the four most promising planets of the First Galaxy—our Earth or Sol Three, Velantia, Rigel Four, and Palain Seven—breeding programs, to develop the highest mentality of which each race was capable, were begun as soon as intelligent life appeared.

On our Earth there were only two blood lines, since humanity has only two sexes. One was a straight male line of descent, and was always named Kinnison, or its equivalent. Civilizations rose and fell; Arisia surreptitiously lifting them up, Eddore callously knocking them down. Pestilences raged, and wars, and famines, and holocausts, and disasters that decimated entire populations again and again; but the direct male line of descent of the Kinnisons was never broken.

The other line, sometimes male and sometimes female, which was to culminate in the female penultimate of the Arisian program, was equally persistent and was characterized throughout its prodigious length by a peculiarly spectacular shade of red-bronze–auburn hair and equally striking gold-flecked, tawny eyes. Atlantis fell, but the red-headed, yellow-eyed child of red-haired Captain Phryges had been sent to North Maya, and lived. Patroclus, the red-headed gladiator, begot a red-haired daughter before he was cut down. And so it went.

World Wars One, Two, and Three, occupying as they did only a few moments of Arisian–Eddorian time, formed merely one incident in the eons-long game. Immediately after that incident, Gharlane of Eddore made what proved to be an error. Knowing nothing of the Arisians, he assumed that the then completely ruined Tellus would not require his personal attention again for many hundreds of Tellurian years, and went elsewhere; to Rigel Four, to Palain Seven, and to Velantia Two, or Delgon, where he found that his creatures, the Overlords, were not progressing satisfactorily. He spent quite a little time there; during which the men of Earth, aided by the Arisians, made a rapid recovery from the ravages of atomic warfare and very rapid advances in both sociology and technology.

Virgil Samms, the auburn-haired, tawny-eyed Crusader who was to become the first wearer of Arisia's Lens, took advantage of the demoralization to institute an effective planetary police force. Then, with the advent of interplanetary flight, he was instrumental in forming the Interplanetary League. As head of the Triplanetary Service he took a leading part in the brief war with the Nevians, a race of highly intelligent amphibians who used allotropic iron as a source of atomic power.*

Gharlane of Eddore came back to the Solarian System as Gray Roger, the enigmatic and practically immortal scourge of space, only to find his every move so completely blocked that he could not kill two ordinary human beings, Conway Costigan and Clio Marsden. Nor were these two, in spite of some belief to the contrary, anything but what they seemed. Neither of them ever knew that they were being protected. Gharlane's blocker was in fact an Arisian fusion; the four-ply mentality which was to become known to every Lensman of the Patrol as Mentor of Arisia.

The inertialess drive, which made an interstellar trip a matter of minutes instead of lifetimes, brought with it such an increase in crime, and made detection of criminals so difficult, that law enforcement broke down almost completely. As Samms himself expressed it:

'How can legal processes work efficiently—work at all, for that matter—when a man can commit a murder or a pirate can loot a space-ship and be a hundred parsecs away before the crime is even discovered? How can a Tellurian John Law find a criminal on a strange world that knows nothing of our Patrol, with a completely alien language—maybe no language at all—when it takes months even to find out who and where—if any—the native police officers are?'

Also there was the apparently insuperable difficulty of identification of authorized personnel. Triplanetary's best scientists had done their best in the way of a non-counterfeitable badge—the historic Golden Meteor, which upon touch impressed upon the toucher's consciousness an unpronounceable,—unspellable syllable—but that best was not enough. What physical science could devise and synthesize, physical science could analyze and duplicate; and that analysis and duplication had caused trouble indeed.

Triplanetary needed something vastly better than its meteor. In fact, without a better, its expansion into an intersystemic organization would probably be impossible. It needed something to identify a Patrolman, anytime and anywhere. This something must be impossible of duplication or imitation—ideally, it should kill, painfully, any entity attempting imposture. It should oper-

* For a complete treatment of matters up to this point, including the discovery of the inertialess—'free'—space-drive, the Nevian War, and the mind-to-mind meeting of Mentor of Arisia and Gharlane of Eddore, see *Triplanetary*, Panther Books.

ate as a telepath or endow its wearer with telepathic power—how else could a Tellurian converse with peoples such as the Rigellians, who could not talk, see, or hear?

Both Solarian Councillor Virgil Samms and his friend of old, Commissioner of Public Safety Roderick Kinnison, knew these things; but they also knew how utterly preposterous their thoughts were; how utterly and self-evidently impossible such a device was.

But Arisia again came to the rescue. The scientist working on the meteor problem, one Dr. Nels Bergenholm—who, all unknown to even his closest associates, was a form of flesh energized at various times by various Arisians—reported to Virgil Samms that:

(1) Physical science could not then produce what was needed, and probably could never do so. (2) Although it could not be explained by any symbology known to man, there was—there *must* be—a science of the mind; a science whose tangible products physical science could neither analyze nor imitate. (3) Virgil Samms, by going to Arisia, could obtain *exactly* what was needed.

'Arisia! Of all the hells in space, why Arisia?' Kinnison demanded. 'How? Don't you know that nobody can get anywhere near that damn planet?'

'I *know* that the Arisians are very well versed in that science. I *know* that if Virgil Samms goes to Arisia he will obtain the symbol he needs. I *know* that he will never obtain it otherwise. As to *how* I know these things—I can't—I just—I *know* them, I tell you!'

And since Bergenholm was already as well known for uncannily accurate 'hunches' as for a height of genius bordering on insanity, the two leaders of Civilization did not press him further, but went immediately to the hitherto forbidden planet. They were—apparently—received hospitably enough, and were given Lenses by Mentor of Arisia; Lenses which, it developed, were all that Bergenholm had indicated, and more.

The Lens is a lenticular structure of hundreds of thousands of tiny crystalloids, built and tuned to match the individual life force—the ego, the personality—of one individual entity. While not, strictly speaking, alive, it is endowed with a sort of pseudo-life by virtue of which it gives off a strong, characteristically-changing, polychromatic light as long as it is in circuit with the living mentality with which it is in synchronization. Conversely, when worn by anyone except its owner, it not only remains dark, but it kills; so strongly does its pseudo-life interfere with any life to which it is not attuned. It is also a telepathic communicator of astounding power and range—and other things.

Back on Earth, Samms set out to find people of Lensman caliber to send to Arisia. Kinnison's son, Jack, Jack's friend Mason Northrop, Conway Costigan, and Samms' daughter Virgilia—who had inherited her father's hair and eyes and who was the most accomplished muscle-reader of her time—went first. The boys got Lenses, but Jill did not. Mentor, who was to her senses a woman seven feet tall—it should be mentioned here that no two entities who ever saw Mentor ever saw the same thing—told her that she did not then and never would need a Lens.

Frederick Rodebush, Lyman Cleveland, young Bergenholm and a couple of commodores of the Patrol—Clayton of North America and Schweikert of Europe—just about exhausted Earth's resources. Nor were the other Solarian planets very helpful, yielding only three Lensmen—Knobos of Mars, DelNalten of Venus, and Rularion of Jove. Lensman material was very scarce stuff.

Knowing that his proposed Galactic Council would have to be made up exclusively of Lensmen, and that it should represent as many solar systems as possible, Samms visited the various systems which had been colonized by humanity, then went on: to Rigel Four, where he found Dronvire the Explorer, who was of Lensman grade; and next to Pluto, where he found Pilinixi the Dexitroboper, who very definitely was not; and finally to Palain Seven, an ultra-frigid world where he found Tallick, who might—or might not—go to Arisia some day. And Virgil Samms, being physically tough and mentally a real crusader, survived these various ordeals.

For some time the existence of the newly-formed Galactic Patrol was precarious indeed. Archibald Isaacson, head of Interstellar Spaceways, wanting a monopoly of interstellar trade, first tried bribery; then, joining forces with the machine of Senator Morgan and Boss Towne, assassination. The other Lensmen and Jill saved Samms' life; after which Kinnison took him to the safest place on Earth—deep underground beneath the Hill; the tremendously fortified, superlatively armed fortress which had been built to be the headquarters of the Triplanetary Service.

But even there the First Lensman was attacked, this time by a fleet of space-ships in full battle array. By that time, however, the Galactic Patrol had a fleet of its own, and again the Lensmen won.

Knowing that the final and decisive struggle would of necessity be a political one, the Patrol took over the Cosmocrat party and set out to gather detailed and documentary evidence of corrupt and criminal activities of the Nationalists, the party then in power. Roderick ('Rod the Rock') Kinnison ran for President of North America against the incumbent Witherspoon; and after a knock-down-and-drag-out political battle with Senator Morgan, the voice of the Morgan–Towne–Isaacson machine, he was elected.

And Morgan was murdered—supposedly by disgruntled gangsters; actually by his Kalonian boss, who was in turn a minion of Eddore—simply because he had failed.*

North America was the most powerful continent of Earth; Earth was the mother planet, the leader and the boss. Hence, under the sponsorship of the Cosmocratic government of North America, the Galactic Council and its arm, the Galactic Patrol, came into their own. At the end of R. K. Kinnison's term of office, at which time he resumed his interrupted duties as Port Admiral of the Patrol, there were a hundred planets adherent to Civilization. In ten years there were a thousand; in a hundred years a million; and it is sufficient characterization of the government of the Galactic Council to say that in the long history of Civilization no planet has ever withdrawn from it.

Time went on. The prodigiously long blood-lines, so carefully manipulated by Mentor of Arisia, neared culmination. Lensman Kimball Kinnison was graduated Number One of his class—as a matter of fact, although he did not know it, he was Number One of his time. And his female counterpart and complement, Clarrissa MacDougall of the red–bronze–auburn hair and the gold-flecked tawny eyes, was a nurse in the Patrol's Hospital at Prime Base.

Shortly after graduation Kinnison was called in by Port Admiral Haynes. Space piracy had become an organized force; and, under the leadership of someone or something known as 'Boskone', had risen to such heights of power as to threaten seriously the Patrol itself. In one respect Boskonia was ahead of the Patrol; its scientists having developed a source of power vastly greater than any known to Civilization. Pirate ships, faster than the Patrol's fastest cruisers and yet more heavily armed than its most powerful battleships, had been doing as

* *First Lensman* (Panther Books).

they pleased throughout all space.

For one particular purpose the engineers of the Patrol had designed and built one ship—the *Brittania*. She was the fastest thing in space, but for offense she had only one weapon, the 'Q-gun'. Kinnison was put in command of this vessel with orders to: (1) Capture a late-model pirate vessel; (2) Learn her secrets of power; and (3) Transmit the information to Prime Base.

He found and took such a ship. Sergeant Peter vanBuskirk led the stormy party of Valerians—men of human ancestry, but of extraordinary size, strength, and agility because of the enormous gravitation of the planet Valeria—in wiping out those of the pirate crew not killed in the battle between the two vessels.

The *Brittania*'s scientists secured the desired data. It could not be transmitted to Prime Base, however, as the pirates were blanketing all channels of communication. Boskonian warships were gathering for the kill, and the crippled Patrol ship could neither run nor fight. Therefore each man was given a spool of tape bearing a complete record of everything that had occurred; and, after setting up a director-by-chance to make the empty ship pursue an unpredictable course in space, and after rigging bombs to destroy her at the first touch of a ray, the Patrolmen paired off by lot and took to the lifeboats.

The erratic course of the cruiser brought her near the lifeboat manned by Kinnison and vanBuskirk and there the pirates tried to stop her. The ensuing explosion was so violent that flying wreckage disabled practically the entire personnel of one of the attacking ships, which did not have time to go free before the crash. The two Patrolmen boarded the pirate vessel and drove her toward Earth, reaching the solar system of Velantia before the Boskonians headed them off. Again taking to their lifeboat, they landed on the planet Delgon, where they were rescued from a horde of Catlats by one Worsel—later to become Lensman Worsel of Velantia—a highly intelligent winged reptile.

By means of improvements upon Velantian thought-screens the three destroyed a group of the Overlords of Delgon, a sadistic race of monsters who had been preying upon the other peoples of the system by sheer power of mind. Worsel then accompanied the two Patrolmen to Velantia, where all the resources of the planet were devoted to the preparation of defenses against the expected attack of the Boskonians. Several other lifeboats reached Velantia, guided by Worsel's mind working through Kinnison's ego and Lens.

Kinnison intercepted a message from Helmouth, who 'spoke for Boskone', and traced his communicator beam, thus getting his first line on Boskone's Grand Base. The pirates attacked Velantia, and six of their warships were captured. In these six ships, manned by Velantian crews, the Patrolmen again set out for Earth and Prime Base.

Then Kinnison's Bergenholm, the generator of the force which makes inertialess flight possible, broke down, so that he had to land upon Trenco for repairs. Trenco, the tempestuous, billiard-ball-smooth planet where it rains forty seven feet and five inches every night and where the wind blows at over eight hundred miles per hour—the Trenco, the source of thionite, the deadliest of all deadly drugs—Trenco, whose weirdly-charged ether and atmosphere so distort beams and vision that it can be policed only by such beings as the Rigellians, who possess the sense of perception instead of those of sight and hearing!

Lensman Tregonsee, of Rigel Four, then in command of the Patrol's wandering base on Trenco, supplied Kinnison with a new Bergenholm and he again set out for Tellus.

Meanwhile Helmuth had decided that some one particular Lensman must be the cause of all his set-backs; and that the Lens, a complete enigma to all Boskonians, was in some way connected with Arisia. That planet had always been dreaded and shunned by all spacemen. No Boskonian who had ever approached that planet could be compelled, even by the certainty of death, to go near it again.

Thinking himself secure by virtue of thought-screens given him by a being from a higher-echelon planet named Ploor, Helmuth went alone to Arisia, determined to learn all about the Lens. There he was punished to the verge of insanity, but was permitted to return to his Grand Base alive and sane: 'Not for your own good, but for the good of that struggling young Civilization which you oppose.'

Kinnison reached Prime Base with the all-important data. By building super-powerful battleships, called 'maulers', the Patrol gained a temporary advantage over Boskonia, but a stalemate soon ensued. Kinnison developed a plan of action whereby he hoped to locate Helmuth's Grand Base, and asked Port Admiral Haynes for permission to follow it. In lieu of that, however, Haynes told him that he had been given his Release; that he was an Unattached Lensman—a 'Gray' Lensman, popularly so-called, from the color of the plain leather uniforms they wear. Thus he earned the highest honor possible for the Galactic

Patrol to give, for the Gray Lensman works under no supervision or direction whatever. He is responsible to no one; to nothing save his own conscience. He is no longer a cog in the immense machine of the Galactic Patrol: wherever he may go he *is* the Patrol!

In quest of a second line to Grand Base, Kinnison scouted a pirate stronghold on Aldebaran I. Its personnel, however, were not even near-human, but were Wheelmen, possessed of the sense of perception; hence Kinnison was discovered before he could accomplish anything and was very seriously wounded. He managed to get back to his speedster and to send a thought to Port Admiral Haynes, who rushed ships to his aid. In Base Hospital Surgeon-Marshal Lacy put him back together; and during a long and quarrelsome convalescence, Nurse Clarrissa MacDougall held him together. And Lacy and Haynes connived to promote a romance between nurse and Lensman.

As soon as he could leave the hospital he went to Arisia in the hope that he might be given advanced training; something which had never before been attempted. Much to his surprise he learned that he had been expected to return for exactly such training. Getting it almost killed him, but he emerged from the ordeal vastly stronger of mind than any human being had ever been before; and possessed of a new sense as well—the sense of perception, a sense somewhat analogous to sight, but of much greater power, depth, and scope, and not dependent on light.

After trying out his new mental equipment by solving a murder mystery on Radelix, he went to Boyssia II, where he succeeded in entering an enemy base. He took over the mind of a communications officer and waited for a chance to get his second, all-important line to Grand Base. An enemy ship captured a hospital ship of the Patrol and brought it in to Boyssia. Nurse MacDougall, head nurse of the ship, working under Kinnison's instructions, stirred up trouble which soon became mutiny. Helmuth took a hand from Grand Base, thus enabling the Lensman to get his second line.

The hospital ship, undetectable by virtue of Kinnison's nullifier, escaped from Boyssia II and headed for Earth at full blast. Kinnison, convinced that Helmuth was really Boskone himself, found that the intersection of the two lines, and therefore the pirates' Grand Base, lay in Star Cluster AC 257–4736, well outside the galaxy. Pausing only long enough to destroy the Wheelmen of Aldebaran I, he set out to investigate Helmuth's headquarters. He found a stronghold impregnable to any attack the

Patrol could throw against it; manned by thought-screened personnel. His sense of perception was suddenly cut off—the pirates had erected a thought-screen around their whole planet. He then returned to Prime Base deciding en route that boring from within was the only possible way to take that stupendous fortress.

In consultation with the Port Admiral the zero hour was set at which time the massed Grand Fleet of the Patrol was to attack Grand Base with every projector it could bring to bear.

Pursuant to his plan, Kinnison again visited Trenco, where the Patrol forces extracted for him some fifty kilograms of thionite; the noxious drug which, in microgram inhalations, makes the addict experience all the sensations of doing whatever it is that he wishes most ardently to do. The larger the dose, the more intense and exquisite the sensations—resulting sooner or later, in a super-ecstatic death.

Thence to Helmuth's planet; where, working through the unshielded brain of a dog, he let himself into the central dome. Here, just before the zero minute, he released his thionite into the air-stream, thus wiping out all the pirates except Helmuth himself, who, in his ultra-shielded inner bomb-proof, could not be affected.

The Patrol attacked precisely on schedule, but Helmuth would not leave his retreat, even to try to save his base. Therefore Kinnison had to go in after him. Poised in the air of the inner dome there was an enigmatic, sparkling ball of force which the Lensman could not understand, and of which he was therefore very suspicious.

But the storming of that quadruply-defended inner stronghold was exactly the task for which Kinnison's new and ultra-cumbersome armor had been designed; so in he went. He killed Helmuth in armor-to-armor combat.*

Kinnison was pretty sure that that force-ball was keyed to some particular pattern, and suspected—correctly—that it was in part an inter-galactic communicator. Hence he did not think into it until he was in the flagship with Port Admiral Haynes; until all kinds of recorders and analyzers had been set up. Then he did so—and Grand Base was blasted out of existence by duodec bombs placed by the pirates themselves and triggered by the force-ball. The detectors showed a hard, tight communications line running straight out toward the Second Galaxy. Helmuth was not Boskone.

* *Galactic Patrol* (Panther Books).

Scouting the Second Galaxy in his super-powerful battleship *Dauntless*, Kinnison met and defeated a squadron of Boskonian war-vessels. He landed upon the planet Medon, whose people had been fighting a losing war against Boskone. The Medonians, electrical wizards who had already installed inertia-neutralizers and a space-drive, moved their world across inter-galactic space to our First Galaxy.

With the cessation of military activity, however, the illicit traffic in habit-forming drugs had increased tremendously, and Kinnison, deducing that Boskone was back of the drug syndicate, decided that the best way to find the real leader of the enemy was to work upward through the drug ring.

Disguised as a dock walloper, he frequented the saloon of a drug baron, and helped to raid it; but although he secured much information, his disguise was penetrated.

He called a Conference of Scientists to devise means of building a gigantic bomb of negative matter. Then, impersonating a Tellurian secret-service agent who lent himself to the deception, he tried to investigate the stronghold of Prellin of Bronseca, one of Boskone's regional directors. This disguise also failed and he barely managed to escape.

Ordinary disguises having proved useless, Kinnison became Wild Bill Williams; once a gentleman of Aldebaran II, now a space-rat meteor miner. He made of himself an almost bottomless drinker of the hardest beverages known to space. He became a drug fiend—a bentlam eater—discovering that his Arisian-trained mind could function at full efficiency even while his physical body was completely stupefied. He became widely known as the fastest, deadliest performer with twin DeLameters ever to strike the asteroid belts.

Through solar system after solar system he built up an unimpeachable identity as a hard-drinking, wildly-carousing bentlam-eating, fast-shooting space-hellion; a lucky or a very skilful meteor miner; a derelict who had been an Aldebaranian gentleman once and who would be again if he should ever strike it rich.

Physically helpless in a bentlam stupor, he listened in on a zwilnik conference and learned that Edmund Crowninshield, of Tressilia III, was also a regional director of the enemy.

Boskone formed an alliance with the Overlords of Delgon, and through a hyper-spatial tube the combined forces again attacked humanity. Not simple slaughter this time, for the Overlords tortured their captives and consumed their life forces in sadistic orgies. The Conference of Scientists solved the mystery of the tube and the *Dauntless* counter-attacked through it, returning victorious.

Wild Bill Williams struck it rich at last. Abandoning the low dives in which he had been wont to carouse, he made an obvious effort to become again an Aldebaranian gentleman. He secured an invitation to visit Crowninshield's resort—the Boskonian, believing that Williams was basically a booze- and drug-soaked bum, wanted to get his quarter-million credits.

In a characteristically wild debauch, Kinnison–Williams did squander a large part of his new fortune; but he learned from Crowninshield's mind that one Jalte, a Kalonian by birth, was Boskone's galactic director; and that Jalte had his headquarters in a star cluster just outside the First Galaxy. Pretending bitter humiliation and declaring that he would change his name and disappear, the Gray Lensman left the planet—to investigate Jalte's base.

He learned that Boskone was not a single entity, but a council. Jalte did not know very much about it, but his superior, one Eichmil, who lived on the planet Jarnevon, in the Second Galaxy, would know who and what Boskone really was.

Therefore Kinnison and Worsel went to Jarnevon. Kinnison was captured and tortured—there was at least one Overlord there—but Worsel rescued him before his mind was damaged and brought him back with his knowledge intact. Jarnevon was peopled by the Eich, a race almost as monstrous as the Overlords. The Council of Nine which ruled the planet was in fact the long-sought Boskone.

The greatest surgeons of the age—Phillips of Posenia and Wise of Medon—demonstrated that they could grow new nervous tissue; even new limbs and organs if necessary. Again Clarrissa MacDougall nursed Kinnison back to health, and this time the love between them could not be concealed.

The Grand Fleet of the Patrol was assembled, and with Kinnison in charge of Operations, swept outward from the First Galaxy. Jalte's planet was destroyed by means of the negasphere—the negative-matter bomb—then on to the Second Galaxy.

Jarnevon, the planet of the Eich, was destroyed by smashing it between two barren planets which had been driven there in the 'free' (inertialess) condition. These planets, having exactly opposite intrinsic velosities, were inerted, one upon each side of the doomed world; and when that frightful collision was over a minor star had come into being.

Grand Fleet returned to our galaxy. Galactic Civilization rejoiced. Prime Base was a center of celebration. Kinnison, supposing that the war was over and that his problem was solved, threw off the Lensman's Load. Marrying his Cris, he declared, was the most important thing in the universe.

But how wrong he was! For even as Lensman and nurse were walking down a corridor of Base Hospital after a conference with Haynes and Lacy regarding that marriage——*

* *Grey Lensman* (Panther Books).

1: Recalled

'Stop, youth!' The voice of Mentor the Arisian thundered silently, deep within the Lensman's brain.

He stopped convulsively, almost in mid-stride, and at the rigid, absent awareness in his eyes Nurse MacDougall's face went white.

'This is not merely the loose and muddy thinking of which you have all too frequently been guilty in the past,' the deeply resonant, soundless voice went on, 'it is simply not thinking at all. At times, Kinnison of Tellus, we almost despair of you. Think, youth, *think*! For know, Lensman, that upon the clarity of your thought and upon the trueness of your perception depends the whole future of your Patrol and of your Civilization; more so now by far than at any time in the past.'

'What'dy'mean, "think"?' Kinnison snapped back thoughtlessly. His mind was a seething turmoil, his emotion an indescribable blend of surprise, puzzlement, and incredulity.

For moments, as Mentor did not reply, the Gray Lensman's mind raced. Incredulity ... becoming tinged with apprehension ... turning rapidly into rebellion.

'Oh, Kim!' Clarrissa choked. A queer enough tableau they made, these two, had they been there to see; the two uniformed figures standing there so strainedly, the nurse's two hands grippings those of the Lensman. She, completely en rapport with him, had understood his every fleeting thought. 'Oh, Kim! They *can't* do that to us ...'

'I'll say they can't!' Kinnison flared. 'By Klono's tungsten teeth, I won't do it! We have a right to happiness, you and I, and we'll ...'

'We'll what?' she asked, quietly. She knew what they had to face; and, strong-souled woman that she was, she was quicker to face it squarely than was he. 'You were just blasting off, Kim, and so was I.'

'I suppose so,' glumly. 'Why in all the nine hells of Valeria did I have to be a Lensman? Why couldn't I have stayed a ...?'

'Because you are you,' the girl interrupted, gently. 'Kimball Kinnison, the man I love. You couldn't do anything else.' Chin up, she was fighting gamely. 'And if I rate Lensman's Mate I can't be a sissy, either. It won't last forever, Kim. Just a little longer to wait, that's all.'

Eyes, steel-gray now, stared down into eyes of tawny, gold-flecked bronze. 'QX, Cris? *Really* QX?' What a world of meaning there was in that cryptic question!

'Really, Kim.' She met his stare unfalteringly. If not entirely unafraid, at least with whole-hearted determination. 'On the beam and on the green, Gray Lensman, all the way. Every long, last millimeter. There, wherever it is—to the very end of whatever road it has to be—and back again. Until it's over. I'll be here. Or somewhere, Kim. Waiting.'

The man shook himself and breathed deep. Hands dropped apart—both knew consciously as well as subconsciously that the less of physical demonstration the better for two such natures as theirs—and Kimball Kinnison, Unattached Lensman, came to grips with his problem.

He began really to think; to think with the full power of his prodigious mind; and as he did so he began to see what the Arisian could have—what he must have—meant. He, Kinison, had gummed up the works. He had made a colossal blunder in the Boskonian campaign. He knew that Mentor, although silent, was still en rapport with him; and as he coldly, grimly, thought the thing through to its logical conclusion he knew, with a dull, sick certainty, what was coming next. It came:

'Ah, you perceive at last some portion of the truth. You see that your confused, superficial thinking has brought about almost irreparable harm. I grant that, in specimens so young of such a youthful race, emotion has its place and its function; but I tell you now in all solemnity that for you the time of emotional relaxation has not yet come. *Think*, youth—*THINK*!' and the ancient Arisian snapped the telepathic line.

As one, without a word, nurse and Lensman retraced their way to the room they had left so shortly before. Port Admiral Haynes and Surgeon-Marshal Lacy still sat upon the nurse's davenport, scheming roseate schemes having to do with the wedding they had so subtly engineered.

'Back so soon? Forget something, MacDougall?' Lacy asked, amiably. Then, as both men noticed the couple's utterly untranslatable expression:

'What happened? Break it out, Kim!' Haynes commanded.

'Plenty, chief,' Kinnison answered, quietly. 'Mentor stopped us before we got to the elevator. Told me I'd put my foot in it up to my neck on that Boskonian thing. That instead of being all buttoned up, my fool blundering has put us farther back than we were when we started.'

'Mentor!'

'*Told* you!'

'Put us back!'

It was an entirely unpremeditated, unconscious duet. The two old officers were completely dumbfounded. Arisians never had come out of their shells, they never would. Infinitely less disturbing would have been the authentic tidings that a brick house had fallen upstairs. They had nursed this romance along *so* carefully, had timed it *so* exactly, and now it had gone *p-f-f-f-t*—it had been taken out of their hands entirely. That thought flashed through their minds first. Then, as catastrophe follows lightning's flash, the real knowledge exploded within their consciousnesses that, in some unguessable fashion or other, the whole Boskonian campaign had gone *p-f-f-f-t*, too.

Port Admiral Haynes, master tactician, reviewed in his keen strategist's mind every phase of the recent struggle, without being able to find a flaw in it.

'There wasn't a loop-hole anywhere,' he said aloud. 'Where do they figure we slipped up?'

'We didn't slip—*I* slipped,' Kinnison stated, flatly. 'When we took Bominger—the fat Chief Zwilnik of Radelix, you know—I took a bop on the head to learn that Boskone had more than one string per bow. Observers, independent, for every station at all important. I learned that fact thoroughly then, I thought. At least, we figured on Boskone's having lines of communication past, not through, his Regional Directors, such as Prellin of Bronseca. Since I changed my line of attack at that point, I did not need to consider whether or not Crowninshield of Tressilia III was by-passed in the same way; and when I had worked my way up through Jalte in his star-cluster to Boskone itself, on Jarnevon, I had forgotten the concept completely. Its possibility didn't even occur to me. That's where I fell down.'

'I still don't see it!' Haynes protested. 'Boskone was the top!'

'Yeah?' Kinnison asked, pointedly. 'That's what I thought—but prove it.'

'Oh.' The Port Admiral hesitated. 'We had no reason to think otherwise ... looked at in that light, this intervention would seem to be conclusive ... but before that there was no ...'

'There were so,' Kinnison contradicted, 'but I didn't see them then. That's where my brain went sour; I should have seen them. Little things, mostly, but significant. Not so much positive as negative indices. Above all, there was nothing whatever to indicate that Boskone actually was the top. That idea was the product of my own wishful and very low-grade thinking, with no basis or foundation in fact or in theory. And now,' he concluded bitterly, 'because my skull is so thick that it takes an idea a hundred years to filter through it—because a sheer, bare fact has to be driven into my brain with a Valerian maul before I can grasp it—we're sunk without a trace.'

'Wait a minute, Kim, we aren't sunk yet,' the girl advised, shrewdly. 'The fact that, for the first time in history, an Arisian has taken the initiative in communication with a human being, means something big—*really* big. Mentor does not indulge in what he calls "loose and muddy' thinking. Every part of every thought he sent carries meaning—plenty of meaning.'

'What do you mean?' As one, the three men asked substantially the same question; Kinnison, by virtue of his faster reactions, being perhaps half a syllable in the lead.

'I don't know, exactly,' Clarrissa admitted. 'I've got only an ordinary mind, and it's firing on half its jets or less right now. But I do know that his thought was 'almost' irreparable, and that he meant precisely that—nothing else. If it had been wholly irreparable he not only would have expressed his thought that way, but he would have stopped you before you destroyed Jarnevon. I know that. Apparently it would have become wholly irreparable if we had got . . .' she faltered, blushing, then went on, '. . . if we had kept on about our own personal affairs. That's why he stopped us. We can win out, he meant, if you keep on working. It's your oyster, Kim . . . it's up to you to open it. You can do it, too—I just *know* you can.'

'But why didn't he stop you before you fellows smashed Boskone?' Lacy demanded, exasperated.

'I hope you're right, Cris—it sounds reasonable,' Kinnison said, thoughtfully. Then, to Lacy:

'That's an easy one to answer, doctor. Because knowledge that comes the hard way is knowledge that really sticks with you. If he had drawn me a diagram before, it wouldn't have helped, the next time I get into a jam. This way it will. I've got to learn how to think, if it cracks my skull.

'*Really* think,' he went on, more to himself than to the other three. 'To think so it counts.'

'Well, what are we going to do about it?' Haynes was—he had to be, to get where he was and to stay where he was—quick on the uptake. 'Or, more specifically, what are you going to do and what am I going to do?'

'What I am going to do will take a bit of mulling over,'

Kinnison replied, slowly. 'Find some more leads and trace them up, is the best that occurs to me right now. Your job and procedure are rather clearer. You remarked out in space that Boskone knew that Tellus was very strongly held. That statement, of course, is no longer true.'

'Huh?' Haynes half-pulled himself up from the davenport, then sank back. 'Why?' he demanded.

'Because we used the negasphere—a negative-matter bomb of planetary anti-mass—to wipe out Jalte's planet, and because we smashed Jarnevon between two colliding planets,' the Lensman explained, concisely. 'Can the present defenses of Tellus cope with either one of those offensives?'

'I'm afraid not . . . no,' the Port Admiral admitted. 'But . . .'

'We can admit no "buts", admiral," Kinnison declared, with grim finality. 'Having used those weapons, we must assume that the Boskonian scientists—we'll have to keep on calling them "Boskonians", I suppose, until we find a truer name—had recorders on them and have now duplicated them. Tellus must be made safe against anything we have ever used; against, as well, everything that, by the wildest stretch of the imagination, we can conceive of the enemy using.'

'You're right . . . I can see that,' Haynes nodded.

'We've been underestimating them right along,' Kinnison went on. 'At first we thought they were merely organized outlaws and pirates. Then, when it was forced upon us that they could match us—overmatch us in some things—we still wouldn't admit that they must be as large and as wide-spread as we are—galactic in scope. We know now that they were wider-spread than we are. Inter-galactic. They penetrated into our galaxy, riddled it, before we knew that theirs was inhabited or inhabitable. Right?'

'To a hair, although I never thought of it in exactly that way before.'

'None of us have—mental cowardice. And they have the advantage,' Kinnison continued, inexorably, 'in knowing that our Prime Base is on Tellus; whereas, if Jarnevon was not in fact theirs, we have no idea whatever where it is. And another point. Was that fleet of theirs a planetary outfit?'

'Well, Jarnevon was a big planet, and the Eich were a mighty warlike race.'

'Quibbling a bit, aren't you, chief?'

'Uh-huh,' Haynes admitted, somewhat sheepishly. 'The probability is very great that no one planet either built or maintained that fleet.'

'And that leads us to expect what?'

'Counter-attack. In force. Everything they can shove this way. However, they've got to rebuild their fleet, besides designing and building the new stuff. We'll have time enough, probably, if we get started right now.'

'But, after all, Jarnevon *may* have been their vital spot,' Lacy submitted.

'Even if that were true, which it probably isn't,' the now thoroughly convinced Port Admiral sided in with Kinnison, 'it doesn't mean a thing, Sawbones. If they should blow Tellus out of space it wouldn't kill the Galactic Patrol. It would hurt it, of course, but it wouldn't cripple it seriously. The other planets of Civilization could, and certainly would, go ahead with it.'

'My thought exactly,' from Kinnison. 'I check you to the proverbial nineteen decimals.'

'Well, there's a lot to do and I'd better be getting at it.' Haynes and Lacy got up to go. 'See you in my office when convenient?'

'I'll be there as soon as I tell Clarrissa goodbye.'

At about the same time that Haynes and Lacy went to Nurse MacDougall's room, Worsel the Velantian arrowed downward through the atmosphere toward a certain flat roof. Leather wings shot out with a snap and in a blast of wind—Velantians can stand eleven Tellurian gravities—he came in his customary appalling landing and dived unconcernedly down a nearby shaft. Into a corridor, along which he wriggled blithely to the office of his old friend, Master Technician La-Verne Thorndyke.

'Verne, I have been thinking,' he announced, as he coiled all but about six feet of his sinuous length into a tight spiral upon the rug and thrust out half a dozen weirdly stalked eyes.

'That's nothing new,' Thorndyke countered. No human mind can sympathize with or even remotely understand the Velantian passion for solid weeks of intense, uninterrupted concentration upon a single thought. 'What about this time? The whichness of the why?'

'That is the trouble with you Tellurians,' Worsel grumbled. 'Not only do you not know how to think, but you . . .'

'Hold on!' Thorndyke interrupted, unimpressed. 'If you've got anything to say, old snake, why not say it? Why circumnavigate total space before you get to the point?'

'I have been thinking about thought...'

'So what?' the technician derided. 'That's even worse. That's a logarithmic spiral if there ever was one.'

'Thought—and Kinnison,' Worsel declared, with finality.

'Kinnison? Oh—that's different. I'm interested—very much so. Go ahead.'

'And his weapons. His DeLameters, you know.'

'No, I don't know, and you know I don't know. What about them?'

'They are so ... so ... so *obvious.*' The Velantian finally found the exact thought he wanted. 'So big, and so clumsy, and so obtrusive. So inefficient, so wasteful of power. No subtlety—no finesse.'

'But that's far and away the best hand-weapon that has ever been developed!' Thorndyke protested.

'True. Nevertheless, a millionth of that power, properly applied, could be at least a million times as deadly.'

'How?' The Tellurian, although shocked, was dubious.

'I have reasoned it out that thought, in any organic being, is and must be connected with one definite organic compound—this one,' the Velantian explained didactically, the while there appeared within the technician's mind the space formula of an incredibly complex molecule; a formula which seemed to fill not only his mind, but the entire room as well. 'You will note that it is a large molecule, one of very high molecular weight. Thus it is comparatively unstable. A vibration at the resonant frequently of any one of its component groups would break it down, and thought would therefore cease.'

It took perhaps a minute for the full import of the ghastly thing to sink into Thorndyke's mind. Then, every fiber of him flinching from the idea, he began to protest.

'But he doesn't need it, Worsel. He's got a mind already that can...'

'It takes much mental force to kill,' Worsel broke in equably. 'By that method one can slay only a few at a time, and it is exhausting work. My proposed method would require only a minute fraction of a watt of power and scarcely any mental force at all.'

'And it would *kill*—it would have to. That reaction could not be made reversible.'

'Certainly,' Worsel concurred. 'I never could understand why you soft-headed, soft-hearted, soft-bodied human beings are so reluctant to kill your enemies. What good does it do merely to stun them?'

'QX—skip it.' Thorndyke knew that it was hopeless to attempt to convince the utterly inhuman Worsel of the fundamental rightness of human ethics. 'But nothing has ever been designed small enough to project such a wave.'

'I realize that. It's design and construction will challenge your inventive ability. Its smallness is its great advantage. He could wear it in a ring, in the bracelet of his Lens; or, since it will be actuated, controlled, and directed by thought, even imbedded surgically beneath his skin.'

'How about backfires?' Thorndyke actually shuddered. 'Protection . . . shielding . . .'

'Details—mere details,' Worsel assured him, with an airy flip of his scimitared tail.

'That's nothing to be running around loose,' the man argued. 'Nobody could tell what killed them, could they?'

'Probably not.' Worsel pondered briefly. 'No. Certainly not. The substance must decompose in the instant of death, from any cause. And it would not be "loose", as you think; it should not become known, even. You would make only the one, of course.'

'Oh. You don't want one, then?'

'Certainly not. What do I need of such a thing? Kinnison only—and only for his protection.'

'Kim can handle it . . . but he's the only being this side of Arisia that I'd trust with one . . . QX, give me the dope on the frequency, wave-form, and so on, and I'll see what I can do.'

2: Invasion via Tube

Port Admiral Haynes newly chosen President of the Galactic Council and by virtue of his double office the most powerful entity of Civilization, set instantly into motion the vast machinery which would make Tellus safe against any possible attack. He first called together his Board of Strategy; the same keen-minded tacticians who had helped him plan the invasion of the Second Galaxy and the eminently successful attack upon Jarnevon. Should Grand Fleet, many of whose component fleets had not yet reached their home planets, be recalled? Not yet—lots of time for that. Let them go home for a while first. The enemy would have to rebuild before they could attack, and there were many more pressing matters.

Scouting was most important. The planets near the galactic rim could take care of that. In fact, they should concentrate upon it, to the exclusion of everything else of warfare's activities. Every approach to the galaxy—yes, the space between the two galaxies and as far into the Second Galaxy as it was safe to penetrate—should be covered as with a blanket. That way, they could not be surprised.

Kinnison, when he heard that, became vaguely uneasy. He did not really have a thought; it was as though he should have had one, but didn't. Deep down, far off, just barely above the threshold of perception an indefinite, formless something obtruded itself upon his consciousness. Tug and haul at it as he would, he could not get the drift. There was *something* he ought to be thinking of, but what in all the iridescent hells from Vandemar to Alsakan was it? So, instead of flitting about upon his declared business, he stuck around; helping the General Staff—and thinking.

And Defense Plan BBT went from the idea men to the draftsmen, then to the engineers. This was to be, primarily, a war of planets. Ships could battle ships, fleets fleets; but, postulating good tactics upon the other side, no fleet, however armed and powered, could stop a planet. That had been proved. A planet had a mass of the order of magnitude of one times ten to the twenty fifth kilograms, and an intrinsic velocity of somewhere around forty kilometers per second. A hundred probably, relative to Tellus, if the planet came from the Second Galaxy. Kinetic energy, roughly, about five times ten to the forty first ergs. No, that was nothing for any possible fleet to cope with.

Also, the attacking planets would of course be inertialess until the last strategic instant. Very well, they must be made inert prematurely, when the Patrol wanted them that way, not the enemy. How? HOW? The Bergenholms upon those planets would be guarded with everything the Boskonians had.

The answer to that question, as worked out by the engineers, was something they called a 'super-mauler'. It was gigantic, cumbersome, and slow; but little faster, indeed, than a free planet. It was like Helmuth's fortresses of space, only larger. It was like the special defense cruisers of the Patrol, except that its screens were vastly heavier. It was like a regular mauler, except that it had only one weapon. All of its incomprehensible mass was devoted to one thing—*power*! It could defend itself; and, if it could get close enough to its objective, it could do plenty of damage—its dreadful primary was the first weapon ever developed capable of cutting a Q-type helix squarely in two.

And in various solar systems, uninhabitable and worthless planets were converted into projectiles. Dozens of them, possessing widely varying masses and intrinsic velocities. One by one they flitted away from their parent suns and took up positions—not too far away from our Solar System, but not too near.

And finally Kinnison, worrying at his tantalizing thought as a dog worries a bone, crystallized it. Prosaically enough, it was an extremely short and flamboyantly waggling pink skirt which catalyzed the reaction; which acted as the seed of the crystallization. Pink—a Chickladorian—Xylpic the Navigator—Overlords of Delgon. Thus flashed the train of thought, culminating in:

'Oh, so *that's* it!' he exclaimed, aloud. 'A TUBE—just as sure as hell's a mantrap!' He whistled raucously at a taxi, took the wheel himself, and broke—or at least bent—most of the city's traffic ordinances in getting to Haynes' office.

The Port Admiral was always busy, but he was never too busy to see Gray Lensman Kinnison; especially when the latter demanded the right of way in such terms as he used then.

'The whole defense set-up is screwy,' Kinnison declared. 'I thought I was overlooking a bet, but I couldn't locate it. Why should they fight their way through inter-galactic space and through sixty thousand parsecs of planet-infested galaxy when they don't have to?' he demanded. 'Think of the length of the supply line, with our bases placed to cut it in a hundred places, no matter how they route it. It doesn't make sense. They'd have to out-weigh us in an almost impossibly high ratio, unless they have an improbably superior armament.'

'Check.' The old warrior was entirely unperturbed. 'Surprised you didn't see that long ago. We did. I'll be very much surprised if they attack at all.'

'But you're going ahead with all this just as though . . .'

'Certainly. Something *may* happen, and we can't be caught off guard. Besides, it's good training for the boys. Helps morale, no end.' Haynes' nonchalant air disappeared and he studied the younger man keenly for moments. 'But Mentor's warning certainly meant something, and you said "when they don't have to". But even if they go clear around the galaxy to the other side—an impossibly long haul—we're covered. Tellus is far enough in so they can't possibly take us by surprise. So—spill it!'

'How about a hyper-spatial tube? They know exactly where we are, you know.'

'Um ... m ... m.' Haynes was taken aback. 'Never thought of it ... possible, distinctly a possibility. A duodec bomb, say, just far enough underground ...'

'Nobody else thought of it, either, until just now,' Kinnison broke in. 'However, I'm afraid of duodec—don't see how they could control it accurately enough at this three dimensional distance. Too deep, it wouldn't explode at all. What I don't like to think of, though, is a negasphere. Or a planet, perhaps.'

'Ideas? Suggestions?' the admiral snapped.

'No—I don't know anything about that stuff. How about putting our Lenses on Cardynge?'

'That's a thought!' and in seconds they were in communication with Sir Austin Cardynge, Earth's mightiest mathematical brain.

'Kinnison, how many times must I tell you that I am not to be interrupted?' the aged scientist's thought was a crackle of fury. 'How can I concentrate upon vital problems if every young whippersnapper in the System is to perpetrate such abominable, such outrageous intrusions ...'

'Hold it, Sir Austin—hold everything!' Kinnison soothed. 'I'm sorry. I wouldn't have intruded if it hadn't been a matter of life or death. But it would be worse intrusion, wouldn't it, if the Boskonians sent a planet about the size of Jupiter—or a negasphere—through one of their extra-dimensional vortices into your study? That's exactly what they're figuring on doing.'

'What-what-what?' Cardynge snapped, like a string of firecrackers. He quieted down, then, and thought. And Sir Austin Cardynge *could* think, upon occasion and when he felt so inclined; could think in the abstruse symbology of pure mathematics with a cogency equalled by few minds in the universe. Both Lensmen perceived those thoughts, but neither could understand or follow them. No mind not a member of the Conference of Scientists could have done so.

'They can't!' of a sudden the mathematician cackled, gleefully disdainful. 'Impossible—quite definitely impossible. There are laws governing such things, Kinnison, my impetuous and ignorant young friend. The terminus of the necessary hyper-tube could not be established within such proximity to the mass of the sun. This is shown by . . .'

'Never mind the proof—the fact is enough,' Kinnison interposed, hastily. 'How close to the sun could it be established?'

'I couldn't say, off-hand,' came the cautiously scientific reply. 'More than one astronomical unit, certainly, but the computation of the exact distance would require some little time. It would, however, be an interesting, if minor, problem. I will solve it for you, if you like, and advise you of the exact minimum distance.'

'Please do so—thanks a million,' and the Lensmen disconnected.

'The conceited old goat!' Haynes snorted. 'I'd like to smack him down!'

'I've felt like it more than once, but it wouldn't do any good. You've got to handle him with gloves—besides, you can afford to make concessions to a man with a brain like that.'

'I suppose so. But how about that infernal tube? Knowing that it can not be set up within or very near Tellus helps some, but not enough. We've got to know where it is—*if* it is. Can you detect it?'

'Yes. That is, I can't, but the specialists can, I think. Wise of Medon would know more about that than anyone else. Why wouldn't it be a thought to call him over here?'

'It would that,' and it was gone.

Wise of Medon and his staff came, conferred, and departed. Sir Austin Cardynge solved his minor problem, reporting that the minimum distance from the sun's center to the postulated center of the terminus of the vortex—actually, the geometrical origin of the three-dimensional figure which was the hyper-plane of intersection—was one point two six four seven, approximately, astronomical units; the last figure being tentative and somewhat uncertain because of the rapidly-moving masses of Jupiter . . .

Haynes cut the tape—he had no time for an hour of mathematical dissertation—and called in his execs.

'Full-globe detection of hyper-spatial tubes,' he directed, crisply. 'Kinnison will tell you exactly what he wants. Hipe!'

Shortly thereafter, five-man speedsters, plentifully equipped with new instruments, flashed at full drive along courses carefully calculated to give the greatest possible coverage in the shortest possible time.

Unobtrusively the loose planets closed in; close enough so that at least three or four of them could reach any designated point in one minute or less. The outlying units of Grand Fleet, too, were pulled in. That fleet was not actually mobilized—yet—but every vessel in it was kept in readiness for instant action.

'No trace,' came the report from the Medonian surveyors, and Haynes looked at Kinnison, quizzically.

'QX, chief—glad of it,' the Gray Lensman answered the unspoken query. 'If it was up, that would mean they were on the way. Hope they don't get a trace for two months yet. But I'm next-to-positive that that's the way they're coming and the longer they put it off the better—there's a possible new projector that will take a bit of doping out. I've got to do a flit—can I have the *Dauntless*?'

'Sure—anything you want—she's yours anyway.'

Kinnison went. And, wonder of wonders, he took Sir Austin Cardynge with him. From solar system to solar system, from planet to planet, the mighty *Dauntless* hurtled at the incomprehensible velocity of full maximum blast; and every planet so visited was the home world of one of the most cooperative—or, more accurately, one of the least non-cooperative—members of the Conference of Scientists. For days brilliant but more or less unstable minds struggled with new and obdurate problems; struggled heatedly and with friction, as was their wont. Few if any of those mighty intellects would have really enjoyed a quietly studious session, even had such a thing been possible.

Then Kinnison returned his guests to their respective homes and shot his flying warship-laboratory back to Prime Base. And, even before the *Dauntless* landed, the first few hundreds of a fleet which was soon to be numbered in the millions of meteor-miners' boats began working like beavers to build a new and exactly-designed system of asteroid belts of iron meteors.

And soon, as such things go, new structures began to appear here and there in the void. Comparatively small, these things were; tiny, in fact, compared to the Patrol's maulers. Unarmed, too; carrying nothing except defensive screen. Each was, apparently, simply a power-house; stuffed skin full of atomic motors, exciters, intakes, and generators of highly peculiar design and pattern. Unnoticed except by gauntly haggard Thorndyke and his experts, who kept dashing from one of the strange craft to another, each took its place in a succession of precisely-determined relationships to the sun.

Between the orbits of Mars and of Jupiter, the new, sharply-defined rings of asteroids moved smoothly. Most of Grand Fleet formed an enormous hollow hemisphere. Throughout all nearby space the surveying speedsters and flitters rushed madly hither and yon. Uselessly, apparently, for not one needle of the vortex-detectors stirred from its zero-pin.

As nearly as possible at the Fleet's center there floated the flagship. Technically the *Z9M9Z*, socially the *Directrix*, ordinarily simply *GFHQ*, that ship had been built specifically to control the operations of a million separate flotillas. At her million-plug board stood—they had no need, ever, to sit—two hundred blocky, tentacle-armed Rigellians. They were waiting, stolidly motionless.

Intergalactic space remained empty. Interstellar ditto, ditto. The flitters flitted, fruitlessly.

But if everything out there in the threatened volume of space seemed quiet and serene, things in the *Z9M9Z* were distinctly otherwise. Haynes and Kinnison, upon whom the heaviest responsibilities rested, were tensely ill at ease.

The admiral had his formation made, but he did not like it at all. It was too big, too loose, to cumbersome. The Boskonian fleet might appear anywhere, and it would take him far, far too long to get any kind of a fighting formation made, anywhere. So he worried. Minutes dragged—he wished that the pirates would hurry up and start something!

Kinnison was even less easy in his mind. He was not afraid of negaspheres, even if Boskonia should have them; but he was afraid of fortified, mobile planets. The super-maulers were big and powerful, of course, but they very definitely were not planets; and the big, new idea was mighty hard to jell. He didn't like to bother Thorndyke by calling him—the master technician had troubles of his own—but the reports that were coming in were none too cheery. The excitation was wrong or the grid action was too unstable or the screen potentials were too high or too low or too something. Sometimes they got a concentration, but it was just as apt as not to be a spread flood instead of a tight beam. To Kinnison, therefore, the minutes fled like seconds—but every minute that space remained clear was one more precious minute gained.

Then, suddenly, it happened. A needle leaped into significant figures. Relays clicked, a bright red light flared into being, a gong clanged out its raucous warning. A fractional instant later ten thousand other gongs in ten thousand other ships came brazenly to life as the discovering speedster automatically sent out its number and position; and those other ships—survivors all—flashed toward that position and dashed frantically about. Theirs the task to determine, in the least number of seconds possible, the approximate location of the center of emergence.

For Port Admiral Haynes, canny old tactician that he was, had planned his campaign long since. It was standing plain in his tactical tank—to englobe the entire space of emergence of the foe and to blast them out of existence before they could maneuver. If he could get into formation before the Boskonians appeared it would be a simple slaughter—if not, it might be otherwise. Hence seconds counted; and hence he had had high-speed computers working steadily for weeks at the computation of courses for every possible center of emergence.

'Get me that center—fast!' Haynes barked at the surveyors, already blasting at maximum.

It came in. The chief computer yelped a string of numbers. Selected loose-leaf binders were pulled down, yanked apart, and distributed on the double, leaf by leaf. And:

'Get it over there! Especially the shock-globe!' the Port Admiral yelled.

For he himself could direct the engagement only in broad; details must be left to others. To be big enough to hold in any significant relationship the millions of lights representing vessels, fleets, planets, structures, and objectives, the Operations tank of the *Directrix* had to be seven hundred feet in diameter; and it was a sheer physical impossibility for any ordinary mind either to perceive that seventeen million cubic feet of space as a whole or to make any sense at all out of the stupendously bewildering maze of multi-colored lights crawling and flashing therein.

Kinnison and Worsel had handled Grand Fleet Operations during the battle of Jarnevon, but they had discovered that they could have used some help. Four Rigellian Lensmen had been training for months for that all-important job, but they were not yet ready. Therefore the two old masters and one new one now labored at GFO: three tremendous minds, each supplying something that the others lacked. Kinnison of Tellus, with his hard, flat driving urge, his unconquerable, unstoppable will to do. Worsel of Velantia, with the prodigious reach and grasp which had enabled him, even without the Lens, to scan mentally a solar system eleven light-years distant. Tregonsee of Rigel IV, with the vast, calm certainty, the imperturbable poise peculiar to his long-lived, solemn race. Second Stage Lensmen all, graduates of Arisian advanced training; minds linked, basically, together into one mind by a wide-open three-way; superficially free, each to do his assigned third of the gigantic task.

Smoothly, effortlessly, those three linked minds went to work at the admiral's signal. Orders shot out along tight beams of thought of the stolid hundreds of Rigellian switchboard operators, and thence along communicator beams to the pilot rooms, wherever stationed. Flotillas, squadrons, sub-fleets flashed smoothly toward their newly-assigned positions. Super-maulers moved ponderously toward theirs. The survey ships, their work done, vanished. They had no business anywhere near what was coming next. Small they were, and defenseless; a speedster's screens were as efficacious as so much vacuum against the forces about to be unleashed. The power houses also moved. Maintaining rigidly their cryptic mathematical relationships to each other and the sun, they went as a whole into a new one with respect to the circling rings of tightly-packed meteors and the invisible, non-existent mouth of the Boskonian vortex.

Then, before Haynes' formation was nearly complete, the Boskonian fleet materialized. Just that—one instant space was empty; the next it was full of warships. A vast globe of battle-wagons, in perfect fighting formation. They were not free, but inert and deadly.

Haynes swore viciously under his breath, the Lensmen pulled themselves together more tensely; but no additional orders were given. Everything that could possibly be done was already being done.

Whether the Boskonians expected to meet a perfectly-placed fleet or whether they expected to emerge into empty space, to descend upon a defenseless Tellus, is not known or knowable. It is certain, however, that they emerged in the best possible formation to meet anything that could be brought to bear. It is also certain that, had the enemy had a *Z9M9Z* and a Kinnison–Worsel–Tregonsee combination scanning its Operations Tank, the outcome might well have been otherwise than it was.

For that ordinarily insignificant delay, that few minutes of time necessary for the Boskonians' orientation, was exactly that required for those two hundred smoothly-working Rigellians to get Civilization's shock-globe into position.

A million beams, primaries raised to the hellish heights possible only to Medonian conductors and insulation, lashed out almost as one. Screens stiffened to the urge of every generable watt of defensive power. Bolt after bolt of quasi-solid lightning struck and struck and struck again. Q-type helices bored, gouged, and searingly bit. Rods and cones, planes and shears of incredibly condensed pure force clawed, tore, and ground in mad abandon. Torpedo after torpedo, charged to the very skin with duodec, loosed its horribly detonant cargo against flinching wall-shields, in such numbers and with such violence as to fill all circumambient space with an atmosphere of almost planetary density.

Screen after screen, wall-shield after wall-shield, in their hundreds and their thousands, went down. A full eighth of the Patrol's entire count of battleships was wrecked, riddled, blown apart, or blasted completely out of space in the paralyzing cataclysmic violence of the first, seconds-long, mind-shaking, space-wracking encounter. Nor could it have been otherwise; for this encounter had not been at battle range. Not even at point-blank range; the warring monsters of the void were packed practically screen to screen.

But not a man died—upon Civilization's side at least—even though practically all the myriad of ships composing the inner sphere, the shock-globe, was lost. For they were automatics, manned by robots; what little superintendence was necessary had been furnished by remote control. Indeed it is possible, although perhaps not entirely probable, that the shock-globe of the foe was similarly manned.

That first frightful meeting gave time for the reserves of the Patrol to get there, and it was then that the superior Operations control of the *Z9M9Z* made itself tellingly felt. Ship for ship, beam for beam, screen for screen, the Boskonians were, perhaps equal to the Patrol; but they did not have the perfection of control necessary for unified action. The field was too immense, the number of contending units too enormously vast. But the mind of each of the three Second-Stage Lensmen read aright the flashing lights of his particular volume of the gigantic tank and spread their meaning truly in the infinitely smaller space-model beside which Port Admiral Haynes, Master Tactician, stood. Scanning the entire space of battle as a whole, he rapped out general orders—orders applying, perhaps, to a hundred or to five hundred planetary fleets. Kinnison and his fellows broke these orders down for the operators, who in turn told the admirals and vice-admirals of the fleets what to do. They gave detailed orders to the units of their commands, and the line officers, knowing exactly what to do and precisely how to do it, did it with neatness and dispatch.

There was no doubt, no uncertainty, no indecision or wavering. The line officers, even the admirals, knew nothing, could know nothing of the progress of the engagement as a whole. But they had worked under the *Z9M9Z* before. They knew that the maestro Haynes did know the battle as a whole. They knew that he was handling them as carefully and as skillfully as a master of chess plays his pieces upon the square-filled board. They knew that Kinnison or Worsel or Tregonsee was assigning no task too difficult of accomplishment. They knew that they could not be taken by surprise, attacked from some unexpected and unprotected direction; knew that, although in those hundreds of thousands of cubic miles of space there were hundreds of thousands of highly inimical and exceedingly powerful ships of war, none of them were or shortly could be in a position to do them serious harm. If there had been, they would have been pulled out of there, *beaucoup* fast. They were as safe as anyone in a warship in such a war could expect, or even hope, to be. Therefore they acted instantly; directly, whole-heartedly, and efficiently; and it was the Boskonians who were taken, repeatedly and by the thousands, by surprise.

For the enemy, as has been said, did not have the Patrol's smooth perfection of control. Thus several of Civilization's fleets, acting in full synchronization, could and repeatedly did rush upon one unit of the foe; englobing it, blasting it out of existence, and dashing back to stations; all before the nearest-by fleets of Boskone knew even that a threat was being made. Thus ended the second phase of the battle, the engagement of the two Grand Fleets, with the few remaining thousands of Boskone's battleships taking refuge upon or near the phalanx of planets which had made up their center.

Planets. Seven of them. Armed and powered as only a planet can be armed and powered; with fixed-mount weapons impossible of mounting upon a lesser mobile base, with fixed-mount intakes and generators which only planetary resources could excite or feed. Galactic Civilization's war-vessels fell back. Attacking a full-armed planet was no part of their job. And as they fell back the super-maulers moved ponderously up and went to work. This was their dish; for this they had been designed. Tubes, lances, stillettoes of unthinkable energies raved against their mighty screens; bouncing off, glancing away, dissipating themselves in space-torturing discharges as they hurled themselves upon the nearest ground. In and in the monsters bored, inexorably taking up their positions directly over the ultra-protected domes which, their commanders knew, sheltered the vitally important Bergenholms and controls. They then loosed forces of their own. Forces of such appalling magnitude as to burn out in a twinkling of an eye projector-shells of a refractoriness to withstand for ten full seconds the maximum output of a first-class battleship's primary batteries!

The resultant beam was of very short duration, but of utterly intolerable poignancy. No material substance could endure it even momentarily. It pierced instantly the hardest, tightest wall-shield known to the scientists of the Patrol. It was the only known thing which could cut or rupture the ultimately stubborn fabric of a Q-type helix. Hence it is not to be wondered at that as those incredible needles of ravening energy stabbed and stabbed and stabbed again at Boskonian domes every man of the Patrol, even Kimball Kinnison, fully expected those domes to go down.

But those domes held. And those fixed-mount projectors hurled back against the super-maulers forces at the impact of which course after course of fierce-driven defensive screen flamed through the spectrum and went down.

'Back! Get them back!' Kinnison whispered, white-lipped, and the attacking structures sullenly, stubbornly gave way.

'Why?' gritted Haynes. 'They're all we've got.'

'You forget the new one, chief—give us a chance.'

'What makes you think it'll work?' the old admiral flashed the searing thought. 'It probably won't—and if it doesn't . . .'

'If it doesn't,' the younger man shot back, 'we're no worse off than now to use the maulers. But we've got to use the sunbeam *now* while those planets are together and before they start toward Tellus.'

'QX,' the admiral assented; and, as soon as the Patrol's maulers were out of the way:

'Verne?' Kinnison flashed a thought. 'We can't crack 'em. Looks like it's up to you—what do you say?'

'Jury-rigged—don't know whether she'll light a cigarette or not—but here she comes!'

The sun, shining so brightly, darkened almost to the point of invisibility. War-vessels of the enemy disappeared, each puffing out into a tiny but brilliant sparkle of light.

Then, before the beam could effect the enormous masses of the planets, the engineers lost it. The sun flashed up—dulled—

brightened—darkened—wavered. The beam waxed and waned irregularly; the planets began to move away under the urgings of their now thoroughly scared commanders.

Again, while millions upon millions of tensely straining Patrol officers stared into their plates, haggard Thorndyke and his sweating crews got the sunbeam under control—and, in a heart-stopping wavering fashion, held it together. It flared—sputtered—ballooned out—but very shortly, before they could get out of its way, the planets began to glow. Ice-caps melted, then boiled. Oceans boiled, their surfaces almost exploding into steam. Mountain ranges melted and flowed sluggishly down into valleys. The Boskonian domes of force went down and stayed down.

'QX, Kim—let be,' Haynes ordered. 'No use overdoing it. Not bad-looking planets; maybe we can use them for something.'

The sun brightened to its wonted splendor, the planets began visibly to cool—even the Titanic forces then at work had heated those planetary masses only superficially.

The battle was over.

'What in all the purple hells of Palain did you do, Haynes, and how?' demanded the *Z9M9Z*'s captain.

'He used the whole damned solar system as a vacuum tube!' Haynes explained, gleefully. 'Those power stations out there, with all their motors and intake screens, are simply the power leads. The asteroid belts, and maybe some of the planets, are the grids and plates. The sun is . . .'

'Hold on, chief!' Kinnison broke in. 'That isn't quite it. You see, the directive field set up by the . . .'

'Hold on yourself!' Haynes ordered, briskly. 'You're too damned scientific, just like Sawbones Lacy. What do Rex and I care about technical details that we can't understand anyway? The net result is what counts—and that was to concentrate upon those planets practically the whole energy output of the sun. Wasn't it?'

'Well, that's the main idea,' Kinnison conceded. 'The energy equivalent, roughly, of four million one hundred and fifty thousand tons per second of disintegrating matter.'

'*Whew!*' the captain whistled. 'No wonder it frizzled 'em up.'

'I can say now, I think, with no fear of successful contradiction, that Tellus *is* strongly held,' Haynes stated, with conviction. 'What now, Kim old son?'

'I think they're done, for a while,' the Gray Lensman pondered. 'Cardynge can't communicate through the tube, so probably they can't; but if they managed to slip an observer through they may know how almighty close they came to licking us. On the other hand, Verne says that he can get the bugs out of the sunbeam in a couple of weeks—and when he does, the next zwilnik he cuts loose at is going to get a surprise.'

'I'll say so,' Haynes agreed. 'We'll keep the surveyors on the prowl, and some of the Fleet will always be close by. Not all of it, of course—we'll adopt a schedule of reliefs—but enough of it to be useful. That ought to be enough, don't you think?'

'I think so—yes,' Kinnison answered, thoughtfully. 'I'm just about positive that they won't be in shape to start anything here again for a long time. And I had better get busy, sir, on my own job—I've got to put out a few jets.'

'I suppose so,' Haynes admitted.

For Tellus *was* strongly held, now—so strongly held that Kinnison felt free to begin again the search upon whose successful conclusion depended, perhaps, the outcome of the struggle between Boskonia and Galactic Civilization.

3: Lyrane the Matriarchy

When the forces of the Galactic Patrol blasted Helmuth's Grand Base out of existence and hunted down and destroyed his secondary bases throughout this galaxy, Boskone's military grasp upon Civilization was definitely broken. Some minor bases may have escaped destruction, of course. Indeed, it is practically certain that some of them did so, for there are comparatively large volumes of our Island Universe which have not been mapped, even yet, by the planetographers of the Patrol. It is equally certain, however, that they were relatively few and of no real importance. For warships, being large, cannot be carried around or concealed in a vest pocket—a war-fleet must of necessity be based upon a celestial object not smaller than a very large asteroid. Such a base, laying close enough to any one of

Civilization's planets to be of any use, could not be hidden successfully from the detectors of the Patrol.

Reasoning from analogy, Kinnison quite justifiably concluded that the back of the drug syndicate had been broken in similar fashion when he had worked upward through Bominger and Strongheart and Crowninshield and Jalte to the dread council of Boskone itself. He was, however, wrong.

For, unlike the battleship, thionite is a vest-pocket commodity. Unlike the space-fleet base, a drug-baron's headquarters can be and frequently is small, compact, and highly mobile. Also, the galaxy is huge, the number of planets in it immense, the total count of drug addicts utterly incomprehensible. Therefore it had been found more efficient to arrange the drug hook-up in multiple series-parallel, instead of in the straight en-cascade sequence which Kinnison thought that he had followed up.

He thought so at first, that is, but he did not think so long. He had thought, and he had told Haynes, as well as Gerrond of Radelix, that the situation was entirely under control; that with the zwilnik headquarters blasted out of existence and with all of the regional heads and many of the planetary chiefs dead or under arrest, all that the Enforcement men would have to cope with would be the normal bootleg trickle. In that, too, he was wrong. The lawmen of Narcotics had had a brief respite, it is true; but in a few days or weeks, upon almost as many planets as before, the illicit traffic was again in full swing.

After the Battle of Tellus, then, it did not take the Gray Lensman long to discover the above facts. Indeed, they were pressed upon him. He was, however, more relieved than disappointed at the tidings, for he knew that he would have material upon which to work. If his original opinion had been right, if all lines of communication with the now completely unknown ultimate authorities of the zwilniks had been destroyed, his task would have been an almost hopeless one.

It would serve no good purpose here to go into details covering his early efforts, since they embodied, in principle, the same tactics as those which he had previously employed. He studied, he analyzed, he investigated. He snooped and he spied. He fought; upon occasion he killed. And in due course—and not too long a course—he cut into the sign of what he thought must be a key zwilnik. Not upon Bronseca or Radelix or Chickladoria, or any other distant planet, but right upon Tellus!

But he could not locate him. He never saw him on Tellus. As

a matter of cold fact, he could not find a single person who had ever seen him or knew anything definite about him. These facts, of course, only whetted Kinnison's keeness to come to grips with the fellow. He might not be a very big shot, but the fact that he was covering himself up so thoroughly and so successfully made it abundantly evident that he was a fish well worth landing.

This wight, however, proved to be as elusive as the proverbial flea. He was never there when Kinnison pounced. In London he was a few minutes late. In Berlin he was a minute or so too early, and the ape didn't show up at all. He missed him in Paris and in San Francisco and in Shanghai. The guy sat down finally in New York, but still the Gray Lensman could not connect—it was always the wrong street, or the wrong house, or the wrong time, or something.

Then Kinnison set a snare which should have caught a microbe—and *almost* caught his zwilnik. He missed him by one mere second when he blasted off from New York Space-Port. He was so close that he saw his flare, so close that he could slap onto the fleeing vessel the beam of the CRX tracer which he always carried with him.

Unfortunately, however, the Lensman was in mufti at the time, and was driving a rented flitter. His speedster—altogether too spectacular and obvious a conveyance to be using in a hush-hush investigation—was at Prime Base. He didn't want the speedster, anyway, except inside the *Dauntless*. He'd go organized this time to chase the lug clear out of space, if he had to. He shot in a call for the big cruiser, and while it was coming he made luridly sulphurous inquiry.

Fruitless. His orders had been carried out to the letter, except in the one detail of not allowing any vessel to take off. This take-off absolutely could not be helped—it was just one of those things. The ship was a Patrol speedster from Deneb V, registry number so-and-so. Said he was coming in for servicing. Came in on the north beam, identified himself properly—Lieutenant Quirkenfal, of Deneb V, he said it was, and it checked. . . .

It would check, of course. The zwilnik that Kinnison had been chasing so long certainly would not be guilty of any such raw, crude work as a faulty identification. In fact, right then he probably looked just as much like Quirkenfal as the lieutenant himself did.

'He wasn't in any hurry at all,' the information went on. 'He waited around for his landing clearance, then slanted in on his assigned slide to the service pits. In the last hundred yards, though, he shot off to one side and sat down, *plop*, broadside on, clear over there in the far corner of the field. But he wasn't down but a second, sir. Long before anybody could get to him—before the cruisers could put a beam on him, even—he blasted off as though the devil was on his tail. Then you came along, sir, but we did put a CRX tracer on him. . . .'

'I did that much, myself,' Kinnison stated, morosely. 'He stopped just long enough to pick up a passenger—my zwilnik, of course—then flitted . . . and you fellows let him get away with it.'

'But we couldn't help it, sir,' the official protested. 'And anyway, he couldn't possibly have . . .'

'He sure could. You'd be surprised no end at what that bimbo can do.'

Then the *Dauntless* flashed in; not asking but demanding instant right of way.

'Look around, fellows, if you like, but you won't find a damned thing,' Kinnison's uncheering conclusion came back as he sprinted toward the dock into which his battleship had settled. 'The lug hasn't left a loose end dangling yet.'

By the time the great Patrol ship had cleared the stratosphere Kinnison's CRX, powerful and tenacious as it was, was just barely registering a line. But that was enough. Henry Henderson, Master Pilot, stuck the *Dauntless*' needle nose into that line and shoved into the driving projectors every watt of 'oof' that those Brobdingnagian creations would take.

They had been following the zwilnik for three days now, Kinnison reflected, and his CRX's were none too strong yet. They were overhauling him mighty slowly; and the *Dauntless* was supposed to be the fastest thing in space. That bucket up ahead had plenty of legs—must have been souped up to the limit. This was apt to be a long chase, but he'd get that bozo if he had to chase him on a geodesic line along the hyper-dimensional curvature of space clear back to Tellus where he started from!

They did not have to circumnavigate total space, of course, but they did almost leave the galaxy before they could get the fugitive upon their plates. The stars were thinning out fast; but still, hazily before them in a vastness of distance, there stretched a milky band of opalescence.

'What's coming up, Hen—a rift?' Kinnison asked.

'Uh-huh, Rift Ninety Four,' the pilot replied. 'And if I remember right, that arm up ahead is Dunstan's region and it has never been explored. I'll have the chart-room check up on it.'

'Never mind; I'll go check it myself—I'm curious about this whole thing.'

Unlike any smaller vessel, the *Dauntless* was large enough so that she could—and hence as a matter of course did—carry every space-chart issued by all the various Boards and Offices and Bureaus concerned with space, astronomy, astrogation, and planetography. She had to, for there were usually minds aboard which were apt at any time to become intensely and unpredictably interested in anything, anywhere. Hence it did not take Kinnison long to obtain what little information there was.

The vacancy they were approaching was Rift Ninety Four, a vast space, practically empty of stars, lying between the main body of the galaxy and a minor branch of one of its prodigious spiral arms. The opalescence ahead was the branch—Dunstan's Region. Henderson was right; it had never been explored.

The Galactic Survey, which has not even yet mapped at all completely the whole of the First Galaxy proper, had of course done no systematic work upon such outlying sections as the spiral arms. Some such regions were well known and well mapped, it is true; either because its own population, independently developing means of space-flight, had come into contact with our Civilization upon its own initiative or because private exploration and investigation had opened up profitable lines of commerce. But Dunstan's Region was bare. No people resident in it had ever made themselves known; no private prospecting, if there had ever been any such, had revealed anything worthy of exploitation or development. And, with so many perfectly good uninhabited planets so much nearer to Galactic Center, it was of course much too far out for colonization.

Through the rift, then, and into Dunstan's Region the *Dauntless* bored at the unimaginable pace of her terrific full-blast drive. The tracers' beams grew harder and more taut with every passing hour; the fleeting speedster itself grew large and clear upon the plates. The opalescence of the spiral arm became a firmament of stars. A sun detached itself from that firmament; a dwarf of Type G. Planets appeared.

One of these in particular, the second out, looked so much like Earth that it made some of the observers homesick. There were the familiar polar ice-caps, the atmosphere and stratosphere, the high-piled, billowy masses of clouds. There were vast blue oceans, there were huge, unfamiliar continents glowing with chlorophyllic green.

At the spectroscopes, at the bolometers, at the many other instruments men went rapidly and skillfully to work.

'Hope the ape's heading for Two, and I think he is,' Kinnison remarked, as he studied the results. 'People living on that planet would be human to ten places, for all the tea in China. No wonder he was so much at home on Tellus ... Yup, it's Two—there, he's gone inert.'

'Whoever is piloting that can went to school just one day in his life and that day it rained and the teacher didn't come,' Henderson snorted. 'And he's trying to balance her down on her tail—look at her bounce and flop around! He's just begging for a crack-up.'

'If he makes it it'll be bad—plenty bad,' Kinnison mused. 'He'll gain a lot of time on us while we're rounding the globe on our landing spiral.'

'Why spiral, Kim? Why not follow him down, huh? Our intrinsic is no worse than his—it's the same one, in fact.'

'Get conscious, Hen. This is a superbattlewagon—just in case you didn't know it before.'

'So what? I can certainly handle this super a damn sight better than that ground-gripper is handling that scrap-heap down there.' Henry Henderson, Master Pilot Number One of the Service, was not bragging. He was merely voicing what to him was the simple and obvious truth.

'Mass is what. Mass and volume and velocity and inertia and power. You never stunted this much mass before, did you?'

'No, but what of it? I took a course in piloting once, in my youth.' He was then a grand old man of twenty-eight or thereabouts. 'I can line up the main rear center pipe onto any grain of sand you want to pick out on that field, and hold her there until she slags it down.'

'If you think you can spell "able", hop to it!'

'QX, this is going to be fun.' Henderson gleefully accepted the challenge, then clicked on his general-alarm microphone. 'Strap down, everybody, for inert maneuvering, Class Three, on the tail. Tail over to belly landing. Hipe!'

The Bergenholms were cut and as the tremendously massive super-dreadnought, inert, shot off at an angle under its Tellurian intrinsic velocity, Master Pilot Number One proved his rating. As much a virtuoso of the banks and tiers of blast keys and levers before him as a concert organist is of his instrument, his hands and feet flashed hither and yon. Not music?—the bellowing, crescendo thunders of those jets *were* music to the hard-boiled space-hounds who heard them. And in response to the exact placement and the precisely-measured power of those blasts the great sky-rover spun, twisted, and bucked as her prodigious mass was forced into motionlessness relative to the terrain beneath her.

Three G's, Kinnison reflected, while this was going on. Not bad—he'd guessed it at four or better. He could sit up and take notice at three, and he did so.

This world wasn't very densely populated, apparently. Quite a few cities, but all just about on the equator. Nothing in the temperate zones at all; even the highest power revealed no handiwork of man. Virgin forest, untouched prairie. Lots of roads and things in the torrid zone, but nothing anywhere else. The speedster was making a rough and unskillful, but not catastrophic landing.

The field which was their destination lay just outside a large city. Funny—it wasn't a space-field at all. No docks, no pits, no ships. Low, flat buildings—hangars. An air-field, then, although not like any air-field he knew. Too small. Gyros? 'Copters? Didn't see any—all little ships. Crates—biplanes and tripes. Made of wire and fabric. Wotta woil, wotta woil!

The *Dauntless* landed, fairly close to the now deserted speedster.

'Hold everything, men,' Kinnison cautioned. 'Something funny here. I'll do a bit of looking around before we open up.'

He was not surprised that the people in and around the airport were human to at least ten places of classification; he had expected that from the planetary data. Nor was he surprised at the fact that they wore no clothing. He had learned long since that, while most human or near-human races—particularly the women—wore at least a few ornaments, the wearing of clothing as such, except when it was actually needed for protection, was far more the exception than the rule. And, just as a Martian, out of deference to conventions, wears a light robe upon Tellus, Kinnison as a matter of course stripped to his evenly-tanned hide when visiting planets upon which nakedness was *de rigeur.* He had attended more than one state function, without a quibble or a qualm, tastefully attired in his Lens.

No, the startling fact was that there was not a man in sight anywhere around the place; there was nothing male perceptible as far as his sense of perception could reach. Women were laboring, women were supervising, women were running the machines. Women were operating the airplanes and servicing them. Women were in the offices. Women and girls and little girls and girl babies filled the waiting rooms and the automobile-like conveyances parked near the airport and running along the streets.

And, even before Kinnison had finished uttering his warning, while his hand was in the air reaching for a spy-ray switch, he felt an alien force attempting to insinuate itself into his mind.

Fat chance! With any ordinary mind it would have succeeded, but in the case of the Gray Lensman it was just like trying to stick a pin unobtrusively into a panther. He put up a solid block automatically, instantaneously; then, a fraction of a second later, a thought-tight screen enveloped the whole vessel.

'Did any of you fellows . . .' he began, then broke off. They wouldn't have felt it, of course; their brains could have been read completely with them none the wiser. He was the only Lensman aboard, and even most Lensmen couldn't . . . this was his oyster. But *that* kind of stuff, on such an apparently backward planet as this? It didn't make sense, unless that zwilnik . . . ah, this *was* his oyster, absolutely!

'Something funnier even than I thought—thought-waves,' he calmly continued his original remark. 'Thought I'd better undress to go out there, but I'm not going to. I'd wear full armor, except that I may need my hands or have to move fast. If they get insulted at my clothes I'll apologize later.'

'But listen, Kim, you can't go out there alone—especially without armor!'

'Sure I can. I'm not taking any chances. You fellows couldn't do me much good out there, but you can here. Break out a 'copter and keep a spy-ray on me. If I give you the signal, go to work with a couple of narrow needle-beams. Pretty sure that I won't need any help, but you can't always tell.'

The airlock opened and Kinnison stepped out. He had a high-powered thought-screen, but he did not need it—yet. He had his DeLameters. He had also a weapon deadlier by far even than those mighty portables; a weapon so utterly deadly that he had not used it. He did not need to test it—since Worsel had said that it would work, it would. The trouble with it was that it could not merely disable: if used at all it killed, with complete and grim finality. And behind him he had the full awful power of the *Dauntless*. He had nothing to worry about.

Only when the space-ship had settled down upon and into the hard-packed soil of the airport could those at work there realize just how big and how heavy the visitor was. Practically everyone stopped work and stared, and they continued to stare as Kinnison strode toward the office. The Lensman had landed upon many strange planets, he had been met in divers fashions and with various emotions; but never before had his presence stirred up anything even remotely resembling the sentiments written so plainly upon these women's faces and expressed even more plainly in their seething thoughts.

Loathing, hatred, detestation—not precisely any one of the three, yet containing something of each. As though he were a monstrosity, a revolting abnormality that should be destroyed on sight. Beings such as the fantastically ugly, spider-like denizens of Dekanore VI had shuddered at the sight of him, but their thoughts were mild compared to these. Besides, that was natural enough. Any human being would appear a monstrosity to such as those. But these women were human; as human as he was. He didn't get it, at all.

Kinnison opened the door and faced the manager, who was standing at that other-worldly equivalent of a desk. His first glance at her brought to the surface of his mind one of the peculiarities which he had already unconsciously observed. Here, for the first time in his life, he saw a woman without any touch whatever of personal adornment. She was tall and beautifully proportioned, strong and fine; her smooth skin was tanned to a rich and even brown. She was clean, almost blatantly so.

But she wore no jewelry, no bracelets, no ribbons; no decoration of any sort or kind. No paint, no powder, no touch of perfume. Her heavy, bushy eyebrows had never been plucked or clipped. Some of her teeth had been expertly filled, and she had a two-tooth bridge that would have done credit to any Tellurian dentist—but her hair! It, too, was painfully clean, as was the white scalp beneath it, but aesthetically it was a mess. Some of it reached almost to her shoulders, but it was very evident that whenever a lock grew long enough to be a bother she was wont to grab it and hew it off, as close to the skull as possible, with whatever knife, shears, or other implement came readiest to hand.

These thoughts and the general inspection did not take any appreciable length of time, of course. Before Kinnison had taken two steps toward the manager's desk, he directed a thought:

'Kinnison of Sol III—Lensman, Unattached. It is possible,

however, that neither Tellus nor the Lens are known upon this planet?'

'Neither is known, nor does anyone of Lyrane care to know anything of either,' she replied coldly. Her brain was keen and clear; her personality vigorous, striking, forceful. But, compared with Kinnison's doubly-Arisian-trained mind, hers was woefully slow. He watched her assemble the mental bolt which was intended to slay him then and there. He let her send it, then struck back. Not lethally, not even paralyzingly, but solidly enough so that she slumped down, almost unconscious, into a nearby chair.

'It's good technique to size a man up before you tackle him, sister,' he advised her when she had recovered. 'Couldn't you tell from the feel of my mind-block that *you* couldn't crack it?'

'I was afraid so,' she admitted, hopelessly, 'but I had to kill you if I possibly could. Since you are the stronger you will of course kill me.' Whatever else these peculiar women were, they were stark realists. 'Go ahead—get it over with.... But it *can't* be!' Her thought was a wail of protest. 'I do not grasp your thought of a "man", but you are certainly a male; and no mere *male* can be—can *possibly* be, ever—as strong as a person.'

Kinnison got that thought perfectly, and it rocked him. She did not think of herself as a woman, a female, at all. She was simply a *person.* She could not understand even dimly Kinnison's reference to himself as a man. To her, 'man' and 'male' were synonymous terms. Both meant sex, and nothing whatever except sex.

'I have no intention of killing you, or anyone else upon this planet,' he informed her levelly, 'unless I absolutely have to. But I have chased that speedster over there all the way from Tellus, and I intend to get the man that drove it here, if I have to wipe out half of your population to do it. Is that perfectly clear?'

'That is perfectly clear, male.' Her mind was fuzzy with a melange of immiscible emotions. Surprise and relief that she was not to be slain out of hand; disgust and repugnance at the very idea of such a horrible, monstrous male creature having the audacity to exist; stunned, disbelieving wonder at his unprecedented power of mind; a dawning comprehension that there were perhaps some things which she did not know: these and numerous other conflicting thoughts surged through her mind. 'But there was no male within the space-traversing vessel which you think of as a "speedster",' she concluded, surprisingly.

And he knew that she was not lying. 'Damnation!' he snorted to himself. 'Fighting *women* again!'

'Who was she, then—it, I mean,' he hastily corrected the thought.

'It was our elder sister . . .'

The thought so translated by the man was not really 'sister'. That term, having distinctly sexual connotations and implications, would never have entered the mind of any 'person' of Lyrane II. 'Elder child of the same heritage' was more like it.

'. . . and another person from what it claimed was another world,' the thought flowed smoothly on. 'An entity, rather, not really a person, but you would not be interested in that, of course.'

'Of course I would,' Kinnison assured her. 'In fact, it is this other person, and not your elderly relative, in whom I am interested. But you say that it is an entity, not a person. How come? Tell me all about it.'

'Well, it looked like a person, but it wasn't. Its intelligence was low, its brain power was small. And its mind was upon things . . . its thought were so . . .'

Kinnison grinned at the Lyranian's efforts to express clearly thoughts so utterly foreign to her mind as to be totally incomprehensible.

'You don't know what that entity was, but I do,' he broke in upon her floundering. "It was a person who was also, and quite definitely, a female. Right?'

'But a person couldn't—couldn't possibly—be a female!' she protested. 'Why, even biologically, it doesn't make sense. There are no such things as females—there can't be!' and Kinnison saw her viewpoint clearly enough. According to her sociology and conditioning there could not be.

'We'll go into that later,' he told her. 'What I want now is this female zwilnik. Is she—or it—with your elder relative now?'

'Yes. They will be having dinner in the hall very shortly.'

'Sorry to bother, but you'll have to take me to them—right now.'

'Oh, may I? Since I could not kill you myself, I must take you to them so they can do it. I have been wondering how I could force you to go there,' she explained, naively.

'Henderson?' The Lensman spoke into his microphone—thought-screens, of course, being no barrier to radio waves. 'I'm going after the zwilnik. This woman here is taking me. Have the 'copter stay over me, ready to needle anything I tell them to. While I'm gone go over that speeder with a fine-tooth comb, and when you get everything we want, blast it. It and the *Dauntless* are the only spacecraft on the planet. These janes are man-haters and mental killers, so keep your thought-screens up. Don't let them down for a fraction of a second, because they've got plenty of jets and they're just as sweet and reasonable as a cageful of cateagles. Got it?'

'On the tape, chief,' came instant answer. 'But don't take any chances, Kim. Sure you can swing it alone?'

'Jets enough and to spare,' Kinnison assured him, curtly. Then, as the Tellurians' helicopter shot into the air, he again turned his thought to the manager.

'Let's go,' he directed, and she led him across the way to a row of parked ground-cars. She manipulated a couple of levers and smoothly, if slowly, the little vehicle rolled away.

The distance was long and the pace was slow. The woman was driving automatically, the while her every sense was concentrated upon finding some weak point, some chink in his barrier, through which to thrust at him. Kinnison was amazed—stumped—at her fixity of purpose; at her grimly single-minded determination to make an end of him. She was out to get him, and she wasn't fooling.

'Listen, sister,' he thought at her, after a few minutes of it; almost plaintively, for him. 'Let's be reasonable about this thing. I told you I didn't want to kill you; why in all the iridescent hells of space are you so dead set on killing me? If you don't behave yourself, I'll give you a treatment that will make your head ache for the next six months. Why don't you snap out of it, you dumb little lug, and be friends?'

This thought jarred her so that she stopped the car, the better to stare directly and viciously into his eyes.

'Be *friends*? With a *male*?' The thought literally seared its way into the man's brain.

'Listen, half-wit!' Kinnison stormed, exasperated. 'Forget your narrow-minded, one-planet prejudices and think for a minute, if you can think—use that pint of bean soup inside your skull for something besides hating me all over the place. Get this—I am no more a male than you are the kind of a female that you think, by analogy, such a creature would have to be if she could exist in a sane and logical world.'

'Oh.' The Lyranian was taken aback at such cavalier instruction. 'But the others, those in your so-immense vessel they are of a certainty males,' she stated with conviction. 'I understood what you told them via your telephone-with-out-conductors. You have mechanical shields against the thought which kills. Yet you do not have to use it, while the others—males indubitably—do. You yourself are not entirely male; your brain is almost as good as a person's.'

'Better, you mean,' he corrected her. 'You're wrong. All of us of the ship are men—all alike. But a man on a job can't concentrate all the time on defending his brain against attack, hence the use of thought-screens. I can't use a screen out here, because I've got to talk to you people. See?'

'You fear us, then, so little?' she flared, all of her old animosity blazing out anew. 'You consider our power, then, so small a thing?'

'Right. Right to a hair,' he declared, with tightening jaw. But he did not believe it—quite. This girl was just about as safe to play around with as five-feet-eleven of coiled bush-master, and twice as deadly.

She could not kill him mentally. Nor could the elder sister—whoever she might be—and her crew; he was pretty sure of that. But if they couldn't do him in by dint of brain it was a foregone conclusion that they would try brawn. And brawn they certainly had. This jade beside him weighted a hundred sixty five or seventy, and she was trained down fine. Hard, limber, and fast. He might be able to lick three or four of them—maybe half a dozen—in a rough-and-tumble brawl; but more than that would mean either killing or being killed. Damn it all! He'd never killed a woman yet, but it looked as though he might have to start in pretty quick now.

'Well, let's get going again,' he suggested, 'and while we're en route let's see if we can't work out some basis of cooperation—a sort of live-and-let-live arrangement. Since you understood the orders I gave the crew, you realize that our ship carries weapons capable of razing this entire city in a space of minutes.' It was a statement not a question.

'I realize that.' The thought was muffled in helpless fury. 'Weapons, weapons—always *weapons*! The eternal *male*! If it were not for your huge vessel and the peculiar airplane hovering over us I would claw your eyes out and strangle you with my bare hands!'

'That would be a good trick if you could do it,' he countered, equably enough. 'But listen, you frustrated young murderess. You have already shown yourself to be, basically, a realist in facing physical facts. Why not face mental, intellectual facts in the same spirit?'

'Why, I do, of course. I *always* do!'

'You do not,' he contradicted, sharply. 'Males, according to your lights, have two—and only two—attributes. One, they breed. Two, they fight. They fight each other, and everything else, to the death and at the drop of a hat. Right?'

'Right, but . . .'

'But nothing—let me talk. Why didn't you breed the combativeness out of your males, hundreds of generations ago?'

'They tried it once, but the race began to deteriorate,' she admitted.

'Exactly. Your whole set-up is cock-eyed—unbalanced. You can think of me only as a male—one to be destroyed on sight, since I am not like one of yours. Yet, when I could kill you and had every reason to do so, I didn't. We can destroy you all, but we won't unless we must. What's the answer?'

'I don't know,' she confessed, frankly. Her frenzied desire for killing abated, although her ingrained antipathy and revulsion did not. 'In some ways, you do seem to have some of the instincts and qualities of a . . . almost of a person.'

'I am a person . . .'

'You are *not*! Do you think that I am to be misled by the silly coverings you wear?'

'Just a minute. I am a person of a race having two *equal* sexes. Equal in every way. Numbers, too—one man and one woman . . .' and he went on to explain to her, as well as he could, the sociology of Civilization.

'Incredible!' she gasped the thought.

'But true,' he assured her. 'And now you are going to lay off me and behave yourself, like a good little girl, or am I going to have to do a bit of massaging on your brain? Or wind that beautiful body of yours a couple of times around a tree? I'm asking this for your own good, kid, believe me.'

'Yes, I do believe you,' she marveled. 'I am becoming convinced that . . . that perhaps you are a person—at least of a sort—after all.'

'Sure I am—that's what I've been trying to tell you for an hour. And cancel that "of a sort", too . . .'

'But tell me,' she interrupted, 'a thought you used— "beautiful". I do not understand it. What does it mean, "beautiful body"?'

'Holy Klono's whiskers!' If Kinnison had never been

stumped before, he was now. How could he explain beauty, or music, or art, to this ... this matriarchal savage? How explain cerise to a man born blind? And above all, who had ever heard of having to explain to a woman—to any woman, anywhere in the whole macrocosmic universe—that she in particular was beautiful?

But he tried. In her mind he spread a portrait of her as he had seen her first. He pointed out to her the graceful curves and lovely contours, the lithely flowing lines, the perfection of proportion and modeling and symmetry, the flawlessly smooth, firm-textured skin, the supple, hard-trained fineness of her whole physique. No soap. She tried, in brow-furrowing concentration, to get it, but in vain. It simply did not register.

'But that is merely efficiency, everything you have shown,' she declared. 'Nothing else. I must be so, for my own good and for the good of those to come. But I think that I have seen some of your beauty,' and in turn she sent into his mind a weirdly distorted picture of a human woman. The zwilnik he was following, Kinnison decided instantly.

She would be jeweled, of course, but not that heavily—a horse couldn't carry that load. And no woman ever born put paint on that thick, or reeked so of violent perfume, or plucked her eyebrows to such a thread, or indulged in such a hair-do.

'If that is *beauty*, I want none of it,' the Lyranian declared.

Kinnison tried again. He showed her a waterfall, this time, in a stupendous gorge, with appropriate cloud formations and scenery. That, the girl declared, was simply erosion. Geological formations and meteorological phenomena. Beauty still did not appear. Painting, it appeared to her, was a waste of pigment and oil. Useless and inefficient—for any purpose of record the camera was much faster and much more accurate. Music—vibrations in the atmosphere—would of necessity be simply a noise; and noise—any kind of noise—was not efficient.

'You poor little devil.' The Lensman gave up. 'You poor, ignorant, soul-starved little devil. And the worst of it is that you don't even realize—and never can realize—what you are missing.'

'Don't be silly.' For the first time, the woman actually laughed. 'You are utterly foolish to make such a fuss about such trivial things.'

Kinnison quit, appalled. He knew, now, that he and this apparently human creature beside him were as far apart as the Galactic Poles in every essential phase of life. He had heard of matriarchies, but he had never considered what a real matriarchy, carried to its logical conclusion, would be like.

This was it. For ages there had been, to all intents and purposes, only one sex; the masculine element never having been allowed to rise above the fundamental necessity of reproducing the completely dominant female. And that dominant female had become, in every respect save the purely and necessitously physical one, absolutely and utterly sexless. Men, upon Lyrane II, were dwarfs about thirty inches tall. They had the temper and the disposition of a mad Radeligian cateagle, the intellectual capacity of a Zabriskan fontema. They were not regarded as people, either at birth or at any subsequent time. To maintain a static population, each person gave birth to one person, on the grand average. The occasional male baby—about one in a hundred—did not count. He was not even kept at home, but was taken immediately to the 'maletorium', in which he lived until attaining maturity.

One man to a hundred or so women for a year, then death. The hundred persons had their babies at twenty-one or twenty-two years of age—they lived to an average age of a hundred years—then calmly blasted their male's mind and disposed of his carcass. The male was not exactly an outcast; not precisely a pariah. He was tolerated as a necessary adjunct to the society of persons, but in no sense whatever was he a member of it.

The more Kinnison pondered this hook-up the more appalled he became. Physically, these people were practically indistinguishable from human, Tellurian, Caucasian women. But mentally, intellectually, in every other way, how utterly different! Shockingly, astoundingly so to any really human being, whose entire outlook and existence is fundamentally, however unconsciously or subconsciously, based upon and conditioned by the prime division of life into two cooperant sexes. It didn't seem, at first glance, that such a cause could have such terrific effects; but here they were. In cold reality, these women were no more human than were the ... the Eich. Take the Posenians, or the Rigellians, or even the Velentians. Any normal, stay-at-home Tellurian woman would pass out cold if she happened to stumble onto Worsel in a dark alley at night. Yet the members of his repulsively reptilian-appearing race, merely because of having a heredity of equality and cooperation between the sexes, were in essence more nearly human than were these tall, splendidly-built, actually and intrinsically beautiful creatures of Lyrane II!

'This is the hall,' the person informed him, as the car came to a halt in front of a large structure of plain gray stone. 'Come with me.'

'Gladly,' and they walked across the peculiarly bare grounds. They were side by side, but a couple of feet apart. She had been altogether too close to him in the little car. She did not want this male—or *any* male—to touch her or to be near her. And, considerably to her surprise, if the truth were to be known, the feeling was entirely mutual. Kinnison would have preferred to touch a Borovan slime-lizard.

They mounted the granite steps. They passed through the dull, weather-beaten portal. They were still side by side—but they were now a full yard apart.

4: Kinnison Captures . . .

'Listen, my beautiful but dumb guide,' Kinnison counseled the Lyranian girl as they neared their objective. 'I see that you're forgetting all your good girl-scout resolutions and are getting all hot and bothered again. I'm telling you now for the last time to watch your step. If that zwilnik person has even a split second's warning that I'm on her tail all hell will be out for noon, and I don't mean perchance.'

'But I must notify the Elder One that I am bringing you in,' she told him. 'One simply does not intrude unannounced. It is not permitted.'

'QX. Stick to the announcement, though, and don't put out any funny ideas or I'll lay you out cold. I'll send a thought along, just to make sure.'

But he did more than that, for even as he spoke his sense of perception was already in the room to which they were going. It was a large room, and bare; filled with tables except for a clear central space upon which at the moment a lithe and supple person was doing what seemed to be a routine of acrobatic dancing, interspersed with suddenly motionless posings and posturings of extreme technical difficulty. At the tables were seated a hundred or so Lyranians, eating.

Kinnison was not interested in the floor show, whatever it was, nor in the massed Lyranians. The zwilnik was what he was after. Ah, there she was, at a ringside table—a small, square table seating four—near the door. Her back was to it—good. At her left, commanding the central view of the floor, was a red-head, sitting in a revolving, reclining chair, the only such seat in the room. Probably the Big Noise herself—the Elder One. No matter, he wasn't interested in her, either—yet. His attention flashed back to his proposed quarry and he almost gasped.

For she, like Dessa Desplaines, was an Aldebaranian, and she was everything that the Desplaines woman had been—more so, if possible. She was a seven-sector callout, a thionite dream if there ever was one. And jewelry! This Lyranian tiger hadn't exaggerated that angle very much, at that. Her breast-shields were of gold and platinum filigree, thickly studded with diamonds, emeralds, and rubies, in intricate designs. Her shorts, or rather trunks, made of something that looked like glamorete, blazed with gems. A cleverly concealed dagger, with a jeweled haft and a vicious little fang of a blade. Rings, even a thumb-ring. A necklace which was practically a collar flashed all the colors of the rainbow. Bracelets, armlets, anklets, and knee-bands. High-laced dress boots, jeweled from stem to gudgeon. Ear-rings, and a meticulous, micrometically precise coiffure held in place by at least a dozen glittering buckles, combs and barrettes.

'Holy Klono's brazen tendons!' the Lensman whistled to himself, for every last, least one of those stones was the clear quill. 'Half a million credits if it's a millo's worth!'

But he was not particularly interested in this jeweler's vision of what the well-dressed lady zwilnik will wear. There were other, far more important things. Yes, she had a thought-screen. It was off, and its battery was mighty low, but it would still work; good thing he had blocked the warning. And she had a hollow tooth, too, but he'd see to it that she didn't get a chance to swallow its contents. She knew plenty, and he hadn't chased her this far to let her knowledge be obliterated by that hellish Boskonian drug.

They were at the door now. Disregarding the fiercely-driven mental protests of his companion, Kinnison flung it open, stiffening up his mental guard as he did so. Simultaneously he invaded the zwilnik's mind with a flood of force, clamping down so hard that she could not move a single voluntary muscle.

Then, paying no attention whatever to the shocked surprise of the assembled Lyranians, he strode directly up to the Aldebaranian and bent her head back into the crook of his elbow. Forcibly but gently he opened her mouth. With thumb and forefinger he deftly removed the false tooth. Releasing her then, mentally and physically, he dropped his spoil to the cement floor and ground it savagely to bits under his hard and heavy heel.

The zwilnik screamed wildly, piercingly at first. However, finding that she was getting no results, from Lensman or Lyranian, she subsided quickly into alerty watchful waiting.

Still unsatisfied, Kinnison flipped out one of his DeLameters and flamed the remains of the capsule of worse than paralyzing fluid, caring not a whit that his vicious portable, even in that brief instant, seared a hole a foot deep into the floor. Then and only then did he turn his attention to the redhead in the boss's chair.

He had to hand it to Elder Sister—through all this sudden and to her entirely unprecedented violence of action she hadn't turned a hair. She had swung her chair around so that she was facing him. Her back was to the athletic dancer who, now holding a flawlessly perfect pose, was going on with the act as though nothing out of the ordinary were transpiring. She was leaning backward in the armless swivel chair, her right foot resting upon its pedestal. Her left ankle was crossed over her right knee, her left knee rested lightly against the table's top. Her hands were clasped together at the nape of her neck, supporting her red-thatched head; her elbows spread abroad in easy, indolent grace. Her eyes, so deeply, darkly green as to be almost black stared up unwinkingly into the Lensman's—'insolently' was the descriptive word that came first to his mind.

If the Elder Sister was supposed to be old, Kinnison reflected as he studied appreciatively the startlingly beautiful picture which the artless Chief Person of this tribe so unconsciously made, she certainly belied her looks. As far as looks went, she really qualified—whatever it took, she in abundant measure had. Her hair was not really red, either. It was a flamboyant, gorgeous auburn, about the same color as Clarrissa's own, and just as thick. And it wasn't all haggled up. Accidentally, of course, and no doubt because on her particular job her hair didn't get in the way very often, it happened to be a fairly even, shoulder-length bob. What a mop! And damned if it wasn't wavy! Just as she was, with no dolling up at all, she'd be a primary beam on any man's planet. She had this zwilnik houri here, knockout that she was and with all her war-paint and feathers, blasted clear out of the ether. But this queen bee had a sting; she was still boring away at his shield. He'd better let her know that she didn't even begin to have enough jets to swing *that* load.

'QX, ace, cut the gun!' he directed, crisply. 'Ace', from him, was a complimentary term indeed. 'Pipe down—that's all of that kind of stuff from you. I stood for this much of it, just to show you that you can't get to the first check-station with that kind of fuel, but enough is a great plenty.' At the sheer cutting power of the thought, rebroadcast no doubt by the airport manager, Lyranian activity throughout the room came to a halt. This was decidedly out of the ordinary. For a male mind—any male mind—to be able even momentarily to resist that of the meanest person of Lyrane was starkly unthinkable. The Elder's graceful body tensed, into her eyes there crept a dawning doubt, a peculiar, wondering uncertainty. Of fear there was none; all these sexless Lyranian women were brave to the point of foolhardiness.

'You tell her, draggle-pate,' he ordered his erstwhile guide. 'It took me hell's own time to make you understand that I mean business, but you talk her language—see how fast you can get the thing through Her Royal Nibs's skull.'

It did not take long. The lovely, dark-green eyes held conviction, now; but also a greater uncertainty.

'It will be best, I think, to kill you now, instead of allowing you to leave . . .' she began.

'*Allow* me to leave!' Kinnison exploded. 'Where do you get such funny ideas as that killing stuff? Just who, Toots, is going to keep me from leaving?'

'This.' At the thought of weirdly conglomerate monstrosity which certainly had not been in the dining hall an instant before leaped at Kinnison's throat. It was a frightful thing indeed, combining the worst features of the reptile and the feline, a serpent's head upon a panther's body. Through the air it hurtled, terrible claws unsheathed to rend and venomous fangs out-thrust to stab.

Kinnison had never before met that particular form of attack, but he knew instantly what it was—knew that neither leather nor armor of proof nor screen of force could stop it. He knew that the thing was real only to the woman and himself, that it was not only invisible, but non-existent to everyone else. He also knew how ultimately deadly the creature was, knew that if claw or fangs should strike him he would die then and there.

Ordinarily very efficient, to the Lensman this method of slaughter was crude and amateurish. No such figment of any other mind could harm him unless he knew that it was coming; unless his mind was given ample time in which to appreciate—in reality, to manufacture—the danger he was in. And in *that* time *his* mind could negate it. He had two defenses. He could deny the monster's existence, in which case it would simply disappear. Or, a much more difficult, but technically a much nicer course, would be to take over control and toss it back at her.

Unhesitatingly he did the latter. In mid-leap the apparition swerved, in a full right-angle turn, directly toward the quietly-poised body of the Lyranian. She acted just barely in time; the madly-reaching claws were within scant inches of her skin when they vanished. Her eyes widened in frightened startlement; she was quite evidently shaken to the core by the Lensman's viciously skillful riposte. With an obvious effort she pulled herself together.

'Or these, then, if I must,' and with a sweeping gesture of thought she indicated the roomful of her Lyranian sisters.

'How?' Kinnison asked, pointedly.

'By force of numbers; by sheer weight and strength. You can kill many of them with your weapons, of course, but not enough or quickly enough.'

'You yourself would be the first to die,' he cautioned her; and, since she was en rapport with his very mind, she knew that it was not a threat, but the stern finality of fact.

'What of that?' He in turn knew that she, too, meant precisely that and nothing else.

He had another weapon, but she would not believe it without a demonstration, and he simply could not prove that weapon upon an unarmed, defenseless woman, even though she was a Lyranian.

Stalemate.

No, the 'copter. 'Listen, Queen of Sheba, to what I tell my boys,' he ordered, and spoke into his microphone.

'Ralph? Stick a one-second needle down through the floor here; close enough to make her jump, but far enough away so as not to blister her fanny.'

At his word a narrow, but ragingly incandescent pencil of destruction raved downward through ceiling and floor. So inconceivably hot was it that if it had been a fraction larger, it would have ignited the Elder Sister's very chair. Effortlessly, insatiably it consumed everything in its immediate path, radiating the while the entire spectrum of vibrations. It was unbearable, and the auburn-haired creature did indeed jump, in spite of herself—half-way to the door. The rest of the hitherto imperturbable persons clustered together in panic-stricken knots.

'You see, Cleopatra,' Kinnison explained, as the dreadful needle-beam expired, 'I've got plenty of stuff if I want to—or have to—use it. The boys up there will stick a needle like that through the brain of any one or everyone in this room if I give the word. I don't want to kill any of you unless it's necessary, as I explained to your misbarbered friend here, but I am leaving here alive and all in one piece, and I'm taking this Aldebaranian along with me, in the same condition. If I must, I'll lay down a barrage like that sample you just saw, and only the zwilnik and I will get out alive. How about it?'

'What are you going to do with the stranger?' the Lyranian asked, avoiding the issue.

'I'm going to take some information away from her, that's all. Why? What were you going to do with her yourselves?'

'We were—and are going to kill it,' came flashing reply. The lethal bolt came even before the reply; but, fast as the Elder One was, the Gray Lensman was faster. He blanked out the thought, reached over and flipped on the Aldebaranian's thought-screen.

'Keep it on until we get to the ship, sister,' he spoke aloud in the girl's native tongue. 'Your battery's low, I know, but it'll last long enough. These hens seem to be strictly on the peck.'

'I'll say they are—you don't know the half of it.' Her voice was low, rich, vibrant. 'Thanks, Kinnison.'

'Listen, Red-Top, what's the percentage in playing so dirty?' the Lensman complained then. 'I'm doing my damndest to let you off easy, but I'm all done dickering. Do we go out of here peaceably, or do we fry you and your crew to cinders in your own lard, and walk out over the grease spots? It's strictly up to you, but you'll decide right here and right now.'

The Elder One's face was hard, her eyes flinty. Her fingers were curled into ball-tight fists. 'I suppose, since we cannot stop you, we must let you go free,' she hissed, in helpless but controlled fury. 'If by giving my life and the lives of all these others we could kill you, here and now would you two die ... but as it is, you may go.'

'But why all the rage?' the puzzled Lensman asked. 'You

strike me as being, on the whole, reasoning creatures. You in particular went to Tellus with this zwilnik here, so you should know . . .'

'I *do* know,' the Lyranian broke in. 'That is why I would go to any length, pay any price whatever, to keep you from returning to your own world, to prevent the inrush of your barbarous hordes here . . .'

'Oh! So *that's* it!' Kinnison exclaimed. 'You think that some of our people might want to settle down here, or to have traffic with you?'

'Yes.' She went into a eulogy concerning Lyrane II, concluding, 'I have seen the planets and the races of your so-called Civilization, and I detest them and it. Never again shall any of us leave Lyrane; nor, if I can help it, shall any stranger ever come here.'

'Listen, angel-face!' the man commanded. 'You're as mad as a Radeligian cateagle—you're as cockeyed as Trenco's ether. Get this, and get it straight. To any really intelligent being of any one of forty million planets, your whole Lyranian race would be a total loss with no insurance. You're a God-forsaken, spiritually and emotionally starved, barren, mentally ossified, and completely monstrous mess. If I, personally, never see either you or your planet again, that will be exactly twenty seven minutes too soon. This girl here thinks the same of you as I do. If anybody else ever hears of Lyrane and thinks he wants to visit it, I'll take him out of—I'll knock a hip down on him if I have to, to keep him away from here. Do I make myself clear?'

'Oh, yes—perfectly!' she fairly squealed in school-girlish delight. The Lensman's tirade, instead of infuriating her further, had been sweet music to her peculiarly insular mind. 'Go, then, at once—hurry! Oh, please, hurry! Can you drive the car back to your vessel, or will one of us have to go with you?'

'Thanks. I could drive your car, but it won't be necessary. The 'copter will pick us up.'

He spoke to the watchful Ralph, then he and the Aldebaranian left the hall, followed at a careful distance by the throng. The helicopter was on the ground, waiting. The man and the woman climbed aboard.

'Clear ether, persons!' The Lensman waved a salute to the crowd and the Tellurian craft shot into the air.

Thence to the *Dauntless*, which immediately did likewise, leaving behind her, upon the little airport, a fused blob of metal that had once been the zwilnik's speedster. Kinnison studied the white face of his captive, then handed her a tiny canister.

'Fresh battery for your thought-screen generator; yours is about shot.' Since she made no motion to accept it, he made the exchange himself and tested the result. It worked. 'What's the matter with you, kid, anyway? I'd say you were starved, if I hadn't caught you at a full table.'

'I am starved,' the girl said, simply. 'I couldn't eat there. I knew they were going to kill me, and it . . . it sort of took away my appetite.'

'Well, what are we waiting for? I'm hungry, too—let's go eat.'

'Not with you, either, any more than with them. I thanked you, Lensman, for saving my life there, and I meant it. I thought then and still think that I would rather have you kill me than those horrible, monstrous women, but I simply can't eat.'

'But I'm not even thinking of killing you—can't you get that through your skull? I don't make war on women; you ought to know that by this time.'

'You will have to.' The girl's voice was low and level. 'You didn't kill any of those Lyranians, no, but you didn't chase them a million parsecs, either. We have been taught ever since we were born that you Patrolmen always torture people to death. I don't quite believe that of you personally, since I have had a couple of glimpses into your mind, but you'll kill me before I'll talk. At least, I hope and I believe that I can hold out.'

'Listen, girl.' Kinnison was in deadly earnest. 'You are in no danger whatever. You are just as safe as though you were in Klono's hip pocket. You have some information that I want, yes, and I will get it, but in the process I will neither hurt you nor do you mental or physical harm. The only torture you will undergo will be that which, as now, you give yourself.'

'But you called me a . . . a zwilnik, and they *always* kill them,' she protested.

'Not always. In battles and in raids, yes. Captured ones are tried in court. If found guilty, they used to go into the lethal chambers. Sometimes they do yet, but not usually. We have mental therapists now who can operate on a mind if there's anything there worth saving.'

'And you think that I will wait to stand trial, in the entirely negligible hope that your bewhiskered, fossilized therapists will find something in me worth saving?'

'You won't have to,' Kinnison laughed. 'Your case has already been decided—in your favor. I am neither a policeman nor a Narcotics man; but I happen to be qualified as judge, jury, and executioner. I am a therapist to boot. I once saved a worse zwilnik than you are, even though she wasn't such a knockout. Now do we eat?'

'Really? You aren't just . . . just giving me the needle?'

The Lensman flipped off her screen and gave her unmistakable evidence. The girl, hitherto so unmovedly self-reliant, broke down. She recovered quickly, however, and in Kinnison's cabin she ate ravenously.

'Have you a cigarette?' She sighed with repletion when she could hold no more food.

'Sure. Alsakanite, Venerian, Tellurian, most anything—we carry a couple of hundred different brands. What would you like?'

'Tellurian, by all means. I had a package of Camerfields once—they were gorgeous. Would you have those, by any chance?'

'Uh-huh,' he assured her. 'Quartermaster! Carton of Camerfields, please.' It popped out of the pneumatic tube in seconds. 'Here you are sister.'

The glittery girl drew the fragrant smoke deep down into her lungs.

'Ah, that tastes good! Thanks, Kinnison—for everything. I'm glad you kidded me into eating; that was the finest meal I ever ate. But it won't take, really. I've never broken yet, and I won't break now. If I do, I won't be worth a damn, to myself or to anybody else, from then on.' She crushed out the butt. 'So let's get on with the third degree. Bring on your rubber hose and your lights and your drip-can.'

'You're still on the wrong foot, Toots,' Kinnison said, pityingly. What a frightful contrast there was between her slimly rounded body, in its fantastically gorgeous costume, and the stark somberness of her eyes! 'There'll be no third degree, no hose, no lights, nothing like that. In fact, I'm not even going to talk to you until you've had a good long sleep. You don't look hungry any more, but you're still not in tune, by seven thousand kilocycles. How long has it been since you really slept?'

'A couple of weeks, at a guess. Maybe a month.'

'Thought so. Come on; you're going to sleep now.'

The girl did not move. 'With whom?' she asked, quietly. Her voice did not quiver, but stark terror lay in her mind and her hand crept unconsciously toward the hilt of her dagger.

'Holy Klono's claws!' Kinnison snorted, staring at her in wide-eyed wonder. 'Just what kind of a bunch of hyenas do you think you've got into, anyway?'

'Bad,' the girl replied, gravely. 'Not the worst possible, perhaps, but from my standpoint plenty bad enough. What can I expect from the Patrol except what I do expect? You don't need to kid me along, Kinnison. I can take it, and I'd a lot rather take it standing up, facing it, than have you sneak up on me with it after giving me your shots in the arm.'

'What somebody has done to you is a sin and a shrieking shame,' Kinnison declared, feelingly. 'Come on, you poor little devil.' He picked up sundry pieces of apparatus, then, taking her arm, he escorted her to another, almost luxuriously furnished cabin.

'That door,' he explained carefully, 'is solid chrome-tungsten-molybdenum steel. The lock can't be picked. There are only two keys to it in existence, and here they are. There's a bolt, too, that's proof against anything short of a five-hundred-ton hydraulic jack, or an atomic-hydrogen cutting torch. Here's a full-coverage screen, and a twenty-foot spy-ray block. There is your stuff out of the speedster. If you want help, or anything to eat or drink, or anything else that can be expected aboard a ship like this, there's the communicator. QX?'

'Then you really mean it? That I . . . that you . . . I mean . . .'

'Absolutely,' he assured her. 'Just that. You are completely the master of your destiny, the captain of your soul. Good-night.'

'Good-night, Kinnison. Good-night, and th . . . thanks.' The girl threw herself face downward upon the bed in a storm of sobs.

Nevertheless, as Kinnison started back toward his own cabin, he heard the massive bolt click into its socket and felt the blocking screens go on.

5: . . . Illona of Lonabar

Some twelve or fourteen hours later, after the Aldebaranian girl had had her breakfast, Kinnison went to her cabin.

'Hi, Cutie, you look better. By the way, what's your name, so we'll know what to call you?'

'Illona.'

'Illona what?'

'No what—just Illona, that's all.'

'How do they tell you from other Illonas, then?'

'Oh, you mean my registry number. In the Aldebaranian language there are not the symbols—it would have to be "The Illona who is the daughter of Porlakent the potter who lives in the house of the wheel upon the road of . . ." '

'Hold everything—we'll call you Illona Potter.' He eyed her keenly. 'I thought your Aldebaranian wasn't so hot—didn't seem possible that I could have got *that* rusty. You haven't been on Aldebaran II for a long time, have you?'

'No, we moved to Lonabar when I was about six.'

'Lonabar? Never heard of it—I'll check up on it later. Your stuff was all here, wasn't it? Did any of the red-headed person's things get mixed in?'

'Things?' She giggled sunnily, then sobered in quick embarrassment. 'She didn't carry any. They're horrid, I think—positively *indecent*—to run around that way.'

'Hm . . . m. Glad you brought the point up. You've got to put on some clothes aboard this ship, you know.'

'Me?' she demanded. 'Why, I'm fully dressed . . .' She paused, then shrank together visibly. 'Oh! Tellurians—I remember, all those coverings! You mean, then . . . you think I'm shameless and indecent too?'

'No. Not at all—yet.' At his obvious sincerity Illona unfolded again. 'Most of us—especially the officers—have been on so many different planets, had dealings with so many different types and kinds of entities, that we're used to anything. When we visit a planet that goes naked, we do also, as a matter of course; when we hit one that muffles up to the smothering point we do that, too. "When in Rome, be a Roman candle", you know. The point is that we're at home here, you're the visitor. It's all a matter of convention, of course; but a rather important one. Don't you think so?'

'Covering up, certainly. Uncovering is different. They told me to be sure to, but I simply *can't*. I tried it back there, but I felt *naked*!'

'QX—we'll have the tailor make you a dress or two. Some of the boys haven't been around very much, and you'd look pretty bare to them. Everything you've got on, jewelery and all, wouldn't make a Tellurian sun-suit, you know.'

'Then have them hurry up the dress, please. But this isn't jewelery, it is...'

'Jet back, beautiful. I know gold, and platinum, and...'

'The metal is expensive, yes,' Illona conceded. 'These alone,' she tapped one of the delicate shields, 'cost five days of work. But base metal stains the skin blue and green and black, so what can one do? As for the beads, they are synthetic—junk. Poor girls, if they buy it themselves, do not wear jewelery, but beads, like these. Half a day's work buys the lot.'

'What!' Kinnison demanded.

'Certainly. Rich girls only, or poor girls who do not work, wear real jewelry, such as ... the Aldebaranian has not the words. Let me think at you, please?'

'Sorry, nothing there that I recognize at all,' Kinnison answered, after studying a succession of thought-images of multi-colored, spectacular gems. 'That's one to file away in the book, too, believe me. But as to that "junk" you've got draped all over yourself—half a day's pay—what do you work at for a living, when you work?'

'I'm a dancer—like this.' She leaped lightly to her feet and her left boot whizzed past her ear in a flashingly fast high kick. Then followed a series of gyrations and contortions, for which the Lensman knew no names, during which the girl seemed a practically boneless embodiment of suppleness and grace. She sat down; meticulous hairdress scarcely rumpled, not a buckle or bracelet awry, breathing hardly one count faster.

'Nice.' He applauded briefly. 'Hard for me to evaluate such talent as that—I thought you were a pilot. However, on Tellus or any one of a thousand other planets I could point out to you, you can sell that "junk" you're wearing for—at a rough guess—about fifty thousand day's work.'

'Impossible!'

'True, nevertheless. So, before we land, you'd better give them to me, so that I can send them to a bank for you, under guard.'

'If I land.' As Kinnison spoke Illona's manner changed;

darkened as though an inner light had been extinguished. 'You have been so friendly and nice, I was forgetting where I am and the business ahead. Putting it off won't make it any easier. Better be getting on with it, don't you think?'

'Oh, that? That's all done, long ago.'

'What?' she almost screamed. 'It isn't! It *couldn't* be!'

'Sure. I got most of the stuff I wanted last night, while I was changing your thought-screen battery. Menjo Bleeko, your big-shot boss, and so on.'

'You didn't! But ... you must have, at that, to know it ... but you didn't hurt me, or anything ... you couldn't have operated—changed me, because I have all my memories ... or seem to ... I'm not an idiot, I mean any more than usual ...'

'You've been taught a good many sheer lies, and quite a few half truths,' he informed her, evenly. 'For instance, what did they tell you that hollow tooth would do to you when you broke the seal?'

'Make my mind a blank. But one of their doctors would get hold of me very soon and give me the antidote that would restore me exactly as I was before.'

'That is one of the half truths. It would certainly have made your mind a blank, but only by blasting most of your memory files out of existence. Their therapists would "restore" you by substituting other memories for your real ones—whatever other ones they pleased.'

'How horrible! How perfectly ghastly! That was why you treated it so, then; as though it were a snake. I wondered at your savagery toward it. But how, really, do I know that you are telling the truth?'

'You don't,' he admitted. 'You will have to make your own decisions after acquiring full information.'

'You are a therapist,' she remarked, shrewdly. 'But if you operated on my mind you didn't "save" me because I still think exactly the same as I always did about the Patrol and everything pertaining to it ... or do I? ... Or is this ...' her eyes widened with a startling possibility.

'No, I didn't operate,' he assured her. 'No such operation can possibly be done without leaving scars—breaks in the memory chains—that you can find in a minute if you look for them. There are no breaks or blanks in any chain in your mind.'

'No—at least, I can't find any,' she reported after a few minutes' thought. 'But why didn't you? You can't turn me loose this way, you know—a z ... an enemy of your society.'

'You don't need saving,' he grinned. 'You believe in absolute good and absolute evil, don't you?'

'Why of course—certainly! *Everybody* must!'

'Not necessarily. Some of the greatest thinkers in the universe do not.' His voice grew somber, then lightened again. 'Such being the case, however, all you need to "save" yourself is experience, observation, and knowledge of both sides of the question. You're a colossal little fraud, you know.'

'How do you mean?' She blushed vividly, her eyes wavered.

'Pretending to be such a hard-boiled egg. 'Never broke yet.' Why should you break, when you've never been under pressure?'

'I have so!' she flared. 'What do you suppose I'm carrying this knife for?'

'Oh, that.' He mentally shrugged the wicked little dagger aside as he pondered. 'You little lamb in wolf's clothing ... but at that, your memories may, I think, be altogether too valuable to monkey with ... there's something funny about this whole matrix—*damned* funny. Come clean, baby-face—why?'

'They told me to,' she admitted, wriggling slightly. 'To act tough—really tough. As though I were an adventuress who had been everywhere and had done ... done everything. That the worse I acted the better I would get along in your Civilization.'

'I suspected something of the sort. And what did you zwil—excuse me, you folks—go to Lyrane for, in the first place?'

'I don't know. From chance remarks I gathered that we were to land on one of the planets—any one, I supposed—and wait for somebody.'

'What were you, personally, going to do?'

'I don't know that, either—not exactly, that is. It was to take some kind of a ship somewhere, but I don't know what, or when, or where, or why, or whether I was to go alone or take somebody. Whoever it was that we were going to meet was going to give us orders.'

'How come those women killed your men? Didn't they have thought-screens, too?'

'No. They weren't agents—just soldiers. They shot about a dozen of the Lyranians when we first landed, just to show their authority, then they dropped dead.'

'Um. Poor technique, by typically Boskonian. Your trip to Tellus was more or less accidental, then?'

'Yes. I wanted her to take me back to Lonabar, but she wouldn't. She couldn't have, anyway, because she didn't know any more about where it is than I did.'

'Huh?' Kinnison blurted. 'You don't know where your own home planet is? What the hell kind of a pilot are you, anyway?'

'Oh, I'm not really a pilot. Just what they made me learn after we left Lonabar, so I'd be able to make that trip. Lonabar wasn't shown on any of the charts we had aboard. Neither was Lyrane—that was why I had to make my own chart, to get back there from Tellus.'

'But you *must* know *something*!' Kinnison fumed. 'Stars? Constellations? The Galaxy—the Milky Way?'

'The Milky Way, yes. By its shape, Lonabar isn't anywhere near the center of the galaxy. I've been trying to remember if there were any noticeable star configurations, but I can't. You see, I wasn't the least bit interested in such things, then.'

'Hell's Brazen Hinges! You *can't* be *that* dumb—*nobody* can! Any Tellurian infant old enough to talk knows either the Big Dipper or the Southern Cross! Hold it—I'm coming in and find out for myself.'

He came—but he did not find out.

'Well, I guess people can be that dumb, since you so indubitably are,' he admitted then. 'Or—maybe—aren't there any?'

'Honestly, Lensman, I don't know. There were lots of stars, of course ... if there were any striking configurations I might have noticed them; but I might not have, too. As I said, I wasn't the least bit interested.'

'That was very evident,' dryly. 'However, excuse me, please, for talking so rough.'

'Rough? Of course, sir,' Illona giggled. 'That wasn't rough, comparatively—and nobody ever apologized before—I'd like awfully well to help you, sir, if I possibly can.'

'I know you would, Toots, and thanks. To get back onto the beam, what put it into Helen's mind to go to Tellus?'

'She learned about Tellus and the Patrol from our minds—none of them could believe at first that there were any inhabited worlds except their own—and wanted to study them at first hand. She took our ship and made me fly it.'

'I see. I'm not surprised. I thought that there was something remarkably screwy about those activities—they seemed so aimless and so barren of results—but I couldn't put my finger on it. And we crowded her so close that she decided to flit for home. You could see her, but nobody else could—that she didn't want to.'

'That was it. She said that she was being hampered by a mind of power. That was you, of course?'

'And others. Well, that's that, for a while.'

He called the tailor in. No, he didn't have a thing to make a girl's dress out of, especially not a girl like that. She should wear glamorette, and sheer—very sheer. He didn't know a thing about ladies' tailoring, either; he hadn't made a gown since he was knee-high to a duck. All he had in the shop was coat-linings. Perhaps nylon would do, after a fashion. He remembered now, he did have a bolt of nylon that wasn't any good for linings—not stiff enough, and red. Too heavy, of course, but it would drape well.

It did. She came swaggering back, an hour or so later, the hem of her skirt swishing against the tops of her high-laced boots.

'Do you like it?' she asked, pirouetting gayly.

'Fine!' he applauded, and it was. The tailor had understated tremendously both his ability and the resources of his shop.

'Now what? I don't have to stay in my room all the time now, please?'

'I'll say not. The ship is yours. I want you to get acquainted with every man on board. Go anywhere you like—except the private quarters, of course—even to the control room. The boys all know that you're at large.'

'The language—but I'm talking English now!'

'Sure. I've been giving it to you right along. You know it as well as I do.'

She stared at him in awe. Then, her natural buoyancy asserting itself, she flirted out of the room with a wave of her hand.

And Kinnison sat down to think. A girl—a kid who wasn't dry behind the ears yet—wearing beads worth a full grown fortune, sent somewhere ... to do what? Lyrane II, a perfect matriarchy. Lonabar, a planet of zwilniks that knew all about Tellus, but wasn't on any Patrol chart, sending expeditions to Lyrane. To the system, perhaps not specifically to Lyrane II. Why? For what? To do what? Strange, new jewels of fabulous value. What was the hook-up? It didn't make any kind of sense yet ... not enough data ...

And faintly, waveringly, barely impinging upon the outermost, most tenuous fringes of his mind he felt something: the groping, questing summons of an incredibly distant thought.

'Male of Civilization ... Person of Tellus ... Kinnison of Tellus ... Lensman Kinnison of Sol III ... Any Lensbearing officer of the Galactic Patrol...' Endlessly the desperately urgent, almost imperceptible thought implored.

Kinnison stiffened. He reached out with the full power of his mind, seized the thought, tuned to it, and hurled a reply—and when *that* mind really pushed a thought, it traveled.

'Kinnison of Tellus acknowledging!' His answer fairly crackled on its way.

'You do not know my name,' the stranger's thought came clearly now. 'I am the "Toots", the 'Rep-Top", the "Queen of Sheba", the "Cleopatra", the Elder Person of Lyrane II. Do you remember me, Kinnison of Tellus?'

'I certainly do!' he shot back. What a brain—what a *terrific* brain—that sexless woman had!

'We are invaded by manlike beings in ships of space, who wear screens against our thoughts and who slay without cause. Will you help us with your ship of might and your mind of power?'

'Just a sec, Toots—*Henderson*!' Orders snapped. The *Dauntless* spun end-for-end.

'QX, Helen of Troy,' he reported then. 'We're on our way back there at maximum blast. Say, that name "Helen of Troy" fits you better than anything else I have called you. You don't know it, of course, but that other Helen launched a thousand ships. You're launching only one; but believe me, Babe, the old *Dauntless* is SOME ship!'

'I hope so.' The Elder Person, ignoring the by-play, went directly to the heart of the matter in her usual pragmatic fashion. 'We have no right to ask; you have every reason to refuse...'

'Don't worry about that, Helen. We're all good little Boy Scouts at heart. We're supposed to do a good deed every day, and we've missed a lot of days lately.'

'You are what you call "kidding", I think.' A matriarch could not be expected to possess a sense of humor. 'But I do not lie to you or pretend. We did not, do not now, and never will like you or yours. With us now, however, it is that you are much the lesser of two terrible evils. If you will aid us now we will tolerate your Patrol; we will even promise to endure others of your kind.'

'And that's big of you, Helen, no fooling.' The Lensman was really impressed. The plight of the Lyranians must be desperate indeed. 'Just keep a stiff upper lip, all of you. We're coming loaded for bear, and we are not exactly creeping.'

Nor were they. The big cruiser had plenty of legs and she was using them all; the engineers were giving her all the oof her drivers would take. She was literally blasting a hole through space; she was traveling so fast that the atoms of substance in the interstellar vacuum, merely wave-forms though they were, simply could not get out of the flyer's way. They were being blasted into nothingness against the *Dauntless*' wall-shields.

And throughout her interior the Patrol ship, always in complete readiness for strife, was being gone over again with microscopic thoroughness, to be put into more readiness, if possible, even than that.

After a few hours Illona danced back to Kinnison's 'con' room, fairly bubbling over.

'Why, they're marvelous, Lensman!' she cried, 'simply *marvelous*!'

'What are marvelous?'

'The boys,' she enthused. 'All of them. They're here because they *want* to be—why, the officers don't even have whips! They *like* them, actually! The officers who push the little buttons and things and those who walk around and look through the little glass things and even the gray-haired old man with the four stripes, why they like them all! And the boys were all putting on guns when I left—why, I never heard of such a thing!—and they're just simply *crazy* about you. I thought it was awfully funny you took off your guns as soon as the ship left Lyrane and you don't have guards around you all the time because I thought sure somebody would stab you in the back or something but they don't even want to and that's what's so marvelous and Hank Henderson told me...'

'Save it!' he ordered. 'Jet back, angel-face, before you blow a fuse.' He had been right in not operating—this girl was going to be a mine of information concerning Boskonian methods and operations, and all without knowing it. 'That's what I've been trying to tell you about our Civilization; that it's based on the freedom of the individual to do pretty much as he pleases, as long as it is not to the public harm. And, as far as possible, equality of all the entities of Civilization.'

'Uh-huh, I know you did,' she nodded brightly, then sobered quickly, 'but I couldn't understand it. I can't understand it yet; I can scarcely believe that you all are so ... you know, don't you, what would happen if this were a Lonabarian ship and I would go running around talking to officers as though I were their equal?'

'No—what?'

'It's inconceivable, of course; it simply couldn't happen. But if it did, I would be punished terribly—perhaps though, at a first offense, I might be given only a twenty-scar whipping.' At his lifted eyebrow she explained, 'One that leaves twenty scars that show for life.

'That's why I'm acting so intoxicated, I think. You see, I...' she hesitated shyly, 'I'm not used to being treated as anybody's equal, except of course other girls like me. Nobody is, on Lonabar. Everybody is higher or lower than you are. I'm going to simply love this when I get used to it.' She spread both arms in a sweeping gesture. 'I'd like to *squeeze* this whole ship and everybody in it—I just can't wait to get to Tellus and really *live* there!'

'That's a thing that has been bothering me,' Kinnison confessed, and the girl stared wonderingly at his serious face. 'We're going into battle, and we can't take time to land you anywhere before the battle starts.'

'Of course not. Why should you?' she paused, thinking deeply. 'You're not worrying about *me*, surely? Why, you're a high officer! Officers don't care whether a girl gets shot or not, do they?' the thought was obviously, utterly new.

'We do. It's extremely poor hospitality to invite a guest aboard and then have her killed. All I can say, though, is that if our number goes up ... I still don't see how I could have done anything else.'

'Oh ... thanks, Gray Lensman. Nobody ever spoke to me like that before. But I wouldn't land if I could. I like Civilization. If you ... if you don't win, I couldn't go to Tellus anyway, so I'd much rather take my chances here than not, sir, really. I'll *never* go back to Lonabar, in any case.'

'At-a-girl, Toots!' He extended his hand. She looked at it dubiously, then hesitantly stretched out her own. But she learned fast; she put as much pressure into the brief handclasp as Kinnison did. 'You'd better flit now, I've got work to do.'

'Can I go up top? Hank Henderson is going to show me the primaries.'

'Sure. Go anywhere you like. Before the trouble starts I'll take you down to the center and put you into a suit.'

'Thanks, Lensman!' the girl hurried away and Kinnison Lensed the master pilot.

'Henderson? Kinnison. Official. Illona just told me about the primaries. They're QX—but no etchings.'

'Of course not, sir.'

'And please pass a word around for me. I know as well as anybody does that she doesn't belong aboard; but it couldn't be helped and I'm getting rid of her as soon as I possibly can. In the meantime she's my personal responsibility. So—no passes. She's strictly off limits.'

'I'll pass the word, sir.'

'Thanks.' The Gray Lensman broke the connection and got into communication with Helen of Lyrane, who gave him a resume of everything that had happened.

Two ships—big ships, immense space-cruisers—appeared near the airport. Nobody saw them coming, they came so fast. They stopped, and without warning or parley destroyed all the buildings and all the people nearby with beams like Kinnison's needle-beam, except much larger. Then the ships landed and men disembarked. The Lyranians killed ten of them by direct mental impact or by monsters of the mind, but after that everyone who came out of the vessel wore thought-screens and the persons were quite helpless. The enemy had burned down and melted a part of the city, and as a further warning were then making formal plans to execute publicly a hundred leading Lyranians—ten for each man they had killed.

Because of the screens no communication was possible, but the invaders had made it clear that if there was one more sign of resistance, or even of non-cooperation, the entire city would be beamed; every living thing in it blasted out of existence. She herself had escaped so far. She was hidden in a crypt in the deepest sub-cellar of the city. She was, of course, one of the ones they wanted to execute, but finding any of Lyrane's leaders would be extremely difficult, if not impossible. They were still searching, with many persons as highly unwilling guides. They had indicated that they would stay there until the leaders were found; that they would make the Lyranians tear down their city, stone by stone, until they *were* found.

'But how could they know who you leaders are?' Kinnison wanted to know.

'Perhaps one of our persons weakened under their torture,' Helen replied equably. 'Perhaps they have among them a mind of power. Perhaps in some other fashion. What matters it? The thing of importance is that they do know.'

'Another thing of importance is that it'll hold them there until we get there,' Kinnison thought. 'Typical Boskonian technique, I gather. It won't be many hours now. Hold them off if you can.'

'I think that I can,' came tranquil reply. 'Through mental contact each person acting as guide knows where each of us hidden ones is, and is avoiding all our hiding-places.'

'Good. Tell me all you can about those ships, their size, shape, and armament.'

She could not, it developed, give him any reliable information as to size. She thought that the present invaders were smaller than the *Dauntless*, but she could not be sure. Compared to the little airships which were the only flying structures with which she was familiar, both Kinnison's ship and those now upon Lyrane were so immensely huge that trying to tell which was larger was very much like attempting to visualize the difference between infinity squared and infinity cubed. On shape, however, she was much better; she spread in the Lensman's mind an accurately detailed picture of the two space-ships which the Patrolman intended to engage.

In shape they were ultra-fast, very much like the *Dauntless* herself. Hence they certainly were not maulers. Nor, probably, were they first-line battleships, such as had composed the fleet which had met Civilization's Grand Fleet off the edge of the Second Galaxy. Of course, the Patrol had had in that battle ultra-fast shapes which were ultra-powerful as well—such as this same *Dauntless*—and it was a fact that while Civilization was designing and building, Boskonia could very well have been doing the same thing. On the other hand, since the enemy could not logically be expecting real trouble in Dunstan's Region, these buckets might very well be second-line or out-of-date stuff . . .

'Are those ships lying on the same field we landed on?' he asked at that point in his cogitations.

'Yes.'

'You can give me pretty close to an actual measurement of the difference, then,' he told her. 'We left a hole in that field practically our whole length. How does it compare with theirs?'

'I can find that out, I think,' and in due time she did so; reporting that the *Dauntless* was the longer, by some twelve times a person's height.

'Thanks, Helen.' Then, and only then, did Kinnison call his officers into consultation in the control room.

He told them everything he had learned and deduced about the two Boskonian vessels which they were about to attack. Then, heads bent over a visitank, the Patrolmen began to discuss strategy and tactics.

6: Back to Lyrane

As the *Dauntless* approached Lyrane II so nearly that the planet showed a perceptible disk upon the plates, the observers began to study their detectors carefully. Nothing registered, and a brief interchange of thoughts with the Chief Person of Lyrane informed the Lensman that the two Boskonian warships were still grounded. Indeed, they were going to stay grounded until after the hundred Lyrian leaders, most of whom were still safely hidden, had been found and executed, exactly as per announcement. The strangers had killed many persons by torture and were killing more in attempts to make them reveal the hiding-places of the leaders, but little if any real information was being obtained.

'Good technique, perhaps, from a bull-headed, dictatorial standpoint, but it strikes me as being damned poor tactics,' grunted Malcolm Craig, the *Dauntless'* grizzled captain, when Kinnison had relayed the information.

'I'll say it's poor tactics,' the Lensman agreed. 'If anybody of Helmuth's caliber were down there one of those heaps would be out on guard, flitting all over space.'

'But how could they be expecting trouble 'way out here, nine thousand parsecs from anywhere?' argued Chatway, the Chief Firing Officer.

'They ought to be—that's the point.' This from Henderson. 'Where do we land, Kim, did you find out?'

'Not exactly; they're on the other side of the planet from here, now. Good thing we don't have to get rid of a Tellurian intrinsic this time—it'll be a near thing as it is.' And it was.

Scarcely was the intrinsic velocity matched to that of the planet when the observers reported that the airport upon which the enemy lay was upon the horizon. Inertialess, the *Dauntless* flashed ahead, going inert and into action simultaneously when within range of the zwilnik ships. Within range of one of them, that is; for short as the time had been, the crew of one of the Boskonian vessels had been sufficiently alert to get her away. The other one did not move; then or ever.

The Patrolmen acted with the flawless smoothness of long practice and perfect teamwork. At the first sign of zwilnik activity as revealed by his spy-rays, Nelson, the Chief Communications officer, loosed a barrage of ethereal and sub-ethereal interference through which no communications beam or signal could be driven. Captain Craig barked a word into his microphone and every dreadful primary that could be brought to bear erupted as one weapon. Chief Pilot Henderson, after a casual glance below, cut in the Bergenholms, tramped in his blasts, and set the cruiser's narrow nose into his tracer's line. Once glance was enough. He needed no orders as to what to do next. It would have been apparent to almost anyone, even to one of the persons of Lyrane, that that riddled, slashed, three-quarters fused mass of junk never again would be or could contain aught of menace. The Patrol ship had not stopped: had scarcely even paused. Now, having destroyed half of the opposition *en passant*, she legged it after the remaining half.

'Now what, Kim?' asked Captain Craig. 'We can't englobe him and he no doubt mounts tractor shears. We'll have to use the new tractor zone, won't we?' Ordinarily the gray-haired four-striper would have made his own decisions, since he and he alone fought his ship; but these circumstances were far from ordinary. First, any Unattached Lensman, wherever he was, was the boss. Second, the tractor zone was new; so brand new that even the *Dauntless* had not as yet used it. Third, the ship was on detached duty, assigned directly to Kinnison to do with as he willed. Fourth, said Kinnison was high in the confidence of the Galactic Council and would know whether or not the present situation justified the use of the new mechanism.

'If he can cut a tractor, yes,' the Lensman agreed. 'Only one ship. He can't get away and he can't communicate—safe enough. Go to it.'

The Tellurian ship was faster than the Boskonian; and, since she had been only seconds behind at the start, she came within striking distance of her quarry in short order. Tractor beams reached out and seized; but only momentarily did they hold. At the first pull they were cut cleanly away. No one was surprised; it had been taken for granted that all Boskonian ships would by this time have been equipped with tractor shears.

These shears had been developed originally by the scientists of the Patrol. Immediately following that invention, looking forward to the time when Boskone would have acquired it, those same scientists set themselves to the task of working out something which would be just as good as a tractor beam for combat purposes, but which could not be cut. They got it finally—a globular shell of force, very much like a meteorite screen except double in phase. That is, it was completely impervious to matter moving in either direction, instead of only to that moving inwardly. Even if exact data as to generation, gauging, distance, and control of this weapon were available—which they very definitely are not—it would serve no good end to detail them here. Suffice it to say that the *Dauntless* mounted tractor zones, and had ample power to hold them.

Closer up the Patrol ship blasted. The zone snapped on, well beyond the Boskonian, and tightened. Henderson cut the Bergenholms. Captain Craig snapped out orders and Chief Firing Officer Chatway and his boys did their stuff.

Defensive screens full out, the pirate stayed free and tried to run. No soap. She merely slid around upon the frictionless inner surface of the zone. She rolled and she spun. Then she went inert and rammed. Still no soap. She struck the zone and bounced; bounced with all of her mass and against all the power of her driving thrust. The impact jarred the *Dauntless* to her very skin; but the zone's anchorages had been computed and installed by top-flight engineers and they held. And the zone itself held. It yielded a bit, but it did not fail and the shear-planes of the pirates could not cut it.

Then no other course being possible, the Boskonians fought. Of course, theoretically, surrender was possible, but it simply was not done. No pirate ship ever had surrendered to a Patrol force, however large; none ever would. No Patrol ship had ever surrendered to Boskone—or would. That was the unwritten, but grimly understood code of this internecine conflict between two galaxy-wide and diametrically-opposed cultures; it was and had to be a war of utter and complete extermination. Individuals or small groups might be captured bodily, but no ship, no individual, even, ever, under any conditions, surrenders. The fight was—always and everywhere—to the death.

So this one was. The enemy was well-armed of her type, but her type simply did not carry projectors of sufficient powers to crush the *Dauntless'* hard-held screens. Nor did she mount screens heavy enough to withstand for long the furious assault of the Patrol ship's terrific primaries.

As soon as the pirate's screens went down the firing stopped; that order had been given long since. Kinnison wanted information, he wanted charts, he wanted a few living Boskonians. He got nothing. Not a man remained alive aboard the riddled hulk, the chart-room contained only heaps of fused ash. Everything which might have been of use to the Patrol had been destroyed, either by the Patrol's own beams or by the pirates themselves after they saw they must lose.

'Beam it out,' Craig ordered, and the remains of the Boskonian warship disappeared.

Back toward Lyrane II, then, the *Dauntless* went, and Kinnison again made contact with Helen, the Elder Sister. She had emerged from her crypt and was directing affairs from her—'office' is perhaps the word—upon the top floor of the city's largest building. The search for the Lyranian leaders, the torture and murder of the citizens, and the destruction of the city had stopped, all at once, when the grounded Boskonian cruiser had been blasted out of commission. The directing intelligences of the raiders had remained, it developed, within the 'safe' confines of their vessel's walls; and when they ceased directing, their minions in the actual theater of operations ceased operating. They had been grouped uncertainly in an open square, but at the first glimpse of the returning *Dauntless* they had dashed into the nearest large building, each man seizing one, or sometimes two persons as he went. They were now inside, erecting defenses and very evidently intending to use the Lyranians both as hostages and as shields.

Motionless now, directly over the city, Kinnison and his officers studied through their spy-rays the number, armament, and disposition of the enemy force. There were one hundred and thirty of them, human to about six places. They were armed with the usual portable weapons carried by such parties. Originally they had had several semi-portable projectors, but since all heavy stuff must be powered from the mother-ship, it had been abandoned long since. Surprisingly, though they wore full armor, Kinnison had expected only thought-screens, since the Lyranians had no offensive weapons save those of the mind; but apparently either the pirates did not know that or else were guarding against surprise.

Armor was—and is—heavy, cumbersome, a handicap to fast action, and a nuisance generally; hence for the Boskonians to have dispensed with it would not have been poor tactics. True, the Patrol *did* attack, but that could not have been what was expected. In fact, had such an attack been in the cards, that Boskonian punitive party would not have been on the ground at all. It was equally true that canny old Helmuth, who took nothing whatever for granted, would have had his men in armor. However, he would have guarded much more completely against surprise ... but few commanders indeed went to such lengths of precaution as Helmuth did. Thus Kinnison pondered.

'This ought to be as easy as shooting fish down a well—but you'd better put out space-scouts just the same,' he decided, as he Lensed a thought to Lieutenant Peter vanBuskirk. 'Bus? Do you see what we see?'

'Uh-huh, we've been peeking a bit,' the huge Dutch–Valerian responded, happily.

'QX. Get your gang wrapped up in their tinware. I'll see you at the main lower stabbard lock in ten minutes.' He cut off and turned to an orderly. 'Break out my G-P cage for me, will you, Spike? And I'll want the 'copters—tell them to get hot.'

'But listen, Kim!'

'You can't do that, Kinnison!' came simultaneously from Chief Pilot and Captain, neither of whom could leave the ship in such circumstances as these. They, the vessel's two top officers, were bound to her; while the Lensman although ranking both of them, even aboard the ship, was not and could not be bound by anything.

'Sure I can—you fellows are just jealous, that's all,' Kinnison retorted, cheerfully. 'I not only can, I've *got* to go with the Valerians. I need a lot of information, and I can't read a dead man's brain—yet.'

While the storming party was assembling the *Dauntless* settled downward, coming to rest in the already devastated section of the town, as close as possible to the building in which the Boskonans had taken refuge.

One hundred and two men disembarked: Kinnison, vanBuskirk, and the full company of one hundred Valerians. Each of those space-fighting wild-cats measured seventy eight inches or more from sole to crown; each was composed of four hundred or more pounds of the fantastically powerful, rigid, and reactive brawn, bone, and sinew necessary for survival upon a planet having a surface gravity almost three times that of small, feeble Terra.

Because of the women held captive by the pirates, the Valerians carried no machine rifles, no semi-portables, no heavy stuff at all; only their DeLameters and of course their space-axes. A Valerian trooper without his space-axe? Unthinkable! A dire weapon indeed, the space-axe. A combination and sublimation of battle-axe, mace, bludgeon, and lumberman's picaroon; thirty pounds of hard, tough, space-tempered alloy; a weapon of potentialities limited only by the physical strength and bodily agility of its wielder. And vanBuskirk's Valerians had both—plenty of both. One-handed, with simple flicks of his incredible wrist, the smallest Valerian of the *Dauntless*' boarding party could manipulate his atrocious weapon as effortlessly as, and almost unbelievably faster than, a fencing master handles his rapier or an orchestra conductor waves his baton.

With machine-like precision the Valerians fell in and strode away; vanBuskirk in the lead, the helicopters hovering overhead, the Gray Lensman bringing up the rear. Tall and heavy, strong and agile as he was—for a Tellurian—he had no business in that front line, and no one knew that fact better than he did. The puniest Valerian of the company could do in full armor a standing high jump of over fourteen feet against one Tellurian gravity; and could dodge, feint, parry, and swing with a blinding speed starkly impossible to any member of any of the physically lesser breeds of man.

Approaching the building they spread out, surrounded it; and at a signal from a helicopter that the ring was complete the assault began. Doors and windows were locked, barred, and barricaded, of course; but what of that? A few taps of the axes and a few blasts of the DeLameters took care of things very nicely; and through the openings thus made there leaped, dove, rolled, or strode the space-black-and-silver warriors of the Galactic Patrol. Valerians, than whom no fiercer race of hand to hand fighters has ever been known—no bifurcate race, and but very few others, however built or shaped, have ever willingly come to grips with the armored axe-men of Valeria!

Not by choice, then, but of necessity and in sheer desperation the pirates fought. In the vicious beams of their portables the stone walls of the room glared a baleful red; in spots even were pierced through. Old-fashioned pistols barked, spitting steel-jacketed lead. But the G-P suits were screened against lethal beams by generators capable of withstanding anything of lesser power than a semi-portable projector; G-P armor was proof against any projectile possessing less energy than that hurled by the high-caliber machine rifle. Thus the Boskonian beams splashed off the Valerians' screen in torrents of man-made lightning and in pyrotechnic displays of multi-colored splendor, their bullets ricocheted harmlessly as spent, mis-shapen blobs of metal.

The Patrolmen did not even draw their DeLameters during their inexorable advance. They knew that the pirates' armor was as capable as theirs, and the women were not to die if death for them could possibly be avoided. As they advanced the enemy fell back toward the center of the great room; holding there with the Lyranians forming the outer ring of their roughly-circular formation; firing over the women's heads and between their naked bodies.

Kinnison did not want those women to die. It seemed, however, that die they must, from the sheer, tremendous reflection from the Valerians' fiercely radiant screens, if the Patrolmen persisted in their advance. He studied the enemy formation briefly, then flashed an order.

There ensued a startling and entirely unorthodox maneuver, one possible only to the troopers there at work, as at Kinnison's command every Valerian left the floor in a prodigious leap. Over the women's heads, over the heads of the enemy; but in mid-leap, as he passed over, each patrolman swung his axe at a Boskonian helmet with all the speed and all the power he could muster. Most of the enemy died then and there, for the helmet has never been forged which is able to fend the beak of a space-axe driven as each of those was driven. The fact that the Valerians were nine or ten feet off the floor at the time made no difference whatever. They were space-fighters, trained to handle themselves and their weapons in any position or situation; with or without gravity, with or without even inertia.

'You persons—run! Get out of here! SCRAM!' Kinnison fairly shouted the thought as the Valerians left the floor, and the matriarchs obeyed—frantically. Through doors and windows they fled, in all directions and at the highest possible speed.

But in their enthusiasm to strike down the foe, not one of the Valerians had paid any attention to the exact spot upon which he was to land; or, if he did, someone else got there either first or just barely second. Besides, there was not room for them all in the center of the ring, For seconds, therefore, confusion reigned and a boiler-works clangor resounded for a mile around as a hundred and one extra-big and extra-heavy men, a writhing, kicking, pulling tangle of armor, axes, and equipment, jammed into a space which half their number would have filled over-full. Sulphurous Valerian profanity and sizzling deep-space oaths blistered the very air as each warrior struggled madly to right himself, to get one more crack at a pirate before somebody else beat him to it.

During this terrific melee some of the pirates released their screens and committed suicide. A few got out of the room, but not many. Nor far; the men in the helicopters saw to that. They had needle-beams, powered from the *Dauntless*, which went through the screens of personal armor as a knife goes through ripe cheese.

'Save it, guys—hold everything!' Kinnison yelled as the tangled mass of Valerians resolved itself into erect and warlike units. 'No more axe-work—don't let them kill themselves—catch them ALIVE!'

They did so, quickly and easily. With the women out of the way, there was nothing to prevent the Valerians from darting right up to the muzzles of the foes' DeLameters. Nor could the enemy dodge, or run, half fast enough to get away. Armored, shielded hands batted the weapons away—if an arm or leg broke in the process, what the hell?—and the victim was held motionless until his turn came to face the mind-reading Kinnison.

Nothing. Nothing, flat. A string of zeros. And, bitterly silent, Kinnison led the way back to the *Dauntless*. The men he wanted, the ones who knew anything, were the ones who killed themselves, of course. Well, why not? In like case, officers of the Patrol had undoubtedly done the same. The live ones didn't know where their planet was, could give no picture even of where it lay in the galaxy, did not know where they were going, nor why. Well, so what? Wasn't ignorance the prime characteristic of the bottom layers of dictatorships everywhere? If they had known anything, they would have been under compulsion to kill themselves, too, and would have done it.

In his own room in the *Dauntless* his black mood lightened somewhat and he called the Elder Person.

'Helen of Troy? I suppose that the best thing we can do now, for your peace of mind, prosperity, well-being, et cetera, is to drill out of here as fast as Klono and Noshabkeming will let us. Right?'

'Why, I ... you ... um ... that is...' The matriarch was badly flustered at the Lensman's bald summation of her attitude. She did not want to agree, but she certainly did not want these males around a second longer than was necessary.

'Just as well say it, because it goes double for me—you can play it clear across the board, Toots, that if I ever see you again it will be because I can't get out of it.' Then, to his chief pilot:

'QX, Hen, give her the oof—back to Tellus.'

7: Wide-Open N-Way

Serenely the mighty *Dauntless* bored her way homeward through the ether, at the easy touring blast—for her—of some eighty parsecs an hour. The engineers inspected and checked their equipment, from the instrument-needles to blast-nozzles; relining, repairing, replacing anything and everything which showed any signs of wear or strain because of what the big vessel had just gone through. Then they relaxed into their customary routine of killing time—the games of a dozen planets and the vying with each other in the telling of outrageously untruthful stories.

The officers on watch lolled at ease in their cushioned seats, making much ado of each tiny thing as it happened, even the changes of watch. The Valerians, as usual, remained invisible in their own special quarters. There the gravity was set at twenty seven hundred instead of at the Tellurian normal of nine hundred eighty, there the atmospheric pressure was forty pounds to the square inch, there the temperature was ninety six degrees Fahrenheit, and there vanBuskirt and his fighters lived and moved and had their drills of fantastic violence and stress. They were irked less than any of the others by montony; being, as has been intimated previously, neither mental nor intellectual giants.

And Kinnison, mirror-polished gray boots stacked in all their majestic size upon a corner of his desk, leaned his chair precariously backward and thought in black concentration. It *still* didn't make any kind of sense. He had just enough clues—fragments of clues—to drive a man nuts. Menjo Bleeko was the man he wanted. On Lonabar. To find one was to find the other, but how in the steaming hells of Venus was he going to find either of them? It might seem funny not to be able to find a thing as big as a planet—but since nobody knew where it was, by fifty thousand parsecs, and since there were millions and skillions and whillions of planets in the galaxy, a random search was quite definitely out. Bleeko was a zwilnik, or tied in with zwilniks, of course; but he could read a million zwilnik minds without finding, except by merest chance, one having any contact with or knowledge of the Lonabarian.

The Patrol had already scoured—fruitlessly—Aldebaran II for any sign, however slight, pointing toward Lonabar. The planetographers had searched the files, the charts, the libraries thoroughly. No Lonabar. Of course, they had suggested—what a help!—they might know it under some other name. Personally, he didn't think so, since no jeweler throughout the far-flung bounds of Civilization had as yet been found who could recognize or identify any of the items he had described.

Whatever avenue or alley of thought Kinnison started along, he always ended up at the jewels and the girl. Illona, the squirrel-brained, romping, joyous little imp who by now owned in fee simple half of the ship and nine-tenths of the crew. Why in Palain's purple hells couldn't she have had a brain? How could *anybody* be dumb enough not to know the galactic co-ordinates of their own planet? Not even to know *anything* that could help locate it? But at that, she was probably about as smart as most—you couldn't expect any other woman in the galaxy to have a mind like Mac's...

For minutes, then, he abandoned his problem and reveled in visions of the mental and physical perfections of his fiancee. But this was getting him nowhere, fast. The girl or the jewels—which? They were the only real angles he had.

He sent out a call for her, and in a few minutes she came swirling in. How different she was from what she had been! Gone were the somberness, the dread, the terror which had oppressed her; gone were the class-conscious inhibitions against which she had been rebelling, however subconsciously, since childhood. Here she was *free*! The boys were free, *everybody* was free! She had expanded tremendously—unfolded. She was living as she had never dreamed it possible to live. Each new minute was an adventure in itself. Her black eyes, once so dull, sparkled with animation; radiated her sheer joy in living. Even her jet-black hair, seemed to have taken on a new luster and gloss, in its every, precisely-arranged wavelet.

'Hi, Lensman!' she burst out, before Kinnison could say a word or think a thought in greeting. 'I'm *so* glad you sent for me, because there's something I've been wanting to ask you since yesterday. The boys are going to throw a blow-out, with all kinds of stunts, and they want me to do a dance. QX, do you think?'

'Sure. Why not?'

'Clothes,' she explained. 'I told them I couldn't dance in a dress, and they said I wasn't supposed to, that acrobats didn't wear dresses when they performed on Tellus, that my regular clothes were just right. I said they were trying to string me and they swore they weren't—said to ask the Old Man...' she broke off, two knuckles jammed into her mouth, expressive eyes wide in sudden fright. 'Oh, excuse me, sir,' she gasped. 'I didn't . . .'

''Smatter? What bit you?' Kinnison asked, then got it. 'Oh—the "Old Man", huh? QX, angel-face, that's standard nomenclature in the Patrol. Not with you folks, though, I take it?'

'I'll say not,' she breathed. She acted as though a catastrophe had been averted by the narrowest possible margin. 'Why, if anybody got caught even *thinking* such a thing, the whole crew would go into the steamer that very minute. And if I would dare to say "Hi" to Menjo Bleeko. . . !' she shuddered.

'Nice people,' Kinnison commented.

'But are you sure that the . . . that I'm not getting any of the boys into trouble?' she pleaded. 'For, after all, none of them ever dare call you that to your face, you know.'

'You haven't been around enough yet,' he assured her. 'On duty, no; that's discipline—necessary for efficiency. And I haven't hung around the wardrooms much of late—been too busy. But at the party you'll be surprised at some of the things they call me—if you happen to hear them. You've been practicing—keeping in shape?'

'Uh-huh,' she confessed. 'In my room, with the spy-ray-block on.'

'Good. No need to hide, though, and no need to wear dresses any time you're practicing—the boys were right on that. But what I called you in about is that I want you to help me. Will you?'

'Yes, sir. In anything I can—*anything*, sir,' she answered instantly.

'I want you to give me every scrap of information you possibly can about Lonabar; its customs and habits, its work and its play—everything, even its money and its jewelry.' This last apparently an after-thought. 'To do so, you'll have to let me into your mind of your own free will—you'll have to cooperate to the limit of your capability. QX?'

'That will be quite all right, Lensman,' she agreed, shyly. 'I know now that you aren't going to hurt me.'

Illona did not like it at first, there was no question of that. And small wonder. It is an intensely disturbing thing to have your mind invaded, knowingly, by another; particularly when that other is the appallingly powerful mind of Gray Lensman Kimball Kinnison. There were lots of things she did not want exposed, and the very effort not to think of them brought them ever and ever more vividly to the fore. She squirmed mentally and physically: her mind was for minutes a practically illegible turmoil. But she soon steadied down and, as she got used to the new sensations, she went to work with a will. She could not increase the planetographical knowledge which Kinnison had already obtained from her, but she was a mine of information concerning Lonabars' fine gems. She knew all about every one of them, with the completely detailed knowledge one is all too apt to have of a thing long and intensely desired, but supposedly forever out of reach.

'Thanks, Illona.' It was over; the Lensman knew as much as she did about everything which had any bearing upon his quest. 'You've helped a lot—now you can flit.'

'I'm glad to help, sir, really—any time. I'll see you at the party, then, if not before.' Illona left the room in a far more subdued fashion than she had entered it. She had always been more than half afraid of Kinnison; just being near him did things to her which she did not quite like. And this last thing, this mind-searching interview, did not operate to quiet her fears. It gave her the screaming meamies, no less!

And Kinnison, alone in his room, started to call for a tight beam to Prime Base, then changed his mind and Lensed a thought—gingerly and diffidently enough—to Port Admiral Haynes.

'Certainly I'm free!' came instant response. 'To *you* I'm free twenty four hours of every day. Go ahead.'

'I want to try something that I don't know whether can be done or not. A wide-open, Lens-to-Lens conference with all the Lensmen, especially all Unattached Lensmen, who can be reached. Can it be done?'

'Whew!' Haynes whistled. 'I've been in such things up to a hundred or so ... no reason why it wouldn't work. Most of the people you want know me, and those who don't can tune in through someone who does. If everybody tunes to me at the same time, we'll all be en rapport with each other.'

'It's QX, then? The reason I ...'

'Skip it, son. No use explaining twice—I'll get it when the others do. I'll take care of it. It'll take some little time... Would hour twenty, tomorrow, be soon enough?'

'That'll be fine. Thanks a lot, chief.'

The next day dragged, even for the always-busy Kinnison. He prowled about, aimlessly. He saw the spectacular Aldebaranian several times, noticing something which tied in very nicely with a fact he had half-seen in the girl's open mind before he could dodge it—that whenever she made a twosome with any man, the man was Henry Henderson.

'Blasted, Hen?' he asked, casually, when he came upon the pilot in a corner of a ward-room, staring fixedly at nothing.

'Out of the ether,' Henderson admitted. 'However, I *haven't* been making any passes. No use telling you that, though.'

There wasn't. Unattached Lensmen, as well as being persons of supreme authority, are supremely able mind-readers, Verbum sap.

'I know you haven't.' Then, answering the unasked question: 'No, I haven't been reading your mind. Nor anybody else's, except Illona's. I've read hers, up and down and crosswise.'

'Oh ... so you know, then ... say, Kim, can I talk to you for a minute? *Really* talk, I mean?'

'Sure. On the Lens?'

'That'd be better.'

'Here you are. About Illona, the beautiful Aldebaranian zwilnik, I suppose.'

'Don't, Kim.' Henderson actually flinched, physically. 'She isn't a zwilnik, really—she *can't* be—I'd bet my last millo on that?'

'Are you telling me or asking me?'

'I don't know.' Henderson hesitated. 'I've been wanting to ask you ... you've got a lot of stuff we haven't, you know ... whether she ... I mean if I ... Oh, hell! Kim, is there any reason why I shouldn't ... well, er ... get married?'

'Millions of reasons why you should, Hen. Everybody ought to.'

'Damnation, Kim! That isn't what I meant, and you know it!'

'Think straight, then.'

'QX. Sir, would Unattached Lensman Kimball Kinnison approve of my marriage to Illona Potter, if I've got jets enough to swing it?'

Mighty clever, the Lensman thought. Since the men of the Patrol were notoriously averse to going sloppy about it, he had wondered just how the pilot was going to phrase his question. He had done it very neatly, by tossing the buck right back at him. But he wouldn't go sloppy, either. This 'untarnished-meteors-upon-the-collars-of-our-heroes' stuff was QX for swivel-tongued spellbinders, but not for anybody else. So:

'As far as I know—and I bashfully admit that I know it

all—the answer is yes.'

'Great!' Henderson came to life with a snap. 'Now, if ... but I don't suppose you'd ...' the thought died away.

'I'll say I wouldn't. Unethical no end. I might cheat just a little bit, though. She probably won't do much worse than beat your brains out with a two-inch spanner if you ask her. And only about half of the twenty one hundred or so other guys aboard this heap are laying awake nights trying to figure out ways of beating your time.'

'Huh? *Those* apes? Watch my jets!' Henderson strode away, doubts all resolved; and Kinnison, seeing that hour twenty was very near, went to his own room.

It is difficult for any ordinary mind to conceive of its being in complete accord with any other, however closely akin. Consider, then, how utterly impossible it is to envision that merging of a hundred thousand, or five hundred thousand, or a million—nobody ever did know how many Lensmen tuned in that day—minds so utterly different that no one human being can live long enough even to see each of the races there represented! Probably less than half of them were even approximately human. Many were not mammals, many were not warm-blooded. Not all, by far, were even oxygen-breathers—oxygen, to many of those races, was sheerest poison. Nevertheless, they had much in common. All were intelligent; most of them very highly so; and all were imbued with the principles of freedom and equality for which Galactic Civilization stood and upon which it was fundamentally based.

That meeting was staggering, even to Kinnison's mind. It was appalling—yet it was ultimately thrilling, too. It was one of the greatest, one of the most terrific thrills of the Lensman's long life.

'Thanks, fellows, for coming in,' he began simply. 'I will make my message very short. As Haynes may have told you, I am Kinnison of Tellus. It will help greatly in locating the head of the Boskonian culture if I can find a certain planet, known to me only by the name of Lonabar. It's people are human beings to the last decimal; its rarest jewels are these,' and he spread in the collective mind a perfect, exactly detailed and pictured description of the gems. 'Does any one of you know of such a planet? Has any one of you ever seen a stone like any of these?'

A pause—a heart-breakingly long pause. Then a faint, soft, diffident thought appeared; appeared as though seeping slowly from a single cell of that incredibly linked, million-fold-composite Lensman's BRAIN.

'I waited to be sure that no one else would speak, as my information is very meager, and unsatisfactory, and old,' the thought apologized.

Kinnison started, but managed to conceal his surprise from the linkage. That thought, so diamond-clear, so utterly precise, must have come from a Second-Stage Lensman—and since it was neither Worsel nor Tregonsee, there must be another one he had never heard of!

'Whatever its nature, any information at all is very welcome,' Kinnison replied, without perceptible pause. 'Who is speaking, please?'

'Nadreck of Palain VII, Unattached. Many cycles ago I secured, and still have in my possession, a crystal—or rather, a fragment of a super-cooled liquid—like one of the red gems you showed us; the one having practically all its transmittance in a very narrow band centering at point seven zero zero.'

'But you do not know what planet it came from—is that it?'

'Not exactly,' the soft thought went on. 'I saw it upon its native planet, but unfortunately I do not now know just what or where that planet was. We were exploring at the time, and had visited many planets. Not being interested in any world having an atmosphere of oxygen, we paused but briefly, nor did we map it. I was interested in the fusion because of its peculiar filtering effect. A scientific curiosity merely.'

'Could you find that planet again?'

'By checking back upon the planets we did map, and by retracing our route, I should be able to—yes, I am certain that I can do so.'

'And when Nadreck of Palain VII admits to being certain of anything,' another thought appeared, 'nothing in the macrocosmic universe is more certain.'

'I thank you, Twenty Four of Six, for the expression of confidence.'

'And I thank both of you particularly as well as all of you collectively,' Kinnison broadcast. Intelligences by the millions broke away from the linkage. As soon as the two were alone:

'You're Second Stage, aren't you?'

'Yes. I felt a need. I was too feeble. A certain project was impossible, since it was so dangerous as to involve a distinct possibility of personal harm. Therefore Mentor gave me advanced treatment, to render me somewhat less feeble than I theretofore was.'

'I see.'

Kinnison didn't see, at all, since this was his first contact with a Palainian mind. Who ever heard of a Lensman refusing a job because of personal risk? Lensmen *always* went in ... no matter how scared he was, *of course* he went in ... that was the Code ... human Lensmen, that is ... There were a lot of things he didn't know, and other races could be—*must* be—different. He was astounded that there could be *that* much difference; but after all, since the guy was an L2, he certainly had enough of what it took to more than make up for any lacks. How did he know how short of jets he himself looked, in the minds of other Second Stage Lensmen? These thoughts flashed through his mind, behind his impervious shield, and after only the appropriate slight pause his thought went smoothly on:

'I had known of only Worsel of Velantia and Tregonsee of Rigel Four, besides myself. I don't need to tell you how terrifically glad I am that there are four of us instead of three. But at the moment the planet Lonabar is, I believe, more important to my job than anything else in existence. You will map it for me, and send the data to me at Prime Base?'

'I will map the planet and will myself bring the data to you at Prime Base. Do you want some of the gems, also?'

'I don't think so.' Kinnison thought swiftly. 'No, better not. They'll be harder to get now, and it might tip our hand too much. I'll get them myself, later. Will you inform me, through Haynes, when to expect you?'

'I will so inform you. I will proceed at once, with speed.'

'Thanks a million, Nadreck—clear ether!'

The ship sped on, and as it sped Kinnison continued to think. He attended the 'blowout'. Ordinarily he would have been right in the thick of it; but this time, young though he was and enthusiastic, he simply could not tune in. Nothing fitted, and until he could see a picture that made some kind of sense he could not let go. He listened to the music with half an ear, he watched the stunts with only half an eye.

He forgot his problem for a while when, at the end, Illona Potter danced. For Lonabarian acrobatic dancing is not like the Tellurian art of the same name. Or rather, it is like it, except more so—much more so. An earthly expert would be scarcely a novice on Lonabar, and Illona was a Lonabarian expert. She had been training, intensively, all her life, and even in Lonabar's chill social and psychological environment she had loved her work. Now, reveling as she was in the first realization of liberty of thought and of person, and inspired by the heart-felt applause of the space-hounds so closely packed into the hall, she put on something more than an exhibition of coldly impersonal skill and limberness. And the feelings, both of performer and of spectators, were intensified by the fact that, of all the repertoire of the *Dauntless*' superb orchestra, Illona liked best to dance to the stirring strains of 'Our Patrol'. 'Our Patrol', which any man who has ever worn the space-black-and-silver will say is the greatest, grandest, most glorious, most terrific piece of music that ever was or ever will be written, played, or sung! Small wonder, then, that the dancer really 'gave'; or that the mighty cruiser's walls almost bulged under the applause of Illona's 'boys' at the end of her first number.

They kept her at it until the captain stopped it, to keep the girl from killing herself. 'She's worn down to a nub,' he declared, and she was. She was trembling. She was panting, her almost-lacquered-down hair stood out in wild disorder. Her eyes were starry with tears—happy tears. Then the ranking officers made short speeches of appreciation and the spectators carried the actors—actual carrying, in Illona's case, upon an improvised throne—off for refreshments.

Back in his quarters, Kinnison tackled his problem again. He could work out something on Lonabar now, but what about Lyrane? It tied in, too—there was an angle there, somewhere. To get it, though, somebody would have to get close to—really friendly with—the Lyranians. Just looking on from the outside wouldn't do. Somebody they could trust and would confide in—and they were so damnably, so fanatically non-cooperative! A man couldn't get a millo's worth of real information—he could read any one mind by force, but he'd never get the right one. Neither could Worsel or Tregonsee or any other non-human Lensman; the Lyranians just simply didn't have the galactic viewpoint. No, what he wanted was a human woman Lensman, and there weren't any...

At the thought he gasped; the pit of his stomach felt cold. Mac! She was more than half Lensman already—she was the only un-Lensed human being who had ever been able to read his thoughts... But he didn't have the gall, the sheer, brazen crust, to shove a load like that onto *her* ... or did he? Didn't the job come first? Wouldn't she be big enough to see it that way? Sure she would! As to what Haynes and the rest of the Lensmen would think ... let them think! In this, he had to make his own decisions . . .

He couldn't. He sat there for an hour; teeth locked until his jaws ached, fists clenched.

'I can't make that decision alone,' he breathed, finally. 'Not jets enough by half,' and he shot a thought to distant Arisia and Mentor the Sage.

'This intrusion is necessary,' he thought coldly, precisely. 'It seems to me to be wise to do this thing which has never before been done. I have no data, however, upon which to base a decision and the matter is grave. I ask, therefore—is it wise?'

'You do not ask as to repercussions—consequences, either to yourself or to the woman?'

'I ask what I asked.'

'Ah, Kinnison of Tellus, you truly grow. You at last learn to think. It is wise,' and the telepathic link snapped.

Kinnison slumped down in relief. He had not known what to expect. He would not have been surprised if the Arisian had pinned his ears back; he certainly did not expect either the compliment or the clear-cut answer. He knew that Mentor would give him no help whatever in any problem which he could possibly solve alone; he was just beginning to realize that the Arisian *would* aid him in matters which were absolutely, intrinsically, beyond his reach.

Recovering, he flashed a call to Surgeon-Marshal Lacy.

'Lacy? Kinnison. I would like to have Sector Chief Nurse Clarrissa MacDougall detached at once. Please have her report to me here aboard the *Dauntless*, en route, at the earliest possible moment of rendezvous.'

'Huh? What? You can't . . . you wouldn't . . .' the old Lensman gurgled.

'No, I wouldn't. The whole Corps will know it soon enough, so I might as well tell you now. I'm going to make a Lensman out of her.'

Lacy exploded then, but Kinnison had expected that.

'Seal it!' he counseled, sharply. 'I'm not doing it entirely on my own—Mentor of Arisia made the final decision. Prefer charges against me if you like, but in the meantime please do as I request.'

And that was that.

8: Cartiff the jeweler

A few hours before the time of rendezvous with the cruiser which was bringing Clarrissa out to him, the detectors picked up a vessel whose course, it proved, was set to intersect their own. A minute or so later a sharp, clear thought came through Kinnison's Lens.

'Kim? Raoul. Been flitting around out Arisia way, and they called me in and asked me to bring you a package. Said you'd be expecting it. QX?'

'Hi, Spacehound! QX.' Kinnison had very decidedly not been expecting it—he had been intending to do the best he could without it—but he realized instantly, with a thrill of gladness, what it was. 'Inert? Or can't you stay?'

'Free. Got to make a rendezvous. Can't take time to inert—that is, if you'll inert the thing in your cocoon. Don't want it to hole out on you, though.'

'Can do. Free it is. Pilot room! Prepare for inertialess contact with vessel approaching. Magnets. Messenger coming aboard—free.'

The two speeding vessels flashed together, at all their unimaginable velocities, without a thump or jar. Magnetic clamps locked and held. Airlock doors opened, shut, opened; and at the inner port Kinnison met Raoul LeForge, his class-mate through the four years at Wentworth Hall. Brief but hearty greetings were exchanged, but the visitor could not stop. Lensmen are busy men.

'Fine seeing you, Kim—be sure and inert the thing—clear ether!'

'Same to you, ace. Sure I will—think I want to vaporize half of my ship?'

Indeed, inerting the package was the Lensman's first care, for in the free condition it was a frightfully dangerous thing. Its intrinsic velocity was that of Arisia, while the ship's was that of Lyrane II. They might be forty or fifty miles per second apart; and if the *Dauntless* should go inert that harmless-looking package would instantly become a meteorite inside the ship. At the thought of that velocity he paused. The cocoon would stand it—but would the Lens? Oh, sure, Mentor knew what was coming; the Lens would be packed to stand it.

Kinnison wrapped the package in heavy gauze, then in roll

after roll of spring-steel mesh. He jammed heavy steel rings into the ends, then clamped the whole thing into a form with high-alloy bolts an inch in diameter. He poured in two hundred pounds of metallic mercury, filling the form to the top. Then a cover, also bolted on. This whole assembly went into the 'coccon', a cushioned, heavily-padded affair suspended from all four walls, ceiling, and floor by every shock-absorbing device known to the engineers of the Patrol.

The *Dauntless* inerted briefly at Kinnison's word and it seemed as though a troop of elephants were running silently amuck in the cocoon room. The package to be inerted weighed no more than eight ounces—but eight ounces of mass, at a relative velocity of fifty miles per second, possesses a kinetic energy by no means to be despised.

The frantic lurchings and bouncings subsided, the cruiser resumed her free flight, and the man undid all he had done. The Arisian package looked exactly as before, but it was harmless now; it had the same intrinsic velocity as did everything else aboard the vessel.

Then the Lensman pulled on a pair of insulating gloves and opened the package; finding, as he had expected, that the packing material was a dense, viscious liquid. He poured it out and there was the Lens—Cris's Lens! He cleaned it carefully, then wrapped it in heavy insulation. For of all the billions of unnumbered billions of living entities in existence, Clarrissa MacDougall was the only one whose flesh could touch that apparently innocuous jewel with impunity. Others could safely touch it while she wore it, while it glowed with its marvelously polychromatic cold flame; but until she wore it and unless she wore it its touch meant death to any life to which it was not attuned.

Shortly thereafter another Patrol cruiser hove in sight. This meeting, however, was to be no casual one, for the nurse could not be inerted from the free state in the *Dauntless*' cocoon. No such device ever built could stand it—and those structures are stronger far than is the human frame. Any adjustment which even the hardest, toughest spacehound can take in a cocoon is measured in feet per second, not in miles.

Hundreds of miles apart, the ships inerted and their pilots fought with supreme skill to make the two intrinsics match. And even so the vessels did not touch, even nearly. A space-line was thrown; the nurse and her space-roll were quite unceremoniously hauled aboard.

Kinnison did not meet her at the airlock, but waited for her in his con room; and the details of that meeting will remain unchronicled. They were young, they had not seen each other for a long time, and they were very much in love. It is evident, therefore, that Patrol affairs were not the first matters to be touched upon. Nor, if the historian has succeeded even partially in portraying truly the characters of the two persons involved, is it either necessary or desirable to go at any length into the argument they had as to whether or not she should be inducted so cavalierly into a service from which her sex had always, automatically, been barred. He did not want to make her carry that load, but he had to; she did not—although for entirely different reasons—want to take it.

He shook out the Lens and, holding it in a thick-folded corner of the insulating blanket, flicked one of the girl's fingertips across the bracelet. Satisfied by the fleeting flash of color which swept across the jewel, he snapped the platinum-iridium band around her left wrist, which it fitted exactly.

She stared for a minute at the smoothly, rhythmically flowing colors of the thing so magically sprung to life upon her wrist; awe and humility in her glorious eyes. Then:

'I can't, Kim. I simply can't. I'm not worthy of it,' she choked.

'None of us are, Cris. We can't be—but we've got to do it, just the same.'

'I suppose that's true—it would be so, of course ... I'll do my best ... but you know perfectly well, Kim, that I'm not—can't ever be—a real Lensman.'

'Sure you can. Do we have to go over all that again? You won't have some of the technical stuff that we got, of course, but you carry jets that no other Lensman ever has had. You're a real Lensman; don't worry about that—if you weren't, do you think they would have made that Lens for you?'

'I suppose not ... it must be true, even though I can't understand it. But I'm simply scared to death of the rest of it, Kim.'

'You needn't be. It'll hurt, but not more than you can stand. Don't think we'd better start that stuff for a few days yet, though; not until you get used to using your Lens. Coming at you, Lensman!' and he went into Lens-to-Lens communication, broadening it gradually into a wide-open two-way.

She was appalled at first, but entranced some thirty minutes later, when he called the lesson to a halt.

'Enough for now,' he decided. 'It doesn't take much of that

stuff to be a great plenty, at first.'

'I'll say it doesn't,' she agreed. 'Put this away for me until next time, will you, Kim? I don't want to wear it all the time until I know more about it.'

'Fair enough. In the meantime I want you to get acquainted with a new girl-friend of mine,' and he sent out a call for Illona Potter.

'*Girl*-friend!'

'Uh-huh. Study her. Educational no end, and she may be important. Want to compare notes with you on her later, is why I'm not giving you any advance dope on her—here she comes.'

'Mac, this is Illona,' he introduced them informally. 'I told them to give you the cabin next to hers,' he added, to the nurse. 'I'll go with you to be sure everything's on the green.'

It was, and the Lensman left the two together.

'I'm awfully glad you're here,' Illona said, shyly. 'I've heard *so* much about you, Miss...'

'"Mac" to you, my dear—all my friends call me that,' the nurse broke in. 'And you don't want to believe everything you hear, especially aboard this space-bucket.' Her lips smiled, but her eyes were faintly troubled.

'Oh, it was nice,' Illona assured her. 'About what a grand person you are, and what a wonderful couple you and Lensman Kinnison make—why, you really *are* in love with him, aren't you?' This in surprise, as she studied the nurse's face.

'Yes,' unequivocally. 'And you love him, too, and that makes it...'

'Good heavens, no!' the Aldebaranian exclaimed, so positively that Clarrissa jumped.

'What? You don't? *Really?*' Gold-flecked, tawny eyes stared intensely into engagingly candid eyes of black. The nurse wished then that she had left her Lens on, so she could tell whether this bejeweled brunette hussy was telling the truth or not.

'Certainly not. That's what I meant—I'm simply scared to death of him. He's so ... well, so overpowering—he's so much more—tremendous—than I am. I didn't see how any girl could possibly love him—but I understand now how you could, perhaps. You're sort of—terrific—yourself, you know. I feel as though I ought to call you "Your Magnificence" instead of just plain "Mac".'

'Why, I'm no such thing!' Clarrissa exclaimed; but she softened noticeably, none the less. 'And I think that I'm going to like you a lot.'

'Oh ... h ... h-honestly?' Illona squealed. 'It sounds too good to be true, you're so marvelous. But if you do, I think that Civilization will be everything that I've been afraid—*so* afraid—that it couldn't possibly be!'

No longer was it a feminine Lensman investigating a female zwilnik; it was two girls—two young, intensely alive, human girls—who chattered on and on.

Days passed. Clarissa learned some of the uses of her Lens. Then Kimball Kinnison, Second-Stage Lensman, began really to bear down. Since such training has been described in detail elsewhere, it need be said here only that Clarrissa MacDougall had mental capacity enough to take it without becoming insane. He suffered as much as she did; after every mental bout he was as spent as she was; but both of them stuck relentlessly to it.

He did not make a Second Stage Lensman of her, of course. He couldn't. Much of the stuff was too hazy yet; more of it did not apply. He gave her everything, however, which she could handle and which would be of any use to her in the work she was to do; including the sense of perception. He did it, that is, with a modicum of help; for, once or twice, when he faltered or weakened, not knowing exactly what to do or not being quite able to do it, a stronger mind than his was always there.

At length, approaching Tellus fast, the nurse and Kinnison had a final conference; the consultation of two Lensmen settling the last details of procedure in a long-planned and highly important campaign.

'I agree with you that Lyrane II is a key planet,' she was saying, thoughtfully. 'It must be, to have those expeditions from Lonabar and the as yet unknown planet "X" centering there.'

'"X" certainly, and don't forget the possibility of "Y" and "Z" and maybe others,' he reminded her. 'The Lyrane-Lonabar linkage is the only one we're sure of. With you on one end of that and me on the other, it'll be funny if we can't trace out some more. While I'm building up an authentic identity to tackle Bleeko, you'll be getting chummy with Helen of Lyrane. That's about as far ahead as we can plan definitely right now, since this groundwork can't be hurried too much.'

'And I report to you often—frequently, in fact.' Clarrissa widened her expressive eyes at her man.

'At least,' he agreed. 'And I'll report to you between times.'

'Oh, Kim, it's nice, being a Lensman!' She snuggled closer. Some way or other, the conference had become somewhat personal. 'Being en rapport will be almost as good as being together—we can stand it, that way, at least.'

'It'll help a lot, ace, no fooling. That was why I was afraid to go ahead with it on my own hook. I couldn't be sure that my feelings were not in control, instead of my judgment—if any.'

'I'd have been certain that it was your soft heart instead of your hard head if it hadn't been for Mentor,' she sighed, happily. 'As it is, though, everything's on the green.'

'All done with Illona?'

'Yes, the darling ... she's the *sweetest* thing, Kim ... and a storehouse of information if there ever was one. You and I know more of Boskonian life than anyone of Civilization ever knew before, I'm sure. And it's *so* ghastly! We *must* win, Kim ... we simply *must*, for the good of all creation!'

'We will.' Kinnison spoke with grim finality.

'But back to Illona. She can't go with me, and she can't stay here with Hank aboard the *Dauntless* taking me back to Lyrane, and you can't watch her. I'd hate to think of anything happening to her, Kim.'

'It won't,' he replied, comfortably. 'Ilyowicz won't sleep nights until he has her as the top-flight solo dancer in his show—even though she doesn't have to work for a living any more ...'

'She will, though, I think. Don't you?'

'Probably. Anyway, a couple of Haynes' smart girls are going to be her best friends, wherever she goes. Sort of keep an eye on her until she learns the ropes—it won't take long. We owe her that much, I figure.'

'That much, at least. You're seeing to the selling of her jewelry yourself, aren't you?'

'No, I had a new thought on that. I'm going to buy it myself—or rather, Cartiff is. They're making up a set of paste imitations. Cartiff has to buy a stock somewhere; why not hers?'

'That's a thought—there's certainly enough of them to stock a wholesaler ... "Cartiff"—I can see that sign,' she snickered. 'Almost microscopic letters, severely plain, in the lower right-hand corner of an immense plate-glass window. One gem in the middle of an acre of black velvet. Cartiff, the most peculiar, if not quite the most exclusive, jeweler in the galaxy. And nobody except you and me knows anything about him. Isn't that something?'

'Everybody will know about Cartiff pretty soon,' he told her.

'Found any flaws in the scheme yet?'

'Nary a flaw.' She shook her head. 'That is, if none of the boys over-do it, and I'm sure they won't. I've got a picture of it,' and she giggled merrily. 'Think of a whole gang of sleuths from the Homicide Division chasing poor Cartiff, and never quite catching him!'

'Uh-huh—a touching picture indeed. But there goes the signal, and there's Tellus. We're about to land.'

'Oh, I want to see!' and she started to get up.

'Look, then,' pulling her down into her original place at his side. 'You've got the sense of perception now, remember; you don't need visiplates.'

And side by side, arms around each other, the two Lensmen watched the docking of their great vessel.

It landed. Jewelers came aboard with their carefully-made wares. Assured that the metal would not discolor her skin, Illona made the exchange willingly enough. Beads were beads, to her. She could scarcely believe that she was now independently wealthy—in fact, she forgot all about her money after Ilyowicz had seen her dance.

'You see,' she explained to Kinnison, 'there were two things I wanted to do until Hank gets back—travel around a lot and learn all I can about your Civilization. I wanted to dance, too, but I didn't see how I could. Now I can do all three, and get paid for doing them besides—isn't that *marvelous*?—and Mr. Ilyowicz said you said it was QX. Is it, really?'

'Right,' and Illona was off.

The Dauntless was serviced and Clarrissa was off, to far Lyrane.

Lensman Kinnison was supposedly off somewhere, also, when Cartiff appeared. Cartiff, the ultra-ultra; the Oh! so exclusive! Cartiff did not advertise. He catered, word spread fast, to only the very upper flakes of the upper crust. Simple dignity was Cartiff's key-note, his insidiously-spread claim; the dignified simplicity of immense wealth and impeccable social position.

What he actually achieved, however, was something subtly different. His simplicity was just a hair off-beam; his dignity was an affected, not a natural, quality. Nobody with less than a million credits ever got past his door, it is true. However, instead of being the real *creme de la creme* of Earth, Cartiff's clients were those who pretended to belong to, or who were trying to force an entrance into, that select stratum. Cartiff was a snob of snobs; he built up a clientele of snobs; and, even more than in his admittedly flawless gems, he dealt in equally high-proof snobbery.

Betimes came Nadreck, the Second Stage Lensman of Palain VII, and Kinnison met him secretly at Prime Base. Soft-voiced, apologetic, diffident; even though Kinnison now knew that the Palainian had a record of accomplishment as long as any one of his arms. But it was not an act, not affectation. It was simply a racial trait, for the intelligent and civilized race of that planet is in no sense human. Nadreck was utterly, startlingly unhuman. In his atmosphere there was no oxygen, in his body there flowed no aqueous blood. At his normal body temperature neither liquid water nor gaseous oxygen could exist.

The seventh planet out from any sun would of course be cold, but Kinnison had not thought particularly about the point until he felt the bitter radiation from the heavily-insulated suit of his guest, perceived how fiercely its refrigerators were laboring to keep its internal temperature down.

'If you will permit it, please, I will depart at once,' Nadreck pleaded, as soon as he had delivered his spool and his message. 'My heat dissipators, powerful though they are, cannot cope much longer with this frightfully high temperature.'

'QX, Nadreck, I won't keep you. Thanks a million. I'm mighty glad to have had this chance of getting acquainted with you. We'll see more of each other, I think, from now on. Remember, Lensman's Seal on all this stuff.'

'Of course, Kinnison. You will understand, however, I am sure, that none of our races of Civilization are even remotely interested in Lonabar—it is as hot, as poisonous, as hellish generally as is Tellus itself!' The weird little monstrosity scuttled out.

Kinnison went back to Cartiff's; and very soon thereafter it became noised abroad that Cartiff was a crook. He was a cheat, a liar, a robber. His stones were synthetic; he made them himself. The stories grew. He was a smuggler; he didn't have an honest gem in his shop. He was a zwilnik, an out-and-out pirate; a red-handed murderer who, if he wasn't there already, certainly ought to be in the big black book of the Galactic Patrol. This wasn't just gossip, either; everybody saw and spoke to men who had seen unspeakable things with their own eyes.

Thus Cartiff was arrested. He blasted his way out, however, before he could be brought to trial, and the newscasters blazed with that highly spectacular, murderous jail-break. Nobody actually saw any lifeless bodies. Everybody, however, saw the Telenews broadcasts of the shattered walls and the sheeted forms; and, since such pictures are and always have been just as convincing as the real thing, everybody knew that there had been plenty of mangled corpses in those ruins and that Cartiff was a fugitive murderer. Also, everybody knew that the Patrol never gives up on a murderer.

Hence it was natural enough that the search for Cartiff, the jeweler-murderer should spread from planet to planet and from region to region. Not exactly obtrusively, but inexorably, it did so spread; until finally anyone interested in the subject could find upon any one of a hundred million planets unmistakable evidence that the Patrol wanted one Cartiff, description so-and-so, for murder in the first degree.

And the Patrol was thorough. Wherever Cartiff went or how, they managed to follow him. At first he disguised himself, changed his name, and stayed in the legitimate jewelry business; apparently the only business he knew. But he never could get even a start. Scarcely would his shop open than he would be discovered and forced again to flee.

Deeper and deeper he went, then, into the noisome society of crime. A fence now—still and always he clung to jewelry. But always and ever the bloodhounds of the law were baying at his heels. Whatever name he used was nosed aside and 'Cartiff!' they howled; so loudly that a thousand million words came to know that hated name.

Perforce he became a traveling fence, always on the go. He flew a dead-black ship, ultra-fast, armed and armored like a super-dreadnought, crewed—according to the newscasts—by the hardest-boiled gang of cut-throats in the known universe. He traded in, and boasted of trading in, the most blood-stained, the most ghost-ridden gems of a thousand worlds. And, so trading, hurling defiance the while into the teeth of the Patrol, establishing himself ever more firmly as one of Civilization's cleverest and most implacable foes, he worked zig-zag-wise and not at all obviously toward the unexplored spiral arm in which the planet Lonabar lay. And as he moved farther and farther away from the Solarian System his stock of jewels began to change. He had always favored pearls—the lovely, glorious things so characteristically Tellurian—and those he kept. The diamonds, however, he traded away; likewise the emeralds, the rubies, the sapphires, and some others. He kept and accumulated Borovan fire-stones, Manarkan star-drops, and a hundred other gorgeous gems, none of which would be 'beads' upon the planet which was his goal.

As he moved farther he also moved faster; the Patrol was hopelessly outdistanced. Nevertheless, he took no chances. His villainous crew guarded his ship; his bullies guarded him wherever he went—surrounding him when he walked, standing behind him while he ate, sitting at either side of the bed in which he slept. He was a king-snipe now.

As such he was accosted one evening as he was about to dine in a garish restaurant. A tall, somewhat fish-faced man in faultless evening dress approached. His arms were at his sides, fingers bent into the 'I'm not shooting' sign.

'Captain Cartiff, I believe. May I seat myself at your table, please?' the stranger asked, politely, in the lingua franca of deep space.

Kinnison's sense of perception frisked him rapidly for concealed weapons. He was clean. 'I would be very happy, sir, to have you as my guest,' he replied, courteously.

The stranger sat down, unfolded his napkin, and delicately allowed it to fall into his lap, all without letting either of his hands disappear from sight, even for an instant, beneath the table's top. He was an old and skillful hand. And during the excellent meal the two men conversed brilliantly upon many topics, none of which were of the least importance. After it Kinnison paid the check, despite the polite protestations of his *vis-a-vis*. Then:

'I am simply a messenger, you will understand, nothing else,' the guest observed. 'Number One has been checking up on you and has decided to let you come in. He will receive you tonight. The usual safeguards on both sides, of course—I am to be your guide and guarantee.'

'Very kind of him, I'm sure.' Kinnison's mind raced. Who could this Number One be? The ape had a thought-screen on, so he was flying blind. Couldn't be a real big shot, though, so soon—no use monkeying with him at all. 'Please convey my thanks, but also my regrets.'

'What?' the other demanded. His veneer of politeness had sloughed off, his eyes were narrow, keen, and cold. 'You know what happens to independent operators around here, don't you? Do you think you can fight *us*?'

'Not fight you, no.' The Lensman elaborately stifled a yawn. He now had a clue. 'Simply ignore you—if you act up, squash you like bugs, that's all. Please tell your Number One that I do not split my take with anybody. Tell him also that I am looking for a choicer location to settle down upon than any I have found as yet. If I do not find such a place near here, I shall move on. If I do find it I shall take it, in spite of God, man, or the devil.'

The stranger stood up, glaring in quiet fury, but with both hands still above the table. 'You want to make it a war, then, Captain Cartiff!' he gritted.

'Not "Captain" Cartiff, please,' Kinnison begged, dipping one paw delicately into his finger-bowl. ' "Cartiff" merely, my dear fellow, if you don't mind. Simplicity, sir, and dignity; those two are my key-words.'

'Not for long,' prophesied the other. 'Number One'll blast you out of the ether before you swap another stone.'

'The Patrol has been trying to do that for some time now, and I'm still here,' Kinnison reminded him, gently. 'Caution him, please, in order to avoid bloodshed, not to come after me in only one ship, but a fleet; and suggest that he have something hotter than Patrol primaries before he tackles me at all.'

Surrounded by his bodyguards, Kinnison left the restaurant, and as he walked along he reflected. Nice going, this. It would get around fast. This Number One couldn't be Bleeko; but the king-snipe of Lonabar and its environs would hear the news in short order. He was now ready to go. He would flit around a few more days—give this bunch of zwilniks a chance to make a pass at him if they felt like calling his bluff—then on to Lonabar.

9: Cartiff the Fence

Kinnison did not walk far, nor reflect much, before he changed his mind and retraced his steps; finding the messenger still in the restaurant.

'So you got wise to yourself and decided to crawl while the crawling's good, eh?' he sneered, before the Lensman could say a word. 'I don't know whether the offer is still good or not.'

'No—and I advise you to muffle your exhaust before somebody pulls one of your legs off and rams it down your throat.' Kinnison's voice was coldly level. 'I came back to tell you to tell your Number One that I'm calling his bluff. You know Checuster?'

'Of course.' The zwilnik was plainly discomfited.

'Come along, then, and listen, so you'll know I'm not running a blazer.'

They sought a booth, wherein the native himself got Checuster on the visiplate.

'Checuster, this is Cartiff.' The start of surprise and the expression of pleased interest revealed how well that name was known. 'I'll be down at your old warehouse day after tomorrow night about this time. Pass the word around that if any of the boys have any stuff too hot for them to handle conveniently, I'll buy it: paying for it in either Patrol credits or bar platinum, whichever they like.'

He then turned to the messenger. 'Did you get that straight, Lizard-Puss?'

The man nodded.

'Relay it to Number One,' Kinnison ordered and strode off. This time he got to his ship, which took off at once.

Cartiff had never made a habit of wearing visible arms, and his guards, while undoubtedly fast gun-men, were apparently only that. Therefore there was no reason for Number One to suppose that his mob would have any noteworthy difficulty in cutting this upstart Cartiff down. He was, however, surprised; for Cartiff did not come afoot or unarmed.

Instead, it was an armored car that brought the intruding fence through the truck-entrance into the old warehouse. Not a car, either; it was more like a twenty-ton tank except for the fact that it ran upon wheels, not treads. It was screened like a cruiser; it mounted a battery of projectors whose energies, it was clear to any discerning eye, nothing short of battle-screen could handle. The thing rolled quietly to a stop, a door swung open, and Kinnison emerged. He was neither unarmed nor unarmored now. Instead, he wore a full suit of G-P armor or a reasonable facsimile thereof, and carried a semi-portable projector.

'You will excuse the seeming discourtesy, men,' he announced, 'when I tell you that a certain Number One has informed me that he will blast me out of the ether before I swap a stone on this planet. Stand clear, please, until we see whether he meant business or was just warming up his jets. Now, Number One, if you're around, come and get it!'

Apparently the challenged party was not present, for no overt move was made. Neither could Kinnison's sense of perception discover any sign of unfriendly activity within its range. Of mind-reading there was none, for every man upon the floor was, as usual, both masked and screened.

Business was slack at first, for those present were not bold souls and the Lensman's overwhelmingly superior armament gave them very seriously to doubt his intentions. Many of them, in fact, had fled precipitately at the first sight of the armored truck, and of these more than a few—Number One's thugs, no doubt—did not return. The others, however, came filtering back as they perceived that there was to be no warfare and as cupidity overcame their timorousness. And as it became evident to all that the stranger's armament was for defense only, that he was there to buy or to barter and not to kill and thus to steal, Cartiff trafficked ever more and more briskly, as the evening wore on, in the hottest gems of the planet.

Nor did he step out of character for a second. He was Cartiff the fence, all the time. He drove hard bargains, but not too hard. He knew jewels thoroughly by this time, he knew the code, and he followed it rigorously. He would give a thousand Patrol credits, in currency good upon any planet of Civilization or in bar platinum good anywhere, for an article worth five thousand, but which was so badly wanted by the law that its then possessor could not dispose of it at all. Or, in barter, he would swap for that article another item, worth fifteen hundred or so, but which was not hot—at least, not upon that planet. Fair enough—so fair that it was almost morning before the silently-running truck slid into its storage inside the dead-black space-ship.

Then, insofar as Number One, the Patrol, and Civilization was concerned, Cartiff and his outfit simply vanished. The zwilnik sub-chief hunted him viciously for a space, then bragged of how he had run him out of the region. The Patrol, as usual, was on a cold scent. The general public forgot him completely in the next sensation to arise.

Fairly close although he then was to the rim of the galaxy, Kinnison did not take any chances at all of detection in a line toward that rim. The spiral arm beyond Rift Eighty Five was unexplored. It had been of so little interest to Civilization that even its various regions were nameless upon the charts, and the Lensman wanted it to remain that way, at least for the time being. Therefore he left the galaxy in as nearly a straight nadir line as he could without coming within detection distance of any trade route. Then, making a prodigious loop, so as to enter the spiral arm from the nadir direction, he threw Nadreck's map into the pilot tank and began the computations which would enable him to place correctly in that three-dimensional chart the brilliant point of light which represented his ship.

In this work he was ably assisted by his chief pilot. He did not have Henderson now, but he did have Watson, who rated Number Two only be the hair-splitting of the supreme Board of Examiners. Such hair-splitting was, of course, necessary; otherwise no difference at all could have been found within the ranks of the first fifty of the Patrol's Master Pilots to say nothing of the first three or four. And the rest of the crew did whatever they could.

For it was only in the newscasts that Cartiff's crew was one of murderous and villainous pirates. They were in fact volunteers; and, since everyone is familiar with what that means in the Patrol, that statement is as informative as a book would be.

The chart was sketchy and incomplete, of course; around the flying ships were hundreds, yes thousands, of stars which were not in the chart at all; but Nadreck had furnished enough reference points so that the pilots could compute their orientation. No need to fear detectors now, in these wild, waste spaces; they set a right-line course for Lonabar and followed it.

As soon as Kinnison could make out the continual outlines of the planet he took over control, as he alone of the crew was upon familiar ground. He knew everything about Lonabar that Illona had ever learned; and, although the girl was a total loss as an astronaut, she did know her geography.

Kinnison docked his ship boldly at the spaceport of Lonia, the planet's largest city and its capital. With equal boldness he registered as 'Cartiff'; filling in some of the blank spaces in the space-port's routine registry form—not quite truthfully, perhaps—and blandly ignoring others. The armored truck was hoisted out of the hold and made its way to Lonia's largest bank, into which it disgorged a staggering total of bar platinum, as well as sundry coffers of hard, gray steel. These last items went directly into a private vault, under the watchful eyes and ready weapons of Kinnison's own guards.

The truck rolled swiftly back to the space-port and Cartiff's ship took off—it did not need servicing at the time—ostensibly for another planet unknown to the Patrol, actually to go, inert, into a closed orbit around Lonabar and near enough to it to respond to a call in seconds.

Immense wealth can command speed of construction and service. Hence, in a matter of days, Cartiff was again in business. His salon was, upon a larger and grander scale, a repetition of his Tellurian shop. It was simple, and dignified, and blatantly expensive. Costly rugs covered the floor, impeccable works of art adorned the walls, and three precisely correct, flawlessly groomed clerks displayed, with the exactly right air of condescending humility, Cartiff's wares before those who wished to view them. Cartiff himself was visible, ensconced within a magnificent plate-glass-and-gold office in the rear, but he did not ordinarily have anything to do with customers. He waited; nor did he wait long before there happened that which he expected.

One of the super-perfect clerks coughed slightly into a microphone.

'A gentleman insists upon seeing you personally, sir,' he announced.

'Very well, I will see him now. Show him in, please,' and the visitor was ceremoniously ushered into the Presence.

'This is a very nice place you have here, Mr. Cartiff, but did it ever occur to you that...'

'It never did and it never will,' Kinnison snapped. He still lolled at ease in his chair, but his eyes were frosty and his voice carried an icy sting. 'I quit paying protection to little shots a good many years ago. Or are you from Menjo Bleeko?'

The visitor's eyes widened. He gasped, as though even to utter that dread name was sheer sacrilege. 'No, but Number...'

'Save it, slob!' The cold venom of that crisp but quiet order set the fellow back onto his heels. 'I am thoroughly sick of this thing of every half-baked tin-horn zwilnik in space calling himself Number One as soon as he can steal enough small change to hire an ape to walk around behind him packing a couple of blasters. If that louse of a boss of yours has a name, use it. If he hasn't call him "The Louse". But cancel that Number One stuff. In my book there is no Number One in the whole damned universe. Doesn't your mob know yet who and what Cartiff is?'

'What do we care?' the visitor gathered courage visibly. 'A good big bomb...'

'Clam it, you squint-eyed slime-lizard!' The Lensman's voice was still low and level, but his tone bit deep and his words drilled in. 'That stuff?' he waved inclusively at the magnificent hall. 'Sucker-bait, nothing more. The whole works cost only a hundred thousand. Chicken feed. It wouldn't even nick the edge of the roll if you blew up ten of them. Bomb it any time you feel the urge. But take notice that it would make me sore—plenty sore—and that I would do things about it; because I'm in a big game, not this petty-larceny racketeering and chiseling your mob is doing, and when a toad gets in my way I step on it. So go back and tell that'—sulphurously and copiously qualified—'Number One of yours to case a job a lot more thoroughly than he did this one before he starts throwing his weight around. Now scram, before I feed your carcass to the other rats around here!'

Kinnison grinned inwardly as the completely deflated gangster slunk out. Good going. It wouldn't take long for *that* blast to get action. This little-shot Number One wouldn't dare to lift a hand, but Bleeko would have to. That was axiomatic, from the very nature of things. It was very definitely Bleeko's move next. The only moot point was as to which His Nibs would do first—talk or act. He would talk, the Lensman thought. The prime reward of being a hot-shot was to have people know it and bend the knee. Therefore, although Cartiff's salon was at all times in complete readiness for any form of violence, Kinnison was practically certain that Menjo Bleeko would send an emissary before he started the rough stuff.

He did, and shortly. A big, massive man was the messenger; a man wearing consciously an aura of superiority, of boundless power and force. He did not simply come into the shop—he made an entrance. All three of the clerks literally cringed before him, and at his casually matter-of-fact order they hazed the already uncomfortable customers out of the shop and locked the doors. Then one of them escorted the visitor, with a sickening servility he had never thought of showing toward his employer and with no thought of consulting Cartiff's wishes in the matter, into Cartiff's private sanctum. Kinnison knew at first glance that this was Ghundrith Khars, Bleeko's right-hand man. Khars, the notorious, who knelt only to His Supremacy, Menjo Bleeko himself; and to whom everyone else upon Lonabar and its subsidiary planets kneeled. The visitor waved a hand and the clerk fled in disorder.

'Stand up, worm, and give me that...' Khars began, loftily.

'Silence, fool! Attention!' Kinnison rasped, in such a drivingly domineering tone that the stupefied messenger obeyed involuntarily. The Lensman, psychologist par excellence that he was, knew that this man, with a background of twenty years of blind, dumb obedience to Bleeko's every order, simply could not cope with a positive and self-confident opposition. 'You will not be here long enough to sit down, even if I permitted it in my presence, which I definitely do not. You came here to give me certain instructions and orders. Instead, you are going to listen merely; I will do all the talking.

'First. The only reason you did not die as you entered this place is that neither you nor Menjo Bleeko knows any better. The next one of you to approach me in this fashion dies in his tracks.

'Second. Knowing as I do the workings of that which your bloated leech of a Menjo Bleeko calls his brain, I know that he has a spy-ray on us now. I am not blocking it out as I want him to receive ungarbled—and I know that you would not have the courage to transmit it accurately to His Foulness—everything I have to say.

'Third. I have been searching for a long time for a planet that I like. This is it. I fully intend to stay here as long as I please. There is plenty of room here for both of us without crowding.

'Fourth. Being essentially a peaceable man, I came in peace and I prefer a peaceable arrangement. However, let it be distinctly understood that I truckle to no man or entity; dead, living, or yet to be born.

'Fifth. Tell Bleeko from me to consider very carefully and very thoroughly an iceberg; its every phase and aspect. That is all—you may go.'

'Bub-bub-but,' the big man stammered. 'An *iceberg*?'

'An iceberg, yes—just that,' Kinnison assured him. 'Don't bother to try to think about it yourself, since you've got nothing to think with. But His Putrescence Bleeko, even though he is a mental, moral, and intellectual slime-lizard, can think—at least in a narrow, mean, small-souled sort of way—and I advise him in all seriousness to do so. Now get the hell out of here, before I burn the seat of your pants off.'

Khars got, gathering together visibly the shreds of his self-esteem as he did so; the clerks staring the while in dumbfounded amazement. Then they huddled together, eyeing the owner of the establishment with a brand-new respect—a subservient respect, heavily laced with awe.

'Business as usual, boys,' he counseled them, cheerfully enough. 'They won't blow up the place until after dark.'

The clerks resumed their places then and trade did go on,

after a fashion; but Cartiff's force had not recovered its wonted blasé aplomb even at closing time.

'Just a moment.' The proprietor called his employees together and, reaching into his pocket, distributed among them a sheaf of currency. 'In case you don't find the shop here in the morning, you may consider yourselves on vacation at full pay until I call you.'

They departed, and Kinnison went back to his office. His first care was to set up a spy-ray block—a block which had been purchased upon Lonabar and which therefore certainly pervious to Bleeko's instruments. Then he prowled about, apparently in deep and anxious thought. But as he prowled, the eavesdroppers did not, could not know that his weight set into operation certain devices of his own highly secret installation, or that when he finally left the shop no really serious harm could be done to it except by an explosion sufficiently violent to demolish the neighborhood for blocks around. The front wall would go, of course. He wanted it to go; otherwise there would be neither reason nor excuse for doing that which for days he had been ready to do.

Since Cartiff lived rigorously to schedule and did not have a spy-ray block in his room, Bleeko's methodical and efficient observers always turned off their beams when the observee went to sleep. This night, however, Kinnison was not really asleep, and as soon as the ray went off he acted. He threw on his clothes and sought the street, where he took a taxi to a certain airport. There he climbed into a prop-and-rocket job already hot and waiting.

Hanging from her screaming props the fantastically powerful little plane bulleted upward in a vertical climb, and as she began to slow down from lack of air her rockets took over. A tractor reached out, seizing her gently. Her wings retracted and she was drawn into Cartiff's great spaceship; which, a few minutes later, hung poised above one of the largest, richest jewel-mines of Lonabar.

This mine was, among others, Menjo Bleeko's personal property. Since over-production would glut the market, it was being worked by only one shift of men; the day-shift. It was now black night; the usual guards were the only men upon the premises. The big black ship hung there and waited.

'But suppose they don't, Kim?' Watson asked.

'Then we'll wait here every night until they do,' Kinnison replied, grimly. 'But they'll do it tonight, for all the tea in

China. They'll have to, to save Bleeko's face.'

And they did. In a couple of hours the observer at a high-powered plate reported that Cartiff's salon had just been blown to bits. Then the Patrolmen went into action.

Bleeko's mobsmen hadn't killed anybody at Cartiff's, therefore the Tellurians wouldn't kill anybody here. Hence, while ten immense beam-dirigible torpedoes were being piloted carefully down shafts and along tunnels into the deepest bowels of the workings, the guards were given warning that, if they got into their flyers fast enough, they could be fifty miles away and probably safe by zero time. They hurried.

At zero time the torpedoes let go as one. The entire planet quivered under the trip-hammer shock of detonating duodec. For those frightful, those appalling charges had been placed, by computations checked and rechecked, precisely where they would wreak the most havoc, the utmost possible measure of sheer destruction. Much of the rock, however hard, around each one of those incredible centers of demolition was simply blasted out of existence. That is the way duodec, in massive charges, works. Matter simply cannot get out of its way in the first instant of its detonation; matter's own inherent inertia forbids.

Most of the rock between the bombs was pulverized the merest fraction of a second later. Then, the distortedly-spherical explosion fronts merging, the total incomprehensible pressure was exerted as almost pure lift. The field above the mine-works lifted, then; practically as a mass at first. But it could not remain as such. It could not move fast enough as a whole; nor did it possess even a minute fraction of the tensile strength necessary to withstand the stresses being applied. Those stresses, the forces of the explosions, were to all intents and purposes irresistible. The crust disintegrated violently and almost instantaneously. Rock crushed grindingly against rock; practically the whole mass reducing in the twinkling of an eye to an impalpable powder.

Upward and outward, then, the ragingly compressed gases of detonation drove, hurling everything before them. Chunks blew out sidewise, flying for miles; the mind-staggeringly enormous volume of dust was hurled upward clear into the stratosphere.

Finally that awful dust-cloud was wafted aside, revealing through its thinning haze a strangely and hideously altered terrain. No sign remained of the buildings or the mechanisms of Bleeko's richest mine. No vestige was left to show that anything built by or pertaining to man had ever existed there. Where those works had been there now yawned an absolutely featureless crater; a crater whose sheer geometrical perfection of figure revealed with shocking clarity the magnitude of the cataclysmic forces which had wrought there.

Kinnison, looking blackly down at that crater, did not feel the glow of satisfaction which comes of a good deed well done. He detested it—it made him sick at the stomach. But, since he had had it to do, he had done it. Why in all the nine hells of Valeria did he have to be a Lensman, anyway?

Back to Lonia, then, the Lensman made his resentful way, and back to bed.

And in the morning, early, workmen began the reconstruction of Cartiff's place of business.

10: Bleeko and the Iceberg

Since Kinnison's impenetrable shields of force had confined the damage to the store's front, it was not long before Cartiff's reopened. Business was and remained brisk; not only because of what had happened, but also because Cartiff's top-lofty and arrogant snobbishness had an irresistible appeal to the upper layers of Lonabar's peculiarly stratified humanity. The Lensman, however, paid little enough attention to business. Outwardly, seated at his ornate desk in haughty grandeur, he was calmness itself, but inwardly he was far from serene.

If she had figured things right, and he was pretty sure that he had, it was up to Bleeko to make the next move, and it would pretty nearly have to be a peaceable one. There was enough doubt about it, however, to make the Lensman a bit jittery inside. Also, from the fact that everybody having any weight at all wore thought-screens, it was almost a foregone conclusion that they had been warned against, and were on the lookout for, THE Lensman—that never-to-be-sufficiently-damned Lensman who had already done so much hurt to the Boskonian cause. That they now thought that one to be a well-hidden, unknown Director of Lensmen, and not an actual operative, was little protection. If he made one slip they'd have him, cold.

He hadn't slipped yet, they didn't suspect him yet; he was sure of those points. With these people to suspect was to act, and his world-circling ship, equipped with every scanning, spying, and eavesdropping device known to science, would have informed him instantly of any untoward development anywhere upon or near the planet. And his fight with Bleeko was, after all, natural enough and very much in character. It was of the very essence of Boskonian culture that king-snipes should do each other to death with whatever weapons came readiest to hand. The underdog was always trying to kill the upper, and if the latter was not strong enough to protect his loot, he deserved everything he got. A callous philosophy, it is true, but one truly characteristic of Civilization's inveterate foes.

The higher-ups never interfered. Their own skins were the only ones in which they were interested. They would, Kinnison reflected, probably check back on him, just to insure their own safety, but they would not take sides in this brawl if they were convinced that he was, as he appeared to be, a struggling young racketeer making his way up the ladder of fame and fortune as best he could. Let them check—Cartiff's past had been fabricated especially to stand up under precisely that investigation, no matter how rigid it were to be!

Hence Kinnison waited, as calmly as might be, for Bleeko to move. There was no particular hurry, especially since Cris was finding heavy going and thick ether at her end of the line, too. They had been in communication at least once every day, usually oftener; and Clarrissa had reported seethingly, in near-masculine, almost-deep-space verbiage, that that damned red-headed hussy of a Helen was a hard nut to crack.

Kinnison grinned sourly every time he thought of Lyrane II. Those matriarchs certainly were a rum lot. They were a pig-headed, self-centered, mulishly stubborn bunch of cock-eyed knotheads, he decided. Non-galaxy-minded; as short-sightedly anti-social as a flock of mad Radeligian cateagles. He'd better ... no, he hadn't better, either—he'd have to lay off. If Cris, with all her potency and charm, with all her drive and force of will, with all her sheer power of mind and of Lens, couldn't pierce their armor, what chance did any other entity of Civilization have of doing it? Particularly any male creature? He'd like to half-wring their beautiful necks, all of them; but that wouldn't get him to the first check-station, either. He'd just have to wait until she broke through the matriarchs' crust—

she'd do it, too, by Klono's prehensile tail!—and then they'd really ride the beam.

So Kinnison waited ... and waited ... and waited. When he got tired of waiting he gave a few more lessons in snobbishness and in the gentle art of self-preservation to the promising young Lonabarian thug whom he had selected to inherit the business, lock, stock, and barrel—including goodwill, if any—if, as, and when he was done with it. Then he waited some more; waited, in fact, until Bleeko was forced, by his silent pressure to act.

It was not an overt act, nor an unfriendly—he simply called him up on the visiphone.

'What do you think you're trying to do?' Bleeko demanded, his darkly handsome face darker than ever with wrath.

'You.' Kinnison made succinct answer. 'You should have taken my advice about pondering the various aspects of an ice-berg.'

'Bah!' the other snorted. 'That silliness?'

'Not as silly as you think. That was a warning, Bleeko, that the stuff showing above the surface is but a very small portion of my total resources. But you could not or would not learn by precept. You had to have it the hard way. Apparently, however, you have learned. That you have not been able to locate my forces I am certain. I am almost as sure that you do not want to try me again, at least until you have found out what you do not know. But I can give you no more time—you must decide now, Bleeko, whether it is to be peace or war between us. I still prefer a peaceful settlement, with an equitable division of the spoils; but if you want war, so be it.'

'I have decided upon peace,' the Lonabarian said, and the effort of it almost choked him. 'I, Menjo Bleeko the Supreme, will give you a place beside me. Come to me here, at once, so that we may discuss the terms of peace.'

'We will discuss them now,' Kinnison insisted.

'Impossible! Barred and shielded as this room is ...'

'It would be,' Kinnison interrupted with a nod, 'for you to make such an admission as you have just made.'

'... I do not trust unreservedly this communication line. If you join me now, you may do so in peace. If you do not come to me, here and now, it is war to the death.'

'Fair enough, at that,' the Lensman admitted. 'After all, you've got to save your face, and I haven't—yet. And if I team up with you I can't very well stay out of your palace forever. But before I come there I want to give you three things—a reminder, a caution, and a warning. I remind you that our first exchange of amenities cost you a thousand times as much as it did me. I caution you to consider again, and more carefully this time, the iceberg. I warn you that if we again come into conflict you will lose not only a mine, but everything you have, including your life. So see to it that you lay no traps for me. I come.'

He went out into the shop. 'Take over, Sport,' he told his gangster protege. 'I'm going up to the palace to see Menjo Bleeko. If I'm not back in two hours, and if your grapevine reports that Bleeko is out of the picture, what I've left in the store here is yours until I come back and take it away from you.'

'I'll take care of it, Boss—thanks,' and the Lensman knew that in true Lonabarian gratitude the youth was already, mentally, slipping a long, keen knife between his ribs.

Without a qualm, but with every sense stretched to the limit and in instant readiness for any eventuality, Kinnison took a cab to the palace and entered its heavily-guarded portals. He was sure that they would not cut him down before he got to Bleeko's room—that room would surely be the one chosen for the execution. Nevertheless, he took no chances. He was supremely ready to slay instantly every guard within range of his sense of perception at the first sign of inimical activity. Long before he came to them, he made sure that the beams which were set to search him for concealed weapons were really search-beams and not lethal vibrations.

And as he passed those beams each one of them reported him clean. Rings, of course; a stick-pin, and various other items of adornment. But Cartiff, the great jeweler, would be expected to wear very large and exceedingly costly gems. And the beam has never been projected which could penetrate those Worsel-designed, Thorndyke-built walls of force; to show that any one of those flamboyant gems was not precisely what it appeared to be.

Searched, combed minutely, millimeter by cubic millimeter, Kinnison was escorted by a heavily-armed quartette of Bleeko's personal guards into His Supremacy's private study. All four bowed as he entered—but they strode in behind him, then shut and locked the door.

'You fool!' Bleeko gloated from behind his massive desk. His face flamed with sadistic joy and anticipation. 'You trusting, greedy fool! I have you exactly where I want you now. How easy! How simple! This entire building is screened and shielded—by *my* screens and shields. Your friends and accomplices, whoever or wherever they are, can neither see you nor know what is to happen to you. If your ship attempts your rescue it will be blasted out of the ether. I will, personally, gouge out your eyes, tear off your nails, strip your hide from your quivering carcass...' Bleeko was now, in his raging exaltation, fairly frothing at the mouth.

'That would be a good trick if you could do it,' Kinnison remarked, coldly. 'But the real fact is that you haven't even tried to use that pint of blue mush that you call a brain. Do you think me an utter idiot? I put on an act and you fell for it...'

'Seize him, guards! Silence his yammering—tear out his tongue!' His Supremacy shrieked, leaping out of his chair as though possessed.

The guards tried manfully, but before they could touch him—before any one of them could take one full step—they dropped. Without being touched by material object or visible beam, without their proposed victim having moved a muscle, they died and fell. Died instantly, in their tracks; died completely, effortlessly, painlessly, with every molecule of the all-important compound without which life cannot even momentarily exist shattered instantaneously into its degradation products; died not knowing even that they died.

Bleeko was shaken, but he was not beaten. Needle-ray men, sharpshooters all, were stationed behind those walls. Gone now the dictator's intent to torture his victim to death. Slaying him out of hand would have to suffice. He flashed a signal to the concealed marksmen, but that order too went unobeyed. For Kinnison had perceived the hidden gunmen long since, and before any of them could align his sights or press his firing stud each one of them ceased to live. The zwilnik then flipped on his communicator and gobbled orders. Uselessly; for death sped ahead. Before any mind at any switchboard could grasp the meaning of the signal, it could no longer think.

'You fiend from hell!' Bleeko screamed, in mad panic now, and wrenched open a drawer in order to seize a weapon of his own. Too late. The Lensman had already leaped, and as he landed he struck—not gently. Lonabar's tyrant collapsed upon the thick-piled rug in a writhing, gasping heap; but he was not unconscious. To suit Kinnison's purpose he could not be unconscious; he had to be in full possession of his mind.

The Lensmen crooked one brawny arm around the zwilnik's neck in an unbreakable strangle-hold and flipped off his thought-screen. Physical struggles were of no avail: the attacker knew exactly what to do to certain nerves and ganglia to paralyze all such activity. Mental resistance was equally futile against the overwhelmingly superior power of the Tellurian's mind. Then, his subject quietly passive, Kinnison tuned in and began his search for information. Began it—and swore soulfully. This *couldn't* be so ... it didn't make any kind of sense ... but there it was.

The ape simply didn't know a thing about any ramification whatever of the vast culture to which Civilization was opposed. He knew all about Lonabar and the rest of the domain which he had ruled with such an iron hand. He knew much—altogether too much—about humanity and Civilization, and plainly to be read in his mind were the methods by which he had obtained those knowledges and the brutally efficient precautions he had taken to make sure that Civilization would not in turn learn of him.

Kinnison scowled blackly. His deductions simply *couldn't* be that far off ... and besides, it wasn't reasonable that this guy was the top or that he had done all that work on his own account ... He pondered deeply, staring unseeing at Bleeko's placid face; and as he pondered, some of the jigsaw blocks of the puzzle began to click into a pattern.

Then, ultra-carefully, with the utmost nicety of which he was capable, he again fitted his mind to that of the dictator and began to trace, one at a time, the lines of memory. Searching, probing, coursing backward and forward along those deeply-buried time-tracks, until at last he found the breaks and the scars. For, as he had told Illona, a radical mind-operation cannot be performed without leaving marks. It is true that upon cold, unfriendly Jarnevon, after Worsel had so operated upon Kinnison's mind, Kinnison himself could not perceive that any work had been done. But that, be it remembered, was before any actual change had occurred; before the compulsion had been applied. The false memories supplied by Worsel were still latent, non-existent; the true memory chains, complete and intact, were still in place.

The lug's brain had been operated upon, Kinnison now knew, and by an expert. What the compulsion was, what combination of thought-stimuli it was that would restore those now non-existent knowledges, Kinnison had utterly no means of finding out. Bleeko himself, even subconsciously, did not know. It was, it had to be, something external, a thought-pattern impressed upon Bleeko's mind by the Boskonian higher-up whenever he wanted to use him; and to waste time in trying to solve *that* problem would be the sheerest folly. Nor could he discover how that compulsion had been or could be applied. If he got his orders from the Boskonian high command direct, there would have to be an inter-galactic communicator; and it would in all probability be right here, in Bleeko's private rooms. No force-ball, or anything else that could take its place, was to be found. Therefore Bleeko was, probably, merely another Regional Director, and took orders from someone here in the First Galaxy.

Lyrane? The possibility jarred Kinnison. No real probability pointed that way yet, however; it was simply a possibility, born of his own anxiety. He wouldn't worry about it—yet.

His study of the zwilnik's mind, unproductive although it was of the desired details of things Boskonian, had yielded one highly important fact. His Supremacy of Lonabar had sent at least one expedition to Lyrane II; yet there was no present memory in his mind that he had ever done so. Kinnison had scanned those files with surpassing care, and knew positively that Bleeko did not now know even that such a planet as Lyrane II existed.

Could he, Kinnison, be wrong? Could somebody other than Menjo Bleeko have sent that ship? Or those ships, since it was not only possible, but highly probable, that that voyage was not an isolated instance? No, he decided instantly. Illona's knowledge was far too detailed and exact. Nothing of such importance would be or could be done without the knowledge and consent of Lonabar's dictator. And the fact that he did not now remember it was highly significant. It meant—it *must* mean—that the new Boskone or whoever was back of Boskone considered the solar system of Lyrane of such vital importance that knowledge of it must never, under any circumstances, get to Star A Star, the detested, hatred, and feared Director of Lensmen of the Galactic Patrol! And Mac was on Lyrane II—ALONE! She had been safe enough so far, but . . .

'Cris!' he sent her an insistent thought.

'Yes, Kim?' came flashing answer.

'Thank Klono and Noshabkeming! You're QX, then?'

'Of course. Why shouldn't I be, the same as I was this morning?'

'Things have changed since then,' he assured her, grimly. 'I've finally cracked things open here, and I find that Lonabar is simply a dead end. It's a feeder for Lyrane, nothing else. It's not a certainty, of course, but there's a very distinct possibility that

Lyrane is IT. If it is, I don't need to tell you that you're on a mighty hot spot. So I want you to quit whatever you're doing and run. Hide. Crawl into a hole and pull it in after you. Get into one of Helen's deepest crypts and have somebody sit on the lid. And do it right now—five minutes ago would have been better.'

'Why, Kim!' she giggled. 'Everything here is exactly as it has always been. And surely, you wouldn't have a Lensman hide, would you? Would you, yourself?'

That question was, they both knew, unanswerable. 'That's different,' he of course protested, but he knew that it was not. 'Well, anyway, be careful,' he insisted. 'More careful than you ever were before in your life. Use everything you've got, every second, and if you notice anything, however small, the least bit out of the way, let me know, right then.'

'I'll do that. You're coming, of course.' It was a statement, not a question.

'I'll say I am—in force! 'Bye, Cris—BE CAREFUL!' and he snapped the line. He had a lot to do. He had to act fast, and had to be right—and he couldn't take all day in deciding, either.

His mind flashed back over what he had done. Could he cover up? Should he cover up, even if he could? Yes and no. Better not even try to cover Cartiff up, he decided. Leave that trail just as it was; wide and plain—up to a certain point. This point, right here. Cartiff would disappear here, in Bleeko's palace.

He was done with Cartiff, anyway. They would smell a rat, of course—it stunk to high heaven. They might not—they probably would not—believe that he had died in the ruins of the palace, but they wouldn't know that he hadn't. And they would think that he hadn't found out a thing, and he would keep them thinking so as long as he could. The young thug in Cartiff's would help, too, all unconsciously. He would assume the name and station, of course, and fight with everything Kinnison had taught him. That *would* help—Kinnison grinned as he realized just how much it would help.

The real Cartiff would have to vanish as completely, as absolutely without a trace as was humanly possible. They would figure out in time that Cartiff had done whatever was done in the palace, but it was up to him to see to it that they could never find out how it was done. Wherefore he took from Menjo's mind every iota of knowledge which might conceivably be of use to him thereafter. Then Menjo Bleeko died and the Lensman strode along corridors and down stairways. And wherever he went, there went Death.

This killing griped Kinnison to the core of his being, but it had to be. The fate of all Civilization might very well depend upon the completeness of his butchery this day; upon the sheer mercilessness of his extermination of every foe who might be able to cast any light, however dim, upon what he had just done.

Straight to the palace arsenal he went, where he labored briefly at the filling of a bin with bombs. A minute more to set a timer and he was done. Out of the building he ran. No one stayed him; nor did any, later, say that they had seen him go. He dumped a dead man out of a car and drove it away at reckless speed. Even at that, however, he was almost too slow—hurtling stones from the dynamited palace showered down scarcely a hundred feet behind his screeching wheels.

He headed for the space-port; then, changing his mind, braked savagely as he sent Lensed instructions to Watson. He felt no compunction about fracturing the rules and regulations made and provided for the landing of space-ships at space-ports everywhere by having his vessel make a hot-blast, unauthorized, and quite possibly highly destructive to pick him up. Nor did he fear pursuit. The big shots were, for the most part, dead. The survivors and the middle-sized shots were too busy by far to waste time over an irregular incident at a space-port. Hence nobody would give anybody any orders, and without explicit orders no Lonabarian officer would act. No, there would be no pursuit. But They—the Ones Kinnison was after—would interpret truly every such irregular incident; wherefore there must not be any.

Thus it came about that when the speeding ground-car was upon an empty stretch of highway, with nothing in sight in any direction, a space-ship eased down upon muffled under-jets directly above it. A tractor beam reached down; car and man were drawn upward and into the vessel's hold. Kinnison did not want the car, but he could not leave it there. Since many cars had been blown out of existence with Bleeko's palace, for this one to disappear would be natural enough; but for it to be found abandoned out in the open country would be a highly irregular and an all too revealing occurrence.

Upward through atmosphere and stratosphere the black cruiser climbed; out into inter-stellar space she flashed. Then, while Watson coaxed the sleek flyer to do even better than her prodigious best, Kinnison went to his room and drilled a thought to Prime Base and Port Admiral Haynes.

'Kinnison. Are you too busy to give me a couple of minutes?'

'You always have the right-of-way, Kim, you know that—you're the most important thing in the galaxy right now,' Haynes said, soberly.

'Well, a minute or so wouldn't make any difference—not *that* much difference, anyway,' Kinnison replied, uncomfortably. 'I don't like to Lens you unless I have to,' and he began his report.

Scarcely had he started, however, when he felt a call impinge upon his own Lens. Clarrissa was calling him from Lyrane II.

'Just a sec, admiral! Come in, Cris—make it a three-way with Admiral Haynes!'

'You told me to report anything unusual, no matter what,' the girl began. 'Well, I finally managed to get chummy enough with Helen so she'd really talk to me. The death-rate from airplane crashes went up sharply a while ago and is still rising. I am reporting that fact as per instructions.'

'Hm . . . m . . . m. What kind of crashes?' Kinnison asked.

'That's the unusual feature of it. Nobody knows—they just disappear.'

'WHAT?' Kinnison yelled the thought, so forcibly that both Clarrissa and Haynes winced under its impact.

'Why, yes,' she replied, innocently—somewhat too innocently. 'But as to what it means . . .'

'You know what it means, don't you?' Kinnison snapped.

'I don't *know* anything. I can do some guessing, of course, but for the present I'm reporting a fact, not personal opinions.'

'QX. That fact means that you *do*, right now, crawl into the deepest, most heavily thought-screened hole in Lyrane and stay there until I, personally, come and dig you out,' he replied, grimly. 'It means, Admiral Haynes, that I want Worsel and Tregonsee as fast as I can get them—not orders, of course, but very, *very* urgent requests. And I want vanBuskirk and his gang of Valerians, and Grand Fleet, with all the trimmings, within easy striking distance of Dunstan's Region as fast as you can possibly get them there. And I want . . .'

'Why all the excitement, Kim?' Haynes demanded. 'You're 'way ahead of me, both of you. Give!'

'I don't *know* anything, either,' Kinnison emphasized the verb very strongly. 'However, I suspect a lot. Everything, in fact, grading downward from the Eich. I'd say Overlords, except that I don't see how . . . what do you think, Cris?'

'What I think is too utterly fantastic for words—my visualization of the Cosmic All calls for another Eich-Overlord alliance.'

'Could be, I guess. That would...'

'But they were all destroyed, weren't they?' Haynes interrupted.

'Far from it.' This from the nurse. 'Would the destruction of Tellus do away with all mankind? I am beginning to think that the Eich are to Boskonia exactly what we are to Civilization.'

'So am I,' Kinnison agreed. 'And, such being the case, I'm going to get in touch with Nadreck of Palain Seven—I think I know his pattern well enough to Lens him from here.'

'Nadreck? Your new playfellow? Why?' Clarrissa asked, curiously.

'Because he's a frigid-blooded, poison-breathing, second-stage Gray Lensman,' Kinnison explained. 'As such he is much closer to the Eich, in every respect, than we are, and may very well have an angle that we haven't.' And in a few minutes the Palanian Lensman became en rapport with the group.

'An interesting development, truly,' his soft thought came in almost wistfully when the situation had been made clear to him. 'I fear greatly that I cannot be of any use, but I am not doing anything of importance at the moment and will be very glad indeed to give you whatever slight assistance may be possible to one of my small powers. I come at speed to Lyrane II.'

11: Alcon of Thrale

Kinnison had not underestimated the power and capacity of his as yet unknown opposition. Well it was for him and for his Patrol that he was learning to think; for, as has already been made clear, this phase of the conflict was not essentially one of physical combat. Material encounters did occur, it is true, but they were comparatively unimportant. Basically, fundamentally, it was brain against brain; the preliminary but nevertheless prodigious skirmishing of two minds—or, more accurately, two teams of minds—each trying, even while covering up its own tracks and traces, to get at and to annihilate the other.

Each had certain advantages.

Boskonia—although we know now that Boskone was by no means the prime mover in that dark culture which opposed Civilization so bitterly, nevertheless 'Boskonia' it was and still is being called—for a long time had the initiative, forcing the Patrol to wage an almost purely defensive fight. Boskonia knew vastly more about Civilization than Civilization knew about Boskonia. The latter, almost completely unknown, had all the advantages of stealth and of surprise; her forces could and did operate from undeterminable points against precisely-plotted objectives. Boskonia had the hyper-spatial tube long before the Conference of Scientists solved its mysteries; and even after the Patrol could use it it could do Civilization no good unless and until something could be found at which to aim it.

Civilization, however, had the Lens. It had the backing of the Arisians; maddeningly incomplete and unsatisfactory though that backing seemed at times to be. It had a few entities, notably one Kimball Kinnison, who were learning to think really efficiently. Above all, it had a massed purpose, a loyalty, an esprit de corps back-boning a morale which the whip-driven ranks of autocracy could never match and which the whip-wielding drivers could not even dimly understand.

Kinnison, then, with all the powers of his own mind and the minds of his friends and co-workers, sought to place and to identify the real key mentality at the destruction of which the mighty Boskonian Empire must begin to fall apart; that mentality in turn was trying with its every resource to find and to destroy the intellect which, pure reason showed, was the one factor which had enabled Civilization to throw the fast-conquering hordes of Boskonia back into their own galaxy.

Now, from our point of vantage in time and space, we can study at leisure and in detail many things which Kimball Kinnison could only surmise and suspect and deduce. Thus, he knew definitely only the fact that the Boskonian organization did not collapse with the destruction of the planet Jarnevon.

We know now, however, all about the Thrallian solar system and about Alcon of Thrale, its unlamented Tyrant. The planet Thrale—planetographically speaking, Thrallis II—so much like Tellus that its natives, including the unspeakable Alcon, were human practically to the limit of classification; and about Onlo, or Thrallis IX, and its monstrous natives. We know now that the duties and the authorities of the Council of Boskone were taken over by Alcon of Thrale; we now know how, by reason of his absolute control over both the humanity of Thrale and the monstrosities of Onlo, he was able to carry on.

Unfortunately, like the Eich, the Onlonians simply cannot be described by or to man. This is, as is already more or less widely known, due to the fact that all such non-aqueous, sub-zero-blooded, non-oxygen-breathing peoples have of necessity a metabolic extension into the hyper dimension; a fact which makes even their three-dimensional aspect subtly incomprehensible to any strictly three-dimensional mind.

Not all such races, it may be said here, belonged to Boskonia. Many essentially similar ones, such as the natives of Palain VII, adhered to our culture from the very first. Indeed, it has been argued that sexual equality is the most important criterion of that which we know as Civilization. But, since this is not a biological treatise, this point is merely mentioned, not discussed.

The Onlonians, then, while not precisely describable to man, were very similar to the Eich—as similar, say, as a Posenian and a Tellurian are to each other in the perception of a Palainian. That is to say practically identical; for to the unknown and incomprehensible senses of those frigid beings the fact that the Posenian possess four arms, eight hands, and no eyes at all, as compared with the Tellurian's simply paired members, constitutes a total difference to slight as to be negligible.

But to resume the thread of history, we are at liberty to know things that Kinnison did not. Specifically, we may observe and hear a conference which tireless research has reconstructed in toto. The place was upon chill, dark Onlo, in a searingly cold room whose normal condition of utter darkness was barely ameliorated by a dim blue glow. The time was just after Kinnison had left Lonabar for Lyrane II. The conferees were Alcon of Thrale and his Onlonian cabinet officers. The armor-clad Tyrant, in whose honor the feeble illumination was, lay at ease in a reclining chair; the pseudo-reptilian monstrosities were sitting or standing in some obscure and inexplicable fashion at a long, low bench of stone.

'The fact is,' one of the Onlonians was radiating harshly, 'that our minions in the other galaxy could not or would not or simply did not think. For years things went so smoothly that no one had to think. The Great Plan, so carefully worked out, gave every promise of complete success. It was inevitable, it seemed, that that entire galaxy would be brought under our domination, its Patrol destroyed, before any inkling of our purpose could be perceived by the weaklings of humanity.

'The Plan took cognizance of every known factor of any importance. When, however, an unknown, unforeseeable factor, the Lens of the Patrol, became of real importance, that Plan of course broke down. Instantly upon the recognition of an unconsidered factor the Plan should have been revised. All action should have ceased until that factor had been evaluated and neutralized. But no—no one of our commanders in that galaxy or handling its affairs ever thought of such a thing...'

'It is you who are not thinking now,' the Tyrant of Thrale broke in. 'If any underling had dared any such suggestion you yourself would have been among the first to demand his elimination. The Plan should have been revised, it is true; but the fault does not lie with the underlings. Instead, it lies squarely with the Council of Boskone ... by the way, I trust that those six of that Council who escaped destruction upon Jarnevon by means of their hyper-spatial tube have been dealt with?'

'They have been liquidated,' another officer replied.

'It is well. They were supposed to think, and the fact that they neither coped with the situation nor called it to your attention until it was too late to mend matters, rather than any flaw inherent in the Plan, is what has brought about the present intolerable situation.

'Underlings are not supposed to think. They are supposed to report facts; and, if so requested, opinions and deductions. Our representatives there were well-trained and skillful. They reported accurately, and that was all that was required of them. Helmuth reported truly, even though Boskone discredited his reports. So did Prellin, and Crowninshield, and Jalte. The Eich, however, failed in their duties of supervision and correlation; which is why their leaders have been punished and their operators have been reduced in rank—why we have assumed a task which, it might have been supposed and was supposed, lesser minds could have and should have performed.

'Let me caution you now that to underestimate a foe is a fatal error. Lan of the Eich prated largely upon this very point, but in the eventuality he did in fact underestimate very seriously the resources and the qualities of the Patrol; with what disastrous consequences we are all familiar. Instead of thinking he attempted to subject a purely philosophical concept, the Lens, to a mathematical analysis. Neither did the heads of our military branch think at all deeply, or they would not have tried to attack Tellus until after this new and enigmatic factor had been resolved. Its expeditionary force vanished without sign or signal—in spite of its primaries, its negative-matter bombs, its supposedly irresistible planets—and Tellus still circles untouched about Sol its sun. The condition is admittedly not to be borne; but I have always said, and I now do and shall insist, that no further action be taken until the Great Plan shall have been so revised as reasonably to take into account the Lens . . . What of Arisia?' he demanded of a third cabineteer.

'It is feared that nothing can be done about Arisia at present,' that entity replied. 'Expeditions have been sent, but they were dealt with as simply and as effectively as were Lan and Amp of the Eich. Planets have also been sent, but they were detected by the Patrol and were knocked out by far-ranging dirigible planets of the enemy. However, I have concluded that Arisia, of and by itself, is not of prime immediate importance. It is true that the Lens did in all probability originate with the Arisians. It is hence true that the destruction of Arisia and its people would be highly desirable, in that it would insure that no more Lenses would be produced. Such destruction would not do away, however, with the myriads of the instruments which are already in use and whose wearers are operating so powerfully against us. Our most pressing business, it seems to me, is to hunt down and exterminate all Lensmen; particularly the one whom Jalte called THE Lensman; whom Eichmil was informed by Lensman Morgan, was known to even other Lensmen only as Star A Star. In that connection, I am forced to wonder—is Star A Star in reality only one mind?'

'That question has been considered both by me and by your chief psychologist,' Alcon made answer. 'Frankly, we do not know. We have not enough reliable data upon which to base a finding of fact. Nor does it matter in the least. Whether one or two or a thousand, we must find and we must slay until it is feasible to resume our orderly conquest of the universe. We must also work unremittingly upon a plan to abate the nuisance which is Arisia. Above all, we must see to it with the utmost diligence that no iota of information concerning us ever reaches any member of the Galactic Patrol—I do not want either of our worlds to become as Jarnevon now is.'

'Hear! Bravo! Nor I!' came a chorus of thoughts, interrupted by an emanation from one of the sparkling force-ball inter-galactic communicators.

'Yes? Alcon acknowledging,' the Tyrant took the call.

It was a zwilnik upon far Lonabar, reporting through Lyrane

VIII everything that Cartiff had done. 'I do not know—I have no idea—whether or not this matter is either unusual or important,' the observer concluded. 'I would, however, rather report ten unimportant things than miss one which might later prove to have had significance.'

'Right. Report received,' and discussion raged. Was this affair actually what it appeared upon the surface to be, or was it another subtle piece of the work of that never-to-be-sufficiently-damned Lensman?

The observer was recalled. Orders were given and were carried out. Then, after it had been learned that Bleeko's palace and every particle of its contents had been destroyed, that Cartiff had vanished utterly, and that nobody could be found upon the face of Lonabar who could throw any light whatever upon the manner or the time of his going; then, after it was too late to do anything about it, it was decided that this must have been the work of THE Lensman. And it was useless to storm or to rage. Such a happening could not have been reported sooner to so high an office; the routine events of a hundred million worlds simply could not be considered at that level. And since this Lensman never repeated—his acts were always different, alike only in that they were drably routine acts until their crashing finales—the Boskonian observers never had been and never would be able to report his activities in time.

'But he got nothing *this* time, I am certain of that,' the chief psychologist exulted.

'How can you be so sure?' Alcon snapped.

'Because Menjo Bleeko of Lonabar knew nothing whatever of our activities or of our organization except at such times as one of my men was in charge of his mind,' the scientist gloated. 'I and my assistants know mental surgery as those crude hypnotists the Eich never will know it. Even our lowest agents are having those clumsy and untrustworthy false teeth removed as fast as my therapists can operate upon their minds.'

'Nevertheless, you are even now guilty of underestimating,' Alcon reproved him sharply, energizing a force-ball communicator. 'It is quite eminently possible that he who wrought so upon Lonabar may have been enabled—by pure chance, perhaps—to establish a linkage between that planet and Lyrane . . .'

The cold, crisply incisive thought of an Eich answered the Tyrant's call.

'Have you of Lyrane perceived or encountered any unusual occurrences or indications?' Alcon demanded.

'We have not.'

'Expect them, then,' and the Thrallian despot transmitted in detail all the new developments.

'We always expect new and untoward things,' the Eich more than half sneered. 'We are prepared momently for anything that can happen, from a visitation by Star A Star and any or all of his Lensmen up to an attack by the massed Grand Fleet of the Galactic Patrol. Is there anything else, Your Supremacy?'

'No. I envy you your self-confidence and assurance, but I mistrust exceedingly the soundness of your judgment. That is all.' Alcon turned his attention to the psychologist. 'Have you operated upon the minds of those Eich and those self-styled Overlords as you did upon that of Menjo Bleeko?'

'No!' the mind-surgeon gasped. 'Impossible! Not physically, perhaps, but would not such a procedure interfere so seriously with the work that it . . .'

'That is your problem—solve it,' Alcon ordered, curtly. 'See to it, however it is solved, that no traceable linkage exists between any of those minds and us. Any mind capable of thinking such thoughts as those which we have just received is not to be trusted.'

As has been said, Kinnison-ex-Cartiff was en route for Lyrane II while the foregoing conference was taking place. Throughout the trip he kept in touch with Clarrissa. At first he tried, with his every artifice of diplomacy, cajolery, and downright threats, to make her lay off; he finally invoked all his Unattached Lensman's transcendental authority and ordered her summarily to lay off.

No soap. How did he get that way, she wanted furiously to know, to be ordering her around as though she were an uncapped probe? She was a Lensman, too, by Klono's curly whiskers! Solving this problem was her job—nobody else's—and she was going to do it. She was on a definite assignment—his own assignment, too, remember—and she wasn't going to be called off of it just because he had found out all of a sudden that it might not be quite as safe as dunking doughnuts at a down-river picnic. What kind of a sun-baked, space-tempered crust did he have to pull a crack like that on *her*? Would he have the bare-faced, unmitigated gall to spring a thing like that on any other Lensman in the whole cock-eyed universe?

That stopped him—cold. Lensmen always went in; that was the Code. For any Tellurian Lensman, anywhere, to duck or to dodge because of any personal danger was sheerly, starkly unthinkable. The fact that she was, to him, the sum total of all the femininity of the galaxy could not be allowed any weight whatever; any more than the converse aspect had ever been permitted to sway him. Fair enough. Bitter, but inescapable. This was one—just one—of the consequences which Mentor had foreseen. He had foreseen it, too, in a dimly unreal sort of way, and now that it was here he'd simply have to take it. QX.

'But be careful, anyway,' he surrendered. 'Awfully careful—as careful as I would myself.'

'I could be ever so much more careful than that and still be pretty reckless.' Her low, entrancing chuckle came through as though she were present in person. 'And by the way, Kim, did I ever tell you that I am fast getting to be a gray Lensman?'

'You always were, ace—you couldn't very well be anything else.'

'No—I mean actually gray. Did you ever stop to consider what the laundry problem would be on this heathenish planet?'

'Cris, I'm surprised at you—what do you need of a laundry?' he derided her, affectionately. 'Here you've been blasting me to a cinder about not taking your Lensmanship seriously enough, and yet you are violating one of the prime tenets—that of conformation to planetary customs. Shame on you!'

He felt her hot blush across all those parsecs of empty space. 'I tried it at first, Kim, but it was just simply *terrible*!'

'You've got to learn how to be a Lensman or else quit throwing your weight around like you did a while back. No back chat, either, you insubordinate young jade, or I'll take that Lens away from you and heave you into the clink.'

'You and what regiment of Valerians? Besides, it didn't make any difference,' she explained, triumphantly. 'These matriarchs don't like me one bit better, no matter what I wear or don't wear.'

Time passed, and in spite of Kinnison's highly disquieting fears, nothing happened. Right on schedule the Patrol ship eased down to a landing at the edge of the Lyranian airport. Clarrissa was waiting; dressed now, not in nurse's white, but in startlingly nondescript gray shirt and breeches.

'Not the gray leather of my station, but merely dirt color,' she explained to Kinnison after the first fervent greetings. 'These women are clean enough physically, but I simply haven't got a thing fit to wear. Is your laundry working?'

It was, and very shortly Sector Chief Nurse Clarrissa Mac-

Dougall appeared in her wonted immaculately-white, stiffly-starched uniform. She would not wear the Grays to which she was entitled; nor would she—except when defying Kinnison—claim as her right any one of the perquisites or privileges which were so indubitably hers. She was not, never had been, and never would or could be a *real* Lensman, she insisted. At best, she was only a synthetic—or an imitation—or a sort of amateur—or maybe a 'Red' Lensman—handy to have around, perhaps, for certain kinds of jobs, but absolutely and definitely not a regular Lensman. And it was this attitude which was to make the Red Lensman not merely tolerated, but loved as she was loved by Lensmen, Patrolmen, and civilians alike throughout the length, breadth, and thickness of Civilization's bounds.

The ship lifted from the airport and went north into the uninhabited temperate zone. The matriarchs did not have anything the Tellurians either needed or wanted; the Lyranians disliked visitors so openly and so intensely that to move away from the populated belt was the only logical and considerate thing to do.

The *Dauntless* arrived a day later, bringing Worsel and Tregonsee; followed closely by Nadreck in his ultra-refrigerated speedster. Five Lensmen, then, studied intently a globular map of Lyrane II which Clarrissa had made. Four of them, the oxygen-breathers, surrounded it in the flesh, while Nadreck was with them only in essence. Physically he was far out in the comfortably sub-zero reaches of the stratosphere, but his mind was en rapport with theirs; his sense of perception scanned the markings upon the globe as carefully and as accurately as did theirs.

'This belt which I have colored pink,' the female Lensman explained, 'corresponding roughly to the torrid zone, is the inhabited area of Lyrane II. Nobody lives anywhere else. Upon it I have charted every unexplained disappearance that I have been able to find out about. Each of these black crosses is where one such person lived. The black circle—or circles, for frequently there are more than one—connected to each cross by a black line, marks the spot—or spots—where that person was seen for the last time or times. If the black circle is around the cross it means that she was last seen at home.'

The crosses were distributed fairly evenly all around the globe and throughout the populated zone. The circles, however tended markedly to concentrate upon the northern edge of that zone; and practically all of the encircled crosses were very close to the northern edge of the populated belt.

'Almost all the lines intersect at this point here,' she went on, placing a finger-tip near the north pole of the globe. 'The few that don't could be observational errors, or perhaps the person was seen there before she really disappeared. If it *is* Overlords, their cavern must be within about fifty kilometers of the spot I've marked here. However, I couldn't find any evidence that any Eich have ever been here; and if they haven't I don't see how the Overlords could be here, either. That, gentlemen of the Second Stage, is my report; which I fear, is neither complete nor conclusive.'

'You err, Lensman MacDougall.' Nadreck was the first to speak. 'It is both. A right scholarly and highly informative piece of work, eh, friend Worsel?'

'It is so ... it is indeed so,' the Velantian agree, the while a shudder rippled along the thirty-foot length of his sinuous body. 'I suspected many things, but not this ... certainly not this, ever, away out here.'

'Nor I.' Tregonsee's four horn-lipped, toothless mouths snapped open and shut; his cabled arms writhed.

'Nor I,' from Kinnison. 'If I had, you'd never've got that Lens, Clarrissa May MacDougall.'

His voice was the grimmest she had ever heard it. He was picturing to himself her lovely body writhing in torment; stretched, twisted, broken; forgetting completely that his thoughts were as clear as a tri-di to all the others.

'If they had detected *you* ... you know what they'd do to get hold of a mind and a vital force such as yours ...'

He shook himself and drew a tremendously deep breath of relief. 'But thank God they didn't. So all I've got to say is that if we ever have any kids and they don't bawl when I tell 'em about this, I'll certainly give 'em something to bawl about!'

12: Helen Goes North

'But listen, Kim!' Clarrissa protested. 'All four of you are assuming that I've dead-centered the target. I thought probably I was right, but since I couldn't find any Eich traces, I expected a lot of argument.'

'No argument,' Kinnison assured her. 'You know how they work. They tune in on some one mind, the stronger and more vital the better. In that connection, I wonder that Helen is still around—the ones who disappeared were upper-bracket minds, weren't they?'

She thought a space. 'Now that you mention it, I believe so. Most of them, certainly.'

'Thought so. That clinches it, if it needed clinching. They tune in; then drag 'em in in a straight line.'

'But that would be so *obvious*!' she objected.

'It was not obvious, Clarrissa,' Tregonsee observed, 'until your work made it so: a task which, I would like to say here, could not have been accomplished by any other entity of Civilization.'

'Thanks, Tregonsee. But they're smart enough to ... you'd think they'd vary their technique, at least enough to get away from those dead straight lines.'

'They probably can't,' Kinnison decided. 'A racial trait, bred into 'em for ages. They've always worked that way; probably can't work any other way. The Eich undoubtedly told 'em to lay off those orgies, but they probably couldn't do it—the vice is too habit-forming to break, would be my guess. Anyway, we're all in agreement that it's the Overlords?'

They were.

'And there's no doubt as to what we do next?'

There was none. Two great ships, the incomparable *Dauntless* and the camouflaged warship which had served Kinnison-Cartiff so well, lifted themselves into the stratosphere and headed north. The Lensmen did not want to advertise their presence and there was no great hurry, therefore both vessels had their thought-screens out and both rode upon baffled jets.

Practically all of the crewmen of the *Dauntless* had seen Overlords in the substance; so far as is known they were the only human beings who had ever seen an Overlord and had lived to tell of it. Twenty two of their former fellows had been Overlords and had died. Kinnison, Worsel, and vanBuskirk had slain Overlords in unscreened hand-to-hand combat in the fantastically incredible environment of a hyper-spatial tube—that uncanny medium in which man and monster could and did occupy the same space at the same time without being able to touch each other; in which the air or pseudo-air is thick and viscous; in which the only substance common to both sets of dimensions and thus available for combat purposes is dureum—a synthetic material so treated and so saturated as to be of enormous mass and inertia.

It is easier to imagine, then, than to describe the emotion which seethed through the crew as the news flew around that the business next in order was the extirpation of a flock of Overlords.

'How about a couple or three nice duodec torpedoes, Kim, steered right down into the middle of that cavern and touched off—POWIE!—slick, don't you think?' Henderson insinuated.

'Aw, let's not, Kim!' protested vanBuskirk, who, as one of the three Overlord-slayers, had been called into the control room. 'This ain't going to be in a tube, Kim; it's in a cavern on a planet—made to order for axe-work. Let me and the boys put on our screens and bash their ugly damn skulls in for 'em—how about it, huh?'

'Not duodec, Hen ... not yet, anyway,' Kinnison decided. 'As for axe-work, Bus—maybe, maybe not. Depends. We want to catch some of them alive, so as to get some information ... but you and your boys will be good for that, too, so you might as well go and start getting them ready.' He turned his thought to his snakish comrade-in-arms.

'What do you think, Worsel, is this hide-out of theirs heavily fortified, or just hidden?'

'Hidden, I would say from what I know of them—well hidden,' the Velantian replied, promptly. 'Unless they have changed markedly; and, like you, I do not believe that a race so old can change that much. I could tune them in, but it might very well do more harm than good.'

'Certain to, I'm afraid.' Kinnison knew as well as did Worsel that a Velantian was the tastiest dish which could be served up to any Overlord. Both knew also, however, the very real mental ability of the foe; knew that the Overlords would be sure to suspect that any Velantian so temptingly present upon Lyrane II must be there specifically for the detriment of the Delgonian race; knew that they would almost certainly refuse the proffered bait. And not only would they refuse to lead Worsel to their caverns, but in all probability they would cancel even their ordinary activities, thus making it impossible to find them at all, until they had learned definitely that the hook-bearing tid-bit and its accomplices had left the Lyranian solar system entirely. 'No, what we need right now is a good, strong-willed Lyranian.'

'Shall we go back and grab one? It would take only a few minutes,' Henderson suggested, straightening up at his board.

'Uh-uh,' Kinnison demurred. 'That might smell a bit on the cheesy side, too, don't you think, fellows?' and Worsel and Tregonsee agreed that such a move would be ill-advised.

'Might I offer a barely tenable suggestion?' Nadreck asked diffidently.

'I'll say you can—come in.'

'Judging by the rate at which Lyranians have been vanishing of late, it would seem that we would not have to wait too long before another one comes hither under her own power. Since the despised ones will have captured her themselves, and themselves will have forced her to come to them, no suspicion will be or can be aroused.'

'That's a thought, Nadreck—that *is* a thought!' Kinnison applauded. 'Shoot us up, will you, Hen? 'Way up, and hover over the center of the spread of intersections of those lines. Put observers on every plate that you've got here, and have Communications alert all observers aboard ship. Have half of them search the air all around as far as they can reach for an airplane in flight; have the rest comb the terrain below, both on the surface and underground, with spy-rays, for any sign of a natural or artificial cave.'

'What kind of information do you think they may have, Kinnison?' asked Tregonsee the Rigellian.

'I don't know.' Kinnison pondered for minutes. 'Somebody—around here somewhere—has got some kind of a tie-up with some Boskonian entity or group that is fairly well up the ladder; I'm pretty sure of that. Bleeko sent ships here—one speedster, certainly, and there's no reason to suppose that it was an isolated case...'

'There is nothing to show, either, that it was not an isolated case,' Tregonsee observed, quietly, 'and the speedster landed, not up here near the pole, but in the populated zone. Why? To secure some of the women?' The Rigellian was not arguing against Kinnison; he was, as they all knew, helping to subject every facet of the matter to scrutiny.

'Possibly—but this is a transfer point,' Kinnison pointed out.

'Illona was to start out from here, remember. And those two ships . . . coming to meet her, or perhaps each other, or . . .'

'Or perhaps called there by the speedster's crew, for aid,' Tregonsee completed the thought.

'One, but quite possibly not both,' Nadreck suggested. 'We are agreed, I think, that the probability of a Boskonian connection is sufficiently large to warrant the taking of these Overlords alive in order to read their minds?'

They were; hence the discussion then turned naturally to the question of how this none-too-easy feat was to be accomplished. The two Patrol ships had climbed and were cruising in great, slow circles; the spy-ray men and the other observers were hard at work. Before they had found anything upon or in the ground, however:

'Plane, ho!' came the report, and both vessels, with spy-ray blocks out now as well as thought-screens, plunged silently into a flatly-slanting dive. Directly over the slow Lyranian craft, high above it, they turned as one to match its course and slowed to match its pace.

'Come to life, Kim—don't let them have her!' Clarrissa exclaimed. Being en rapport with them all, she knew that both unhuman Worsel and monstrous Nadreck were perfectly willing to let the helpless Lyranian become a sacrifice; she knew that neither Kinnison nor Tregonsee had as yet given that angle of the affair a single thought. 'Surely, Kim, you don't have to let them kill her, do you? Isn't showing you the gate or whatever it is, enough? Can't you rig up something to do something with when she gets almost inside?'

'Why . . . uh . . . I s'pose so.' Kinnison wrenched his attention away from a plate. 'Oh, sure, Cris. Hen! Drop us down a bit, and have the boys get ready to spear that crate with a couple of tractors when I give the word.'

The plane held its course, directly toward a range of low, barren, precipitous hills. As it approached them it dropped, as though to attempt a landing upon a steep and rocky hillside.

'She can't land there,' Kinnison breathed, 'and Overlords would want her alive, not dead . . . suppose I've been wrong all the time? Get ready, fellows!' he snapped. 'Take her at the very last possible instant—before—she—crashes—NOW!'

As he yelled the command the powerful beams leaped out, seizing the disaster-bound vehicle in a gently unbreakable grip. Had they not done so, however, the Lyranian would not have crashed; for in that last spilt second a section of the rugged hillside fell inward. In the very mouth of that dread opening the little plane hung for an instant, then:

'Grab the woman, quick!' Kinnison ordered, for the Lyranian was very evidently going to jump. And, such was the awful measure of the Overlord's compulsion, she did jump; without a parachute, without knowing or caring what, if anything, was to break her fall. But before she struck ground a tractor beam had seized her, and passive plane and wildly struggling pilot were both borne rapidly aloft.

'Why, Kim, it's *Helen*!' Clarrissa shrieked in surprise, then voice and manner became transformed. 'The poor, poor thing,' she crooned. 'Bring her in at number six lock. I'll meet her there—you fellows keep clear. In the state she's in a shock—especially such a shock as seeing such a monstrous lot of males—would knock her off the beam, sure.'

Helen of Lyrane ceased struggling in the instant of being drawn through the thought-screen surrounding the *Dauntless*. She had not been unconscious at any time. She had known exactly what she had been doing; she had wanted intensely—such was the insidiously devastating power of the Delgonian mind—to do just that and nothing else. The falseness of values, the indefensibility of motivation, simply could not register in her thoroughly suffused, completely blanketed mind. When the screen cut off the Overlord's control, however, thus restoring her own, the shock of realization of what she had done—what she had been forced to do—struck her like a physical blow. Worse than a physical blow, for ordinary physical violence she could understand.

This mischance, however, she could not even begin to understand. It was utterly incomprehensible. She knew what had happened; she knew that her mind had been taken over by some monstrously alien, incredibly powerful mentality, for some purpose so obscure as to be entirely beyond her ken. To her narrow philosophy of existence, to her one-planet insularity of viewpoint and outlook, the very existence, anywhere, of such a mind with such a purpose was in simple fact impossible. For it actually to exist upon her own planet, Lyrane II, was sheerly, starkly unthinkable.

She did not recognize the *Dauntless*, of course. To her all space-ships were alike. They were all invading warships, full of enemies. All things and all beings originating elsewhere than upon Lyrane II were, perforce, enemies. Those outrageous males, the Tellurian Lensman and his cohorts, had pretended not to be inimical, as had the peculiar, white-swathed Tellurian near-person who had been worming itself into her confidence in order to study the disappearances; but she did not trust even them.

She now knew the manner of, if not the reason for, the vanishment of her fellow Lyranians. The tractors of the spaceship had saved her from whatever fate it was that impended. She did not, however, feel any thrill of gratitude. One enemy or another, what difference did it make? Therefore, as she went through the blocking screen and recovered control of her mind, she set herself to fight; to fight with every iota of her mighty mind and with every fiber of her lithe, hard-schooled, tigress' body. The air-lock doors opened and closed—she faced, not an armed and armored male all set to slay, but the white-clad near-person whom she already knew better than she ever would know any other non-Lyranian.

'Oh, Helen!' the girl half sobbed, throwing both arms around the still-braced Chief Person. 'I'm *so* glad that we got to you in time! And there will be no more disappearances, dear—the boys will see to that!'

Helen did not know, really, what disinterested friendship meant. Since the nurse had put her into a wide-open two-way, however, she knew beyond all possibility of doubt that these Tellurians wished her and all her kind well, not ill; and the shock of that knowledge, superimposed upon the other shocks which she had so recently undergone, was more than she could bear. For the first and only time in her hard, busy, purposeful life, Helen of Lyrane fainted; fainted dead away in the circle of the Earth-girl's arms.

The nurse knew that this was nothing serious; in fact, she was professionally quite in favor of it. Hence, instead of resuscitating the Lyranian, she swung the pliant body into a carry—as has been previously intimated, Clarrissa MacDougall was no more a weakling physically than she was mentally—and without waiting for orderlies and stretcher she bore it easily away to her own quarters.

13: In the Cavern

In the meantime the more warlike forces of the *Dauntless* had not been idle. In the instant of the opening of the cavern's doors the captain's talker issued orders, and as soon as the Lyranian was out of the line of fire keen-eyed needle-ray men saw to it that those doors were in no mechanical condition to close. The *Dauntless* settled downward; landed in front of the entrance to the cavern. The rocky, broken terrain meant nothing to her; the hardest, jaggedest boulders crumbled instantly to dust as her enormous mass drove the file-hard, inflexible armor of her mid-zone deep into the ground. Then, while alert beamers watched the entrance and while spy-ray experts combed the interior for other openings which Kinnison and Worsel were already practically certain did not exist, the forces of Civilization formed for the attack.

Worsel was fairly shivering with eagerness for the fray. His was, and with plenty of reason, the bitterest by far of all the animosities there present against the Overlords. For Delgon and his own native planet, Velantia, were neighboring worlds, circling about the same sun. Since the beginning of Velantian space-flight the Overlords of Delgon had preyed upon the Velantians; in fact, the Overlords had probably caused the first Velantian space-ship to be built. They had called them, in a never-ending stream, across the empty gulf of space. They had pinned them against their torture screens, had flayed them and had tweaked them to bits, had done them to death in every one of the numberless slow and hideous fashions which had been developed by a race of sadists who had been specializing in the fine art of torture for thousands upon thousands of years. Then, in the last minutes of the long-drawn-out agony of death, the Overlords were wont to feed, with a passionate, greedy, ineradicably ingrained lust utterly inexplicable to any civilized mind, upon the life-forces which the mangled bodies could no longer contain.

This horrible parasitism went on for ages. The Velantians fought vainly; their crude thought-screens were almost useless until after the coming of the Patrol. Then, with screens that were of real use, and with ships of power and with weapons of might, Worsel himself had taken the lead in the clean-up of Delgon. He was afraid, of course. Any Velantian was and is frightened to the very center of his being by the mere thought of an Overlord. He cannot help it; it is in his heredity, bred into the innermost chemistry of his body; the cold grue of a thousand thousand fiendishly tortured ancestors simply will not be denied or cast aside.

Many of the monsters had succeeded in fleeing Delgon, of course. Some departed in the ships which had ferried their victims to the planet, some were removed to other solar systems by the Eich. The rest were slain; and as the knowledge that a Velantian *could* kill an Overlord gained headway, the emotions toward the oppressors generated within minds such as the Velantians' became literally indescribable. Fear was there yet and in abundance—it simply could not be eradicated. Horror and revulsion. Sheer, burning hatred; and, more powerful than all, amounting almost to an obsession, a clamoring, shrieking, driving urge for revenge which was almost tangible. All these, and more, Worsel felt as he waited, twitching.

The Valerians wanted to go in because it meant a hand-to-hand fight. Fighting was their business, their sport, and their pleasure; they loved it for its own sweet sake, with a simple, wholehearted devotion. To die in combat was a Valerian soldier's natural and much-to-be-desired end; to die in any peaceful fashion was a disgrace and a calamity. They did and do go into battle with very much the same joyous abandon with which a sophomore goes to meet his date in Lover's Lane. And now, to make physical combat all the nicer and juicier, they carried semi-portable tractors and pressors, for the actual killing was not to take place until after the battle proper was over. Blasting the Overlords out of existence would have been simplicity itself: but they were not to die until after they had been forced to divulge whatever they might have of knowledge or of information.

Nadreck of Palain wanted to go in solely to increase his already vast store of knowledge. His thirst for facts was a purely scientific one; the fashion in which it was to be satisfied was the veriest, the most immaterial detail. Indeed, it is profoundly impossible to portray to any human intelligence the serene detachment, the utterly complete indifference to suffering exhibited by practically all of the frigid-blooded races, even those adherent to Civilization, especially when the suffering is being done by an enemy. Nadreck did know, academically and in a philological sense, from his reading, the approximate significance of such words as 'compunction', 'sympathy', and 'squeamishness'; but he would have been astounded beyond measure at any suggestion that they would apply to any such matter-of-fact business as the extraction of data from the mind of an Overlord of Delgon, no matter what might have to be done to the unfortunate victim in the process.

Tregonsee went in simply because Kinnison did—to be there to help out in case the Tellurian should need him.

Kinnison went in because he felt that he had to. He knew full well that he was not going to get any kick at all out of what was going to happen. He was not going to like it, any part of it. Nor did he. In fact, he wanted to be sick—violently sick—before the business was well started. And Nadreck perceived his mental and physical distress.

'Why stay, friend Kinnison, when your presence is not necessary?' he asked, with the slightly pleased, somewhat surprised, hellishly placid mental immobility which Kinnison was later to come to know so well. 'Even though my powers are admittedly small, I feel eminently qualified to cope with such minor matters as the obtainment and the accurate transmittal of that which you wish to know. I cannot understand your emotions, but I realize fully that they are essential components of that which makes you what you fundamentally are. There can be no justification for your submitting yourself needlessly to such stresses, such psychic traumata.'

And Kinnison and Tregonsee, realizing the common sense of the Palainian's statement and very glad indeed to have an excuse for leaving the outrageous scene, left it forthwith.

There is no need to go into detail as to what actually transpired within that cavern's dark and noisome depths. It took a long time, nor was any of it gentle. The battle itself, before the Overlords were downed, was bad enough in any Tellurian eyes. Clad in armor of proof although they were, more than one of the Valerians died. Worsel's armor was shattered and rent, his leather-hard flesh was slashed, burned, and mangled before the last of the monstrous forms was pinned down and helpless. Nadreck alone escaped unscathed—he did so, he explained quite truthfully, because he did not go in there to fight, but to learn.

What followed the battle, however, was infinitely worse. The Delgonians, as has been said, were hard, cold, merciless, even among themselves; they were pitiless and unyielding and refractory in the extreme. It need scarcely be emphasized then, that they did not yield to persuasion either easily or graciously; that their own apparatus and equipment had to be put to its fullest grisly use before those stubborn minds gave up the secrets so grimly and so implacably sought. Worsel, the raging Velantian, used those torture-tools with a vengeful savagery and a snarling ferocity which are at least partially understandable; but Nadreck employed them with a calm capability, a coldly, emotionlessly efficient callousness the mere contemplation of which made icy shivers chase each other up and down Kinnison's spine.

At long last the job was done. The battered Patrol force returned to the *Dauntless*, bringing with them their spoils and their dead. The cavern and its every molecule of contents was bombed out of existence. The two ships took off; Cartiff's heavily-armed 'merchantman' to do the long flit back to Tellus, the *Dauntless* to drop Helen and her plane off at her airport and then to join her sister super-dreadnoughts which were already beginning to assemble in Rift Ninety Four.

'Come down here, will you please, Kim?' came Clarrissa's thought. 'I've been keeping her pretty well blocked out, but she wants to talk to you—in fact, she insists on it—before she leaves the ship.'

'Hm ... that *is* something!' the Lensman exclaimed, and hurried to the nurse's cabin.

There stood the Lyranian queen; a full five inches taller than Clarrissa's five feet six, a good thirty five pounds heavier than her not inconsiderable one hundred and forty five. Hard, fine, supple; erectly poised she stood there, an exquisitely beautiful statue of pale bronze, her flaming hair a gorgeous riot. Head held proudly high, she stared only slightly upward into the Earth-man's quiet, understanding eyes.

'Thanks, Kinnison, for everything that you and yours have done for me and mine,' she said, simply; and held out her right hand in what she knew was the correct Tellurian gesture.

'Uh-uh, Helen,' Kinnison denied, gently, making no motion to grasp the proffered hand—which was promptly and enthusiastically withdrawn. 'Nice, and it's really big of you, but don't strain yourself to like us men too much or too soon; you've got to get used to us gradually. We like you a lot, and we respect you even more, but we've been around and you haven't. You can't be feeling friendly enough yet to enjoy shaking hands with me—you certainly haven't got jets enough to swing *that* load—so this time we'll take the thought for the deed. Keep trying, though, Toots old girl, and you'll make it yet. In the meantime we're all pulling for you, and if you ever need any help, shoot us a call on the communicator we've put aboard your plane. Clear ether, ace!'

'Clear ether, MacDougall and Kinnison!' Helen's eyes were softer than either of the Tellurians had ever seen them before. 'There is, I think, something of wisdom, of efficiency, in what you have said. It may be . . . that is, there is a possibility . . . you of Civilization are, perhaps, persons—of a sort, that is,—after all. Thanks—*really* thanks, I mean, this time—goodbye.'

Helen's plane had already been unloaded. She disembarked and stood beside it; watching, with a peculiarly untranslatable expression, the huge cruiser until it was out of sight.

'It was just like pulling teeth for her to be civil to me,' Kinnison grinned at his fiancee, 'but she finally made the lift. She's a grand girl, that Helen, in her peculiar, poisonous way.'

'Why, Kim!' Clarrissa protested. 'She's nice, really, when you get to know her. And she's so stunningly, so ravishingly beautiful!'

'Uh-huh,' Kinnison agreed, without a trace of enthusiasm. 'Cast her in chilled stainless steel—she'd just about do as she is, without any casting—and she'd make a mighty fine statue.'

'Kim! Shame on you!' the girl exclaimed. 'Why, she's the most perfectly *beautiful* thing I ever saw in my whole life!' Her voice softened. 'I wish I looked like that,' she added wistfully.

'She's beautiful enough—in her way—of course,' the man admitted, entirely unimpressed. 'But then, so is a Radelegian cateagle, so is a spire of frozen helium, and so is a six-foot-long, armor-piercing punch. As for you wanting to look like her—that's sheer tripe, Cris, and you know it. Beside you, all the Helens that ever lived, with Cleopatra, Dessa Desplaines, and Illona Potter thrown in, wouldn't make a baffled flare . . .'

That was, of course, what she wanted him to say; and what followed is of no particular importance here.

Shortly after the *Dauntless* cleared the stratosphere, Nadreck reported that he had finished assembling and arranging the data, and Kinnison called the Lensmen together in his con room for an ultra-private conference. Worsel, it appeared, was still in surgery.

''Smatter, Doc?' Kinnison asked, casually. He knew that there was nothing really serious the matter—Worsel had come out of the cavern under his own power, and a Velantian recovers with startling rapidity from any wound which does not kill him outright. 'Having trouble with your stitching?'

'I'll say we are!' the surgeon grunted. 'Have to bore holes

with an electric drill and use linemen's pliers. Just about through now, though—he'll be with you in a couple of minutes,' and in a very little more than the stipulated time the Velantian joined the other Lensmen.

He was bandaged and taped, and did not move at his customary headlong pace, but he fairly radiated self-satisfaction, bliss, and contentment. He felt better, he declared, than he had at any time since he cleaned out the last of Delgon's caverns.

Kinnison stopped the inter-play of thoughts by starting up his Lensman's projector. This mechanism was something like a tri-di machine, except that instead of projecting sound and three-dimensional color, it operated via pure thought. Sometimes the thoughts of one or more Overlords, at other times the thoughts of the Eich or other beings as registered upon the minds of the Overlords, at still others the thoughts of Nadreck or of Worsel amplifying a preceding thought-passage or explaining some detail of the picture which was being shown at the moment. The spool of tape now being run, with others, formed the Lensmen's record of what they had done. This record would go to Prime Base under Lensman's Seal; that is, only a Lensman could handle it or see it. Later, after the emergency had passed, copies of it would go to various Central Libraries and thus become available to properly accredited students. Indeed, it is only from such records, made upon the scene and at the time by keen-thinking, logical, truth-seeking Lensmen, that such a factual, minuuely-detailed history as this can be compiled; and your historian is supremely proud that he was the first person other than a Lensman to be allowed to study a great deal of this priceless data.

Worsel knew the gist of the report, Nadreck the compiler knew it all; but to Kinnison, Clarrissa, and Tregonsee the unreeling of the tape brought shocking news. For, as a matter of fact, the Overlords had known more, and there was more in the Lyrianian solar system to know, than Kinnison's wildest imaginings had dared to suppose. The system was one of the main focal points for the zwilnik business of an immense volume of space; Lyrane II was the meeting-place, the dispatcher's office, the nerve-center from which thousands of invisible, immaterial lines reached out to thousands of planets peopled by warm-blooded oxygen-breathers. Menjo Bleeko had sent to Lyrane II not one expedition, but hundreds of them; the affair of Illona and her escorts had been the veriest, the most trifling incident.

The Overlords, however, did not know of any Boskonian group in the Second Galaxy. They had no superiors, anywhere. The idea of anyone or any thing anywhere being superior to an Overlord was unthinkable. They did, however, cooperate with—here came the really stunning fact—certain of the Eich who lived upon eternally dark Lyrane VIII, and who managed things for the frigid-blooded, poison-breathing Boskonians of the region in much the same fashion as the Overlords did for the warm-blooded, light-loving races. To make the cooperation easier and more efficient, the two planets were connected by a hyper-spatial tube.

'Just a sec!' Kinnison interrupted, as he stopped the machine for a moment. 'The Overlords were kidding themselves a bit there, I think—they must have been. If they didn't report to or get orders from the Second Galaxy or some other higher-up office, the Eich must have; and since the records and plunder and stuff were not in the cavern, the Eich must have them on Eight. Therefore, whether they realized it or not, the Overlords must have been inferior to the Eich and under their orders. Check?'

'Check,' Nadreck agreed. 'Worsel and I concluded that they knew the facts, but were covering up even in their own minds, to save face. Our conclusions, and the data from which they were derived, are in the introduction—another spool. Shall I get it?'

'By no means—just glad to have the point cleared up, is all. Thanks,' and the showing went on.

The principal reason why the Lyranian system had been chosen for that important headquarters was that it was one of the very few outlying solar systems, completely unknown to the scientists of the Patrol, in which both the Eich and the Overlords could live in their natural environments. Lyrane VIII was, of course, intensely, bitterly cold. This quality is not rare, since nearly all Number Eight planets are; its uniqueness lay in the fact that its atmosphere was almost exactly like that of Jarnevon.

And Lyrane II suited the Overlords perfectly. Not only did it have the correct temperature, gravity, and atmosphere, but also it offered that much rarer thing without which no cavern of Overlords would have been content for long—a native life-form possessing strong and highly vital minds upon which they could prey.

There was more, much more; but the rest of it was not

directly pertinent to the immediate questions. The tape ran out, Kinnison snapped off the projector, and the Lensmen went into a five-way.

Why was not Lyrane II defended? Worsel and Kinnison had already answered that one. Secretiveness and power of mind, not armament, had always been the natural defenses of all Overlords. Why hadn't the Eich interfered? That was easy, too. The Eich looked after themselves—if the Overlords couldn't that was just too bad. The two ships that had come to aid and had remained to revenge had certainly not come from Eight—their crews had been oxygen-breathers. Probably a rendezvous—immaterial anyway. Why wasn't the whole solar system ringed with outposts and screens? Too obvious. Why hadn't the *Daunltess* been detected? Because of her nullifiers; and if she had been spotted by any short-range stuff she had been mistaken for another swilnik ship. They hadn't detected anything out of the way on Eight because it hadn't occurred to anybody to swing an analyzer toward that particular planet. If they did they'd find that Eight was defended plenty. Had the Eich had time to build defenses? They must have had, or they wouldn't be there—they certainly were not taking that kind of chances. And by the way, hadn't they better do a bit of snooping around Eight before they went back to join the *Z9M9Z* and the Fleet? They had.

Thereupon the *Dauntless* faced about and retraced her path toward the now highly important system of Lyrane. In their previous approaches the Patrolmen had observed the usual precautions to avoid revealing themselves to any zwilnik vessel which might have been on the prowl. Those precautions were now intensified to the limit, since they knew that Lyrane VIII was the site of a base manned by the Eich themselves.

As the big cruiser crept toward her goal, nullifies full out and every instrument of detection and reception as attentively outstretched as the whiskers of a tomcat slinking along a black alley at midnight, the Lensmen again pooled their brains in conference.

The Eich. This was going to be NO pushover. Even the approach would have to be figured to a hair; because, since the Boskonians had decided that it would be poor strategy to screen in their whole solar system, it was a cold certainty that they would have their own planets guarded and protected by every device which their inhuman ingenuity could devise. The *Dauntless* would have to stop just outside the range of electro-magnetic detection, for the Boskonians would certainly have a five hundred percent overlap. Their nullifiers would hash up the electors somewhat, but there was no use in taking too many chances. Previously, on right-line courses to and from Lyrane II, that had not mattered, for two reasons—not only was the distance extreme for accurate electro work, but also it would have been assumed that their ship was a zwilnik. Laying a course for Eight, though, would be something else entirely. A zwilnik would take the tube, and they would not, even if they had known where it was.

That left the visuals. The cruiser was a mighty small target at interplanetary distances; but there were such things as electronic telescopes, and the occultation of even a single star might prove disastrous. Kinnison called the chief pilot.

'Stars must be thin in certain regions of the sky out here, Hen. Suppose you can pick us out a line of approach along which we will occult no stars and no bright nebulae?'

'I should think so, Kim—just a sec; I'll see ... Yes, easily. There's a lot of black background, especially to the nadir,' and the conference was resumed.

They'd have to go through the screens of electros in Kinnison's inherently indetectable black speedster. QX, but she was nobody's fighter—she didn't have a beam hot enough to light a match. And besides, there were the thought-screens and the highly-probable other stuff about which the Lensmen could know nothing.

Kinnison quite definitely did not relish the prospect. He remembered all too vividly what had happened when he had scouted the Eich's base on Jarnevon; when it was only through Worsel's aid that he had barely—*just* barely—escaped with his life. And Jarnevon's defenders had probably been exerting only routine precautions, whereas these fellows were undoubtedly cocked and primed for THE Lensman. He would go in, of course, but he'd probably come out feet first—he didn't know any more about their defenses than he had known before, and that was nothing, flat ...

'Excuse the interruption, please,' Nadreck's thought apologized, 'but it would seem to appear desirable, would it not, to induce the one of them possessing the most information to come out to us?'

'Huh?' Kinnison demanded. 'It would, of course—but how in all your purple hells do you figure on swinging *that* load?'

'I am, as you know, a person of small ability,' Nadreck replied in his usual circuitous fashion. 'Also, I am of almost negligible mass and strength. Of what is known as bravery I have no trace—in fact, I have pondered long over that to me incomprehensible quality and have decided that it has no place in my scheme of existence. I have found it much more efficient to perform the necessary tasks in the easiest and safest possible manner, which is usually by means of stealth, deceit, indirection, and other cowardly artifices.'

'Any of those, or all of them, would be QX with me,' Kinnison assured him. 'Anything goes with gusto and glee, as far as the Eich are concerned. What I don't see is how we can put it across.'

'Thought-screens interfered so seriously with my methods of procedure,' the Palainian explained, 'that I was forced to develop a means of puncturing them without upsetting their generators. The device is not generally known, you understand.' Kinnison understood. So did the other Lensmen.

'Might I suggest that the four of you put on heated armor and come with me to my vessel in the hold? It will take some little time to transfer my apparatus and equipment to your speedster.'

'Is it non-ferrous—undetectable?' Kinnison asked.

'Of course,' Nadreck replied in surprise. 'I work, as I told you, by stealth. My vessel is, except for certain differences necessitated by racial considerations, a duplicate of your own.'

'Why didn't you say so?' Kinnison wanted to know. 'Why bother to move the gadget? Why not use your speedster?'

'Because I was not asked. We should not bother. The only reason for using your vessel is so that you will not suffer the discomfort of wearing armor,' Nadreck replied, categorically.

'Cancel it, then,' Kinnison directed. 'You've been wearing armor all the time you were with us—turn about for a while will be QX. Better that way, anyway, as this is very definitely your party, not ours. Not?'

'As you say; and with your permission,' Nadreck agreed. 'Also it may very well be that you will be able to suggest improvements in my device whereby its efficiency may be increased.'

'I doubt it.' The Tellurian's already great respect for this retiring, soft-spoken, 'cowardly' Lensman was increasing constantly. 'But we would like to study it, and perhaps copy it, if you so allow.'

'Gladly,' and so it was arranged.

The *Dauntless* crept along a black-background pathway and stopped. Nadreck, Worsel, and Kinnison—three were enough and neither Clarrissa nor Tregonsee insisted upon going—boarded the Palainian speedster.

Away from the mother-ship it sped upon muffled jets, and through the far-flung, heavily overlapped electro-magnetic detector zones. Through the outer thought-screens. Then, ultra-slowly, as space-speeds go, the speedster moved forward, feeling for whatever other blocking screens there might be.

All three of those Lensmen were in fact detectors themselves—their Arisian-imparted special senses made ethereal, even sub-ethereal, vibrations actually visible or tangible—but they did not depend only upon their bodily senses. That speedster carried instruments unknown to space-pilotry, and the Lensmen used them unremittingly. When they came to a screen they opened it, so insidiously that its generating mechanisms gave no alarms. Even a meteorite screen, which was supposed to forbid the passage of any material object, yielded without protest to Nadreck's subtle manipulation.

Slowly, furtively, a perfectly absorptive black body sinking through blackness so intense as to be almost palpable, the Palainian speedster settled downward toward the Boskonian fortress of Lyrane III.

14: Nadreck at Work

This is perhaps as good a place as any to glance in passing at the fashion in which the planet Lonabar was brought under the aegis of Civilization. No attempt will or can be made to describe it in any detail, since any adequate treatment of it would fill a volume—indeed, many volumes have already been written concerning various phases of the matter—and since it is not strictly germane to the subject in hand. However, some knowledge of the *modus operandi* in such cases is highly desirable for the full understanding of this history, in view of the vast number of planets which Coordinator Kinnison and his associates did have to civilize before the Second Galaxy was made secure.

Scarcely had Cartiff-Kinnison moved out than the Patrol moved in. If Lonabar had been heavily fortified, a fleet of appropriate size and power would have cleared the way. As it was, the fleet which landed was one of transports, not of battleships, and all the fighting from then on was purely defensive.

Propagandists took the lead; psychologists; Lensmen skilled not only in languages but also in every art of human relationships. The case of Civilization was stated plainly and repeatedly, the errors and the fallacies of autocracy were pointed out. A nucleus of government was formed; not of Civilization's imports, but of solid Lonabarian citizens who had passed the Lensmen's tests of ability and trustworthiness.

Under this local government a pseudo-democracy began haltingly to function. At first its progress was painfully slow; but as more and more of the citizens perceived what the Patrol actually was doing, it grew apace. Not only did the invaders allow—yes, foster—free speech and statutory liberty; they suppressed ruthlessly any person or any faction seeking to build a new dictatorship, whatever its nature, upon the ruins of the old. *That* news traveled fast; and laboring always and mightily upon Civilization's side were the always-present, however deeply-buried, urges of all intelligent entities toward self-expression.

There was opposition, of course. Practically all of those who had waxed fat upon the old order were very strongly in favor of its continuance. There were the hordes of the down-trodden who had so long and so dumbly endured oppression that they could not understand anything else; in whom the above-mentioned urges had been beaten and tortured almost out of existence. They themselves were not opposed to Civilization—for them it meant at worst only a change of masters—but those who sought by the same old wiles to re-enslave them were foes indeed.

Menjo Bleeko's sycophants and retainers were told to work or starve. The fat hogs could support the new order—or else. The thugs and those who tried to prey upon and exploit the dumb masses were arrested and examined. Some were cured, some were banished, some were shot.

Little could be done, however, about the dumb themselves, for in them the spark was feeble indeed. The new government nursed that spark along, the while ruling them as definitely, although not as harshly, as had the old; the Lensmen backing the struggling young Civilization knowing full well that in the children or in the children's children of these unfortunates the spark would flame up into a great white light.

It is seen that this government was not, and could not for many years become, a true democracy. It was in fact a benevolent semi-autocracy; autonomous in a sense, yet controlled by the Galactic Council through its representatives, the Lensmen. It was, however, so infinitely more liberal than anything theretofore known by the Lonabarians as to be a political revelation, and since corruption, that cosmos-wide curse of democracy, was not allowed a first finger-hold, the principles of real democracy and of Civilization took deeper root year by year.

To get back into the beam of narrative, Nadreck's blackly indetectable speedster settled to ground far from the Boskonians' central dome; well beyond the far-flung screens. The Lensmen knew that no life existed outside that dome and they knew that no possible sense of perception could pierce those defenses. They did not know, however, what other resources of detection, of offense, or of defence the foe might possess; hence the greatest possible distance at which they could work efficiently was the best distance.

'I realize that it is useless to caution any active mind not to think at all,' Nadreck remarked as he began to manipulate various and sundry controls, 'but you already know from the nature of our problem that any extraneous thought will wreak untold harm. For that reason I beg of you to keep your thought-screens up at all times, no matter what happens. It is, however, imperative that you be kept informed, since I may require aid or advice at any moment. To that end I ask you to hold these electrodes, which are connected to a receptor. Do not hesitate to speak freely to each other or to me; but please use only a spoken language, as I am averse to Lensed thoughts at this juncture. Are we agreed? Are we ready?'

They were agreed and ready. Nadreck actuated his peculiar drill—a tube of force somewhat analogous to a Q-type helix except in that it operated within the frequency-range of thought—and began to increase, by almost infinitesimal increments, its power. Nothing, apparently, happened; but finally the Palainians instruments registered the fact that it was through.

'This is none too safe, friends,' the Palainian announced from one part of his multi-compartmented brain, without distracting any part of his attention from the incredibly delicate operation he was performing. 'May I suggest, Kinnison, in my cowardly way, that you place yourself at the controls and be ready to take us away from this planet at speed and without notice?'

'I'll say you may!' and the Tellurian complied, with alacrity. 'Right now, cowardice is indicated—copiously!'

But through course after course of screen the hollow drill gnawed its cautious way without giving alarm; until at length there began to come through the interloping tunnel a vague impression of foreign thought. Nadreck stopped the helix, then advanced it by tiny steps until the thoughts came in coldly clear—the thoughts of the Eich going about their routine businesses. In the safety of their impregnably shielded dome the proudly self-confident monsters did not wear their personal thought-screens; which, for Civilization's sake, was just as well.

It had been decided previously that the mind they wanted would be that of a psychologist; hence the thought sent out by the Palainian was one which would appeal only to such a mind; in fact, one practically imperceptible to any other. It was extremely faint; wavering uncertainly upon the very threshold of perception. It was so vague, so formless, so inchoate that it required Kinnison's intensest concentration even to recognize it as a thought. Indeed, so starkly unhuman was Nadreck's mind and that of his proposed quarry that it was all the Tellurian Lensman could do to so recognize it. It dealt, fragmentarily and in the merest glimmerings, with the nature and the mechanisms of the First Cause; with the fundamental ego, its *raison d'etre*, its causation, its motivation, its differentiation; with the stupendously awful concepts of the Prime Origin of all things ever to be.

Unhurried, monstrously patient, Nadreck neither raised the power of the thought nor hastened its slow tempo. Stolidly, for minute after long minute he held it, spraying it throughout the vast dome as mist is sprayed from an atomizer nozzle. And finally he got a bite. A mind seized upon that wistful, homeless, incipient thought; took it for its own. It strengthened it, enlarged upon it, built it up. And Nadreck followed it.

He did not force it; he did nothing whatever to cause any suspicion that the thought was or ever had been his. But as the mind of the Eich busied itself with that thought he all unknowingly let down the bars to Nadreck's invasion.

Then, perfectly in tune, the Palainian subtly insinuated into the mind of the Eich the mildly disturbing idea that he had forgotten something, or had neglected to do some trifling thing. This was the first really critical instant, for Nadreck had no idea whatever of what his victim's duties were or what he could have left undone. It had to be something which would take him out of the dome and toward the Patrolman's concealed speedster, but what it was, the Eich would have to develop for himself; Nadreck could not dare to attempt even a partial control at this stage and at this distance.

Kinnison clenched his teeth and held his breath, his big hands clutching fiercely the pilot's bars; Worsel unheedingly coiled his supple body into an ever smaller, ever harder and more compact bale.

'Ah!' Kinnison exhaled explosively. 'It worked!' The psychologist, at Nadreck's impalpable suggestion, had finally thought of the thing. It was a thought-screen generator which had been giving a little trouble and which really should have been checked before this.

Calmly, with the mild self-satisfaction which comes of having successfully recalled to mind a highly elusive thought, the Eich opened one of the dome's unforceable doors and made his unconcerned way directly toward the waiting Lensmen; and as he approached Nadreck stepped up by logarithmic increments the power of his hold.

'Get ready, please, to cut your screens and to synchronize with me in case anything slips and he tries to break away,' Nadreck cautioned; but nothing slipped.

The Eich came up unseeing to the speedster's side and stopped. The drill disappeared. A thought-screen encompassed the group narrowly. Kinnison and Worsel released their screens and also tuned in to the creature's mind. And Kinnison swore briefly, for what they found was meager enough.

He knew a great deal concerning the zwilnik doings of the First Galaxy; but so did the Lensmen; they were not interested in them. Neither were they interested, at the moment, in the files or in the records. Regarding the higher-ups, he knew of two, and only two, personalities. By means of an inter-galactic communicator he received orders from, and reported to, a clearly-defined, somewhat Eich-like entity known to him as Kandron; and vaguely, from occasional stray and unintentional thoughts of this Kandron, he had visualized as being somewhere in the background a human being named Alcon. He supposed that the planets upon which these persons lived were located in the Second Galaxy, but he was not certain, even of that. He had never seen either of them; he was pretty sure that none of his group ever would be allowed to see them. He had no means of tracing them and no desire whatsoever to do so. The only fact he really knew was that at irregular intervals Kandron got into communication with this base of the Eich.

That was all. Kinnison and Worsel let go and Nadreck, with a minute attention to detail which would be wearisome here, jockeyed the unsuspecting monster back into the dome. The native knew full where he had been, and why. He had inspected the generator and found it in good order. Every second of elapsed time was accounted for exactly. He had not the slightest inkling that anything out of the ordinary had happened to him or anywhere around him.

As carefully as the speedster had approached the planet, she departed from it. She rejoined the *Dauntless*, in whose control room Kinnison lined out a solid communicator beam to the *Z9M9Z* and to Port Admiral Haynes. He reported crisply, rapidly, everything that had transpired.

'So our best bet is for you and the Fleet to get out of here as fast as Klono will let you,' he concluded. 'Go straight out Rift Ninety Four, staying as far away as possible from both the spiral arm and the galaxy proper. Unlimber every spotting-screen you've got—put them to work along the line between Lyrane and the Second Galaxy. Plot all the punctures, extending the line as fast as you can. We'll join you at max and transfer to the *Z9M9Z*—her tank is just what the doctors ordered for the job we've got to do.'

'Well, if you say so, I suppose that's the way it's got to be,' Haynes grumbled. He had been growling and snorting under his breath ever since it had become evident what Kinnison's recommendation was to be. 'I don't like this thing of standing by and letting zwilniks thumb their noses at us, like Prellin did on Bronseca. That once was once too damned often.'

'Well, you got him, finally, you know,' Kinnison reminded, quite cheerfully, 'and you can have these Eich, too—sometime.'

'I hope,' Haynes acquiesced, something less than sweetly. 'QX, then—but put out a few jets. The quicker you get out here the sooner we can get back and clean out this hoo-raw's nest.'

Kinnison grinned as he cut his beam. He knew that it would be some time before the Port Admiral could hurl the metal of the Patrol against Lyrane VIII; but even he did not realize just how long a time it was to be.

What occasioned the delay was not the fact that the communicator was in operation only at intervals: so many screens were out, they were spaced so far apart, and the punctures were measured and aligned so accurately that the periods of non-operation caused little or no loss of time. Nor was it the vast distance involved; since, as has already been pointed out, the matter in the inter-galactic void is so tenuous that spaceships are capable of enormously greater velocities than any attainable in the far denser medium filling interstellar space.

No: what gave the Boskonians of Lyrane VIII their greatly lengthened reprieve was simply the direction of the line established by the communicator-beam punctures. Reasoning from analogy, the Lensmen had supposed that it would lead them into a star-cluster, fairly well away from the main body of the Second Galaxy, in either the zenith or the nadir direction. Instead of that, however, when the Patrol surveyors got close enough so that their possible error was very small, it became clear that their objective lay inside the galaxy itself.

'I don't like this line a bit, chief,' Kinnison told the admiral then. 'It'd smell like Limburger to have a fleet of this size and power nosing into their home territory, along what must be one of the hottest lines of communication they've got.'

'Check,' Port Admiral Haynes agreed. 'QX so far, but it would begin to stink pretty quick now. We've got to assume that they know about spotting screens, whether they really do or not. If they do, they'll have this line trapped from stem to gudgeon, and the minute they detect us they'll cut this line out entirely. Then where'll you be?'

'Right back where I started from—that's what I'm yowling about. To make matters worse, it's credits to millos that the ape we're looking for isn't going to be anywhere near the end of this line.'

'Huh? How do you figure that?' Haynes demanded.

'Logic. We're getting up now to where these zwilniks can really think. We've already assumed that they know about our beam tracers and detector nullifiers. Aren't they apt to know that we have inherently indetectable ships and almost perfectly absorptive coatings? Where does that land you?'

'Um . . . m . . . m. I see. Since they can't change the nature of the beam, they'll run it through a series of relays . . . with each leg trapped with everything they can think of . . . at the first sign of interference they'll switch, maybe half way across the galaxy. Also, they might very well switch around once in a while, anyway, just on general principles.'

'Check. That's why you'd better take the fleet back home, leaving Nadreck and me to work the rest of this line with our speedsters.'

'Don't be dumb, son; you can think straighter than that.' Haynes gazed quizzically at the younger man.

'What else? Where am I overlooking a bet?' Kinnison demanded.

'It is elementary tactics, young man,' the admiral instructed, 'to cover up any small, quiet operation with a large and noisy one. Thus, if I want to make an exploratory sortie in one sector I should always attack in force in another.'

'But what would it get us?' Kinnison expostulated. 'What's the advantage to be gained, to make up for the unavoidable losses?'

'Advantage? Plenty! Listen!' Haynes' bushy gray hair fairly bristled in eagerness. 'We've been on the defensive long enough. They must be weak, after their losses at Tellus; and now, before they can rebuild, is the time to strike. It's good tactics, as I said, to make a diversion to cover you up, but I want to do more than that. We should start an actual, serious invasion, right now. When you can swing it, the best possible defense—even in general—is a powerful offense, and we're all set to go. We'll begin it with this fleet, and then, as soon as we're sure that they haven't got enough power to counter-invade, we'll bring over everything that's loose. We'll hit them so hard that they won't be able to worry about such a little thing as a communicator line.'

'Hm . . . m. Never thought of it from that angle, but it'd be nice. We were coming over here sometime, anyway—why not now? I suppose you'll start on the edge, or in a spiral arm, just as though you were going ahead with the conquest of the whole galaxy?'

'Not "just as though",' Haynes declared. 'We *are* going through with it. Find a planet on the outer edge of a spiral arm, as nearly like Tellus as possible . . .'

'Make it nearly enough like Tellus and maybe I can use it for our headquarters on this "coordinator" thing,' Kinnison grinned.

'More truth than poetry in that, fellow. We find it and take over. Comb out the zwilniks with a fine-tooth comb. Make it the biggest, toughest base the universe ever saw—like Jarnevon, only more so. Bring in everything we've got and expand from that planet as a center, cleaning everything out as we go. We'll civilize 'em!'

And so, after considerable ultra-range communicator work, it was decided that the Galactic Patrol would forthwith assume the offensive.

Haynes assembled Grand Fleet. Then, while the two black speedsters kept unobtrusively on with the task of plotting the line, Civilization's mighty armada moved a few thousand parsecs aside and headed at normal touring blast for the nearest outcropping of the Second Galaxy.

There was nothing of stealth in this maneuver, nothing of finesse, excepting in the arrangements of the units. First, far in the van, flew the prodigious, irregular cone of scout cruisers. They were comparatively small, not heavily armed or armored, but they were ultra-fast and were provided with the most powerful detectors, spotters, and locators known. They adhered to no rigid formation, but at the will of their individual commanders, under the direct supervision of Grand Fleet Operations in the *Z9M9Z*, flashed hither and thither ceaselessly—searching, investigating, mapping, reporting.

Backing them up came the light cruisers and the cruising bombers—a new type, this latter, designed primarily to bore in to close quarters and to hurl bombs of negative matter. Third in order were the heavy defensive cruisers. These ships had been developed specifically for hunting down Boskonian commerce raiders within the galaxy. They wore practically impenetrable screen, so that they could lock to and hold even a super-dreadnought. They had never before been used in Grand Fleet formation; but since they were now equipped with tractor zones and bomb-tubes, theoretical strategy found a good use for them in this particular place.

Next came the real war-head—a solidly packed phalanx of maulers. All the ships up ahead had, although in varying degrees, freedom of motion and of action. The scouts had practially nothing else; fighting was not their business. They could fight, a little, if they had to; but they always ran away if they could, in whatever direction was most expedient at the time. The cruising bombers could either take their fighting or leave it alone, depending upon circumstances—in other words, they fought light cruisers, but ran away from big stuff, stinging as they ran. The heavy cruisers would fight anything short of a mauler, but never in formation: they always broke ranks and fought individual dog-fights, ship to ship.

But that terrific spear-head of maulers had no freedom of motion whatever. It knew only one direction—straight ahead. It would swerve aside for an inert planet, but for nothing smaller; and when it swerved it did so as a whole, not by parts. Its function was to blast through—straight through—any possible opposition, if and when that opposition should have been successful in destroying or dispersing the screens of lesser vessels preceding it. A sunbeam was the only conceivable weapon with which that stolid, power-packed mass of metal could not cope; and, the Patrolmen devoutly hoped, the zwilniks didn't have any sunbeams—yet.

A similar formation of equally capable maulers, meeting it head-on, could break it up, of course. Theoretical results and war-game solutions of this problem did not agree, either with each other or among themselves, and the thing had never been put to the trial of actual battle. Only one thing was certain—when and if that trial did come there was bound to be, as in the case of the fabled meeting of the irresistible force with the immovable object, a lot of very interesting by-products.

Flanking the maulers, streaming gracefully backward from their massed might in a parabolic cone, were arranged the heavy battleships and the super-dreadnoughts; and directly behind the bulwark of flying fortresses, tucked away inside the protecting envelope of big battle-wagons, floated the *Z9M9Z*—the brains of the whole outfit.

There were no free planets, no negaspheres of planetary anti-mass, no sunbeams. Such things were useful either in the defense of a Prime Base or for an all-out, ruthlessly destructive attack upon such a base. Those slow, cumbersome, supremely powerful weapons would come later, after the Patrol had selected the planet which they intended to hold against everything the Boskonians could muster. This present expedition had as yet no planet to defend, it sought no planet to destroy. It was the vanguard of Civilization, seeking a suitable foothold in the Second Galaxy and thoroughly well equipped to argue with any force mobile enough to bar its way.

While it has been said that there was nothing of stealth in this approach to the Second Galaxy, it must not be thought that it was unduly blatant or obvious: any carelessness or ostentation would have been very poor tactics indeed. Civilization's Grand Fleet advanced in strict formation, with every routine military precaution. Its nullifiers were full on, every blocking screen was out, every plate upon every ship was hot and was being scanned by alert and keen-eyed observers.

But every staff officer from Port Admiral Haynes down, and practically every line officer as well, knew that the enemy would locate the invading fleet long before it reached even the outer fringes of the galaxy toward which it was speeding. That stupendous tonnage of ferrous metal could not be disguised; nor could it by any possible artifice be made to simulate normal tenant of the space which it occupied.

The gigantic flares of the heavy stuff could not be baffled, and the combined grand flare of the Grand Fleet made a celestial object which would certainly attract the electronic telecopes of plenty of observatories. And the nearest such 'scopes, instruments of incredible powers of resolution, would be able to pick them out, almost ship by ship, against the relatively brilliant background of their own flares.

The Patrolman, however, did not care. This was, and was tended to be, an open, straightforward invasion; the first wave of an attack which would not cease until the Galactic Patrol had crushed Boskonia throughout the entire Second Galaxy.

Grand Fleet bored serenely on. Superbly confident in her awful might, grandly contemptuous of whatever she was to face, she stormed along; uncaring that at that very moment the foe was massing his every defensive arm to hurl her back or to blast her out of existence.

15 : Klovia

As Haynes and the Galactic Council had already surmised, Boskonia was now entirely upon the defensive. She had made her supreme bid in the effort which had failed so barely to overcome the defenses of hard-held Tellus. It was, as has been seen, a very near thing indeed, but the zwilnik chieftains did not and could not know that. Communication through the hyperspatial tube was impossible, no ordinary communicator beam could be driven through the Patrol's scramblers, no Boskonian observers could be stationed near enough to the scene of action to perceive or to record anything that had occurred, and no single zwilnik ship or entity survived to tell of how nearly Tellus had come to extinction.

And, in fine, it would have made no difference in the mind of

Alcon of Thrale if he had known. A thing which was not a full success was a complete failure; to be almost a success meant nothing. The invasion of Tellus had failed. They had put everything they had into that gigantically climactic enterprise. They had shot the whole wad, and it had not been enough. They had, therefore, abandoned for the nonce humanity's galaxy entirely, to concentrate their every effort upon the rehabilitation of their own depleted forces and upon the design and construction of devices of hitherto unattempted capability and power.

But they simply had not had enough time to prepare properly to meet the invading Grand Fleet of Civilization. It takes time—lots of time—to build such heavy stuff as maulers and flying fortresses, and they had not been allowed to have it. They had plenty of lighter stuff, since the millions of Boskonian planets could furnish upon a few hours' notice more cruisers, and even more first-line battleships, than could possibly be used efficiently, but their back-bone of brute force and fire-power was woefully weak.

Since the destruction of a solid center of maulers was, theoretically, improbable to the point of virtual impossibility, neither Boskonia nor the Galactic Patrol had built up any large reserve of such structures. Both would now build up such a reserve as rapidly as possible, of course, but half-built structures could not fight.

The zwilniks had many dirigible planets, but they were *too* big. Planets, as has been seen, are too cumbersome and unwieldly for use against a highly mobile and adequately-controlled fleet.

Conversely, humanity's Grand Fleet was up to its maximum strength and perfectly balanced. It had suffered losses in the defense of Prime Base, it is true; but those losses were of comparatively light craft, which Civilization's inhabited world could replace as quickly as could Boskonia's.

Hence Boskonia's fleet was at a very serious disadvantage as it formed to defy humanity just outside the rim of its galaxy. At two disadvantages, really, for Boskonia then had neither Lensmen nor a *Z9M9Z*; and Haynes, canny old master strategist that he was, worked upon them both.

Grand Fleet so far had held to one right-line course, and upon this line the zwilnik defense had been built. Now Haynes swung aside, forcing the enemy to re-form: they had to engage him, he did not have to engage them. Then, as they shifted—raggedly, as he had supposed and had hoped that they would—

he swung again. Again, and again; the formation of the enemy becoming more and more hopelessly confused with each shift.

The scouts had been reporting constantly; in the seven-hundred-foot lenticular tank of the *Z9M9Z* there was spread in exact detail the disposition of every unit of the foe. Four Rigellian Lensmen, now thoroughly trained and able to perform the task almost as routine, condensed the picture—summarized it—in Haynes' ten-foot tactical tank. And finally, so close that another swerve could not be made, and with the line of flight of his solid fighting core pointing straight through the loosely disorganized nucleus of the enemy, Haynes gave the word to engage.

The scouts, remaining free, flashed aside into their prearranged observing positions. Everything else went inert and bored ahead. The light cruisers and the cruising bombers clashed first, and a chill struck at Haynes' stout old heart as he learned that the enemy did have negative-matter bombs.

Upon that point there had been much discussion. One view was that the Boskonians would have them, since they had seen them in action and since their scientists were fully as capable as were those of Civilization. The other was that, since it had taken all the massed intellect of the Conference of Scientists to work out a method of handling and of propelling such bombs, and since the Boskonians were probably not as cooperative as were the civilized races, they could not have them.

Approximately half of the light cruisers of Grand Fleet were bombers. This was deliberate, for in the use of the new arm there were involved problems which theoretical strategy could not completely solve. Theoretically, a bomber could defeat a conventional light cruiser of equal tonnage one hundred percent of the time, *provided*—here was the rub!—that the conventional cruiser did not blast her out of the ether before she could get her bombs into the vitals of the foe. For, in order to accommodate the new equipment, something of the old had to be decreased: something of power, of armament, of primary or secondary beams, or of defensive screen. Otherwise the size and mass must be so increased that the ship would no longer be a light cruiser, but a heavy one.

And the Patrol's psychologists had had ideas, based upon facts which they had gathered from Kinnison and from Illona and from many spools of tape—ideas by virtue of which it was eminently possible that the conventional light cruisers of Civilization, with their heavier screen and more and hotter beams, could vanquish the light cruisers of the foe, even though they should turn out to be negative-matter bombers.

Hence the fifty-fifty division of types; but, since Haynes was not thoroughly sold upon either the psychologists or their ideas, the commanders of his standard light cruisers had received very explicit and definite orders. If the Boskonians should have bombs and if the high-brows' idea did not pan out, they were to turn tail and run, at maximum and without stopping to ask questions or to get additional instructions.

Haynes had not really believed that the enemy would have negabombs, they were so new and so atrociously difficult to handle. He wanted—but was unable—to believe implicitly in the psychologist's findings. Therefore, as soon as he saw what was happening, he abandoned his tank for a moment to seize a plate and get into full touch with the control room of one of the conventional light cruisers then going into action.

He watched it drive boldly toward a Boskonian vessel which was in the act of throwing bombs. He saw that the agile little vessel's tractor zone was out. He watched the bombs strike that zone and bounce. He watched the tractor-men go to work and he saw the psychologists' idea bear splendid fruit. For what followed was a triumph, not of brute force and striking power, but of morale and manhood. The brain-men had said, and it was now proved, that the Boskonian gunners, low-class as they were and driven to their tasks like the slaves they were, would hesitate long enough before using tractor-beams as pressors so that the Patrolmen could take their own bombs away from them!

For negative matter, it must be remembered, is the exact opposite of ordinary matter. To it a pull is, or becomes, a push; the tractor beam which pulls ordinary matter toward its projector actually pushed negative matter away.

The 'boys' of the Patrol knew that fact thoroughly. They knew all about what they were doing, and why. They were there because they wanted to be, as Illona had so astoundingly found out, and they worked with their officers, not because of them. With the Patrol's gun-crews it was a race to see which crew could capture the first bomb and the most.

Aboard the Boskonian how different it was! There the dumb cattle had been told what to do, but not why. They did not know the fundamental mechanics of the bomb-tubes they operated by rote; did not know that they were essentially tractor-beam projectors. They did know, however, that tractor beams pulled things toward them; and when they were ordered to swing their ordinary tractors upon the bombs which the Patrolmen were so industriously taking away from them, they hesitated for seconds, even under the lash.

This hesitation was fatal. Haynes' gleeful gunners, staring through their special finders, were very much on their toes; seconds were enough. Their fierce-driven tractors seized the inimical bombs in mid-space, and before the Boskonians could be made to act in the only possible opposition hurled them directly backward against the ships which had issued them. Ordinary defensive screen did not affect them; repulsor screen, meteorite- and wall-shields only sucked them inward the faster.

And ordinary matter and negative matter cannot exist in contact. In the instant of touching, the two unite and disappear, giving rise to vast quantities of intensely hard radiation. One negabomb was enough to put any cruiser out of action, but here there were usually three or four at once. Sometimes as many as ten; enough almost, to consume the total mass of a ship.

A bomb struck; ate in. Through solid armor it melted. Atmosphere rushed out, to disappear en route—for air is normal matter. Along beams and trusses the hellish hyper-sphere travelled freakishly, although usually in the direction of greatest mass. It clung, greedily. Down stanchions it flowed; leaving nothing in its wake, flooding all circumambient space with lethal emanations. Into and through converters. Into pressure tanks, which blew up enthusiastically. Men's bodies it did not seem to favor—not massive enough, perhaps—but even them it did not refuse if offered. A Boskonian, gasping frantically for air which was no longer there and already half mad, went completely mad as he struck savagely at the thing and saw his hand and his arm to the shoulder vanish instantaneously, as though they had never been.

Satisfied, Haynes wrenched his attention back to his tank. Most of his light cruisers were through and in the clear; they were reporting by thousands. Losses were very small. The conventional-type cruisers had won either by using the enemies' own bombs, as he had seen them used, or by means of their heavier armor and armament. The bombers had won in almost every case; not by superior force, for in arms and equipment they were to all intents and purposes identical with their opponents, but because of their infinitely higher quality of personnel. To brief it, scarcely a handful of Boskonia's light cruisers got away.

The heavy cruisers came up, broke formation, and went

doggedly to work. They were the blockers. Each took one ship—a heavy cruiser or a battleship—out of the line, and held it out. It tried to demolish it with every weapon it could swing, but even if it could not vanquish its foe, it could and did hang on until some big bruiser of a battleship could come up and administer the *coup de grace*.

And battleships and super-dreadnoughts were coming up in their thousands and their myriads. All of them, in fact, save enough to form a tight globe, packed screen to screen, around the *Z9M9Z*.

Slowly, ponderously, inert, the war-head of maulers came crawling up. The maulers and fortresses of the Boskonians were hopelessly outnumbered and were badly scattered in position. Hence this meeting of the ultra-heavies was not really a battle at all, but a slaughter. Ten or more of Haynes' gigantic structures could concentrate their entire combined fire-power upon any luckless one of the enemy; with what awful effect it would be superfluous to enlarge upon.

When the mighty fortresses had done their work they englobed the *Z9M9Z*, enabling the guarding battleships to join their sister moppers-up; but there was very little left to do. Civilization had again triumphed; and, this time, at very little cost. Some of the pirates had escaped, of course; observers from afar might very well have had scanners and recorders upon the entire conflict; but, whatever of news was transmitted or how, Alcon of Thrale and Boskonia's other master minds would or could derive little indeed of comfort from the happenings of this important day.

'Well, that's probably that—for a while, at least, don't you think?' Haynes asked his Council of War.

It was decided that it was; that if Boskonia could not have mustered a heavier center for her defensive action here, she would be in no position to make any really important attack for months to come.

Grand Fleet, then, was re-formed; this time into a purely defensive and exploratory formation. In the center, of course, was the *Z9M9Z*. Around her was a close-packed quadruple globe of maulers. Outside of them in order, came sphere after sphere of super-dreadnoughts, of battleships, of heavy cruisers, and of light cruisers. Then, not in globe at all, but ranging far and wide, were the scouts. Into the edge of the nearest spiral arm of the Second Galaxy the stupendous formation advanced, and along it it proceeded at dead slow blast. Dead slow, to enable the questing scouts to survey thoroughly each planet of every solar system as they came to it.

And finally an Earth-like planet was found. Several approximately Tellurian worlds had been previously discovered and listed as possibilities; but this one was so perfect that the search ended then and there. Apart from the shape of the continents and the fact that there was somewhat less land-surface and a bit more salt water, it was practically identical with Tellus. As was to be expected, its people were human to the limit of classification. Entirely unexpectedly, however, the people of Klovia—which is as close as English can come to the native name—were not zwilniks. They had never heard of, nor had they ever been approached by, the Boskonians. Space-travel was to them only a theoretical possibility, as was atomic energy.

They had no planetary organization, being still divided politically into sovereign states which were all too often at war with each other. In fact, a world war had just burned itself out, a war of such savagery that only a fraction of the world's population remained alive. There had been no victor, of course. All had lost everything—the survivors of each nation, ruined as they were and without either organization or equipment, were trying desperately to rebuild some semblance of what they had once had.

Upon learning these facts the psychologists of the Patrol breathed deep sighs of relief. This kind of thing was made to order; civilizing this planet would be simplicity itself. And it was. The Klovians did not have to be overawed by a show of superior force. Before this last, horribly internecine war, Klovia had been a heavily industrialized world, and as soon as the few remaining inhabitants realized what Civilization had to offer, that no one of their neighboring competitive states was to occupy a superior position, and that full, world-wide production was to be resumed as soon as was humanly possible, their relief and joy were immeasurable.

Thus the Patrol took over without difficulty. But they were, the Lensmen knew, working against time. As soon as the zwilniks could get enough heavy stuff built they would attack, grimly determined to blast Klovia and everything upon it out of space. Even though they had known nothing about the planet previously, it was idle to hope that they were still in ignorance either of its existence or of what was in general going on there.

Haynes' first care was to have the heaviest metalry of the Galactic Patrol—loose planets, negaspheres, sunbeams, fortresses, and the like—rushed across the void to Klovia at maximum. Then, as well as putting every employable of the new world to work, at higher wages than he had ever earned before, the Patrol imported millions upon millions of men, with their women and families, from hundreds of Earth-like planets in the First Galaxy.

They did not, however, come blindly. They came knowing that Klovia was to be primarily a military base, the most supremely powerful base that had ever been built. They knew that it would bear the brunt of the most furious attacks that Boskone could possibly deliver; they knew full well that it might fall. Nevertheless, men and women, they came in their multitudes. They came with high courage and high determination, glorying in that which they were to do. People who could and did so glory were the only ones who came; which fact accounts in no small part for what Klovia is today.

People came, and worked, and stayed. Ships came, and trafficked. Trade and commerce increased tremendously. And farther and farther abroad, as there came into being upon that formerly almost derelict planet some seventy-odd gigantic defensive establishments, there crept out an ever-widening screen of scout-ships, with all their high-powered feelers hotly outstretched.

Meanwhile Kinnison and frigid-blooded Nadreck had worked their line, leg by tortuous leg, to Onlo and thence to Thrale. A full spool should be devoted to that working alone; but, unfortunately, as space here must be limited to the barest essentials, it can scarcely be mentioned. As Kinnison and Haynes had foreseen, that line was heavily trapped. Luckily, however, it had not been moved so radically that the searchers could not rediscover it; the zwilniks were, as Haynes had promised, very busily engaged with other and more important matters. All of those traps were deadly, and many of them were ingenious indeed—so ingenious as to test to the utmost the 'cowardly' Palainian's skill and mental scope. All, however, failed. The two Lensmen held to the line in spite of the pitfalls and followed it to the end. Nadreck stayed upon or near Onlo, to work in its frightful environment against the monsters to whom he was biologically so closely allied, while the Tellurian went on to try conclusions with Alcon, the Tyrant of Thrale.

Again he had to build up an unimpeachable identity and here there were no friendly thousands to help him do it. He had to get close—*really* close—to Alcon, without antagonizing him or in any way arousing his hair-trigger suspicions. Kinnison had studied that problem for days. Not one of his previously-used artifices would work, even had he dared to repeat a procedure. Also, time was decidedly of the essence.

There was a way. It was not an easy way, but it was fast and, if it worked at all, it would work perfectly. Kinnison would not have risked it even a few months back, but now he was pretty sure that he had jets enough to swing it.

He needed a soldier of about his own size and shape—details were unimportant. The man should not be in Alcon's personal troops, but should be in a closely-allied battalion, from which promotion into that select body would be logical. He should be relatively inconspicuous, yet with a record of accomplishment, or at least of initiative, which would square up with the rapid promotions which were to come.

The details of that man-hunt are interesting, but not of any real importance here, since they did not vary in any essential from other searches which have been described at length. He found him—a lieutenant in the Royal Guard—and the ensuing mind-study was as assiduous as it was insidious. In fact, the Lensman memorized practically every memory-chain in the fellow's brain. Then the officer took his regular furlough and started for home—but he never got there.

Instead, it was Kimball Kinnison who wore the Thralian's gorgeous full-dress uniform and who greeted in exactly appropriate fashion the Thralian's acquaintances and life-long friends. A few of these, who chanced to see the guardsman first, wondered briefly at his changed appearance or thought that he was a stranger. Very few, however, and very briefly; for the Lensman's sense of perception was tensely alert and his mind was strong. In moments, then, those chance few forgot that they had ever had the slightest doubt concerning this soldiers' identity; they knew calmly and as a matter of fact that he was the Traska Gannel whom they had known so long.

Living minds presented no difficulty except for the fact that of course he could not get in touch with everyone who had ever known the real Gannel. However, he did his best. He covered plenty of ground and he got most of them—all that could really matter.

Written records, photographs, and tapes were something else again. He had called Worsel in on the problem long since, and the purely military records of the Royal Guard were QX before

Gannel went on leave. Although somewhat tedious, that task had not proved particularly difficult. Upon a certain dark night a certain light-circuit had gone dead, darkening many buildings. Only one or two sentries or guards saw anything amiss, and they never afterward recalled having done so. And any record that has ever been made can be remade to order by the experts of the Secret Service of the Patrol!

And thus it was also with the earlier records. He had been born in a hospital. QX—that hospital was visited, and thereafter Gannel's baby foot-prints were actually those of infant Kinnison. He had gone to certain schools—those schools' records also were made to conform to the new facts.

Little could be done, however, about pictures. No man can possibly remember how many times he has had his picture taken, or who has the negatives, or to whom he had given photographs, or in what papers, books, or other publications his likeness has appeared.

The older pictures, Kinnison decided, did not count. Even if the likenesses were good, he looked enough like Gannel so that the boy or the callow youth might just about as well have developed into something that would pass for Kinnison in a photograph as into the man which he actually did become. Where was the dividing line? The Lensman decided—or rather, the decision was forced upon him—that it was at his graduation from the military academy.

There had been an annual, in which volume appeared an individual picture, fairly large, of each member of the graduating class. About a thousand copies of the book had been issued, and now they were scattered all over space. Since it would be idle even to think of correcting them all, he could not correct any of them. Kinnison studied that picture for a long time. He didn't like it very well. The cub was just about grown up, and this photo looked considerably more like Gannel than it did like Kinnison. However, the expression was self-conscious, the pose strained—and, after all, people hardly ever looked at old annuals. He'd have to take a chance on that. Later poses—formal portraits, that is; snap-shots could not be considered—would have to be fixed up.

Thus it came about that certain studios were raided very surreptitiously. Certain negatives were abstracted and were deftly re-touched. Prints were made therefrom, and in several dozens of places in Gannel's home town, in albums and in frames, stealthy substitutions were made.

The furlough was about to expire. Kinnison had done everything that he could do. There were holes, of course—there couldn't help but be—but they were mighty small and, if he played his cards right, they would never show up. Just to be on the safe side, however, he'd have Worsel stick around for a couple of weeks or so, to watch developments and to patch up any weak spots that might develop. The Velantian's presence upon Thrale would not create suspicion—there were lots of such folks flitting from planet to planet—and if anybody did get just a trifle suspicious of Worsel, it might be all the better.

Mentor of Arisia, however, knew many things that Kinnison of Tellus did not; he had powers of which Kinnison would never dream. Mentor knew exactly what entity stood behind Tyrant Alcon's throne; knew exactly what it could and would do; knew that this was one of the most critical instants of Civilization's long history.

Wherefore every negative of every picture that had ever been taken of Traska Gannel, and every print and reproduction made therefrom, was made to conform; nowhere, throughout the reaches of space or the vistas of time, was there any iota of evidence that the present Traska Gannel had not borne that name since infancy.

So it was done, and Lieutenant Traska Gannel of the Royal Guard went back to duty.

16: Gannel Fights a Duel

Nadreck, the furtive Palainian, had prepared as thoroughly in his own queerly underhanded fashion as had Kinnison in his bolder one. Nadreck was cowardly, in Earthly eyes, there can be no doubt of that; as cowardly as he was lazy. To his race, however, those traits were eminently sensible; and those qualities did in fact underlie his prodigious record of accomplishment. Being so careful of his personal safety, he had lived long and would live longer: by doing everything in the easiest possible way he had conserved his resources. Why take chances with a highly valuable life? Why be so inefficient as to work hard in the performance of a task when it could always be done in some easy way?

Nadreck moved in upon Onlo, then, absolutely imperceptibly. His dark, cold, devious mind, so closely akin to those of the Onlonians, reached out, indetectably *en rapport* with theirs. He studied, dissected, analyzed, and neutralized their defenses, one by one. Then, his ultra-black speedster securely hidden from their every prying mechanism and sense, although within easy working distance of the control dome itself, he snuggled down into his softly-cushioned resting place and methodically, efficiently, he went to work.

Thus, when Alcon of Thrale next visited his monstrous henchmen, Nadreck flipped a switch and every thought of the zwilniks' conference went permanently on record.

'What have you done, Kandron, about the Lensman?' the Tyrant demanded harshly. 'What have you concluded?'

'We have done very little,' the chief psychologist replied, coldly. 'Beyond the liquidation of a few lensmen—with nothing whatever to indicate that any of them had any leading part in our recent reverses—our agents have accomplished nothing.

'As to conclusions, I have been unable to draw any except the highly negative one that every Boskonian psychologist who has ever summed up the situation has, in some respect or other, been seriously in error.'

'And only *you* are right!' Alcon sneered. 'Why?'

'I am right only in that I admit my inability to draw any valid conclusions,' Kandron replied, imperturbably. 'The available data are too meager, too inconclusive, and above all, too contradictory to justify any positive statements. There is a possibility that there are two Lensmen who have been and are mainly responsible for what has happened. One of these, the lesser, may be—note well that I say "may be", not "is"—a Tellurian or an Aldebaranian or some other definitely human being; the other and by far the more powerful one is apparently entirely unknown, except by his works.'

'Star A Star,' Alcon declared.

'Call him so if you like,' Kandron assented, flatly. 'But this Star A Star is an operator. As the supposed Director of Lensmen he is merely a figment of the imagination.'

'But this information came from the Lensman Morgan!'

Alcon protested. 'He was questioned under the drug of truth; he was tortured and all but slain; the Overlord of Delgon consumed all his life-force except for the barest possible moiety!'

'How do you know all these things?' Kandron asked, unmoved. 'Merely from the report of the Overlords and from the highly questionable testimony of one of the Eich, who was absent from the scene during all of the most important time.

'You suspect, then, that...' Alcon broke off, shaken visibly.

'I do,' the psychologist replied, dryly. 'I suspect very strongly indeed that there is working against us a mind of a power and scope but little inferior to my own. A mind able to overcome that of an Overlord; one able, at least if unsuspected and hence unopposed, to deceive even the admittedly capable minds of the Eich. I suspect that the Lensman Morgan was, if he existed at all, merely a puppet. The Eich took him too easily by far. It is therefore eminently possible that he had no physical actuality of existence...'

'Oh, come, now! Don't be ridiculous!' Alcon snapped. 'With all Boskone there as witnesses? Why, his hand and Lens remained!'

'Improbable, perhaps, I admit—but still eminently possible,' Kandron insisted. 'Admit for the moment that he was actual, and that he did lose a hand—but remember also that the hand and the Lens may very well have been brought along and left there as reassurance; we cannot be sure even that the Lens matched the hand. But admitting all this, I am still of the opinion that Lensman Morgan was not otherwise tortured, that he lost none of his vital force, that he and the unknown I have already referred to returned practically unharmed to their own galaxy. And not only did they return, they must have carried with them the information which was later used by the Patrol in the destruction of Jarnevon.'

'Preposterous!' Alcon snorted. 'Tell me, if you can, upon what facts you have been able to base such fantastic opinions?'

'Gladly,' Kandron assented. 'I have been able to come to no really valid conclusions, and it may very well be that your fresh viewpoint will enable us to succeed where I alone have failed. I will therefore summarize very briefly the data which seem to me most significant. Attend closely, please:

'For many years, as you know, everything progressed smoothly. Our first set-back came when a Tellurian warship, manned by Tellurians and Valerians, succeeded in capturing almost intact one of the most modern and most powerful of our vessels. The Valerians may be excluded from consideration, insofar as mental ability is concerned. At least one Tellurian escaped, in one of our own supposedly derelict, vessels. This one, whom Helmuth thought of, and reported, as "the" Lensman, eluding all pursuers, went to Velantia; upon which planet he so wrought as to steal bodily six of our ships sent there specifically to hunt him down. In those ships he won his way back to Tellus in spite of everything Helmuth and his force could do.

'Then there were the two episodes of the Wheelmen of Aldebaran I. In the first one a Tellurian Lensman was defeated—possibly killed. In the second our base was destroyed—tracelessly. Note, however, that the base next above it in order was, so far as we know, not visited or harmed.

'There was the Boyssia affair, in which the human being Blakeslee did various unscheduled things. He was obviously under the control of some far more powerful mind; a mind which did not appear, then or ever.

'We jump then to this, our own galaxy—the sudden, inexplicable disappearance of the planet Medon.

'Back to theirs again—the disgraceful and closely connected debacles at Shingvors and Antigan. Traceless both, but again neither was followed up to any higher headquarters.'

Nadreck grinned at that, if a Palainian can be said to grin. Those matters were purely his own. He had done what he had been requested to do—thoroughly—no following up had been either necessary or desirable.

'Then Radelix.' Kandron's summary went concisely on. 'The female agents, Bominger, the Kalonian observers—all wiped out. Was or was not some human Lensman to blame? Everyone, from Chester Q. Forsyce down to a certain laborer upon the docks, was suspected, but nothing definite could be learned.

'The senselessly mad crew of the *27L462P*—Wynor—Grantlia. Again completely traceless. Reason obscure, and no known advantage gained, as this sequence also has dropped.'

Nadreck pondered briefly over this material. He knew nothing of any such matters nor, he was pretty sure, did Kinnison. THE Lensman apparently was getting credit for something that must have been accidental or wrought by some internal enemy. QX. He listened again:

'After the affair of Bronseca, in which so many Lensmen were engaged that particularization was impossible, and which again was not followed up, we jump to the Asteroid Euphrosyne,

Miner's Rest, and Wild Bill Williams of Aldebaran II. If it was a concidence that Bill Williams became William Williams and followed our line to Tressilia, it is a truly remarkable one—even though, supposedly, said Williams was so stupefied with drugs as to be incapable either of motion or perception.

'Jalte's headquarters was, apparently, missed. However, it must have been invaded—tracelessly—for it was the link between Tressilia and Jarnevon, and Jarnevon was found and was destroyed.

'Now, before we analyze the more recent events, what do you yourself deduce from the above facts?' Kandron asked.

While the tyrant was cogitating, Nadreck indulged in a minor gloat. This psychologist, by means of impeccable logic and reasoning from definitely known facts, had arrived at such erroneous conclusions! However, Nadreck had to admit, his own performances and those in which Kinnison had acted indetectably, when added to those of some person or persons unknown, did make a really impressive total.

'You may be right,' Alcon admitted finally. 'At least two entirely different personalities and methods of operation. Two Lensmen are necessary to satisfy the above requirements ... and, as far as we know, sufficient. One of the necessary two is a human being, the other an unknown. Cartiff was, of course, the human Lensman. A masterly piece of work, that—but, with the cooperation of the Patrol, both logical and fairly simple. This human being is always in evidence, yet is so cleverly concealed by his very obviousness that nobody ever considers him important enough to be worthy of a close scrutiny. Or ... perhaps ...'

'That is better,' Kandron commented. 'You are beginning to see why I was so careful in saying that the known Tellurian factor "may be", not "is", of any real importance.'

'But he *must* be!' Alcon protested. 'It was a human being who tried and executed our agent; Cartiff was a human being—to name only two.'

'Of course,' Kandron admitted, half contemptuously. 'But we have no proof whatever that any of those human beings actually did, of their own volition, any of the things for which they have been given credit. Thus, it is now almost certain that that widely advertised "mind-ray machine" was simply a battery of spot-lights—the man operating them may very well have done nothing else. Similarly, Cartiff may have been an ordinary gangster controlled by the Lensman—we may as well call him Star A

Star as anything else—or a Lensman or some other member of the Patrol acting as a dummy to distract our attention from Star A Star, who himself did the real work, all unperceived.'

'Proof?' the Tyrant snapped.

'No proof—merely a probability,' the Onlonian stated flatly. 'We *know*, however, definitely and for a fact—visiplates and long-range communicators cannot be hypnotized—that Blakeslee was one of Helmuth's own men. Also that he was the same man, both as a loyal Boskonian of very ordinary mental talents and as an enemy having a mental power which he as Blakeslee never did and never could possess.'

'I see.' Alcon thought deeply. 'Very cogently put. Instead of there being two Lensmen, working sometimes together and sometimes separately, you think that there is only one really important mind and that this mind at times works with or through some Tellurian?'

'But not necessarily the same Tellurian—exactly. And there is nothing to give us any indication whatever as to Star A Star's real nature or race. We cannot even deduce whether or not he is an oxygen-breather ... and that is bad.'

'Very bad,' the Tyrant assented. 'Star A Star, or Cartiff, or both working together, found Lonabar. They learned of the Overlords, or at least of Lyrane II ...'

'By sheer accident, if they learned it there at all, I am certain of that,' Kandron insisted. 'They did not get any information from Menjo Bleeko's mind; there was none there to get.'

'Accident or not, what boots it?' Alcon impatiently brushed aside the psychologists protests. 'They found Bleeko and killed him. A raid upon the cavern of the Overlords of Lyrane II followed immediately. From the reports sent by the Overlords to the Eich of Lyrane VIII we know that there were two Patrol ships involved. One, not definitely identified as Cartiff's, took no part in the real assault. The other, the super-dreadnought *Dauntless*, did that alone. She was manned by Tellurians, Valerians, and at least one Velantian. Since they went to the trouble of taking the Overlords alive, we may take it for granted that they obtained from them all the information they possessed before they destroyed them and their cavern?'

'It is at least highly probable that they did so,' Kandron admitted.

'We have, then, many questions and few answers,' and the Tyrant strode up and down the dimly blue-lit room. 'It would be idle indeed, in view of the facts, to postulate that Lyrane II was left, as were some others, a dead end. Has Star A Star attempted Lyrane VIII! If not, why has he delayed? If so, did he succeed or fail in penetrating the defenses of the Eich? They swear that he did not, that he could not . . .'

'Of course,' Kandron sneered. 'But while asking questions why not ask why the Patrol chose this particular time to invade our galaxy in such force as to wipe out our Grand Fleet? To establish themselves so strongly as to make it necessary for us of the High Command to devote our entire attention to the problem of dislodging them?'

'What!' Alcon exclaimed, then sobered quickly and thought for minutes. 'You think, then, that . . .' His thoughts died away.

'I do so think,' Kandron thought, glumly. 'It is very decidely possible—perhaps even probable—that the Eich of Lyrane VIII were able to offer no more resistance to the penetration of Star A Star than was Jalte the Kalonian. That this massive thrust was timed to cover the insidious tracing of our lines of communication or whatever other leads the Lensman had been able to discover.'

'But the traps—the alarms—the screens and zones!' Alcon exclaimed, manifestly jarred by this new and disquietingly keen thought.

'No alarm was tripped, as you know; no trap was sprung,' Kandron replied, quietly. 'The fact that we have not as yet been attacked here may or may not be significant. Not only is Onlo very strongly held, not only is it located in such a central position that their lines of communication would be untenable, but also . . .'

'Do you mean to admit that *you* may have been invaded and searched—tracelessly?' Alcon fairly shrieked the thought.

'Certainly,' the psychologist replied, coldly. 'While I do not believe that it has been done, the possibility must be conceded. What we could do, we have done; but what science can do, science can circumvent. To finish my thought, it is a virtual certainty that it is not Onlo and I who are their prime objectives, but Thrale and you. Especially you.'

'You may be right. You probably *are* right; but with no data whatever upon who or what Star A Star really is, with no tenable theory as to how he could have done what actually has been done, speculation is idle.'

Upon this highly unsatisfactory note the interview closed. Alcon the Tyrant went back to Thrale; and as he entered his palace grounds he passed within forty inches of his Nemesis.

For Star-A-Star-Kinnison-Traska-Gannel was, as Alcon himself so clearly said, rendered invisible and imperceptible by his own obviousness.

Although obvious, Kinnison was very busy indeed. As a lieutenant of Guardsmen, the officer in charge of a platoon whose duties were primarily upon the ground, he had very little choice of action. His immediate superior, the first lieutenant of the same company, was not much better off. The captain had more authority and scope, since he commanded aerial as well as ground forces. Then, disregarding side-lines of comparative seniority, came the major, the colonel, and finally the general, who was in charge of all the regular armed forces of Thrale's capital city. Alcon's personal troops were of course a separate organization, but Kinnison was not interested in them—yet.

The major would be high enough, Kinnison decided. Big enough to have considerable authority and freedom of motion, and yet not important enough to attract undesirable attention.

The first lieutenant, a stodgy, strictly rule-of-thumb individual, did not count. He could step right over his head into the captaincy. The real Gannel had always, in true zwilnik fashion, hated his captain and had sought in devious ways to undermine him. The pseudo-Gannel despised the captain as well as hating him, and to the task of sapping he brought an ability enormously greater than any which the real Gannel had ever possessed.

Good Boskonian technique was to work upward by stealth and treachery, aided by a carefully-built up personal following of spies and agents. Gannel had already formed such a staff; had already selected the man who, in the natural course of events, would assassinate the first lieutenant. Kinnison retained Gannel's following, but changed subtly its methods of operation. He worked almost boldly. He himself criticized the captain severely, within the hearing of two men whom he knew to belong, body and soul, to his superior.

This brought quick results. He was summoned brusquely to the captain's office; and knowing that the company commander would not dare to have him assassinated there, he went. In that office there were a dozen people: it was evident that the captain intended this rebuke to be a warning to all upstarts.

'Lieutenant Traska Gannel, I have had my eye on you and your subversive activities for some time,' the captain orated. 'Now, purely as a matter of form, and in accordance with paragraph 5, section 724 of General Regulations, you may offer whatever you have of explanation before I reduce you to the ranks for insubordination.'

'I have a lot to say,' Kinnison replied, coolly. 'I don't know what your spies have reported, but to whatever it was I would like to add that having this meeting here as you are having it proves that you are as fat in the head as you are in the belly . . .'

'Silence! Seize him, men!' the captain commanded, fiercely. He was not really fat. He had only a scant inch of equatorial bulge; but that small surplusage was a sore point indeed. 'Disarm him!'

'The first man to move dies in his tracks,' Kinnison countered; his coldly venomous tone holding the troopers motionless. He wore two handweapons more or less similar to DeLameters, and now his hands rested lightly upon their butts. 'I cannot be disarmed until after I have been disrated, as you know very well; and that will never happen. For if you demote me I will take an appeal, as is my right, to the colonel's court; and there I will prove that you are stupid, inefficient, cowardly, and unfit generally to command. You really are, and you know it. Your discipline is lax and full of favoritism; your rewards and punishments are assessed, not by logic, but by whim, passion, and personal bias. Any court that can be named would set you down into the ranks, where you belong, and would give me your place. If this is insubordination and if you want to make something out of it, you pussy-gutted, pusillanimous, brainless tub of lard, cut in your jets!'

The maligned officer half-rose, white-knuckled hands gripping the arms of his chair, then sank back craftily. He realized now that he had blundered; he was in no position to face the rigorous investigation which Gannel's accusation would bring on. But there was a way out. This could now be made a purely personal matter, in which a duel would be *de riguer*. And in Boskonian duelling the superior officer, not the challenged, had the choice of weapons. He was a master of the saber; he had outpointed Gannel regularly in the regimental games. Therefore he choked down his wrath and:

'These personal insults, gratuitous and false as they are, make it a matter of honor,' he declared smoothly. 'Meet me, then, tomorrow, half an hour before sunset, in the Place of Swords. It will be sabers.'

'Accepted,' Kinnison meticulously followed the ritual. 'To first blood or to the death?' This question was superfluous—the stigma of the Lensman's epithets, delivered before such a large group, could not possibly be expunged by the mere letting of a little blood.

'To the death,' curtly.

'So be it, Oh captain!' Kinnison saluted punctiliously, executed a snappy about-face, and marched stiffly out of the room.

QX. This was a fine—strictly according to Hoyle. The captain was a swordsman, of course; but Kinnison was no slouch. He didn't think he'd have to use a thought-beam to help him. He had had five years of intensive training. Quarter-staff, night-stick, club, knife, and dagger; foil, epee, rapier, saber, broadsword, scimitar, bayonet, what-have-you—with practically any nameable weapon any Lensman had to be as good as he was with fists and feet.

The Place of Swords was in fact a circular arena, surrounded by tiers of comfortably-padded seats. It was thronged with uniforms, with civilian formal afternoon dress, and with modish gowns; for such duels as this were sporting events of the first magnitude.

To guard against such trickery as concealed armor, the contestants were almost naked. Each wore only silken trunks and a pair of low shoes, whose cross-ribbed, flexible composition soles could not be made to slip upon the corrugated surface of the cork-like material of the arena's floor.

The colonel himself, as master of ceremonies, asked the usual perfunctory questions. No, reconciliation was impossible. No, the challenged would not apologize. No, the challenger's honor could not be satisfied with anything less than mortal combat. He then took two sabers from an orderly, measuring them to be sure that they were of precisely the same length. He tested each edge for keenness, from hilt to needle point, with an expert thumb. He pounded each hilt with a heavy testing club. Lastily, still in view of the spectators, he slipped a guard over each point and put his weight upon the blades. They bent alarmingly; but neither broke and both snapped back into shape. No spy or agent, everyone then knew, had tampered with either one of those beautiful weapons.

Removing the point-guards, the colonel again inspected those slenderly lethal tips and handed one saber to each of the duelists. He held out a baton, horizontal and shoulder-high. Gannel and the captain crossed their blades upon it. He snapped his stick away and the duel was on.

Kinnison fought in Gannel's fashion exactly; in his characteristic crouch, and with his every mannerism. He was, however, the merest trifle faster than Gannel had ever been—just enough faster so that by the exertion of everything he had of skill and finesse, he managed to make the zwilnik's blade meet steel instead of flesh during the first long five minutes of furious engagement. The guy was good, no doubt of that. His saber came writhing in, to disarm. Kinnison flicked his massive wrist. Steel slithered along steel; hilt clanged against heavy basket hilt. Two mighty right arms shot upward straining to the limit. Breast to hard-ridged breast, left arms pressed against bulging-corded backs, every taut muscle from floor-gripping feet up to powerful shoulders thrown into the effort, the battlers stood motionlessly *en tableau* for seconds.

The ape wasn't fat, at that, Kinnison realized then; he was as hard as cord-wood underneath. Not fat enough, anyway, to be anybody's push-over; although he was probably not in good enough shape to last very long—he could probably wear him down. He wondered fleetingly, if worse came to worst, whether he would use his mind or not. He didn't want to ... but he might have to. Or would he, even then—*could* he? But he'd better snap out of it. He couldn't get anywhere with this body-check business; the zwilnik was just about as strong as he was.

They broke, and in the breaking Kinnison learned a brand new cut. He sensed it coming, but he could not parry or avoid it entirely; and the crowd shrieked wildly as the captain's point slashed into Gannel's trunks and a stream of crimson trickled down Gannel's left leg.

Stamp! Stamp! Cut, thrust, feint, slash and parry, the grim game went on. Again, in spite of all he could do, Kinnison was pinked; this time by a straight thrust aimed at the heart. He was falling away from it, though, so got only half an inch or so of the point in the fleshy part of his left shoulder. It bled spectacularly, however, and the throng yelled ragingly for the kill. Another—he never did know exactly how he got that one—in the calf of his right leg; and the blood-thirsty mob screamed still louder.

Then, the fine edge of the captain's terrific attack worn off, Kinnison was able to assume the offensive. He maneuvered his foe into an awkward position, swept his blade aside, and slashed viciously at the neck. But the Thralian was able partially to cover. He ducked frantically, even while his parrying blade was flashing up. Steel clanged, sparks flew; but the strength of the Lensman's arm could not be entirely denied. Instead of the whole head, however, Kinnison's razor-edged weapon snicked off only an ear and a lock of hair.

Again the spectators shrieked frenzied approval. They did not care whose blood was shed, so long as it *was* shed; and this duel, of two superb swordsmen so evenly matched, was the best they had seen for years. It was, and promised to keep on being, a splendidly gory show indeed.

Again and again the duelists engaged at their flashing top speed; once again each drew blood before the colonel's whistle shrilled.

Time out for repairs: to have either of the contestants bleed to death, or even to the point of weakness, was no part of the code. The captain had out-pointed the lieutenant, four to two, just as he always did in the tournaments; but he now derived very little comfort from the score. He was weakening while Gannel seemed as strong and fast as at the bout's beginning.

Surgeons gave hasty but effective treatment, new and perfect sabers replaced the nicked weapons, the ghastly thing went on. The captain tired slowly but surely; Gannel took, more and more openly and more and more savagely, the offensive.

When it was over Kinnison flipped his saber dexterously, so that its point stuck deep into the softly resilient floor beside that which had once been his captain. Then, while the hilt swung back and forth in slow arcs, he faced one segment of the now satiated throng and crisply saluted the colonel.

'Sir, I trust that I have won honorably the right to be examined for fitness to become the captain of my company?' he asked, formally; and:

'You have, sir,' the colonel as formally replied.

17: Into Nth Space

Kinnison's wounds, being superficial, healed rapidly. He passed the examination handily. He should have; since, although it was rigorous and comprehensive, Traska Gannel himself could have passed and Kinnison, as well as knowing practically everything that the Thralian had ever learned, had his own vast store of knowledge upon which to draw. Also, if necessary, he could have read the answers from the minds of the examiners.

As captain, the real Gannel would have been a hard and brilliant commander, noticeable even among the select group of tried and fire-polished veterans who officered the Guards. Hence Kinnison became so; in fact, considerably more so than most. He was harsh, he was relentless and inflexible; but he was absolutely fair. He did not punish a given breach of discipline with twenty lashes one time and with a mere reprimand the next; fifteen honest, scarring strokes it became for each and every time, whoever the offender. Whatever punishment a man deserved by the book he got, promptly and mercilessly; whatever reward was earned was bestowed with equal celerity, accompanied by a crisply accurate statement of the facts in each case, at the daily parade-review.

His men hated him, of course. His non-coms and lieutenants, besides hating him, kept on trying to cut him down. All, however, respected him and obeyed him without delay and without question, which was all that any Boskonian officer could expect and which was far more than most of them ever got.

Having thus consolidated his position, Kinnison went blithely to work to undermine and to supplant the major. Since Alcon, like all dictators everywhere, was in constant fear of treachery and of revolution, war-games were an almost constant form of drill. The general himself planned and various officers executed the mock attacks, by space, air, and land; the Royal Guards and Alcon's personal troops, heavily outnumbered, always constituted the defense. An elaborate system of scoring had been worked out long since, by means of which the staff officers could study in detail every weak point that could be demonstrated.

'Captain Gannel, you will have to hold passes 25, 26, and 27,' the obviously worried major told Kinnison, the evening before a particularly important sham battle was to take place. The Lensman was not surprised. He himself had insinuated the idea into his superior's mind. Moreover, he already knew, from an intensive job of spying, that his major was to be in charge of the defense, and that the colonel, who was to direct the attacking forces, had decided to route his main column through Pass 27.

'Very well, sir, Kinnison acknowledged. 'I wish to protest formally, however, against those orders. It is manifestly impossible, sir, to hold all three of those passes with two platoons of infantry and one squadron of speedsters. May I offer a suggestion ...'

'You may not,' the major snapped. 'We have deduced that the real attack is coming from the north, and that any activity in your sector will be merely a feint. Orders are orders, captain!'

'Yes, sir,' Kinnison replied, meekly, and signed for the thick sheaf of orders which stated in detail exactly what he was to do.

The next evening, after Kinnison had won the battle by disregarding every order he had been given, he was summoned to the meeting of the staff. He had expected that, too, but he was not at all certain of how it was coming out. It was in some trepidation, therefore, that he entered the lair of the Big Brass Hats.

'Har-rumph!' he was greeted by the adjutant. 'You have been called ...'

'I know why I was called,' Kinnison interrupted, brusquely. 'Before we go into that, however, I wish to prefer charges before the general against Major Delios of stupidity, incompetence, and inefficiency.'

Astonishment resounded throughout the room in a ringing silence, broken finally by the general.

'Those are serious charges indeed, Captain Gannel; but you may state your case.'

'Thank you, sir. First, stupidity: He did not perceive, at even as late a time as noon, when he took all my air away from me to meet the feint from the north, that the attack was not to follow any orthodox pattern. Second, incompetence: The orders he gave me could not possibly have stopped any serious attack through any one of the passes I was supposed to defend. Third, inefficiency: No efficient commander refuses to listen to suggestions from his officers, as he refused to listen to me last night.'

'Your side, Major?' and the staff officers listened to a defence based upon blind, dumb obedience to orders.

'We will take this matter under advisement,' the general announced then. 'Now, Captain, what made you suspect that the colonel was coming through Pass 27?'

'I didn't,' Kinnison replied, mendaciously. 'To reach any one of those passes, however, he would have to come down this valley,' tracing it with his forefinger upon the map. 'Therefore I held my whole force back here at Hill 562, knowing that, warned by my air of his approach, I could reach any one of the passes before he could.'

'Ah. Then, when your air was sent elsewhere?'

'I commandeered a flitter—my own, by the way—and sent it up so high as to be indetectable. I then ordered motor-cycle scouts out, for the enemy to capture; to make the commander of any possible attack or reconnaissance force think that I was still blind.'

'Ah . . . smart work. And then?'

'As soon as my scout reported troop movements in the valley, I got my men ready to roll. When it became certain that Pass 27 was the objective, I rushed everything I had into preselected positions commanding every foot of that pass. Then, when the colonel walked into the trap, I wiped out most of his main column. However, I had a theoretical loss of three-quarters of my men in doing it,' bitterly. 'If I had been directing the defense I would have wiped out the colonel's entire force, ground and air both, with a loss of less than two percent.'

This was strong talk. 'Do you realize, Captain Gannel, that this is sheer insubordination?' the general demanded. 'That you are in effect accusing me also of stupidity in planning and in ordering such an attack?'

'Not at all, sir,' Kinnison replied instantly. 'It was quite evident, sir, that you did it deliberately, to show all of us junior officers the importance of thought. To show us that, while unorthodox attacks may possibly be made by unskilled tacticians, any such attack is of necessity fatally weak if it be opposed by good tactics. In other words, that orthodox strategy is the only really good strategy. Was not that it, sir?'

Whether it was or not, that viewpoint gave the general an out, and he was not slow in taking advantage of it. He decided then and there, and the always subservient staff agreed with him, that Major Delios had indeed been stupid, incompetent, and inefficient; and Captain Gannel forthwith became Major Gannel.

Then the Lensman took it easy. He wangled and finagled various and sundry promotions and replacements, until he was once more surrounded by a thoroughly subsidized personal staff and in good position to go to work upon the colonel. Then, however, instead of doing so, he violated another Boskonian precendent by having a frank talk with the man whom normally he should have been trying to displace.

'You have found out that you can't kill me, colonel,' he told his superior, after making sure that the room was really shielded. 'Also that I can quite possibly kill you. You know that I know more than you do—that all my life, while you other fellows were helling around, I have been working and learning—and that I can, in a fairly short time, take your job away from you without killing you. However, I don't want it.'

'You don't *want* it!' The colonel stared, narrow-eyed. 'What *do* you want, then?' He knew, of course, that Gannel wanted something.

'Your help,' Kinnison admitted, candidly. 'I want to get onto Alcon's personal staff, as adviser. With my experience and training, I figure that there's more in it for me there than here in the Guards. Here's my proposition—if I help you, by showing you how to work out your field problems and in general building you up however I can instead of tearing you down, will you use your great influence with the general and Prime Minister Fossten to have me transferred to the Household?'

'Will I? I'll say I will!' the colonel agreed, with fervor. He did not add 'If I can't kill you first'—that was understood.

And Kinnison did build the colonel up. He taught him things about the military business which that staff officer had never even suspected; he sounded depths of strategy theretofore completely unknown to the zwilnik. And the more Kinnison taught him, the more eager the colonel became to get rid of him. He had been suspicious and only reluctantly cooperative at first; but as soon as he realized that he could not kill his tutor and that if the latter stayed in the Guards it would be only a matter of days—at most of weeks—until Gannel would force himself into the colonelcy by sheer force of merit, he pulled in earnest every wire he could reach.

Before the actual transfer could be effected, however, Kinnison received a call from Nadreck.

'Excuse me, please, for troubling you,' the Palainian apologized, 'but there has been a development in which you may perhaps be interested. This Kandron has been given orders by Alcon to traverse a hyper-spatial tube, the terminus of which will appear at coordinates 217–493–28 at hour eleven of the seventh Thralian day from the present.'

'Fine business! And you want to chase him, huh?' Kinnison jumped at the conclusion. 'Sure—go ahead. I'll meet you there. I'll fake up some kind of an excuse to get away from here and we'll run him ragged...'

'I do not,' Nadreck interrupted, decisively. 'If I leave my work here it will all come undone. Besides, it would be dangerous—foolhardly. Not knowing what lies at the other end of that tube, we could make no plans and could have no assurance of safety, or even of success. You should not go, either—that is unthinkable. I am reporting this matter in view of the possibility that you may think it significant enough to warrant the sending of some observer whose life is of little or no importance.'

'Oh ... uh-huh ... I see. Thanks, Nadreck.' Kinnison did not allow any trace of his real thought to go out before he broke the line. Then:

'Funny ape, Nadreck,' he cogitated, as he called Hayes. 'I don't get his angle at all—I simply can't figure him out... Haynes? Kinnison,' and he reported in full.

'The *Dauntless* has all the necessary generators and equipment, and the place is far enough out so that she can make the approach without any trouble,' the Lensman concluded. 'We'll burn whatever is at the other end of that tube clear out of the ether. Send along as many of the old gang as you can spare. Wish we had time to get Cardynge—he'll howl like a wolf at being left out—but we've got only a week...'

'Cardynge is here,' Haynes broke in. 'He has been working out some stuff for Thorndyke on the sunbeam. He is finished now, though, and will undoubtedly want to go along.'

'Fine!' and explicit arrangements for the rendezvous were made.

It was not unduly difficult for Kinnison to make his absence from duty logical, even necessary. Scouts and observers reported inexplicable interferences with certain communications lines. With thoughts of THE Lensman suffusing the minds of the higher-ups, and because of Gannel's already-demonstrated prowess and keenness, he scarcely had to signify a willingness to investigate the phenomena in order to be directed to do so.

Nor did he pick a crew of his own sycophants. Instead, he chose the five highest ranking privates of the battalion to accompany him upon this supposedly extremely dangerous mission; apparently entirely unaware that two of them belonged to the colonel, two to the general, and one to the captain who had taken his place.

The colonel wished Major Gannel luck—verbally—even while hoping fervently that THE Lensman would make cold meat of him in a hurry; and Kinnison gravely gave his well-wisher thanks as he set out. He did not, however, go near any communications lines; although his spying crew did not realize the fact. They did not realize anything; they did not know even that they became unconscious within five minutes after leaving Thrale.

They remained unconscious while the speedster in which they were was drawn into the *Dauntless'* capacious hold. In the Patrol ship's sick-bay, under expert care, they remained unconscious during the entire duration of their stay on board.

The Patrol pilots picked up Kandron's flying vessel with little difficulty; and, nullifiers full out, followed it easily. When the zwilnik ship slowed down to feel for the vortex the *Dauntless* slowed also, and baffled her driving jets as she sneaked up to the very edge of electro-detector range. When the objective disappeared from three-dimensional space the point of vanishment was marked precisely, and up to that point the Patrol ship flashed in seconds. The regular driving blasts were cut off, the special generators were cut in. Then, as the force-fields of the ship reacted against those of the Boskonian 'shore' station, the Patrolmen felt again in all their gruesome power the appallingly horrible sensations of inter-dimensional acceleration. For that sensation is, literally, indescribable. A man in good training can overcome sea-sickness, air-sickness, and space-sickness. He can overcome the nausea and accustom himself to the queasily terrifying endless-fall sensation of weightlessness. He can become inured to the physical and mental ills accompanying inertialessness. No man ever has, however, been able to get used to inter-dimensional acceleration.

It is best likened to a compression; not as a whole, but atom by atom. A man feels as though he were being twisted—cork-screwed in some monstrously obscure fashion which permits him neither to move from his place nor to remain where he is. It in a painless but utterly revolting transformation, progressing in a series of waves; a re-arrangement, a writhing, crawling distortion, an incomprehensibly impossible extrusion of each ultimate particle of his substance in an unknowable, ordinary non-existent direction.

The period of acceleration over, the *Dauntless* began to travel at uniform velocity along whatever course it was that the tube took. The men, although highly uncomfortable and uneasy, could once more move about and work. Sir Austin Cardynge in particular was actually happy and eager as he flitted from one to another of the automatic recording instruments upon his special panel. He resembled more closely than ever a lean, gray tomcat, Kinnison thought—he almost expected to see him begin to lick his whiskers and purr.

'You see, my ignorant young friend,' the scientist almost did purr as one of the recording pens swung wildly across the ruled paper, 'it is as I told you—the lack of exact data upon even one tiny factor of this extremely complex phenomenon is calamitous. While my notes were apparently complete and were certainly accurate, our experimental tubes did not function perfectly. The time factor was irreconcilable—completely so, in every aspect, even that of departure from and return to normal space—and it is unthinkable that time, one of the fundamental units, is or can be intrinsically variable ...'

'You think so?' Kinnison broke in. 'Look at that,' pointing to the ultimate of timepieces, Cardynge's own triplex chronometer. 'Number One says we've been in this tube for an hour, Number Two says a little over nine minutes, and according to Number Three we won't be starting for twenty minutes yet—it must be running backwards—let's see you comb *that* out of your whiskers!'

'Oh-h ... ah ... a-hum.' But only momentarily was Sir Austin taken aback. 'Ah, I was right all the time!' he cackled gleefully. 'I thought it was practically impossible for me to commit an error to overlook any possibilities, and I have now proved that I did not. Time, in this hyper-spatial region or condition, *is* intrinsically variable, and in major degree!'

'And what does that get you?' Kinnison asked, pointedly.

'Much, my impetuous youngster, much,' Cardynge replied. 'We observe, we note facts. From the observations and facts we theorize and we deduce; thus arriving very shortly at the true inwardness of time.'

'You hope,' the Lensman snorted, dubiously; and in his skepticism he was right and Sir Austin was wrong. For the actual nature and mechanism of time remained, and still constitute, a mystery, or at least an unsolved problem. The Arisians—perhaps—understand time; no other race does.

To some of the men, then, and to some of the clocks and other time-measuring devices, the time seemed—or actually was?—very long; to other and similar beings and mechanisms it seemed—or was—short. Short or long, however, the *Dauntless* did not reach the Boskonian end of the hyper-spatial tube.

In mid-flight there came a crunching, twisting *cloonk*! and an abrupt reversal of the inexplicably horrible interdimensional acceleration—a deceleration as sickeningly disturbing, both physically and mentally, as the acceleration had been.

While within the confines of the hyper-spatial tube every eye of the *Dauntless* had been blind. To every beam upon every frequency, visible or invisible, ether-borne or carried upon the infinitely faster waves of the sub-ether, the murk was impenetrable. Every plate showed the same mind-numbing blankness; a vague, eerily-shifting, quasi-solid blanket of formless, textureless grayness. No lightness or darkness, no stars or constellation or nebulae, no friendly, deep-space blackness—nothing.

Deceleration ceased; the men felt again the wonted homeliness and comfort of normal pseudo-gravity. Simultaneously the gray smear of the visiplates faded away into commonplace areas of jetty black, pierced by the brilliantly dimensionless varicolored points of light which were the familiar stars of their own familiar space.

But were they familiar? Was that our galaxy, or anything like it? They were not. It was not. Kinnison stared into his plate, aghast.

He would not have been surprised to have emerged into three-dimensional space anywhere within the Second Galaxy. In that case, he would have seen a Milky Way; and from its shape, apparent size, and texture he could have oriented himself fairly closely in a few minutes. But the *Dauntless* was not within any lenticular galaxy—nowhere was there any sign of a Milky Way!

He would not have been really surprised to have found himself and his ship out in open inter-galactic space. In that case he would have seen a great deal of dead-black emptiness, blotched with lenticular bodies which were in fact galaxies. Orientation would then have been more difficult; but, with the aid of the Patrol charts, it could have been accomplished. But here there were no galaxies—no nebulae of any kind!

18: Prime Minister Fossten

Here, upon a background of a blackness so intense as to be obviously barren of nebular material, there lay a multitude of blazingly resplendent stars—and nothing except stars. A few hundred were of a visual magnitude of about minus three.

Approximately the same number were of minus two or thereabouts, and so on down; but there did not seem to be a star or other celestial object in that starkly incredible sky of an apparent magnitude greater than about plus four.

'What do you make of this, Sir Austin?' Kinnison asked, quietly. 'It's got me stopped like a traffic light.'

The mathematician ran toward him and the Lensman stared. He had never known Cardynge to hurry—in fact, he was not really running now. He was walking, even though his legs were fairly twinkling in their rapidity of motion. As he approached Kinnison his pace gradually slowed to normal.

'Oh—time must be cock-eyed here, too,' the Lensman observed. 'Look over there—see how fast those fellows are moving, and how slow those others over that way are?'

'Ah, yes. Interesting—intensely interesting. Truly, a most remarkable and intriguing phenomenon,' the fascinated mathematician enthused.

'But that wasn't what I meant. Swing this plate—it's on visual—around outside, so as to get the star aspect and distribution. What do you think of it?'

'Peculiar—I might almost say unique,' the scientist concluded, after his survey. 'Not at all like any normal configuration or arrangement with which I am familiar. We could perhaps speculate, but would it not be preferable to secure data first? Say by approaching a solar system and conducting systematic investigations?'

'Uh-huh,' and again Kinnison stared at the wispy little physicist in surprise. Here was a *man*! 'You're certainly something to tie to, ace, do you know it?' he asked, admiringly. Then, as Cardynge gazed at him questioningly, uncomprehendingly:

'Skip it. Can you feel my thought, Henderson?'

'Yes.'

'Shoot us across to one of those nearer stars, stop, and go inert.'

'QX, chief.' The pilot obeyed.

And in the instant of inerting, the visiplate into which the two men stared went black. The thousands of stars studding the sky a moment before had disappeared as though they had never been.

'Why ... What ... How in all the yellow hells of space can *that* happen?' Kinnison blurted.

Without a word Cardynge reached out and snapped the

plate's receiver over from 'visual' to 'ultra', whereupon the stars reappeared as suddenly as they had vanished.

'Something's screwy somewhere!' the Lensman protested. 'We *can't* have an inert velocity greater than that of light—it's impossible!'

'Few things, if any, can be said definitely to be impossible; and everything is relative, not absolute,' the old scientist declared, pompously. 'This space, for instance. You have not yet perceived, I see, even that you are not in the same three-dimensional space in which we have heretofore existed.'

Kinnison gulped. He was going to protest about that, too, but in the face of Cardynge's unperturbed acceptance of the fact he did not quite dare to say what he had in mind.

'That is better,' the old man declaimed. 'Do not get excited—to do so dulls the mind. Take nothing for granted, do not jump at conclusions—to commit either of those errors will operate powerfully against success. Working hypotheses, young man, must be based upon accurately determined facts; not upon mere guesses, superstitions, or figments of personal prejudices.'

'Bub—bub—but ... QX—skip it!' Nine-tenths of the *Dauntless*' crew would have gone out of control at the impact of the knowledge of what had happened; even Kinnison's powerful mind was shaken. Cardynge, however, was—not seemed to be, but actually was—as calm and as self-contained as though he were in his own quiet study. 'Explain it to me, will you please, in words of as nearly one syllable as possible?'

'Our looser thinkers have for centuries speculated upon the possibility of an entire series of different spaces existing simultaneously, side by side in a hypothetical hyper-continuum. I have never indulged in such time-wasting; but now that actual corroborative data have become available, I regard it as a highly fruitful field of investigation. Two extremely significant facts have already become apparent; the variability of time and the non-applicability of our so-called "laws" of motion. Different spaces, different laws, it would seem.'

'But when we cut our generators in that other tube we emerged into our own space,' Kinnison argued. 'How do you account for that?'

'I do not as yet try to account for it?' Cardynge snapped. 'Two very evident possibilities should already be apparent, even to your feeble brain. One, that at the moment of release your vessel happened to be situated within a fold of our own space. Two, that the collapse of the ship's force-fields aways returns it to its original space, while the collapse of those of the shore station always forces it into some other space. In the latter case, it would be reasonable to suppose that the persons or beings at the other end of the tube may have suspected that we were following Kandron, and, as soon as he landed, cut off their forces deliberately to throw us out of space. They may even have learned that persons of lesser ability, so treated, never return. Do not allow yourself to be at all impressed by any of these possibilities, however, as the truth may very well lie in something altogether different. Bear it in mind that we have as yet very little data upon which to formulate any theories, and that the truth can be revealed only by a very careful, accurate, and thorough investigation. Please note also that I would surely have discovered and evaluated all these unknowns during the course of my as yet incomplete study of our own hyper-spatial tubes; that I am merely continuing here a research in which I have already made noteworthy progress.'

Kinnison really gasped at that—the guy was certainly terrific! He called the chief pilot. 'Go free, Hen, and start flitting for a planet—we've got to sit down somewhere before we can start back home. When you find one, land free. Stay free, and watch your Bergs—I don't have to tell you what will happen if they quit on us.'

Then Thorndyke. 'Verne? Break out some personal neutralizers. We've got a job of building to do—inertialess,' and he explained to both men in flashing thoughts what had happened and what they had to do.

'You grasp the basic idea, Kinnison,' Cardynge approved, 'that it is necessary to construct a station apart from the vessel in which we propose to return to our normal environment. You err grievously, however, in your insistence upon the necessity of discovering a planet, satellite, asteroid, or other similar celestial body upon which to build it.'

'Huh?' Kinnison demanded.

'It is eminently possible—yes, even practicable—for us to use the *Dauntless* as an anchorage for the tube and for us to return in the lifeboats,' Cardynge pointed out.

'What? Abandon this ship? Waste all that time rebuilding all the boats?'

'It is preferable, of course, and more expeditious, to find a planet, if possible,' the scientist conceded. 'However, it is plain that it is in no sense necessary. Your reasoning is fallacious, your phraseology is deplorable. I am correcting you in the admittedly faint hope of teaching you scientific accuracy of thought and of statement.'

'Wow! Wottaman!' Kinnison breathed to himself, as, heroically, he 'skipped it'.

Somewhat to Kinnison's surprise—he had more than half expected that planets would be non-existent in that space—the pilots did find a solid world upon which to land. It was a peculiar planet indeed. It did not move right, it did not look right, it did not feel right. It was waterless, airless, desolate; a senseless jumble of jagged fragments, mostly metallic. It was neither hot nor cold—indeed, it seemed to have no temperature of its own at all. There was nothing whatever right about it, Kinnison declared.

'Oh, yes, there is!' Thorndyke contradicted. 'Time is constant here, whatever its absolute rate may be, these metals are nice to work with, and some of this other stuff will make insulation. Or hadn't you thought of that? Which would be faster, cutting down an intrinsic velocity of fifteen lights to zero or building the projector out of native materials? And if you match intrinsics, what will happen when you hit our normal space again?

'Plenty, probably—uh-huh, faster to use the stuff that belongs here. Careful, though, fella!'

And care was indeed necessary; extreme care that not a particle of matter from the ship was used in the construction and that not a particle of the planet's substance by any mischance got aboard the space-ship.

The actual work was simple enough. Cardynge knew exactly what had to be done. Thorndyke knew exactly how to do it, as he had built precisely similar generators for the experimental tubes upon Tellus. He had a staff of experts; the *Dauntless* carried a machine shop and equipment second to none. Raw material was abundant, and it was an easy matter to block out an inertialess room within which the preojectors and motors were built. And, after they were built, they worked.

It was not the work, then, but the strain which wore Kinnison down. The constant, wearing strain of incesssant vigilance to be sure that the Bergenholms and the small units of the personal neutralizers did not falter for a single instant. He did not lose a man, but again and again there flashed into his mind the ghastly picture of one of his boys colliding with the solid metal of the planet at a relative velocity fifteen times that of light! The strain of the endless checking and rechecking to make certain that there was no exchange of material, however slight, between the ship and the planet.

Above all, the strain of knowing a thing which, apparently, no once else suspected; that Cardynge, with all his mathematical knowledge, was not going to be able to find his way back! He had never spoken of this to the scientist. He did not have to. He knew that without a knowledge of the fundamental distinguishing characteristics of our normal space—a knowledge even less to be expected than that a fish should know the fundamental equations and structure of water—they never could, save by sheerest accident, return to their own space. And as Cardynge grew more and more tensely, unsocially immersed in his utterly insoluble problem, the more and more uneasy the Gray Lensman became. But this last difficulty was resolved first, and in a totally unexpected fashion.

'Ah, Kinnison of Tellus, here you are—I have been considering your case for some twenty nine of your seconds,' a deep, well-remembered voice resounded within his brain.

'Mentor!' he exclaimed, and at the sheer shock of his relief he came very near indeed to fainting. 'Thank Klono and Noshabkeming you found us! How did you do it? How do we get ourselves out of here?'

'Finding you was elementary,' the Arisian replied, calmly. 'Since you were not in your own environment you must be elsewhere. It required but little thought to perceive what was a logical, in fact an inevitable, development. Such being the case, it needed very little additional effort to determine what had happened, and how, and why; likewise precisely where you must now be. As for departure therefrom, your mechanical preparations are both correct and adequate. I could give you the necessary information, but it is rather technically specialized and not negligible in amount; and since your brain is not of infinite capacity, it is better not to fill any part of it with mathematics for which you will have no subsequent use. Put yourself en rapport, therefore, with Sir Austin Cardynge. I will follow.'

He did so, and as mind met mind there ensued a conversation whose barest essentials Kinnison could not even dimly grasp. For Cardynge, as has been said, could think in the universal language of mathematics; in the esoteric symbology which very few minds have ever been able even partially to master. The Lensman did not get it, nor any part of it; he knew only that in that to him completely meaningless gibberish the Arisian was describing to the physicist, exactly and fully, the distinguishing characteristics of a vast number of parallel and simultaneously co-existent spaces.

If that was 'rather' technical stuff, the awed Lensman wondered, what would really deep stuff be like? Not that he wanted to find out! No wonder these mathematical wizards were nuts—went off the beam—he'd be pure squirrel-food if he had half that stuff in *his* skull!

But Sir Austin took to it like a cap lapping up cream or doing away with the canary. He brightened visibly; he swelled; and, when the Arisian had withdrawn from his mind, he preened himself and swaggered as he made meticulous adjustments of the delicate meters and controls which the technicians had already built.

Preparations complete, Cardynge threw in the switches and everything belonging to the *Dauntless* was rushed aboard—everything, that is, that was demonstrably uncontaminated by any particle of Nth-space matter. The spacesuits that had been worn on the planet and everything else, no matter what it was, that could not show an unquestionable bill of health were dumped. The neutralizers, worn so long and cherished so assiduously, were taken off with profound sighs of relief. The vessel was briefly, tentatively inerted. QX—no faster-than-light meteorites tore volatizingly through her mass. So far, so good.

Then the ship's generators were energized and smoothly, effortlessly the big battle-wagon took the inter-dimensional plunge. There came the expected, but nevertheless almost unendurable acceleration; the imperceptible, unloggable flight through the drably featureless grayness; the horrible deceleration. Stars flashed beautifully upon the plates.

'We made it!' Kinnison shouted in relief when he had assured himself that they had emerged into 'real' space inside the Second Galaxy, only a few parsecs away from their point of departure. 'By Klono's golden grin, Sir Austin, you figured it to a red whisker! And when the Society meets, Tuesday week, won't you just blast that ape Weingarde to a cinder? Hot dog!'

'Having the basic data, the solution and the application followed of necessity—automatically—uniquely,' the scientist said, austerely. He was high pleased with himself, he was tremendously flattered by the Lensman's ebullient praise; but not for anything conceivable would he have so admitted.

'Well, the first thing we'd better do is to find out what time of what day it is,' Kinnison went on, as he directed a beam to the Patrol headquarters upon Klovia.

'Better ask 'em the year, too,' Henderson put in, pessimistically—he had missed Illona poignantly—but it wasn't that bad.

In fact, it was not bad at all; they had been gone only a little over a week of Thralian time. This finding pleased Kinnison immensely, as he had been more than half afraid that it had been a month. He could explain a week easily enough, but anything over two weeks would have been tough to handle.

The supplies of the Thralian speedster were adjusted to fit the actual elapsed time, and Worsel and Kinnison engraved upon the minds of the five unconscious Guardsmen completely detailed, even though equally completely fictitious—memories of what they and Major Gannel had done since leaving Thrale. Their memories were not exactly alike, of course—each man had had different duties and experiences, and no two observers see precisely the same things even while watching the same event—but they were very convincing. Also, and fortunately, not even the slightest scars were left by the operations, for in these cases no memory chain had to be broken at any point.

The *Dauntless* blasted off for Klovia; the speedster started for Thrale. Kinnison's crew woke up—without having any inkling that they had ever been unconscious, or that their knowledge of recent events did not jibe exactly with the actual occurrences—and resumed work.

Immediately upon landing, Kinnison turned in a full official report of the mission, giving himself neither too much nor too little credit for what had been accomplished. They had found a Patrol sneak-boat near Line Eleven. They had chased it so many parsecs, upon such-and-such a course, before forcing it to engage. They had crippled it and boarded, bringing away material, described as follows, which had been turned over to Space Intelligence. And so on. It would hold, Kinnison knew; and it would be corroborated fully by the ultra-private reports which his men would make to their real bosses.

The colonel made good; hence with due pomp and ceremony Major Traska Gannel was inducted into the Household. He was given one of the spy-ray-screened cigarette boxes in which Alcon's most trusted officers were allowed to carry their private, secret insignia. Kinnison was glad to get that—he could carry his Lens with him now, if the thing was really ray-proof, instead of leaving it buried in a can outside the city limits.

The Lensman went to his first meeting of the Advisory Cabinet with his mind set on a hair-trigger. He hadn't been around Alcon very much, but he knew that the Tyrant had a stronger mind-shield than any untreated human being had any right to have. He'd have to play this mighty close to his chest—he didn't want any zwilnik reading his mind, yet he didn't want to create suspicion by revealing the fact that he, too, had an impenetrable block.

As he approached the cabinet chamber he walked into a zone of compulsion and practically bounced. He threw up his head; it was all he could do to keep his barriers down. It was general, he knew, not aimed specifically at him—to fight the hypnotist would be to call attention to himself as the only man able either to detect his work or to resist him; would give the whole show away. Therefore he let the thing take hold—with reservations—of his mind. He studied it. He analyzed it. Sight only, eh? QX—he'd let Alcon have superficial control, and he wouldn't put too much faith in anything he saw.

He entered the room; and, during the preliminarys, he reached out delicately, to touch imperceptibly mind after mind. All the ordinary officers were on the level; now he'd see about the prime minister. He'd heard a lot about this Fossten, but had never met him before—he'd see what the guy really had on the ball.

He did not find out, however. He did not even touch his mind, for that worthy also had an automatic block; a block as effective as Alcon's or as Kinnison's own.

Sight was unreliable; how about the sense of perception? He tried it, very daintily and gingerly, upon Alcon's feet, legs, arms, and torso. Alcon was real, and present in the flesh. Then the premier—and he yanked his sense back, cancelled it, appalled. Perception was blocked, at exactly what his eyes told him was the fellow's skin!

That tore it—that busted it wide open. What in all nine prime iridescent hells did that mean? He didn't know of anything except a thought-screen that could stop a sense of perception. He thought intensely. Alcon's mind was bad enough. It had been treated, certainly; mind-shields like that didn't grow naturally on human or near-human beings. Maybe the Eich, or the race of super-Eich to which Kandron belonged, could give mental treatments of that kind. Fossten, though, was worse.

Alcon's boss! Probably not a man at all. It was he, it was clear, and not Alcon, who was putting out the zone of compulsion. An Eich, maybe? No, he was a warm-blooded oxygen-breather; a frigid-blooded super-big-shot would make Alcon come to him. A monster, almost certainly, though; possibly of a type Kinnison had never seen before. Working by remote control? Possibly; but not necessarily. He could be—probably was—right here, inside the dummy or figment or whatever it was that everybody thought was the prime minister—that was it, for all the tea in China . . .

'And what do you think, Major Gannel?' the prime minister asked, smoothly, insinuating his mind into Kinnison's as he spoke.

Kinnison, who knew that they had been discussing an invasion of the First Galaxy, hesitated as though in thought. He *was* thinking, too, and ultra-carefully. If that ape was out to do a job of digging he'd never dig again—QX, he was just checking Gannel's real thoughts against what he was going to say.

'Since I am such a newcomer to this Council I do not feel as though my opinions should be given too much weight,' Kinnison said—and thought—slowly, with the exactly correct amount of obsequiousness. 'However, I have a very decided opinion upon the matter. I believe very firmly that it would be better tactics to consolidate our position here in our own galaxy first.'

'You advise, then, against any immediate action against Tellus?' the prime minister asked. 'Why?'

'I do, definitely. It seems to me that short-sighed, half-prepared measures, based upon careless haste, were the underlying causes of our recent reverses. Time is not an important factor—the Great Plan was worked out, not in terms of days or of years, but of centuries and millenia—and it seems to me self-evident that we should make ourselves impregnably secure, then expand slowly; seeing to it that we can hold, against everything that the Patrol can bring to bear, every planet that we take.'

'Do you realize that you are criticising the chiefs of staff who are in complete charge of military operations?' Alcon asked, venomously.

'Fully,' the Lensman replied, coldly. 'I ventured this opinion because I was asked specifically for it. The chiefs of staff failed, did they not? If they had succeeded, criticism would have been neither appropriate nor forthcoming. As it is, I do not believe that mere criticism of their conduct, abilities, and tactics is sufficient. They should be disciplined and demoted. New chiefs should be chosen; persons abler and more efficient than the present incumbents.'

This was a bomb-shell. Dissentions waxed rife and raucous, but amidst the turmoil the Lensman received from the prime minister a flash of coldly congratulatory approval.

And as Major Traska Gannel made his way back to his quarters two things were starkly plain:

First, he would have to cut Alcon down and himself become the Tyrant of Thrale. It was unthinkable to attack or to destroy this planet. It had too many too promising leads—there were too many things that didn't make sense—above all, there were the stupendous files of information which no one mind could scan in a lifetime.

Second, if he wanted to keep on living he would have to keep his detectors shoved out to maximum—this prime minister was just about as touchy and just about as safe to play with as a hundred kilograms of dry nitrogen iodide!

19: Gannell, Tyrant of Thrale

Nadreck, the Palainian Lensman, had not exaggerated in saying that he could not leave his job, that his work would come undone if he did.

As has been intimated, Nadreck was cowardly and lazy and characterized otherwise by traits not usually regarded by humankind as being noble. He was, however, efficient; and he was now engaged in one of the most colossal tasks ever attempted by any one Lensman. Characteristically, he had told no one, not even Haynes or Kinnison, what it was that he was trying to do—he never talked about a job until after it was done, and his talking then was usually limited to a taped, Lensman's-sealed, tersely factual report. He was 'investigating' Onlo; that was all that anybody knew.

Onlo was at that time perhaps the most heavily fortified planet in the universe. Compared to its massed might Jarnevon was weak; Tellus, except for its sunbeams and its other open-space safeguards, a joke. Onlo's defenses were all, or nearly all, planetary; Kandron's strategy, unlike Haynes', was to let any attacking force get almost down to the ground and then blast it out of existence.

Thus Onlo was in effect one tremendously armed, titanically powered fortress; not one cubic foot of its poisonous atmosphere was out of range of projectors theoretically capable of puncturing any defensive screen possible of mounting upon a mobile base.

And Nadreck, the cowardly, the self-effacing, the apologetic, had tackled Onlo—alone!

Using the technique which has already been described in connection with his highly successful raid upon the Eich stronghold of Lyrane VIII, he made his way through the Onlonian defensive screens and settled down comfortably near one of the gigantic domes. Then, as though time were of no consequence whatever, he proceeded to get acquainted with the personnel. He learned the identifying pattern of each entity and analyzed every one psychologically, mentally, intellectually, and emotionally. He tabulated his results upon the Palainian equivalent of index cards, then very carefully arranged the cards into groups.

In the same fashion he visited and took the census of dome after dome. No one knew that he had been near, apparently he had done nothing; but in each dome as he left it there had been sown seeds of discord and of strife which, at a carefully calculated future time, would yield bitter fruit indeed.

For every mind has some weakness, each intellect some trait of which it does not care to boast, each Achilles his heel. That is true even of Gray Lensmen—and the Onlonians, with their heredity and environment of Boskonianism, were in no sense material from which Lensmen could be made.

Subtly, then, and coldly and callously, Nadreck worked upon the basest passions, the most ignoble traits of that far-from-noble race. Jealousy, suspicion, fear, greed, revenge—quality by quality he grouped them, and to each group he sent series after series of horridly stimulating thoughts.

Jealousy, always rife, assumed fantastic proportions. Molehills became mountains overnight. A passing word became a studied insult. No one aired his grievances, however, for always and everywhere there was fear—fear of discipline, fear of reprisal, fear of betrayal, fear of the double cross. Each monster brooded, sullenly intense. Each became bitterly, gallingly, hatingly aware of an unwarranted and intolerable persecution. Not much of a spark would be necessary to touch off such explosive material as that!

Nadreck left the headquarters dome until the last. In one

sense it was the hardest of all; in another the easiest. It was hard in that the entities there had stronger minds than those of lower station; minds better disciplined, minds more accustomed to straight thinking and to logical reasoning. It was easy, however, in that those minds were practically all at war already—fighting either to tear down the one above or to resist the attacks of those below. Every mind in it already hated, or feared, or distrusted, or was suspicious of or jealous of some other.

And while Nadreck labored thus deviously his wonders to perform, Kinnison went ahead in his much more conventional and straightforward fashion upon Thrale. His first care, of course, was to surround himself with the usual coterie of spies and courtiers.

The selection of this group gave Kinnison many minutes of serious thought. It was natural enough that he had not been able to place any of his own men in the secret service of Alcon or the prime minister, since they both had minds of power. It would not be natural, however, for either of them not to be able to get an agent into his. For to be too good would be to invite a mental investigation which he simply could not as yet permit. He would have to play dumb enough so that his hitherto unsuspected powers of mind would remain unsuspected.

He could, however, do much. Since he knew who the spies were, he was able quite frequently to have his more trusted henchmen discover evidence against them, branding them for what they were. Assassinations were then, of course, very much in order. And even a strong suspicion, even though it could not be documented, was reason enough for a duel.

In this fashion, then, Kinnison built up his entourage and kept it reasonably free from subversive elements; and, peculiarly enough, those elements never happened to learn anything which the Lensman did not want them to know.

Building up a strong personal organization was now easy, for at last Kinnison was a real Boskonian big shot. As a major of the Household he was a power to be toadied to and fawned upon. As a personal adviser to Alcon the Tyrant he was one whose ill-will should be avoided at all costs. As a tactician who had so boldly and yet so altruistically put the skids under the chiefs of staff, thereby becoming a favorite even of the dreaded prime minister, he was marked plainly as a climber to whose coat-tails it would be wise to cling. In short, Kinnison made good in a big—it might almost be said in a stupendous—way.

With such powers at work the time of reckoning could not be

delayed for long. Alcon knew that Gannel was working against him; learned very quickly, since he knew exactly the personnel of Kinnison's 'private' secret service and could read at will any of their minds, that Gannel held most of the trumps. The Tyrant had tried many times to read the major's mind, but the latter, by some subterfuge or other, had always managed to elude his inquisitor without making an issue of the matter. Now, however, Alcon drove in a solid questing beam which, he was grimly determined, would produce results of one kind or another.

It did: but, unfortunately for the Thralian, they were nothing he could use. For Kinnison, instead either of allowing the Tyrant to read his whole mind or of throwing up an all-too-revealing barricade, fell back upon the sheer native power of will which made him unique in his generation. He concentrated upon an all-inclusive negation; which in effect was a rather satisfactory block and which was entirely natural.

'I don't know what you're trying to do, Alcon,' he informed his superior, stiffly, 'but whatever it is I do NOT like it. I think you're trying to hypnotize me. If you are, know now that you can't do it. No possible hypnotic force can overcome my definitely and positively opposed will.'

'Major Gannel, you will . . .' the Tyrant began, then stopped. He was not quite ready yet to come openly to grips with this would-be usurper. Besides, it was now plain that Gannel had only an ordinary mind. He had not even suspected all the prying that had occurred previously. He had not recognized even this last powerful thrust for what it really was; he had merely felt it vaguely and had supposed that it was an attempt at hypnotism!

A few more days and he would cut him down. Hence Alcon changed his tone and went on smoothly, 'It is not hypnotism, Major Gannel, but a sort of telepathy which you cannot understand. It is, however, necessary; for in the case of a man occupying such a high position as yours, it is self-evident that we can permit no secrets whatever to be withheld from us—that we can allow no mental reservations of any kind. You see the justice and necessity of that, do you not?'

Kinnison did. He saw also that Alcon was being superhumanly forbearing. Moreover, he knew what the Tyrant was covering up so carefully—the real reason for this highly unusual tolerance.

'I suppose you're right; but I still *don't* like it,' Gannel grumbled. Then, without either denying or acceding to Alcon's right of mental search, he went to his own quarters.

And there—or thereabouts—he wrought diligently at a thing which had been long in the making. He had known all along that his retinue would be useless against Alcon, hence he had built up an organization entirely separate from, and completely unknown to any member of, his visible following. Nor was this really secret outfit composed of spies or sycophants. Instead, its members were hard, able, thoroughly proven men, each one carefully selected for the ability and the desire to take the place of one of Alcon's present department heads. One at a time he put himself en rapport with them; gave them certain definite orders and instructions.

Then he put on a mechanical thought-screen. Its use could not make the prime minister any more suspicious than he already was, and it was the only way he could remain in character. This screen was, like those of Lonabar, decidedly pervious in that it had an open slit. Unlike Bleeko's, however, which had their slits set upon a fixed frequency, the open channel of this one could be varied, both in width and in wavelength, to any setting which Kinnison desired.

Thus equipped, Kinnison attended the meeting of the Council of Advisers, and to say that he disrupted the meeting is no exaggeration. The other advisers perceived nothing out of the ordinary, of course, but both Alcon and the prime minister were so perturbed that the session was cut very short indeed. The other members were dismissed summarily, with no attempt at explanation. The Tyrant was raging, furious; the premier was alertly, watchfully intent.

'I did not expect any more physical privacy than I have been granted,' Kinnison grated, after listening quietly to a minute or two of Alcon's unbridled language. 'This thing of being spied upon continuously, both by men and mechanisms, while it is insulting and revolting to any real man's self-respect, can—just barely—be borne. I find it impossible, however, to force myself to submit to such an ultimately degrading humiliation as the surrender of the only vestiges of privacy I have remaining; those of my mind. I will resign from the Council if you wish, I will resume my status as an officer of the line, but I cannot and will not tolerate your extinction of the last spark of my self-respect,' he finished stubbornly.

'Resign? Resume? Do you think I'll let you off *that* easily, fool?' Alcon sneered. 'Don't you realize what I'm going to do to you? That, were it not for the fact that I am going to watch you die slowly and hideously, I would have you blasted where you stand?'

'I do not, no, and neither do you,' Gannel answered, as quietly as surprisingly. 'If you were sure of your ability, you would be doing something instead of talking about it.' He saluted crisply, turned, and walked out.

Now the prime minister, as the student of this history already knows, was considerably more than he appeared upon the surface to be. His, not Alcon's, was the voice of authority, although he worked so subtly that the Tyrant himself never did realize that he was little better than a figure-head.

Therefore, as Gannel departed, the premier thought briefly but cogently. This major was smart—too smart. He was too able, he knew too much. His advancement had been just a trifle too rapid. That thought-screen was an entirely unexpected development. The mind behind it was not quite right, either—a glimpse through the slit had revealed a flash of something that might be taken to indicate that Major Gannel had an ability which ordinary Thralians did not have. This open defiance of the Tyrant of Thrale did not ring exactly true—it was not quite in character. If it had been a bluff, it was too good—much too good. If it had not been a bluff, where was his support? How could Gannel have grown so powerful without his, Fossten's, knowledge?

If Major Gannel were bona-fide, all well and good. Boskonia needed the strongest possible leaders, and if any other man showed himself superior to Alcon, Alcon should and would die. However, there was a bare possibility that... Was Gannel bona-fide? That point should be cleared up without delay. And Fossten, after a quizzical, searching, more than half contemptuous inspection of the furiously discomfited Tyrant, followed the rebellious, the contumaceous, the enigmatic Gannel to his rooms.

He knocked and was admitted. A preliminary and entirely meaningless conversation occurred. Then:

'Just when did you leave the Circle?' the visitor demanded, sharply.

'What do you want to know for?' Kinnison shot back. That question didn't mean a thing to him. Maybe it didn't to the big fellow, either—it could be just a catch—but he didn't intend to give any kind of an analyzable reply to any question that this ape asked him.

Nor did he, through thirty minutes of viciously skillful verbal fencing. That conversation was far from meaningless, but it was entirely unproductive of results; and it was a baffled, intensely thoughtful Fossten who at its conclusion left Gannel's quarters. From those quarters he went to the Hall of Records, where he requisitioned the major's dossier. Then to his own private laboratory, where he applied to those records every test known to the scientists of his ultra-suspicious race.

The photographs were right in every detail. The prints agreed exactly with those he himself had secured from the subject not twenty four hours since. The typing was right. The ink was right. Everything checked. And why not? Ink, paper, fiber, and film were in fact exactly what they should have been. There had been no erasures, no alterations. Everything had been aged to the precisely correct number of days. For Kinnison had known that this check-up was coming; and while the experts of the Patrol were not infallible, Mentor of Arisia was.

Even though he had found exactly what he had expected to find, the suspicions of the prime minister were intensified rather than allayed. Besides his own, there were two unreadable minds upon Thrale, where there should have been only one. He knew how Alcon's had been treated—could Gannel's possibly be a natural phenomenon? If not, who had treated it, and why?

There were three, and only three, possibilities. Another Eddorian, another member of the Innermost Circle, working against him? Probably not; his job was too important. The All-Highest would not permit it. The arisian who had been hampering him so long? Much more like. Star A Star? Most likely of all.

Not enough data ... but in any event, circumspection was very definitely indicated. The show-down would come at a time and a place of his own choosing, not the foe's.

He left the palace then, ostensibly to attend a function at the Military Academy. There, too, everything checked. He visited the town in which Gannel had been born—finding no irregularities whatever in the records of the birth. He went to the city in which Gannel had lived for the greater part of his life; where he assured himself that school records, club records, even photographs and negatives, all dead-centered the beam.

He studied the minds of six different persons who had known Gannel from childhood. As one they agreed that the Traska Gannell who was now Traska Gannel was in fact the real Traska Gannel, and could not by any possibility be anyone else. He examined their memory tracks minutely for scars, breaks, or other evidences of surgery; finding none. In fact, none existed, for the therapists who had performed those operations had gone back clear to the very beginnings, to the earliest memories of the Gannel child.

In spite of the fact that all the data thus far investigated were so precisely what they should have been—or because of it—the prime minister was now morally certain that Gannel was, in some fashion or other, completely spurious. Should he go farther, delve into unimportant but perhaps highly revealing side issues? He should. He did so with a minute attention to detail anticipated only by Mentor of Arisia. He found nothing amiss in any particular, but he was still unsatisfied. The mind who had falsified those records so flawlessly—if they had in fact been falsified—had done a beautiful piece of work; as masterly a job as he himself could have done. He himself would have left no traces; neither, in all probability, had the unknown.

Who, then, and why? This was no ordinary plot, no part of any ordinary scheme to overthrow Alcon. It was bigger, deeper, far more sinister. Nothing so elaborate and efficient originating upon Thrale could possibly have been developed and executed without his knowledge and at least his tacit consent. It could not be Eddorian. That narrowed the field to two—the Arisian or Star A Star.

His mind flashed back, reviewing everything that had been ascribed to that mysterious Director of Lensmen. Something clicked.

BLAKESLEE!

This was much finer than the Blakeslee affair, of course; more subtle and more polished by far. It was not nearly as obvious, as blatant, but the basic similarity was nevertheless there. Could this similarity have been accidental? No—unthinkable. In this undertaking accidents could be ruled out—definitely. Whatever had been done had been done deliberately and after meticulous preparation.

But Star A Star *never* repeated . . . Therefore, this time, he *had* repeated; deliberately, to throw Alcon and his psychologists off the trail. But he, Fossten, was not to be deceived by even such clever tactics.

Gannel was, then, really Gannel, just as Blakeslee had really been Blakeslee. Blakeslee had obviously been under control. Here, however, there were two possibilities. First Gannel might be under similar control. Second, Star A Star might have operated upon Gannel's mind so radically as to make an entirely different man of him. Either hypothesis would explain Gannel's extreme reticence in submitting to any except the most superficial mental examination. Each would account for Gannel's calm certainty that Alcon was afraid to attack him openly. Which of these hypotheses was the correct one could be determined later. It was unimportant, anyway, for in either case there was now accounted for the heretofore inexplicable power of Gannel's mind.

In either case it was not Gannel's mind at all, but that of THE Lensman, who was making Gannel act as he could not normally have acted. Somewhere hereabouts, in either case, there actually was lurking Boskonia's Nemesis; the mentality whom above all others Boskonia was raving to destroy; the one Lensman who had never been seen or heard or perceived; the feared and detested Lensman about whom nothing whatever had ever been learned.

That Lensman, whoever he might be, had at last met his match. Gannel, as Gannel, was of no importance whatever; the veriest pawn. But he who stood behind Gannel . . . Ah! . . . He, Gharlane himself, would wait and he would watch. Then, at precisely the correct instant, he would pounce!

And Kinnison, during the absence of the prime minister, worked swiftly and surely. Twelve men died, and as they ceased to live twelve others, grimly ready and thoroughly equipped for any emergency, took their places. And during that same minute of time Kinnison strode in Alcon's private sanctum.

The Tyrant hurled orders to his guards—orders which were not obeyed. He then went for his own weapons, and he was fast—but Kinnison was faster. Alcon's guns and hands disappeared and the sickened Tellurian slugged him into unconsciousness. Then, grimly, relentlessly, he took every item of interest from the Thralian's mind, killed him and assumed forthwith the title and the full authority of the Tyrant of Thrale.

Unlike most such revolutions, this one was accomplished with very little bloodshed and with scarcely any interference with the business of the realm. Indeed, if anything, there was an improvement in almost every respect, since the new men were more thoroughly trained and were more competent than the previous officers had been. Also, they had arranged matters beforehand so that their accessions could be made with a minimum of friction.

They were as yet loyal to Kinnison and to Boskonia; and in a rather faint hope of persuading them to stay that way, without developing any queer ideas about overthrowing him, the Lensman called them into conference.

'Men, you know how you got where you are,' he began, coldly. 'You are loyal to me at the moment. You know that real cooperation is the only way to achieve maximum productivity, and that true cooperation cannot exist in any regime in which the department heads, individually or en mass are trying to do away with the dictator.

'Some of you will probably be tempted very shortly to begin to work against me instead of for me and with me. I am not pleading with you, nor even asking you out of gratitude for what I have done for you, to refrain from such inactivities. Instead, I am telling you as a simple matter of fact that any or all of you, at the first move toward any such disloyalty, will die. In that connection, I know that all of you have been exerting every resource to discover in what manner your predecessors came so conveniently to die, and that none of you have succeeded.'

One by one they admitted that they had not.

'Nor will you, ever. Be advised that I know vastly more than Alcon did, and that I am far more powerful. Alcon, while in no sense a weakling, did not know how to command obedience. I do. Alcon's sources of information were meager and untrustworthy; mine are comprehensive and reliable. Alcon very often did not know that anything was being plotted against him until the thing was well along; I shall always know of the first seditious move. Alcon blustered, threatened and warned; he tortured; he gave some offenders a second chance before he killed. I shall do none of these things. I do not threaten, I do not warn, I do not torture. Above all I give no snake a second chance to strike at me. I execute traitors without bluster or fanfare. For your own good, gentlemen, I advise you in all seriousness to believe that I mean precisely every word I say.'

They slunk out, but Boskonian habit was too strong. Thus, within three days, three of Kinnison's newly appointed head men died. He called another cabinet meeting.

'The three new members have listened to the recording of our first meeting, hence there is no need to repeat what I said at that time,' the Tyrant announced, in a voice so silkily venomous that his listeners cringed. 'I will add to it merely that I will have full cooperation, and only cooperation, if I have to kill all of you and all of your successors to get it. You may go.'

20: Gannel vs. Fossten

This killing made Kinnison ill; physically and mentally sick. It was ruthless, cowardly murder. It was worse than stabbing a man in the back; the poor devils didn't have even the faintest shadow of a chance. Nevertheless he did it.

When he had first invaded the stronghold of the Wheelmen of Aldebaran I, he had acted almost without thought. If there was a chance of success, Lensmen went in. When he had scouted Jarnevon he had thought but little more. True—and fortunately—he took Worsel along; but he did not stop to consider whether or not there were minds in the Patrol better fitted to cope with the problem than was his own. It was his problem, he figured, and it was up to him to solve it.

Now, however, he knew bitterly that he could no longer act in that comparatively thoughtless fashion. At whatever loss of self-esteem, of personal stature, or of standing, he had to revise the Tellurian Lensmen's Code. It griped him to admit it, but Nadreck was right. It was not enough to give his life in an attempt to conquer a half-way station; he must remain alive in order to follow through to completion the job which was so uniquely his. He must *think*, assaying and evaluating every factor of his entire task. Then, without considering his own personal feelings, he must employ whatever forces and methods were best fitted to do the work at the irreducible minimum of cost and of risk.

Thus Kinnison sat unharmed upon the throne of the Tyrant of Thrale, and thus the prime minister returned to the palace to find the fact accomplished. That worthy studied with care every aspect of the situation before he sought an audience with the new potentate.

'Allow me to congratulate you, Tyrant Gannel,' he said, smoothly. 'I cannot say that I am surprised, since I have been watching you and your activities for some little time—with distinct approval, I may add. You have fulfilled—more than fulfilled, perhaps—my expectations. Your regime is functioning superbly; you have established in this very short time a smoothness of operation and an esprit de corps which are decidedly unusual. There are however, certain matters about which it is possible that you are not completely informed.'

'It is possible,' Kinnison agreed, with the merest trace of

irony. 'Such as?'

'In good time. You know, do you not, who is the real authority here upon Thrale?'

'I know who was,' the Tellurian corrected, with the faintest perceptible accent upon the final verb. 'In part only, however, for if you had concerned yourself wholly, the late Alcon would not have made so many nor so serious mistakes.'

'I thank you. You know, of course, the reason for that. I want the Tyrant of Thrale to be the strongest man of Thrale, and I may say without flattery that I believe he now is. And I would suggest that you add 'sire' when you speak to me.'

'I thank you in turn. I will so address you when you call me 'Your Supremacy'—not sooner.'

'We will let it pass for the moment. To come to your question, you apparently do not know that the Tyrant of Thrale, whoever he may be, opens his mind to me.'

'I have never suspected that such a condition has existed in the past. However, please be informed that I trust fully only those who fully trust me; and that thus far in my short life such persons have been few. You will observe that I am still respecting your privacy in that I am allowing your control of my sense of sight to continue. It is not because I trust you, but because your true appearance is to me a matter of complete indifference. For, frankly, I do not trust you at all. I will open my mind to you just exactly as wide as you will open yours to me—no wider.'

'Ah . . . the bravery of ignorance. It is as I thought. You do not realize, Gannel, that I can slay you at any moment I choose, or that a very few more words of defiance from you will be enough.' Fossten did not raise his voice, but his tone was instinct with menace.

'I do not, and neither do you, as I remarked to the then Tyrant Alcon in this very room not long ago. I am sure that you will understand without elaboration the connotations and implications inherent in that remark.' Kinnison's voice also was low and level, freighted in its every clipped syllable with the calm assurance of power. 'Would you be interested in knowing why I am so certain that you will not accept my suggestion of a mutual opening of minds?'

'Very much so.'

'Because I suspect that you are, or are in league with, Star A Star of the Galactic Patrol.' Even at that astounding charge Fossten gave no sign of surprise or of shock. 'I have not been able as yet to obtain any evidence supporting that belief, but I tell you now that when I do so, you die. Not by power of thought, either, but in the beam of my personal ray-gun.'

'Ah—you interest me strangely,' and the premier's hand strayed almost imperceptibly toward an inconspicuous button.

'Don't touch that switch!' Kinnison snapped. He did not quite see why Fossten was letting him see the maneuver, but he would bite, anyway.

'Why not, may I ask? It is merely a . . .'

'I know what it is, and I do not like thought-screens. I prefer that my mind be left free to roam.'

Fossten's thoughts raced in turn. Since the Tyrant was on guard, this was inconclusive. It might—or might not—indicate that Gannel was controlled by or in communication with Star A Star.

'Do not be childish,' he chided. 'You know as well as I do that your accusations are absurd. However, as I reconsider the matter, the fact that neither of us trusts unreservedly the other may not after all be an insuperable obstacle to our working together for the good of Boskonia. I think now more than ever that yours is the strongest Thralian mind, and as such the logical one to wield the Tyrant's power. It would be a shame to destroy you unnecessarily, especially in view of the probability that you will come later of your own accord to see the reasonableness of that which I have suggested.'

'It is possible,' Kinnison admitted, 'but not, I would say, probable.' He thought that he knew why the lug had pulled in his horns, but he wasn't sure. 'Now that we have clarified our attitudes toward each other, have decided upon an armed and suspicious truce, I see nothing to prevent us from working together in a completely harmonious mutual distrust for the good of all. The first thing to do, as I see it, is to devote our every effort to the destruction of the planet Klovia and all the Patrol forces based upon it.'

'Right.' If Fossten suspected that the Tyrant was somewhat less than frank he did not show it, and the conversation became strictly technical.

'We must not strike until we are completely ready,' was Kinnison's first statement, and he repeated it so often thereafter during the numerous conferences with the chiefs of staff that it came almost to be a slogan.

The prime minister did not know that Kinnison's main purpose was to give the Patrol plenty of time to make Klovia utterly impregnable. Fossten could know nothing of the Patrol's sunbeam to which even the mightiest fortress possible for a man to build could offer scarcely more resistance than could the lightest, the most fragile pleasure yacht.

Hence he grew more and more puzzled, more and more at a loss week by week, as Tyrant Gannel kept on insisting upon building up the strongest, the most logically perfect fleet which all the ability of their pooled brains could devise. Once or twice he offered criticisms and suggestions which while defensible according to one theory, would actually have weakened their striking power. These offerings Gannel rejected flatly; insisting, even to an out-and-out break with his co-administrator if necessary, upon the strongest possible armada.

The Tyrant wanted, and declared that he must and would have, more and bigger of everything. More and heavier flying fortresses, more and stronger battleships and super-dreadnoughts, more and faster cruisers and scouts, more and deadlier weapons.

'We want more of everything than our operations officers can possible handle in battle,' he declared over and over and he got them. Then:

'Now, you operations officers, learn how to handle them!' he commanded.

Even the prime minister protested at that, but it was finally accomplished. Fossten was a real thinker. So, in a smaller way, was Kinnison, and between them they worked out a system. It was crudeness and inefficiency incarnate in comparison with the *Z9M9Z*, but it was so much better than anything previously known to the Boskonians that everyone was delighted. Even the suspicious and cynical Fossten began to entertain some doubts as to the infallibility of his own judgment. Tyrant Gannel might be working under his own power, after all.

And these doubts grew apace as the Tyrant drilled his Grand Fleet. He drove the personnel unmercifully, especially the operations officers; as relentlessly as he drove himself. He simply could not be satisfied, his ardor and lust for efficiency were insatiable. His reprimands were scathingly accurate; officer after officer he demoted bitingly during ever more complicated, ever more inhumanly difficult maneuvers; until finally he had what were unquestionably his best men in those supremely important positions. Then, one day:

'QX, Kim, come ahead—we're ready,' Haynes Lensed him, briefly.

For Kinnison had been in touch with the Port Admiral every day. He had learned long since that the prime minister could not detect a Lensed thought, particularly when the Lensman was wearing a thought-screen, as he did practically constantly; wherefore the strategists of the Patrol were as well informed as was Kinnison himself of every move made by the Boskonians.

Then Kinnison called Fossten, and was staring glumly at nothing when the latter entered the room.

'Well, it would seem that we're about as nearly ready as we ever will be,' the Tyrant brooded, pessimistically. 'Have you any suggestions, criticisms, or other contributions to offer, of however minor a nature?'

'None whatever. You have done very well indeed.'

'Unnhh,' Gannel grunted, without enthusiasm. 'You have observed, no doubt, that I have said little if anything as to the actual method of approach?'

The prime minister had indeed noticed that peculiar oversight, and said so. Here, undoubtedly, he thought, was the rub. Here was where Star A Star's minion would get in his dirty work.

'I have thought about it at length,' Kinnison said, still in his brown study. 'But I know enough to recognize and to admit my own limitations. I do know tactics and strategy, and thus far I have worked with known implements toward known objectives. That condition, however, no longer exists. The simple fact is that I do not know enough about the possibilities, the techniques and the potentialities, the advantages and the disadvantages of the hyper-spatial tube as an avenue of approach to enable me to come to a defensible decision one way or the other. I have decided, therefore, that if you have any preference in the matter I will give you full authority and let you handle the approach in any manner you please. I shall of course direct the actual battle, as in that I shall again be upon familiar ground.'

The premier was flabbergasted. This was incredible. Gannel must really be working for Boskonia after all, to make such a decision as that. Still skeptical, unprepared for such a startling development as that one was, he temporized.

'The bad—the *very* bad features of the approach via tube are two,' he pondered aloud. 'We have no means of knowing anything about what happens; and since our previous such venture was a total failure, we must assume that, contrary to our plans and expectations, the enemy was not taken by surprise.'

'Right,' Kinnison concurred, tonelessly.

'Upon the other hand, an approach via open space, while conducive to the preservation of our two lives, would be seen from afar and would certainly be met by an appropriate formation.'

'Check,' came emotionlessly non-committal agreement.

'Haven't you the slightest bias, one way or the other?' Fossten demanded, incredulously.

'None whatever,' the Tyrant was coldly matter-of-fact. 'If I had had any such, I would have ordered the approach made in the fashion I preferred. Having none, I delegated authority to you. When I delegate authority I do so without reservations.'

This was a stopper.

'Let it be open space, then,' the prime minister finally decided.

'So be it.' And so it was.

Each of the component flotillas of Grand Fleet made a flying trip to some nearby base, where each unit was serviced. Every item of mechanism and of equipment was checked and rechecked. Stores were replenished, and munitions—especially munitions. Then the mighty armada, the most frightfully powerful aggregation ever to fly for Boskonia—the mightiest fleet ever assembled anywhere, according to the speeches of the politicians—remade its stupendous formation and set out for Klovia. And as it flew through space, shortly before contact was made with the Patrol's Grand Fleet, the premier called Kinnison into the control room.

'Gannel, I simply can not make you out,' he remarked, after studying him fixedly for five minutes. 'You have offered no advice. You have not interfered with my handling of the Fleet in any way. Nevertheless, I still suspect you of treacherous intentions. I have been suspicious of you from the first . . .'

'With no grounds whatever for your suspicions,' Kinnison reminded him, coldly.

'What? With all the reason possible!' Fossten declared. 'Have you not steadily refused to bare your mind to me?'

'Certainly. Why not? Do we have to go over that again? Just how do you figure that I should so trust any being who refuses to reveal even his true shape to me?'

'That is for your own good. I have not wanted to tell you this, but the truth is that no human being can perceive my true self and retain his sanity.'

Fossten's Eddorian mind flashed. Should he reveal this form of flesh, which was real enough, as Tellurians understood reality? Impossible. Star-A-Star-Gannel was no more Tellurian than Fossten was Thralian. He would not be satisfied with perceiving the flesh; he would bore in for the mind.

'I'll take a chance on that,' Kinnison replied skeptically. 'I've seen a lot of monstrous entities in my time and I haven't conked out yet.'

'There speaks the sheer folly of callow youth; the rashness of an ignorance so abysmal as to be possible only to one of your ephemeral race.' The voice deepened, became more resonant. Kinnison, staring into those inscrutable eyes which he knew did not in fact exist, thrilled forebodingly; the timbre and the overtones of that voice reminded him very disquietingly of something which he could not at the moment recall to mind. 'I forbear to discipline you, not from any doubt as to my ability to do so, as you suppose, but because of the sure knowledge that breaking you by force will destroy your usefulness. On the other hand, it is certain that if you cooperate with me willingly you will be the strongest, ablest leader that Boskonia has ever had. Think well upon these matters, O Tyrant.'

'I will,' the Lensman agreed, more seriously than he had intended. 'But just what, if anything, has led you to believe that I am not working to the fullest and best of my ability for Boskonia?'

'Everything,' Fossten summarized. 'I have been able to find no flaws in your actions, but those actions do not fit in with your unexplained and apparently unexplainable reticence in letting me perceive for myself exactly what is in your mind. Furthermore, you have never even troubled to deny accusations that you are in fact playing a far deeper game than you appear upon the surface to be playing.'

'That reticence I have explained over and over as an overmastering repugnance—call it a phobia if you like,' Kinnison rejoined, wearily. 'I simply can't and won't. Since you cannot understand that, denials would have been entirely useless. Would you believe anything that I could possibly say—that I would swear by everything I hold sacred—whether it was that I am whole-heartedly loyal to Boskonia or that I am in fact Star A Star himself?'

'Probably not,' came the measured reply. 'No, certainly not. Men—especially men such as you, bent ruthlessly upon the acquisition of power—are liars . . . ah, could it, by any chance, be that the reason for your intractability is that you have the effrontery to entertain some insane idea of supplanting ME?'

Kinnison jumped mentally. That tore it—that was a flarelit tip-off. This man—this thing—being—entity—whatever he really was—instead of being just another Boskonian big shot, must be the clear quill—the real McCoy—BOSKONE HIMSELF! The end of the job might be right here! This was—*must* be—the real Brain for whom he had been searching so long; here within three feet of him sat the creature with whom he had been longing so fervently to come to grips!

'The reason is as I have said,' the Tellurian stated, quietly. 'I will attempt to make no secret, however, of a fact which you must already have deduced; that if and when it becomes apparent that you have any authority above or beyond that of the Tyrant of Trale I shall take it away from you. Why not? Now that I have come so far, why should I not aspire to sit in the highest seat of all?'

Hrrummphhh!' the monster—Kinnison could no longer think of him as Fossten, or as the prime minister, or as any thing even remotely human—snorted with such utter, such searing contempt that even the Lensman's burly spirit quailed. 'As well might you attempt to pit your vaunted physical strength against the momentum of an inert planet. Now, youth, have done. The time for temporizing is past. As I have said, I desire to spare you, as I wish you to rule this part of Boskonia as my viceroy. Know, however, that you are in no sense essential, and that if you do not yield your mind fully to mine, here and now, before this coming battle is joined, you most certainly die.' At the grim finality, the calm assured certainty of the pronouncement, a quick chill struck into the Gray Lensman's vitals.

This thing who called himself Fossten ... who or what was he? What was it that he reminded him of? He thought and talked like ... like ... MENTOR! But it *couldn't* be an Arisian, possibly—that wouldn't make sense... But then, it didn't make any kind of sense, anyway, any way you looked at it... Whoever he was, he had plenty of jets—jets enough to lift a freighter off of the north pole of Valeria ... and by the same token, his present line of talk didn't make sense, either—there must be some good reason why he hadn't made a real pass at him long before this, instead of arguing with him so patiently—what could it be? ... Oh, that was it, of course... He needed only a few minutes more, now; he could probably stall off the final show-down that long by crawling a bit—much as it griped him to let this zwilnik think that he was licking his boots...

'Your forebearance is appreciated, sire.' At the apparently unconscious tribute to superiority and at the fact that the hitherto completely self-possessed Tyrant got up and began to pace nervously up and down the control room, the prime minister's austere mien softened appreciably. 'It is, however, a little strange. It is not quite in character; it does not check quite satisfactorily with the facts thus far revealed. I may, perhaps, as you say, be stupid. I may be overestimating flagrantly my own abilities. To one of my temperament, however, to surrender in such a craven fashion as you demand comes hard—extremely, almost unbearably hard. It would be easier, I think, if Your Supremacy would condescend to reveal his true identity, thereby making plainly evident and manifest that which at present must be left to unsupported words, surmise, and not too much conviction.'

'But I told you, and now tell you again, that for you to look upon my real form is to lose your reason!' the creature rasped.

'What do you care whether or not I remain sane?' Kinnison shot his bolt at last, in what he hoped would be taken for a last resurgence of spirit. His time was about up. In less than one minute now the screens of scout cruisers would be in engagement, and either he or the prime minister or both would be expected to be devoting every cell of their brains to the all-important battle of giants. And in that very nick of time he would have to cripple the Bergenholms and thus inert the flagship. 'Could it be that the real reason for your otherwise inexplicable forbearance is that you must know how my mind became as it now is, and that the breaking down of my barriers by mental force will destroy the knowledge which you, for your own security, must have?'

This was the blow-off. Kinnison still paced the room, but his pacing took him nearer and even nearer to a certain control panel. Behind his thought-screen, which he could not now trust, he mustered every iota of his tremendous force of mind and of will. Only seconds now. His left hand, thrust into his breeches pocket, grasped the cigarette case within which reposed his Lens. His right arm and hand were tensely ready to draw and to fire his weapon.

'Die, then! I should have known from the sheer perfection of your work that you were what you really are—Star A Star!'

The mental blast came ahead even of the first word, but the Gray Lensman, supremely ready, was already in action. One quick thrust of his chin flicked off the thought-screen. The shielded cigarette-case flew open, his more-than-half-alive Lens blazed again upon his massive wrist. His blaster leaped out of its scabbard, flaming destruction as it came—a ravening tongue of incandescent fury which licked out of existence in the twinking of an eye the Bergenholms' control panels and the operators clustered before it. The vessel went inert—much work would have to be done before the Boskonian flagship could again fly free!

These matters required only a fraction of a second. Well indeed it was that they did not take longer, for the ever-mounting fury of the prime minister's attack soon necessitated more—much more—than an automatic block, however capable. But Kimball Kinnison, Gray Lensman, Lensman of Lensmen had more—ever so much more—than that!

He whirled, lips thinned over tight-set teeth in a savage fighting grin. Now he'd see what this zwilnik was and what he had. No fear, no doubt of the outcome, entered his mind. He had suffered such punishment as few minds have ever endured in learning to ward off everything that Mentor, one of the mightiest intellects of this or of any other universe, could send; but through that suffering he had learned. This unknown entity was an able operator, of course, but he certainly had a thick, hard crust to think that he could rub *him* out!

So thinking, the Lensman hurled a bolt of his own, a blast of power sufficient to have slain a dozen men—and, amazedly, saw it rebound harmlessly from the premier's hard-held block.

Which of the two combatants was the more surprised it would be hard to say; each had considered his own mind impregnable and invincible. Now, as the prime minister perceived how astoundingly capable a foe he faced, he drove a thought toward Eddore and the All-Highest.

Blocked!

Star A Star and the Arisian, then, were not two, but one!

He ordered the officers on duty to blast their Tyrant down. In vain. For, even so early in that ultimately lethal struggle, he could not spare enough of his mind to control effectively any outsider; and in a matter of seconds there were no minds left throughout that entire room in any condition to be controlled.

For the first reverberations, the ricochets, the spent forces of the monster's attack against Kinnison's shield had wrought grievously among the mentalities of all bystanders. Those forces were deadly—deadly beyond telling—so inimical to and destructive of intelligence that even their transformation products affected tremendously the nervous systems of all within range.

Then, instants later, the spectacle of the detested and searing feared Lens scintillating balefully upon the wrist of their own ruler was an utterly inexpressible shock. Some of the officers tried then to go for their blasters, but it was already too late; their shaking, trembling, almost paralyzed muscles could not be forced to function.

An even worse shock followed almost instantly, for the prime minister, under the incredibly mounting intensity of the Lensman's poignant thrust, found it necessary to concentrate his every iota of power upon his opponent. Fossten's form of flesh dissolved, revealing to all beholders except Kinnison what their prime minister actually was—and he had not been very much wrong in saying that that sight would drive any human being mad. Most of the Boskonians did go mad, then and there; but they did not rush about nor scream. They could not move purposefully, but only twitched and writhed horribly as they lay grotesquely a-sprawl. They could not scream or shriek, but only mouthed and mumbled meaningless burblings.

And ever higher, ever more brilliant flamed the Lens as Kinnison threw all of his prodigious will-power, all of his tremendous, indomitable drive, through it and against the incredibly resistant thing to which he was opposed. This was the supreme, the climactic battle of his life thus far. Ether and sub-ether seethed and boiled invisibly under the frightful violence of the forces there unleashed. The men in the control room lay still; all life rived away. Now death spread throughout the confines of the vast space-ship.

Indomitably, relentlessly, the Gray Lensman held his offense upon that unimaginably high level; his lens flooding the room with intensely coruscant polychromatic light. He did not know, then or ever, how he did it. He never did suspect that he was not alone. It seemed as though his Lens, of its own volition in this time of ultimate need, reached out into unguessable continua and drew therefrom an added, an extra something. But, however it was done, Kinnison and his Lens managed to hold; and under the appalling, the never-ceasing concentration of force the monster's defenses began gradually to weaken and go down.

Then sketchily, patchily, there was revealed to Kinnison's sight and sense of perception—a—a—a—a BRAIN!

There was a body, of sorts, of course—a peculiarly neckless body designed solely to support that gigantic, thin-skulled head. There were certain appendages of limbs, and such-like appurtenances and incidentalia to nourishment, locomotion, and the like; but to all intents and purposes the thing was simply and solely a brain.

Kinnison knew starkly that it was an Arisian—it looked enough like old Mentor to be his twin brother. He would have been stunned, except for the fact that he was far too intent upon victory to let any circumstance, however distracting, affect his purpose. His concentration upon the task in hand was so complete that nothing—literally nothing whatever—could sway him from it.

Step by short, hard, jerky step, Kinnison advanced. Close enough, he selected certain areas upon the sides of that enormous head and with big, hard, open hands he went viciously to work. Right, left, right, left, he slapped those bulging temples brutally, rocking monstrous head and repulsive body from side to side, pendulum-like, with every stunning blow.

His fist would have smashed that thin skull, would perhaps have buried itself deep within the soft tissues of that tremendous brain; and Kinnison did not want to kill his inexplicable opponent—yet. He had to find out first what this was all about.

He knew that he was due to black out soon as he let go, and he intended to addle the thing's senses so thoroughly that he would be completely out of action for hours—long enough to give the Lensman plenty of time in which to recover his strength.

He did so.

Kinnison did not quite faint. He did, however, have to lie down flat upon the floor; as limp, almost, as the dead men so thickly strewn about.

And thus, while the two immense Grand Fleets met in battle, Boskonia's flagship hung inert and silent in space afar; manned by fifteen hundred corpses, one unconscious Brain, and one utterly exhausted Gray Lensman.

21: The Battle of Klovia

Boskonia's Grand Fleet was, as has been said, enormous. It was not as large as that of the Patrol in total number of ships, since no ordinary brain nor any possible combination of such brains could have coordinated and directed the activities of so vast a number of units. Its center was, however, heavier; composed of a number and a tonnage of super-maulers which made it self-evidently irresistible.

In his training of his operations staff Kinnison had not overlooked a single bet, had not made a single move which by its falsity might have excited Premier Fossten's all-too-ready suspicions. They had handled Grand Fleet as a whole in vast, slow maneuvers; plainly the only kind possible to so tremendous a force. Kinnison and his officers had in turn harshly and thoroughly instructed the sub-fleet commanders in the various arts and maneuvers of conquering units equal to or smaller than their own.

That was all; and to the Boskonians, even to Fossten, that had been enough. That was obviously all that was possible. Not one of them realized that Tyrant Gannel very carefully avoided any suggestion that there might be any intermediate tactics, such as that of three or four hundred sub-fleets, too widely spread in space and too numerous to be handled by any ordinary mind or apparatus, to englobe and to wipe out simultaneously perhaps fifty sub-fleets whose commanders were not even in communication with each other. This technique was as yet the exclusive property of the Patrol and the *Z9M9Z*.

And in that exact operation, a closed book to the zwilniks, lay—supposedly and tactically—the Patrol's overwhelming advantage. For Haynes, through his four highly-specialized Rigellian Lensmen and thence through the two hundred Rigellian operator-computers, could perform maneuvers upon any intermediate scale he pleased. He could handle his whole vast Grand Fleet and its every component part—he supposed—as effectively, as rapidly, and almost as easily as a skilled chess player handles his pieces and his pawns. Neither Kinnison nor Haynes can be blamed, however, for the fact that their suppositions were somewhat in error; it would have taken an Arisian to deduce that this battle was not to be fought exactly as they had planned it.

Haynes had another enormous advantage in knowing the exact number, rating, disposition, course, and velocity of every main unit of the aggregation to which he was opposed. And third, he had the sunbeam, concerning which the enemy knew nothing at all and which was now in good working order.

It is needless to say that the sunbeam generators were already set to hurl that shaft of irresistible destruction along the precisely correct line, or that Haynes' Grand Fleet formation had been made with that particular weapon in mind. It was not an orthodox formation; in any ordinary space-battle it would have been sheerly suicidal. But the Port Admiral, knowing for the first time in his career every pertinent fact concerning his foe, knew exactly what he was doing.

His fleet, instead of driving ahead to meet the enemy, remaining inert and practically motionless well within the limits of Klovia's solar system. His heavy stuff, instead of being massed at the center, was arranged in a vast ring. There was no center except for a concealing screen of heavy cruisers.

When the far-flung screens of scout cruisers came into engagement, then, the Patrol scouts near the central line did not fight, but sped lightly aside. So did the light and heavy cruisers and the battleships. The whole vast center of the Boskonians drove onward, unopposed, into—nothing.

Nevertheless, they kept on driving. They could, without orders, do nothing else, and no orders were forthcoming from the flagship. Commanders tried to get in touch with Grand Fleet Operations, but could not; and, in failing, kept on under their original instructions. They had, they could have, no suspicion that any minion of the Patrol was back of what had happened to their top brass. The flagship had been in the safest possible position and no attack had as yet been made. They probably wondered futilely as to what kind of a mechanical breakdown could have immobilized and completely silenced their High Command, but that was—strictly—none of their business. They had had orders, very definite orders, that no matter what happened they were to go on to Klovia and to destroy it. Thus, however wondering, they kept on. They were on the line. They would hold it. They would blast out of existence anything and everything which might attempt to bar their way. They would reach Klovia and they would reduce it to component atoms.

Unresisted, then, the Boskonian center bored ahead into nothing, until Haynes, through his Rigellians, perceived that it had come far enough. Then Klovia's brilliantly shining sun darkened almost to the point of extinction. Along the line of centers, through the space so peculiarly empty of Patrol ships, there came into being the sunbeam—a bar of quasi-solid lightning into which there had been compressed all the energy of well over four million tons *per second* of disintegrating matter.

Scouts and cruisers caught in that ravening beam flashed briefly, like sparks flying from a forge, and vanished. Battleships and super-dreadnoughts the same. Even the solid warhead of fortresses and maulers were utterly helpless. No screen has ever been designed capable of handling that hellish load; no possible or conceivable substance can withstand save momentarily the ardor of a sunbeam. For the energy liberated by the total annihilation of four million tons per second of matter is in fact as irresistible as it is incomprehensible.

The armed and armored planets did not disappear. They contained too much sheer mass for even that inconceivably powerful beam to volatilize in any small number of seconds. Their surfaces, however, melted and boiled. The controlling and powering mechanisms fused into useless pools of molten metal. Inert, then, inactive and powerless, they no longer constituted threats to Klovia's well-being.

The negaspheres also were rendered ineffective by the beam. Their anti-masses were not decreased, of course—in fact, they were probably increased a trifle by the fervor of the treatment—but, with the controlling superstructures volatilized away, they became more of menace to the Boskonian forces than to those of Civilization. Indeed, several of the terrible things were drawn into contact with ruined planets. Then negasphere and planet consumed each other, flooding all nearby space with intensely hard and horribly lethal radiation.

The beam winked out; Klovia's sun flashed on. The sunbeam was—and is—clumsy, unwieldly, quite definitely not rapidly maneuverable. But it had done its work; now the component parts of Civilization's Grand Fleet started in to do theirs.

Since the Battle of Klovia—it was and still is called that, as though it were the only battle which that warlike planet has ever seen—has been fought over in the classrooms of practically every civilized planet of two galaxies, it would be redundant to discuss it in detail here.

It was, of course, unique. No other battle like it has ever been fought, either before or since—and let us hope that no other ever will be. It is studied by strategists, who have offered many thousands of widely variant profundities as to what Port Admiral Haynes should have done. Its profound emotional appeal, however, lies only and sheerly in its unorthodoxy. For in the technically proper space battle there is no hand-to-hand fighting, no purely personal heroism, no individual deeds of valor. It is a thing of logic and of mathematics and of science, the massing of superior fire-power against a well-chosen succession of weaker opponents. When the screens of a space-ship go down that ship is down, her personnel only memories.

But here how different! With the supposed breakdown of the lines of communication to the flagship, the sub-fleets carried on in formation. With the destruction of the entire center, however, all semblance of organization or of cooperation was lost. Every staff officer knew that no more orders would emanate from the flagship. Each knew chillingly that there could be neither escape nor succor. The captain of each vessel, thoroughly convinced that he knew vastly more than did his fleet commander, proceeded to run the war to suit himself. The outcome was fantastic, so utterly bizarre that the *Z9M9Z* and her trained coordinating officers were useless. Science and tactics and the million lines of communication could do nothing against a foe who insisted upon making it a ship-to-ship, yes, a man-to-man affair!

The result was the most gigantic dog-fight in the annals of military science. Ships—Civilization's perhaps as eagerly as Boskonia's—cut off their projectors, cut off their screens, the better to ram, to board, to come to grips personally with the enemy. Scout to scout, cruiser to cruiser, battleship to battleship, the insane contagion spread. Haynes and his staff men swore fulminantly, the Rigellians hurled out orders, but those orders simply could not be obeyed. The dog-fight spread until it filled a good sixth of Klovia's entire solar system.

Board and storm! Armor—DeLameters—axes! The mad blood-lust of hand-to-hand combat, the insensately horrible savagery of our pirate forbears, multiplied by millions and spread out to fill a million million cubic miles of space!

Haynes and his fellows wept unashamed as they stood by helpless, unable to avoid or to prevent the slaughter of so many splendid men, the gutting of so many magnificent ships. It was ghastly—it was appalling—it was WAR!

And far from this scene of turmoil and of butchery lay Boskonia's great flagship, and in her control room Kinnison began to recover. He sat up groggily. He gave his throbbing head a couple of tentative shakes. Nothing rattled. Good—he was QX, he guessed, even if he did feel as limp as nine wet dishrags. Even his Lens felt weak; its usually refulgent radiance was sluggish, wan, and dim. This had taken plenty out of them, he reflected soberly; but he was mighty lucky to be alive. But he'd better get his batteries charged. He couldn't drive a thought across the room, the shape he was in now, and he knew of only one brain in the universe capable of straightening out *this* mess.

After assuring himself that the highly inimical brain would not be able to function normally for a long time to come, the Lensman made his way to the gallery. He could walk without staggering already—fine! There he fried himself a big, thick, rare steak—his never-failing remedy for all the ills to which flesh is heir—and brewed a pot of Thralian coffee; making it viciously, almost corrosively strong. And as he ate and drank his head cleared magically. Strength flowed back into him in waves. His Lens flamed into its normal splendor. He stretched prodigiously; inhaled gratefully a few deep breaths. He was QX.

Back in the control room, after again checking up on the still quiescent brain—he wouldn't trust this Fossten as far as he could spit—he hurled a thought to far-distant Arisia and to Mentor, its ancient sage.

'What's an Arisian doing in this Second Galaxy, working *against* the Patrol? Just what is somebody trying to pull off?' he demanded heatedly, and in a second of flashing thought reported what had happened.

'Truly, Kinnison of Tellus, my mind is not entirely capable,' the deeply reasonant, slow simulacrum of a voice resounded within the Lensman's brain. The Arisian never hurried; nothing whatever, apparently, not even such a cataclysmic upheaval as this, could fluster or excite him. 'It does not seem to be in accord with the visualization of the Cosmic All which I hold at the moment that any one of my fellows is in fact either in the Second Galaxy or acting antagonistically to the Galactic Patrol. It is, however, a truism that hypotheses, theories, and visualizations must fit themselves to known or observed facts, and even your immature mind is eminently able to report truly upon actualities. But before I attempt to revise my visualization to conform to this admittedly peculiar circumstance, we must be very sure indeed of our facts. Are you certain, youth, that the being whom you have beaten into unconsciousness is actually an Arisian?'

'Certainly I'm certain!' Kinnison snapped. 'Why, he's enough like you to have been hatched out of half of the same egg. Take a look!' and he knew that the Arisian was studying every external and internal detail, part, and organ of the erstwhile Fossten of Thrale.

'Ah, it would appear to be an Arisian, at that, youth,' Mentor finally agreed. 'He appears to be old, as you said—as old, perhaps, as I am. Since I have been of the opinion that I am acquainted with every member of my race this will require some little thought—allow me therefore, please, a moment of time.' The Arisian fell silent, presently to resume:

'I have it now. Many millions of years ago—so long ago that it was with some little difficulty that I recalled it to mind—when I was scarcely more than an infant, a youth but little older than myself disappeared from Arisia It was determined then that he was aberrant—insane—and since only an unusually capable mind can predict truly the illogical workings of a diseased and disordered mind for even one year in advance, it is not surprising that in my visualization that unbalanced youth perished long ago. Nor is it surprising that I do not recognize him in the creature before you.'

'Well, aren't you surprised that I could get the best of him?' Kinnison asked, naively. He had really expected that Mentor would compliment him upon his prowess, he figured that he had earned a few pats on the back; but here the old fellow was mooning about his own mind and his own philosophy, and acting as though knocking off an Arisian were something to be taken in stride. And it wasn't, by half!

'No,' came the flatly definite reply. 'You have a force of will, a totalizable and concentrable power, a mental and psychological drive whose capabilities you do not and cannot fully appreciate. I perceived those latent capabilities when I assembled your Lens, and developed them when I developed you. It was their presence which made it certain that you would return here for that development; they made you what you intrinsically are.'

'QX then—skip it. What shall I do with him? It's going to be a real job of work, any way you figure it, for us to keep him alive and harmless until we get him back there to Arisia.'

'We do not want him here,' Mentor replied without emotion. 'He has no present or future place within our society. Nor, however I consider the matter, can I perceive that he has any longer a permissible or condonable place in the all-inclusive

Scheme of Things. He has served his purpose. Destroy him, therefore, forthwith, before he recovers consciousness; lest much and grievous harm befall you.'

'I believe you, Mentor. You said something then, if anybody ever did. Thanks,' and communication ceased.

The Lensman's ray-gun flamed briefly and whatever it was that lay there became a smoking, shapeless heap.

Kinnison noticed then that a call-light was shining brightly upon a communicator panel. This thing must have taken longer than he had supposed. The battle must be over, otherwise all space would still be filled with interference through which no long-range communicator beam could have been driven. Or ... could Boskonia have ... no, that was unthinkable. The patrol *must* have won. This must be Haynes, calling him ...

It was. The frightful Battle of Klovia was over. While many of the Patrol ships had yielded, either by choice or by necessity, to the Boskonians' challenge, most of them had not, and the majority of those who did so yield, came out victorious.

While fighting in any kind of recognized formation against such myriads of independently-operating, wide-spaced individual ships was of course out of the question, Haynes and his aides had been able to work out a technique of sorts. General orders were sent out to sub-fleet commanders, who in turn relayed them to the individual captains by means of visual beams. Single vessels, then, locked to equal or inferior craft—avoiding carefully anything larger than themselves—with tractor zones and held grimly on. If they could defeat the foe, QX. If not, they hung on; until shortly one of the Patrol's maulers—who had no opposition of their own class to face—would come lumbering up. And when the dreadful primary batteries of one of *those* things cut loose that was, very conclusively, that.

Thus Boskonia's mighty fleet vanished from the skies.

The all-pervading interference was cut off and Port Admiral Haynes, not daring to use his Lens in what might be a critical instant, sat down at his board and punched a call. Time after time he punched it. Finally he shoved it in and left it in; and as he stared, minute after minute, into the coldly unresponsive plate his face grew gray and old.

Just before he decided to Lens Kinnison anyway, come what might, the plate lighted up to show the smiling, deeply space-tanned face of the one for whom he had just about given up hope.

'Thank God!' Haynes' exclamation was wholly reverent; his

strained old face lost twenty years in half that many seconds. 'Thank God you're safe. You did it, then?'

'I managed it, but just by the skin of my teeth—I didn't have half a jet to spare. It was Old Man Boskone himself, in person. And you?'

'Clean-up—one hundred point zero zero zero percent.'

'Fine business!' Kinnison exulted. 'Everything's on the exact center of the green, then—come on!'

And Civilization's Grand Fleet went.

The *Z9M9Z* flashed up to visibility, inerted, and with furious driving blasts full ablaze, matched her intrinsic velocity to that of the Boskonian flagship—the only Boskonian vessel remaining in that whole vast volume of space. Tractors and pressors were locked on and balanced. Flexible—or, more accurately, not ultimately rigid—connecting tubes were pushed out and sealed. Hundreds, yes thousands, of men—men in full Thralian uniform—strode through those tubes and into the Thralian ship. The *Z9M9Z* unhooked and a battleship took her place. Time after time the maneuver was repeated, until it seemed as though Kinnison's vessel, huge as she was, could not possibly carry the numbers of men who marched aboard.

Those men were all human or approximately so—nearly enough human, at least, to pass as Thralians under a casual inspection. More peculiarly, that army contained an astounding number of Lensmen. So many Lensmen, it is certain, had never before gathered together into so small a space. But the fact that they were Lensmen was not apparent; their Lenses were not upon their wrists, but were high upon their arms, concealed from even the most prying eyes within the sleeves of their tunics.

Then the captured flagship, her Bergenholms again at work, the *Z9M9Z*, and the battleships which had already assumed the intrinsic velocity possessed originally by the Boskonians, spread out widely in space. Each surrounded itself with a globe of intensely vivid red light. Orders as to course and power flashed out The word was given and spectacular fire flooded space as that vast host of ships, guided by those red beacons, matched in one prodigious and beautiful maneuver its intrinsic velocity to theirs.

Finally, all the intrinsics in exact agreement, Grand Fleet formation was remade. The term 'remade' is used advisedly, since this was not to be a battle formation. For Traska Gannel had long since sent a message to his capital; a terse and truthful message which was, nevertheless, utterly misleading. It was:

'My forces have won, my enemy has been wiped out to the last man. Prepare for a two-world broadcast, to cover both Thrale and Onlo, at hour ten today of my palace time.'

The formation, then, was not one of warfare, but of boasting triumph. It was the consciously proud formation of a Grand Fleet which, secure in the knowledge that it has blasted out of the ether everything which can threaten it, returns victoriously home to receive as its just due the plaudits and the acclaim of the populace.

Well in the van—alone in the van, in fact, and strutting—was the flagship. She, having originated upon Thrale and having been built specifically for a flagship, would be recognized at sight. Back of her came, in gigantic co-axial cones, the sub-fleets; arranged now not class by class of ships, but world by world of origin. One mauler, perhaps, or two; from four or five to a dozen or more battleships; an appropriate number of cruisers and of scouts; all flying along together in a tight little group.

But not all of the Patrol's armada was in that formation. It would have been very poor technique indeed to have had Boskonia's Grand Fleet come back to home ether forty percent larger than it had set out. Besides, the *Z9M9Z* simply could not be allowed to come within detector range of any Boskonian look-out. She was utterly unlike any other vessel ever to fly: she would not, perhaps, be recognized for what she really was, but it would be evident to the most casual observer that she was not and could not be of Thrale or Boskonia.

The *Z9M9Z*, then, hung back—far back—escorted and enveloped by the great number of warships which could not be made to fit into the roll-call of Tyrant's original Grand Fleet.

The sub-fleet which was originally from Thrale could land without arousing any suspicion. Boskonian and Patrol designs were not identical, of course; but the requirements of sound engineering dictated that externals should be essentially the same. The individual ships now bore the correct identifying symbols and insignia. The minor differences could not be perceived until after the vessels had actually landed, and that would be—for the Thralians—entirely too late.

Thralian hour ten arrived. Kinnison, after a long, minutely searching inspection of the entire room, became again in every millimeter Traska Gannel, the Tyrant of Thrale. He waved a hand. The scanner before him glowed: for a full minute he stared into it haughtily, to give his teeming millions of minions ample opportunity to gaze upon the inspiring countenance of His Supremacy the Feared.

He knew that the scanner revealed clearly every detail of the control room behind him, but everything there was QX. There wasn't a chance that some person would fail to recognize a familiar face at any post, for not a single face except his own would be visible. Not a head back of him would turn, not even a rear-quarter profile would show: it would be *lese majeste* of the most intolerable for any face, however inconspicuous, to share the lime-light with that of the Tyrant of Thrale which His Supremacy was addressing his subjects. Serenely and assuredly enough, then. Tyrant Gannel spoke:

'MY people! As you have already been told, my forces have won the complete victory which my foresight and my leadership made inevitable. This milestone of progress is merely a repetition upon a grander scale of those which I have already accomplished upon a somewhat smaller; an extension and a continuation of the carefully considered procedure by virtue of which I shall see to it that My Plan succeeds.

'As one item in that scheduled procedure I removed the weakling Alcon, and in the stead of his rule of oppression, shortsightedness, corruption, favoritism, and greed, I substituted my beneficient regime of fair play, of mutual cooperation for the good of all.

'I have now accomplished the next major step in my program; the complete destruction of the armed forces which might be, which would be employed to hamper and to nullify the development and the fruition of My Plan.

'I shall take the next step immediately upon my return to my palace. There is no need to inform you now as to the details of what I have in mind. In broad, however, it pleases me to inform you that, having crushed all opposition, I am now able to institute and shall proceed at once to institute certain changes in policy, in administration, and in jurisdiction. I assure you that all of these changes will be for the best good of all save the enemies of society.

'I caution you therefore to cooperate fully and willingly with my officers who may shortly come among you with instructions; some of these, perhaps, of a nature not hitherto promulgated upon Thrale. Those of you who do so cooperate will live and will prosper; those who do not will die in the slowest, most hideous fashions which all the generations of Thralian torturers have been able to devise.'

22: The Taking of Thrale

Up to the present, Kinnison's revolution, his self-advancement into the dictatorship, had been perfectly normal; in perfect accordance with the best tenets of Boskonian etiquette. While it would be idle to contend that any of the others of the High Command really approved of it—each wanted intensely that high place for himself—none of them had been strong enough at the moment to challenge the Tyrant effectively and all of them knew that an ineffective challenge would mean certain death. Wherefore each perforce bided his time; Gannel would slip, Gannel would become lax or over-confident—and that would be the end of Gannel.

They were, however, loyal to Boskonia. They were very much in favor of the rule of the strong and the ruthless. They believed implicitly that might made right. They themselves bowed the knee to anyone strong enough to command such servility from them; in turn they commanded brutally an even more abject servility from those over whom they held in practice, if not at law, the power of life and death.

Thus Kinnison knew that he could handle his cabinet easily enough as long as he could make them believe that he was a Boskonian. There was, there could be, no real unity among them under those conditions; each would be fighting his fellows as well as working to overthrow His Supremacy the Tyrant. But they all hated the Patrol and all that it stood for with a whole-hearted fervor which no one adherent to Civilization can really appreciate. Hence at the first sign that Gannel might be in league with the Patrol they would combine forces instantly against him; automatically there would go into effect a tacit agreement to kill him first and then, later, to fight it out among themselves for the prize of the Tyrancy.

And that combined opposition would be a formidable one indeed. Those men were really able. They were as clever and as shrewd and as smart and as subtle as they were hard. They were masters of intrigue; they simply could not be fooled. And if their united word went down the line that Traska Gannel was in fact a traitor to Boskonia, an upheaval would ensue which would throw into the shade the bloodiest revolutions of all history. Everything would be destroyed.

Nor could the Lensman hurl the metal of the Patrol against

Thrale in direct frontal attack. Not only was it immensely strong, but also there were those priceless records, without which it might very well be the work of generations for the Patrol to secure the information which it must, for its own security, have.

No. Kinnison, having started near the bottom and worked up, must now begin all over again at the top and work down; and he must be very, *very* sure that no alarm was given until at too late a time for the alarmed ones to do anything of harm to the Lensman's cause. He didn't know whether he had jets enough to swing the load or not—a lot depended on whether or not he could civilize those twelve devils of his—but the scheme that the psychologists had worked out was a honey and he would certainly give it the good old college try.

Thus Grand Fleet slowed down; and, with the flagship just out of range of the capital's terrific offensive weapons, it stopped. Half a dozen maulers, towing a blackly indetectable, imperceptible object, came up and stopped. The Tyrant called, from the safety of his control room, a conference of his cabinet in the council chamber.

'While I have not been gone very long in point of days,' he addressed them smoothly, via plate, 'and while I of course trust each and every one of you, there are certain matters which must be made clear before I land. None of you has, by any possible chance, made any effort to lay a trap for me, or anything of the kind?' There may have been a trace of irony in the speaker's voice.

They assured him, one and all, that they had not had the slightest idea of even considering such a thing.

'It is well. None of you have discovered, then, that by changing locks and combinations, and by destroying or removing certain inconspicuous but essential mechanisms of an extremely complicated nature—and perhaps substituting others—I made it quite definitely impossible for any one of all of you to render this planet inertialess. I have brought back with me a negasphere of planetary anti-mass, which no power at your disposal can effect. It is here beside me in space; please study it attentively. It should not be necessary for me to inform you that there are countless other planets from which I can rule Boskonia quite as effectively as from Thrale; or that, while I do not relish the idea of destroying my home planet and everything upon it, I would not hesitate to do so if it became a matter of choice between that action and the loss of my life and my position.'

They believed the statement. That was the eminently sensible thing to do. Any one of them would have done the same; hence they knew that Gannel would do exactly what he threatened—if he could. And as they studied Gannel's abysmally black ace of trumps they knew starkly that Gannel could. For they had found out, individually, that the Tyrant had so effectively sabotaged Thrale's Bergenholms that they could not possibly be made operative until after his return. Consequently repairs had not been started—any such activity, they knew, would be a fatal mistake.

By out-guessing and out-maneuvering the members of his cabinet Gannel had once more shown his fitness to rule. They accepted that fact with a good enough grace; indeed, they admired him all the more for the ability thus shown. No one of them had given himself away by any overt moves; they could wait. Gannel would slip yet—quite possibly even before he got back into his palace. So they thought, not knowing that the Tyrant could read at will their most deeply-hidden plans; and, so thinking, each one pledged anew in unreserved terms his fealty and his loyalty.

'I thank you, gentlemen.' The Tyrant did not, and the officers were pretty sure that he did not, believe a word of their protestations. 'As loyal cabinet members, I will give you the honor of sitting in the front of those who welcome me home. Your men and your guards will occupy the front boxes in the Royal Stand. With you and around you will be the entire palace personnel—I want no person except the usual guards inside the buildings or even within the grounds when I land. Back of these you will have arranged the Personal Troops and the Royal Guards. The remaining stands and all of the usual open grounds will be for the common people—first come, first served.

'But one word of caution. You may wear your side-arms, as usual. Bear in mind, however, that armor is neither usual nor a part of your full-dress uniform, and that any armored man or men in or near the concourse will be blasted by a needle-ray before I land. Be advised also that I myself shall be wearing full armor. Furthermore, no vessel of the fleet will land until I, personally, from my private sanctum, order them to do so.'

This situation was another poser; but it, too, they had to take. There was no way out of it, and it was still perfect Boskonian generalship. The welcoming arrangements were therefore made precisely as Tyrant Gannel had directed.

The flagship settled toward ground, her under-jets blasting

unusually viciously because of her tremendous load; and as she descended Kinnison glanced briefly down at the familiar terrain. There was the immense space-field, a dock-studded expanse of burned, scarred, pock-marked concrete and steel. Midway of its extreme northern end, that nearest the palace, was the berth of the flagship, Dock No. I. An eighth of a mile straight north from the dock—the minumum distance possible because of the terrific fury of the under-jets—was the entrance to the palace grounds. At the northern end of the western side of the field, a good three-quarters of a mile from Dock No. I and somewhat more than that distance from the palace gates, were the Stands of Ceremony. That made the Lensman completely the master of the situation.

The flagship landed. Her madly blasting jets died out. A car of state rolled grandly up. Airlocks opened. Kinnison and his bodyguards seated themselves in the car. Helicopters appeared above the stands and above the massed crowds thronging the western approaches to the field; hovering, flitting slowly and watchfully about.

Then from the flagship there emerged an incredible number of armed and armored soldiers. One small column of these marched behind the slowly-moving car of state, but by far the greater number went directly to and through the imposing portals of the palace grounds. The people in general, gathered there to see a major spectacle, thought nothing of these circumstances—who were they to wonder at what the Tyrant of Thrale might choose to do?—but to Gannel's Council of Advisers they were extremely disquieting departures from the norm. There was, however, nothing they could do about them, away out there in the grandstand; and they knew with a stark certainty what those helicopters had orders to do in case of any uprising or commotion anywhere in the crowd.

The car rolled slowly along before the fenced-back, wildly-cheering multitudes, with blaring bands and the columns of armored spacemen marching crisply, swingingly behind it. There was nothing to indicate that those selected men were not Thralians; nothing whatever to hint that over a thousand of them were in fact Lensmen of the Galactic Patrol. And Kinnison, standing stiffly erect in his car, acknowledged gravely, with upraised right arm, the plaudits of his subjects.

The triumphal bus stopped in front of the most out-thrust, the most ornate stand, and through loud-voiced amplifiers the Tyrant invited, as a signal honor, the twelve members of his

Advisory cabinet to ride with him in state to the palace. There were exactly twelve vacant seats in the great coach. The advisers would have to leave their bodyguards and ride alone with the Tyrant: even had there been room, it was unthinkable that any one else's personal killers could ride with the Presence. This was no honor, they knew chillingly, no matter what the mob might think--it looked much more like a death-sentence. But what could they do? They glanced at their unarmored henchmen; then at the armor and the semi-portables of Gannel's own heelers; then at the 'copters now clustering thickly overhead, with the narrow snouts of needle-ray projectors very much in evidence.

They accepted.

It was in no quiet frame of mind, then, that they rode into the pretentious grounds of the palace. They felt no better when, as they entered the council chamber, they were seized and disarmed without a word having been spoken. And the world fairly dropped out from beneath them when Tyrant Gannel emerged from his armor with a Lens glowing upon his wrist.

'Yes, I am a Lensman,' he gravely informed the stupefied but unshrinking Boskonians. 'That is why I know that all twelve of you tried while I was gone to cut me down, in spite of everything I told you and everything you have seen me do. If it were still necessary for me to pose as Traska Gannel I would have to kill you here and now for your treachery. That phase is, however, past.

'I am one of the Lensman whose collective activities you have ascribed to "the" Lensman or to Star A Star. All those others who came with me into the palace are Lensmen. All those outside are either Lensmen or tried and seasoned veterans of the Galactic Patrol. The fleet surrounding this world is the Grand Fleet of that Patrol. The Boskonian force was completely destroyed—every man and every ship except your flagship—before it reached Klovia. In short, the power of Boskonia is broken forever; Civilization is to rule henceforth throughout both galaxies.

'You are the twelve strongest, the twelve ablest men of the planet, perhaps of your whole dark culture. Will you help us to rule according to the principles of Civilization that which has been the Boskonian Empire or will you die?'

The Thralians stiffened themselves rigidly against the expected blasts of death, but only one spoke. 'We are fortunate at least, Lensman, in that you do not torture,' he said, coldly, his lips twisted into a hard, defiant sneer.

'Good!' and the Lensman actually smiled. 'I expected no less. With that solid bottom, all that is necessary is to wipe away a few of your misconceptions and misunderstandings, correct your viewpoints, and . . .'

'Do you think for a second that your therapists can fit *us* into the pattern of your Civilization?' the Boskonian spokesman demanded, bitingly.

'I don't have to think, Lanion—I know,' Kinnison assured him. 'Take them away, fellows, and lock them up—you know where. Everything will go ahead as scheduled.'

It did.

And while the mighty vessels of war landed upon the space-field and while the thronging Lensmen took over post after post in an ever-widening downward course, Kinnison led Worsel and Tregonsee to the cell in which the outspoken Thralian chieftain was confined.

'I do not know whether I can prevent you from operating upon me or not,' Lanion of Thrale spoke harshly, 'but I will try. I have seen the pitiful, distorted wrecks left after such operations and I do not like them. Furthermore, I do not believe that any possible science can eradicate from my subconscious the fixed determination to kill myself the instant you release me. Therefore you had better kill me now, Lensman, and save your time and trouble.'

'You are right, and wrong,' Kinnison replied, quietly. 'It may very well be impossible to remove such a fixation.' He knew that he could remove any such, but Lanion must not know it. Civilization needed those twelve hard, shrewd minds and he had no intention of allowing an inferiority complex to weaken their powers. 'We do not, however, intend to operate, but only and simply to educate. You will not be unconscious at any time. You will be in full control of your own mind and you will know beyond peradventure that you are so in control. We shall engrave, in parallel with your own present knowledges of the culture of Boskonia, the equivalent or corresponding knowledges of Civilization.'

They did so. It was not a short undertaking, nor an easy; but it was thorough and it was finally done. Then Kinnison spoke.

'You now have completely detailed knowledge both of Boskonia and of Civilization, a combination possessed by but few intelligences indeed. You know that we did not alter, did not even touch, any track of your original mind. Being fully en rapport with us, you know that we gave you as unprejudiced a concept of Civilization as we possibly could. Also, you have assimilated completely the new knowledge.'

'That is all true,' Lanion conceded. 'Remarkable, but true. I was, and remained throughout, myself; I checked constantly to be sure of that. I can still kill myself at any moment I choose.'

'Right,' Kinnison did not smile, even mentally, at the unconscious alteration of intent. 'The whole proposition can now be boiled down into one clear-cut question, to which you can formulate an equally clear-cut reply. Would you, Lanion, personally, prefer to keep on as you have been, working for personal power, or would you rather team up with others to work for the good of all?'

The Thralian thought for moments, and as he pondered an expression of consternation spread over his hard-hewn face. 'You mean actually—personally—apart from all consideration of your so-called altruism and your other infantile weaknesses?' he demanded, resistantly.

'Exactly,' Kinnison assured him. 'Which would you *rather* do? Which would you, personally, get the most good—the most fun—out of?'

The bitter conflict was plainly visible in Lanion's bronzed face; so was the direction in which it was going.

'Well ... I'll ... be ... damned! You win, Lensman!' and the ex-Boskonian executive held out his hand. Those were not his words, of course; but as nearly as Tellurian English can come to it, that is the exact sense of his final decision. And the same, or approximately the same, was the decision of each of his eleven fellows, each in his turn.

Thus it was, then, that Civilization won over the twelve recruits who were so potently instrumental in the bloodless conquest of Thrale, and who were later to be of such signal service throughout the Second Galaxy. For they knew Boskonia with a sure knowledge, from top to bottom and from side to side, in every aspect and ramification; they knew precisely where and when and how to work to secure the desired ends. And they worked—*how* they worked!—but space is lacking to go into any of their labors here.

Specialists gathered, of a hundred different sorts; and when, after peace and security had been gained, they began to attack the stupendous files of the Hall of Records, Kinnison finally yielded to Haynes' insistence and moved out to the *Z9M9Z*.

'It's about time, young fellow!' the Port Admiral snapped. 'I've gnawed my finger-nails off just about to the elbow and I still haven't figured out how to crack Onlo. Have you got any ideas?'

'Thrale first,' Kinnison suggested. 'Everything QX here, you sure?'

'Absolutely,' Haynes grunted. 'As strongly held as Tellus or Klovia. Primaries, helices, super-tractors, Bergenholms sunbeam—everything. They don't need us here any longer, any more than a hen needs teeth. Grand Fleet is all set to go, but we haven't been able to work out a feasible plan of campaign. The best way would be not to use the fleet at all, but a sunbeam—but we can't move the sun and Thorndyke can't hold the beam together that far. I don't suppose we could use a negasphere?'

'I don't see how,' Kinnison pondered. 'Ever since we used it first they've been ready for it. I'd be inclined to wait and see what Nadreck works out. He's a wise old owl, that bird—what does he tell you?'

'Nothing. Nothing flat.' Haynes' smile was grimly amused. 'The fact that he is still "investigating"—whatever that means —is all he'll say. Why don't you try him? You know him better than I do or ever will.'

'It wouldn't do any harm,' Kinnison agreed. 'Nor good, either, probably. Funny egg, Nadreck. I'd tie fourteen of his arms into lover's knots if it'd make him give, but it wouldn't—he's really tough.' Nevertheless he sent out a call, which was acknowledged instantly.

'Ah, Kinnison, greetings. I am even now on my way to Thrale and the *Directrix* to report.'

'You are? Fine!' Kinnison exclaimed. 'How did you come out?'

'I did not—exactly—fail, but the work was very incompletely and very poorly done,' Nadreck apologized, the while the Tellurian's mind felt very strongly the Palainian equivalent of a painful blush of shame. 'My report of the affair is going in under Lensman's Seal.'

'But what did you *do*?' both Tellurians demanded as one.

'I scarcely know how to confess to such blundering,' and Nadreck actually squirmed. 'Will you not permit me to leave my shame to the spool of record?'

They would not, they informed him.

'If you must have it, then, I yield. The plan was to make all Onlonians destroy themselves. In theory it was sound and simple, but my execution was pitifully imperfect. My work was so poorly done that the commanding officer in each one of three of the domes remained alive, making it necessary for me to slay those three commanders personally, by the use of crude force. I regret exceedingly the lack of finish of this undertaking, and I apologize profoundly for it. I trust that you will not allow this information to become a matter of public knowledge,' and the apologetic, mentally sweating, really humiliated Palainian broke the connection.

Haynes and Kinnison stared at each other, for moments completely at a loss for words. The Port Admiral first broke the silence.

'Hell's—jingling—bells!' he wrenched out, finally, and waved a hand at the points of light crowding so thickly his tactical tank. 'A thing that the whole damned Grand Fleet couldn't do, and he does it alone, and then he *apologizes* for it as though he ought to be stood up in a corner or sent to bed without any supper!'

'Uh-huh, that's the way he is,' Kinnison breathed, in awe. 'What a brain! . . . what a man!'

Nadreck's black speedster arrived and a three-way conference was held. Both Haynes and Kinnison pressed him for the details of his really stupendous achievement, but he refused positively even to mention any phase of it.

'The matter is closed—finished,' he declared, in a mood of anger and self-reproach which neither of the Tellurians had ever supposed that the gently scientific monster could assume. 'I practically failed. It is the poorest piece of work of which I have been guilty since cubhood, and I desire and I insist that it shall not be mentioned again. If you wish to lay plans for the future, I will be very glad indeed to place at your disposal my small ability—which has now been shown to be even smaller than I had supposed—but if you insist upon discussing my fiasco, I shall forthwith go home. I will *not* discuss it. The record of it will remain permanently under Lensman's Seal. That is my last word.'

And it was. Neither of the two Tellurians mentioned the subject, of course, either then or ever, but many other persons—including your historian—have done so, with no trace whatever of success. It is a shame, it is positively outrageous, that no details are available of the actual fall of Onlo. No human mind can understand why Nadreck will not release his seal, but the bitter fact of his refusal to do so has been made all too plain.

Thus, in all probability, it never will become publicly known how those monstrous Onlonians destroyed each other, nor how Nadreck penetrated the defensive screens of Onlo's embattled domes, nor in what fashions he warred upon the three surviving commanders. These matters, and many others of perhaps equal interest and value, must have been of such an epic nature that it is a cosmic crime that they cannot be recorded here; that this, one of the most important incidents of the campaign, must be mentioned merely and baldly as having happened. But, unless Nadreck relents—and he apparently never does—that is the starkly tragic fact.

Other Lensmen were called in then, and admirals and generals and other personages. It was decided to man the fortifications of Onlo immediately, from the several fleets of frigid-blooded poison-breathers which made up a certain percentage of Civilization's forces. This decision was influenced markedly by Nadreck, who said in part:

'Onlo is a beautiful planet. Its atmosphere is perfect, its climate is ideal; not only for us of Palain VII, but also for the inhabitants of many other planets, such as...' and he mentioned some twenty names. 'While I personally am not a fighter, there are some who are; and while those of a more warlike disposition man Onlo's defenses and weapons, my fellow researchers and I might very well be carrying on with the same type of work which you fire-blooded oxygen-breathers are doing elsewhere.

This eminently sensible suggestion was adopted at once. The conference broke up. The selected sub-fleets sailed. Kinnison went to see Haynes.

'Well, sir, that's it ... I hope ... what do you think? Am I, or am I not, due for a spot of free time?' The Gray Lensman's face was drawn and grim.

'I wish I knew, son ... but I don't.' Eyes and voice were deeply troubled. 'You ought to be ... I hope you are ... but you're the only judge of that, you know.'

'Uh-huh ... that is, I know how to find out ... but I'm afraid to—afraid he'll say no. However, I'm going to see Cris first—talk it over with her. How about having a gig drop me down to the hospital?'

For he did not have to travel very far to find his fiancee. From the time of leaving Lyrane until the taking over of Thrale she had as a matter of course been chief nurse of the hospital ship *Pasteur*, and with the civilizing of that planet she had as automatically become chief nurse of the Patrol's Base Hospital there.

'Certainly, Kim—anything you want, whenever you please.'

'Thanks, chief ... Now that this fracas is finally over—if it is—I suppose you'll have to take over as president of the Galactic Council?'

'I suppose so—after we clean up Lyrane VIII, that you've been holding me away from so long—but I don't relish the thought. And you'll be Coordinator Kinnison.'

'Uh-huh,' gloomily. 'By Klono, I hate to put my Grays away! I'm not going to do it, either, until after we're married and I'm really settled down onto the job.'

'Of course not. You'll be wearing them for some time yet, I'm thinking.' Haynes' tone was distinctly envious. 'Getting *your* job reduced to routine will take a long, long time ... It'll probably take years even to find out what it's really going to be.'

'That's so, too,' Kinnison brightened visibly. 'Well, clear ether, President Haynes!' and he turned away, whistling unmelodiously—in fact, somewhat raucously—through his teeth.

23: Attainment

At Base Hospital it was midnight. The two largest of Thrale's four major moons were visible, close together in the zenith, almost at the full; shining brilliantly from a cloudless, star-besprinkled sky upon the magnificent grounds.

Fountains splashed and tinkled musically. Masses of flowering shrubs, bordering meandering walks, flooded the still air with a perfume almost cloying in its intensity. No one who has once smelled the fragrance of Thralian thorn-flower at midnight will ever forget it—it is as though the poignant sweetness of the mountain syringa has been blended harmoniously with the heavy, entrancing scent of the jasmine and the appealing pungency of the lily-of-the-valley. Statues of gleaming white stone and of glinting metal were spaced infrequently over acres and acres of springy, close-clipped turf. Trees, not over-high but massive of bole and of tremendous spread and thickness of foliage, cast shadows of impenetrable black.

'QX, Cris?' Kinnison Lensed the thought as he entered the grounds: she had known that he was coming. 'Kinda late, I know, but I wanted to see you, and you don't have to punch the clock.'

'Surely, Kim,' and her low, infectious chuckle welled out. 'What's the use of being a Red Lensman, else? This is just right—you couldn't make it any sooner and tomorrow would have been too late.'

They met at the door and with arms around each other strolled wordless down a walk. Across the resilient sward they made their way and to a bench beneath one of the spreading trees.

Kinnison swept her into both arms, hers went eagerly around his neck. How long, how unutterably long it had been since they had stood thus, nurse's white crushed against Lensman's Gray!

They had no need, these Lensmen, of sight. Nor of language. Hence, since words are so pitifully inadequate, no attempt will be made to chronicle the ecstasy of that reunion. Finally, however:

'Now that we're together again I'll *never* let you go,' the man declared aloud.

'If they separate us again it will simply break my heart,' Clarrissa agreed. Then, woman-like, she faced the facts and made the man face them, too. 'Let's sit down, Kim, and have this out. You know as well as I do that we can't go on if ... if we can't ... that's all.'

'I do not,' Kinnison said, flatly. 'We've got a right to *some* happiness, you and I. They can't keep us apart forever, sweetheart—we're going straight through with it this time.'

'Uh-uh, Kim,' she denied gently, shaking her spectacular head. 'What would have happened if we'd have gone ahead before, leaving those horrible Thralians free to ruin Civilization?'

'But Mentor stopped us then,' Kinnison argued. Deep down, he knew that if the Arisian called he would have to answer, but he argued nevertheless. 'If the job wasn't done, he would have stopped us before we got this far—I think.'

'You hope, you mean,' the girl contradicted. 'What makes you think—if you really do—that he might not wait until the ceremony has actually begun?'

'Not a thing in the universe. He might, at that,' Kinnison

confessed, bleakly.

'You've been afraid to ask him, haven't you?'

'But the job must be done!' he insisted, avoiding the question. 'The prime minister—that Fossten—*must* have been the top; there couldn't *possibly* be anything bigger than an Arisian to be back of Boskone. It's unthinkable! They've got no military organization left—not a beam hot enough to light a cigarette or a screen that would stop a firecracker. We have all their records—everything. Why, it's just a matter of routine now for the boys to uproot them completely; system by system, planet by planet.

'Uh-huh.' She eyed him shrewdly, there in the dark. 'Cogent. Really pellucid. As clear as so much crystal—and twice as fragile. If you're so sure, why not call Mentor and ask him, right now? You're not afraid of just the calling part, like I am; you're afraid of what he'll say.'

'I'm going to marry you before I do another lick of work of any kind, anywhere,' he insisted, doggedly.

'I just love to hear you say that, even if I do know you're just popping off!' She snuggled deeper into the curve of his arm. 'I feel that way too, but both of us know very well that if Mentor stops us ... even at the altar ...' her thought slowed, became tense, solemn. 'We're Lensmen, Kim, you and I. We both know exactly what that means. We'll have to muster jets enough, some way or other, to swing the load. Let's call him now, Kim, together. I just simply can't stand this not knowing ... I can't, Kim ... I can't!' Tears come hard and seldom to such a woman as Clarrissa MacDougall; but they came then—and they hurt.

'QX, ace.' Kinnison patted her back and her gorgeous head. 'Let's go—but I tell you now that if he says "no" I'll tell him to go out to the Rim and take a swan-dive off into inter-galactic space.'

She linked her mind with his, thinking in affectionate half-reproach, 'I'd like to, too, Kim, but that's pure balloon juice and you know it. You couldn't ...' she broke off as he hurled their joint thought to Arisia the Old, going on frantically:

'You think at him, Kim, and I'll just listen. He scares me into a shrinking, quivering pulp!'

'QX, ace,' he said again. Then: 'Is it permissible that we do what we are about to do?' he asked crisply of Arisia's ancient sage.

'Ah, 'tis Kinnison and MacDougall; once of Tellus, henceforth of Klovia,' the calmly unsurprised thought rolled in. 'I was expecting you at this time. Any mind, however far from competent, could have visualized this event in its entirety. That which you contemplate is not merely permissible; it has now become necessary,' and as usual, without tapering off or leave-taking, Mentor broke the line.

The two clung together rapturously then for minutes, but something was obtruding itself disquietingly upon the nurse's mind.

'But his thought was "necessary", Kim?' she asked, rather than said. 'Isn't there a sort of a sinister connotation in that, somewhere? What did he mean?'

'Nothing—exactly nothing,' Kinnison assured her, comfortably. 'He's got a complete picture of the macrocosmic universe in his mind—his "Visualization of the Cosmic All", he calls it—and in it we get married now, just as I've been telling you we are going to. Since it gripes him no end to have even the tiniest thing not conform to his visualization, our marriage is NECESSARY, in capital letters. See?'

'Uh-huh ... Oh, I'm *glad*!' she exclaimed. 'That shows you how scared of him I am,' and thoughts and actions became such that, although they were no doubt of much personal pleasure and satisfaction, they do not require detailed treatment here.

Clarrissa MacDougall resigned the next day, without formality or fanfare. That is, she thought that she did so then, and rather wondered at the frictionless ease with which it went through: it had simply not occurred to her that in the instant of being made an Unattached Lensman she had been freed automatically from every man-made restraint. That was one of the few lessons hard for her to learn; it was the only one which she refused consistently even to try to learn.

Nothing was said or done about the ten thousand credits which had been promised her upon the occasion of her fifteen-minutes-long separation from the Patrol following the fall of Jarnevon. She thought about it briefly, but with no real sense of loss. Some way or other, money did not seem important. Anyway, she had some—enough for a fairly nice, if limited, trousseau—in a Tellurian bank. She could undoubtedly get it through the Disbursing Office here.

She took off her Lens and stuffed it into a pocket. That wasn't so good, she reflected. It bulged, and besides, it might fall out; and anyone who touched it would die. She didn't have a bag; in fact, she had with her no civilian clothes at all. Wherefore she put it back on, pausing as she did so to admire the Manarkan star-drop flashing pale fire from the third finger of her left hand. Of Cartiff's whole stock of fine gems, this was the loveliest.

It was not far to the Disbursing Office, so she walked; window-shopping as she went. It was a peculiar sensation, this being out of harness—it felt good, though, at that—and upon arriving at the bank she found to her surprise that she was both well known and expected. An officer whom she had never seen before greeted her cordially and led her into his private office.

'We have been wondering why you didn't pick up your kit, Lensman MacDougall,' he went on, briskly. 'Sign here, please, and press your right thumb in this box here, after peeling off this plastic strip, so.' She wrote in her boldly flowing script, and peeled, and pressed; and watched fascinatedly as her thumb-print developed itself sharply black against the bluish off-white of the Patrol's stationery. 'That transfers your balance upon Tellus to the Patrol's general fund. Now sign and print this, in quadruplicate ... Thank you. Here's your kit. When this book of slips is gone you can get another one at any bank or Patrol station anywhere. It has been a real pleasure to have met you, Lensman MacDougall; come in again whenever you happen to be upon Thrale,' and he escorted her to the street as briskly as he had ushered her in.

Clarrissa felt slightly dazed. She had gone in there to get the couple of hundred credits which represented her total wealth; but instead of getting it she had meekly surrendered her savings to the Patrol and had been given—what? She leafed through the little book. One hundred blue-white slips; small things, smaller than currency bills. A little printing, two lines for description, a blank for figures, a space for signature, and a plastic-covered oblong area for thumb-print. That was all—but what an all! Any one of those slips, she knew, would be honored without hesitation or question for any amount of cash money she pleased to draw; for any object or thing she chose to buy. Anything—absolutely *anything*—from a pair of half-credit stockings up to and beyond a hundred-million-credit space-ship. ANYTHING! The thought chilled her buoyant spirit, took away her zest for shopping.

'Kim, I can't!' she wailed through her Lens. 'Why didn't they give me my own money and let me spend it the way I please?'

'Hold everything, ace—I'll be with you in a sec.' He wasn't—

quite—but it was not long. 'You can get all the money you want, you know—just give them a chit.'

'I know, but all I wanted was my own money. I didn't ask for this stuff!'

'None of that, Cris—when you get to be a Lensman you've got to take what goes with it. Besides, if you spend money foolishly all the rest of your life, the Patrol knows that it will still owe you plenty for what you did on Lyrane II. Where do you want to begin?'

'Brenleer's,' she decided, after she had been partially convinced. 'They aren't the largest, but they give real quality at a fair price.'

At the shop the two Lensmen were recognized at sight and Brenleer himself did the honors.

'Clothes,' the girl said succinctly, with an all-inclusive wave of her hand. 'All kinds of clothes, except white uniforms.'

They were ushered into a private room and Kinnison wriggled as mannequins began to appear in various degrees of enclothement.

'This is no place for me,' he declared. 'I'll see you later, ace. How long—half an hour or so?'

'Half an hour?' The nurse giggled, and:

'She will be here all the rest of today, and most of the time for a week,' the merchant informed him severely—and she was.

'Oh, Kim, I'm having the most *marvelous* time!' she told him excitedly, a few days later. 'But it makes me feel sick to think of how much of the Patrol's money I'm spending.'

'That's what *you* think.'

'Huh? What do you mean?' she demanded, but he would not talk.

She found out, however, after the long-drawn-out business of selecting and matching and designing and fitting was over.

'You've only seen me in real clothes once, and that time you hardly looked at me. Besides, I got myself all prettied up in the beauty shop.' She posed provocatively. 'Do you like me, Kim?'

'*Like* you!' The man could scarcely speak. She had been a seven-sector call-out in faded moleskin breeches and a patched shirt. She had been a thionite dream in uniform. But now—radiantly, vibrantly beautiful, a symphony in her favorite dark green ... 'Words fail, ace. Thoughts, too. They fold up and quit. The universe's best, is all I can say ...'

And—later—they sought out Brenleer.

'I would like to ask you to do me a tremendous favor,' he

said, hesitantly, without filling in any of the blanks upon the blue-white slip the girl had proffered. 'If, instead of paying for these things, you would write upon this voucher the date and "my fall outfit and much of my trousseau were made by Brenleer of Thrale . . ." ' His voice expired upon a wistful note.

'Why . . . I never even thought of such a thing . . . would it be quite ethical, do you think, Kim?'

'You said that he gives value for price, so I don't see why not . . . Lots of things they never let any of us pay for . . .' Then, to Brenleer, 'Never thought of that angle, of what a terrific draw she'd be . . . you're figuring on displaying that chit unobtrusively in a gold and platinum frame four feet square.'

Brenleer nodded. 'Something like that. This will be the most fantastically lucky break a man in my position ever had, if you approve of it.'

'I don't see why not,' Kinnison said again. 'You might as well give him a break, Cris. What tore it was buying so much stuff here, not admitting the fact over your signature and thumbprint.'

She wrote and they went out.

'You mean to tell me I'm so . . . so . . .'

'Famous? Notorious?' he helped out.

'Uh-huh. Or words to that effect.' A touch of fear darkened her glorious eyes.

'All of that, and then some. I never thought of what your buying so much plunder in one store would do, but it'd have the pulling power of a planetary tractor. It's bad enough with us regulars—half the chits we issue are never cashed—but *you* are absolutely unique. The first Lady Lensman—the only Red Lensman—and *what* a Lensman! Wow! As I think it over one gets you a hundred if any chit you ever sign ever will get cashed. There have been collectors, you know, ever since Civilization began—maybe before.'

'But I don't like it!' she stormed.

'That won't change the facts,' he countered, philosophically. 'Are you ready to flit? The *Dauntless* is hot, they tell me.'

'Uh-huh, all my stuff is aboard,' and soon they were en route to Klovia.

The trip was uneventful, and even before they reached that transformed planet it became evident that it was theirs from pole to pole. Their cruiser was met by a horde of space-ships of all types and sizes, which formed a turbulent and demonstrative escort of honor. The seething crowd at the space-port could scarcely be kept out of range of the dreadnought's searing landing-blasts. Half the brass bands of the world, it seemed, burst into 'Our Patrol' as the Lensmen disembarked, and their ground-car and the street along which it slowly rolled were decorated lavishly with deep-blue flowers.

'Thorn-flowers!' Clarrissa choked. 'Thralian thorn-flowers, Kim—how could they?'

'They grow here as well as there, and when they found out that you liked them so well they imported them by the ship-load,' and Kinnison himself swallowed a lump.

Their brief stay upon Klovia was a hectic one indeed. Parties and balls, informal and formal, and at least a dozen Telenews poses every day. Receptions, at which there were presented the personages and the potentates of a thousand planets; at which the uniforms and robes and gowns put the solar spectrum to shame.

And from tens of thousands of planets came Lensmen, to make or to renew acquaintance with the Galactic Coordinator and to welcome into their ranks the Lensman-bride. From Tellus, of course, they came in greatest number and enthusiasm, but other planets were not too far behind. They came from Manarka and Velantia and Chickladoria and Alsakan and Vandemar, from the worlds of Canopus and Vega and Antares, from all over the galaxy. Human, near-human, non-human, monstrous; there even appeared briefly quite large numbers of frigid-blooded Lensmen, whose fiercely-laboring refrigerators chilled the atmosphere for yards around their insulated and impervious suits. All those various beings came with a united purpose, with a common thought—to congratulate Kinnison of Tellus and to wish his Lensman-mate all the luck and all the happiness of the universe.

Kinnison was surprised at the sincerity with which they acclaimed him; he was amazed at the genuineness and the tensity of their adoption of his Clarrissa as their own. He had been afraid that some of them would think he was throwing his weight around when he violated precedent by making her a Lensman. He had been afraid of animosity and ill-will. He had been afraid that outraged masculine pride would set up a sex antagonism. But if any of these things existed, the keenest use of his every penetrant sense could not discover them.

Instead, the human Lensmen literally mobbed her as they took her to their collective bosom. No party, wherever or for what reason held, was complete without her. If she ever had less than ten escorts at once, she was slighted. They ran her ragged, they danced her slippers off, they stuffed her to repletion, they would not let her sleep, they granted her the privacy of a goldfish—and she loved every tumultuous second of it.

She had wanted, as she had told Haynes and Lacy so long ago, a big wedding; but this one was already out of hand and was growing more so by the minute. The idea of holding it in a church had been abandoned long since; now it became clear that the biggest armory of Klovia would not hold even half of the Lensmen, to say nothing of the notables and dignitaries who had come so far. It would simply have to be the Stadium.

Even that tremendous structure could not hold enough people, hence speakers and plates were run outside, clear up to the space-field fence. And, although neither of the principals knew it, this marriage had so fired public interest that Universal Telenews men had already arranged the hook-up which was to carry it to every planet of Civilization. Thus the number of entities who saw and heard that wedding has been estimated, but the figures are too fantastic to be repeated here.

But it was in no sense a circus. No ceremony ever held, in home or in church or in cathedral, was ever more solemn. For when half a million Lensmen concentrate upon solemnity, it prevails.

The whole vast bowl was gay with flowers—it seemed as though a state must have been stripped of blooms to furnish so many—and ferns and white ribbons were everywhere. There was a mighty organ, which pealed out triumphal melody as the bridal parties marched down the aisles, subsiding into a lilting accompaniment as the betrothal couple ascended the white-brocaded stairway and faced the Lensman-Chaplain in the heavily-garlanded little open-air chapel. The minister raised both hands. The massed Patrolmen and nurses stood at attention. A profound silence fell.

'Dearly beloved . . .' The grand old service—short and simple, but utterly impressive—was soon over. Then, as Kinnison kissed his wife, half a million Lensed members were thrust upward in silent salute.

Through a double lane of glowing Lenses the wedding party made its way up to the locked and guarded gate of the space-field where lay the *Dauntless*—the super-dreadnought 'yacht' in which the Kinnisons were to take a honeymoon voyage to distant Tellus. The gate opened. The couple, accompanied by the Port Admiral and the Surgeon Marshal, stepped into the car, which sped out to the battleship; and as it did so the crowd loosed its pent-up feelings in a prolonged outburst of cheering.

And as the newlyweds walked up the gangplank Kinnison turned his head and Lensed a thought to Haynes:

'You've been griping so long about Lyrane VIII, chief—I forgot to tell you—you can go mop up on it now!'

Acknowledgment

Your historian, not wishing to take credit which is not rightfully his, wishes to say here that without the fine cooperation of many persons and entities this history must have been of much less value and importance than it now is.

First, of course, there were the Lensmen. It is unfortunate that Nadreck of Palain VII could not be induced either to release his spool of the Fall of Onlo or to enlarge upon his other undertakings.

Coordinator Kinnison, Worsel of Velantia, and Tregonsee of Rigel IV, however, were splendidly cooperative, giving in personal conversations much highly useful material which is not heretofore of public record. The gracious and queenly Red Lensman also was of great assistance.

Dr. James R. Enright was both prolific and masterly in deducing that certain otherwise necessarily obscure events and sequences must have in fact occurred, and it is gratefully admitted here that the author has drawn heavily upon 'Doctor Jim's' profound knowledge of the mind.

The Galactic Roamers, those intrepid spacemen, assisted no little: E. Everett Evans, their Chief Communications Officer, F. Edwin Counts, Paul Leavy, Jr., Alfred Ashley, to name only a few who aided in the selection, arrangement, and presentation of material.

Verna Trestrail, the exquisite connoisseuse, was of help, not only by virtue of her knowledge of the jewels of Lonabar, but also in her interpretations of many things concerning Illona Potter of which Illona Henderson—characteristically—will not speak.

To all these, and to many others whose help was only slightly less, the writer extends his sincere thanks.

EDWARD E. SMITH.